Also by Adrian Plass

keeping up
with the
Robinsons

Also by Adrian Plass

keeping up
with the
Robinsons

INTERNATIONALLY BESTSELLING AUTHOR

ADRIAN PLASS

■ ZONDERVAN®

ZONDERVAN.com/
AUTHORTRACKER
follow your favorite authors

ZONDERVAN

Keeping Up with the Robinsons
Copyright © 2010 by Adrian Plass

Stress Family Robinson
Copyright © 1995 by Adrian Plass

Stress Family Robinson 2, The Birthday Party
Copyright © 1999 by Adrian Plass

Requests for information should be addressed to:
Zondervan, *Grand Rapids, Michigan* 49530

ISBN 978-0-310-25226-9

Adrian Plass asserts the moral right to be identified as the author of this work.

Cover design: Laura Maitner-Mason
Cover photography or illustration: Jupiter Images
Interior design: Michelle Espinoza

Printed in the United States of America

10 11 12 13 14 15 16 /DCI/ 24 23 22 21 20 19 18 17 16 15 14 13 12 11 10 9 8 7 6 5 4 3 2 1

This book is dedicated to my son, David,
who first used the phrase 'Stress Family Robinson' in 1993
when all six Plasses were touring Queensland, Australia.
Long hot periods of travelling
in the close confines of a relatively small vehicle
may well have contributed to David's small
but productive burst of creativity.

Contents

Book 1: Stress Family Robinson

Chapter 1 / 11
Chapter 2 / 17
Chapter 3 / 33
Chapter 4 / 50
Chapter 5 / 66
Chapter 6 / 76
Chapter 7 / 83
Chapter 8 / 103
Chapter 9 / 120
Chapter 10 / 140
Chapter 11 / 152
Chapter 12 / 169

Book 2: The Birthday Party

1. Saturday / 177
2. Sunday / 234
3. Monday / 273
4. Tuesday / 287
5. Wednesday / 302
6. Thursday / 315
7. Friday / 322
8. Saturday / 325
9. Sunday / 345

Book 1:

Stress Family Robinson

Chapter 1

Let me introduce you to the Robinson family. They go to the same church as I do, which is where I first met them. There are five of them, or seven if you include the two stick-insects, which Felicity Robinson always does. You'll hear quite a lot about those stick-insects later. By the way, I'm not a Robinson myself, although I think, if you asked them, all the family would say that I am nearly one – you'll hear a fair bit about that before we've finished, too. In fact, if you were talking to Felicity, she'd probably say I was absolutely, definitely another Robinson, so, just to confuse you, there are either five, six, seven or eight Robinsons, depending on who you include and who you're talking to.

I'll give myself the benefit of the doubt and start with me, because I'm the one who's telling this story.

My name is Elizabeth Reynolds, although nobody has called me Elizabeth since I was a very small girl, when I was nicknamed 'Dip' by my family for reasons which – yes, you guessed it – you'll hear about later. I'm fifty years old, but not inside, and I was born and grew up in the city of Adelaide in Australia. Nowadays I live in a little terraced house on my own in Standham, the same market town as the Robinsons, in the south of England. I was trained as a nurse, and I think I'm quite a good one, but I've only worked part time at the local hospital for a few years now, and I shall carry on doing that for as long as I can afford it. I enjoy work, but I enjoy lots of other things as well. None of my own family are alive any more, and the people I love most in the world are God and the Robinsons (I hope it's in that order). I drive a yellow Mini called 'Daffodil' because I always wanted one, and the things I enjoy doing most are reading, walking, dreaming and being with the people I love most. Although I laugh a lot when I'm with my friends, I do get very lonely and unhappy sometimes, but I've become a bit of an expert at covering it up – that's one of my main faults. I've never been married and I've never had any children. I wish I had.

When I look in a mirror (I try not to) I see a tallish, rather overweight person who used to have quite a nice figure, but gets bored with living on cottage cheese and crispbread and horrible pink flavoured stuff. There's a reasonably nice, smiley, quite wide face stuck on top of the body, with light blue eyes, a full mouth and fair hair cut short because I get so sick of trying to do something with it. I do like my nose. My nose has style.

One more thing – I love being cuddled, but only by people I like, and it doesn't happen often because I don't look as if I need to be.

The man in the Robinson clan is called Mike. He's in his mid-forties, a fairly tall, nicely shaped sort of chap with a pleasant, mild expression (he goes a sort of plum colour on the rare occasions when he's angry) and reddish-gold hair that's beginning to get a bit see-through on top. For the last two years Mike has been deputy headmaster at a little village junior school two or three miles to the west of Standham. I've never actually been to Mike's school, but from the way he talks about it I should think it's a very calm and well-organized place indeed. I'm sure that all the people there, staff members and children, know exactly where they should be and what they should be doing at any given moment during the day. Mike's wife, Kathy, tells me that her husband's school is a place where naughtiness hardly happens at all. She says that Mike's disciplinary methods consist of either a stern look, which, in this setting, reduces the offending junior to a quivering wreck, or a very slightly raised voice, which presumably leaves him or her for dead. One of the great frustrations of Mike's life is that the regime and atmosphere of his place of work is impossible to duplicate in his own home. Every now and then he declares war on the formless entity which is the Robinson household, producing lists and complex plans designed to transform daily living into something efficient, smooth-running and civilized. He enrages Kathy once every month or so by suggesting that major organizational problems (he means housework) would be solved if she were to introduce some kind of system into her work. These occasional, frenetic attempts to take a dustpan and brush to the untidiness of life are largely ignored by the rest of the family, who know quite well that Mike's lists and plans will be in the bin within forty-eight hours as long as he's not encouraged.

Mike's Christianity is a little bit similar really. He would love the whole thing to be neat and easily manageable, but he does accept – he *has* to accept, as Kathy's husband and the father of three very different children – that life is simply not like that. I don't want to give the wrong idea. Mike is a real Jesus man. He wants to do things right, and he wants to be good, it's just that the pedantic side of him takes over at times. Above all else he is an immensely kind person, who adores his family and genuinely cares about others. I love him for the gentleness and warmth he has shown me.

Definitely one of those people I like to be hugged by.

Kathy Robinson used to be a journalist before her youngest child was born six years ago. Apart from the fact that they both love travelling (and are lucky enough to be able to afford to do quite a lot of it because of money inherited from Kathy's mum and dad) she is different from her husband in just about every way that I can think of. I don't mean that the bond between them is not strong. It is strong, but it jolly well needs to be, to chain such opposites together. He's fair and she's dark; he's generally quite placid in temperament, while she swings wildly from optimism or flippancy to misery and despair; he likes things to be well organized and properly planned, she acts by instinct or inspiration, which, of course, tends to result in great successes and spectacular failures; Mike is essentially an uncomplicated person, whereas Kathy's personality is full of twists and turns and troubles, probably because of the difference in their backgrounds. Kathy's peace, as you will discover, is continually being ambushed by her own childhood trauma, in contrast to Mike, who tells people that he grew up in an atmosphere of 'quiet approval'. Kathy reckons that the approval was not as quiet as all that. She told me the story once of how, at an early stage in their courtship, she visited Mike's parents' home at Christmas time. Mike volunteered to blow up some balloons, and was half-way through inflating the first one, when his mother, who had been watching her son with fond admiration, whispered, 'My goodness, the *breath* in the boy!'

My friend is often very funny, very beautiful when things are going all right, and a staunch ally when troubles come, but she's also a stormy child who is stuck with being a grown-up. She loves her family and is often infuriated beyond measure by them, in particular by Mark, who was so solidly at the centre of his own universe at the time I'm writing about, that he repeatedly brought out all the worst feelings of inadequacy that have plagued Kathy since she first had children.

Kathy must have exhausted God over the years, but I'm sure he's crackers about her.

Finally, she just *loves* Bristol Cream sherry – and so do I.

Jack – yes, his name really is *Jack* Robinson! – is Mike and Kathy's oldest son, and I have always found him utterly delightful. Nineteen years old, you're meeting him at a time when he's moving towards the end of a year out between school and university, during which he's done just enough paid work to avoid excessive hassle from his parents. Tall, long haired and lean, very much like his father in general looks, Jack's easy contentment (and waste of milk – read on!) madden Kathy occasionally, but he's warm and affectionate as well, so she never stays mad with him for long. Jack is at that stage in his life when wisdom and naïvety are constantly elbowing each other aside. Terrific insights and intelligence are coupled with plain silliness, especially when it comes to Mark, with whom he is in a state of virtually unrelieved conflict. Jack's love of somewhat obscure music is probably the most important thing in his life, but his little sister Felicity comes a very close second, and I'm sure the music would be instantly stilled if, for some bizarre reason, a choice needed to be made. That's all I'm going to say about Jack for now.

Mark Robinson is fourteen. Writers of textbooks on parenting who want to specify this age as one that's likely to be difficult could photograph Mark in sullen mood and use him to illustrate their point. He is dark, not very tall for his age, quite broad, and as much like his mother as Jack is like his dad. He is actually a very nice looking boy, but an aura of glowering tension, mainly in the company of adults, tends to obscure this fact a lot of the time. His best friend could not deny that Mark is sometimes quite breathtakingly rude and obtuse. I think this is largely because, like many people of his age, he vaguely believes that the rest of the world (when he notices them) are there merely to swell crowd scenes in which M. Robinson is the central star. Kathy finds him very difficult indeed, and that's putting it mildly.

Most of Mark's free time is spent with his friends, a shadowy group of contemporaries, who seem to drift around our town in the late evenings from one shopwindow-lit whispering point to another in a sort of solid block of conspiring boyhood. I don't suppose they ever do anything very wicked, but they look as if they might. Mark enjoys watching some sports but he isn't very interested in taking part, so most of his energies and interests (apart from kite-flying) are bound up with these friends of his, although he too adores Felicity. He has a good but strangely quiet relationship with his dad.

I'm quite convinced that, as he gets older, Mark will be able to reveal a lot more of the sensitivity that is already there beneath the glowering and crossness. He and I have a good friendship – as long as I keep to the 'rules' – and I hope I still know him when he's older. He's going to be a terrific fellow.

Finally (if we don't include the stick-insects, and I'm not going to in this bit), there's Felicity. Felicity Robinson is six years old, fair haired, shiny-eyed, full of energy and has undoubtedly benefited from the healthy neglect that her older brothers lacked. One of the happiest people I've ever met, she brings in her turn great happiness to those she lives with, and to me. Somehow, the best of Mike and Kathy seems to have been poured into this little girl, and if you think I'm going over the top – well, I don't care. She's a little bit naughty sometimes, and I expect there'll be problems as the years go by, but in the meantime – Felicity is wonderful. In knowing this smallest Robinson I've come closer than I ever thought possible to having a child of my own, and I thank God for her.

There you are, then – those are the Robinsons, and the following pages are all about them and the turbulent way in which they conduct their lives. There's quite a bit about me as well, because I am, after all, entitled to put D.H.R. after my name. What does D.H.R. stand for? I'm not going to tell you – read on and you'll find out.

Chapter 2

There are lots of things about being married that I really like the idea of, but I think some things would drive me completely round the bend. Take, for instance, the way in which husbands and wives seem to have the same arguments over and over again without ever realizing that their word battles have more or less become scripted. The Robinsons are extraordinary in this respect. I never stop marvelling at the way they begin each disagreement as though it's a totally new experience. It's rather sweet I suppose, but an awful waste of time usually.

A good example is the Great Packing Debate. In all the time that I've known them, this regularly repeated row has never varied by more than a word or two, and it always ends in exactly the same way. I love them both dearly, but, in battle mode, Mike and Kathy can be startlingly predictable.

I first witnessed this particular piece of unconsciously rehearsed role-play on a Saturday when the family were due to disappear for a long holiday over the Easter period. Knowing that the packing for America had been put off again and again, and, incredibly, would somehow have to be fitted in before lunch, I'd offered to pop round after breakfast to see if I could help. Arriving at the Robinsons' tall thin Victorian semi-detached at about nine o'clock, I found six-year-old Felicity glowing prettily in the spring sunshine on top of a brick pillar by the gate as she addressed an invisible circle of admirers.

'You are all my very good friends,' she was saying graciously, as I stepped out of Daffodil and locked the door behind me, 'and I love every one of you exactly the same amount. You are all invited to my next birthday party, which will be horse-riding, swimming, jungle-tumble, bowling, ice-skating and deep-pan pizzas.'

'Can I come?' I asked.

'No, Dip,' said Felicity, 'you can come to my real party, which will be Daddy doing tricks that don't work and Mummy getting cross because people won't play the games properly – and a nice tea,' she added, anxious to be absolutely fair.

'Mummy and Daddy up yet?'

'Drinking coffee in the kitchen and sighing and making lists. Jack's gone back upstairs with his headphones on because Mummy said his room looked as if something sad and terrible had happened there.'

'Oh, dear! And Mark?'

'Mark got very cross because he said no one had told him we were going to America today and he'd arranged to go out with his friends. Mummy said only a deaf imbecile could've not known we were going, and if Mark was's interested in his family as he is in his blinking friends he might have a better idea of what was going on. Then Mark said that next time boring guests came round he wouldn't bother to be polite, and he stomped off with his feet sticking out, like a duck in a sulk, and Mummy said she would never have believed that the back of someone's head could be so infuriating.' – Felicity sighed – 'It hasn't been a very good morning, really.'

'It doesn't sound very good,' I agreed, 'but I'm sure it'll get better. It's always difficult when you go away. I've come to lend a hand.'

'You'll have to wait till they've had their packing argument,' said Felicity, solemnly, 'nothing'll happen till they've had that. We've got a secret surprise for you later,' she added mysteriously.

'Oooh, well, I shall look forward to that, I like surprises!'

I found Mike and Kathy slumped over coffee mugs and pieces of paper at the kitchen table. They looked haggard and depressed, not at all like people who were planning to fly to America for a family holiday in a few hours' time. The kitchen looked as if it had drunk too much the night before and woken up wishing it hadn't.

'Hello, Dip,' said Mike, getting up. 'I'm afraid we're not in a very good state this morning – haven't really got moving. You sit down and I'll make you a coffee. One sugar at the moment, isn't it? We're just writing a list of things to do and then – '

'And then,' interrupted Kathy, clutching fistfuls of dark hair close to her scalp, 'we pack three weeks' worth of luggage that should have been done a week ago, scrape the grease off this infernal pit – '

'We prayed over this kitchen when we moved in, Kath,' interposed Mike mildly, setting a coffee of typically Robinsonian darkness before me. 'I don't think you ought to call it an infernal pit. What do you think, Dip?'

'I don't think it – '

'Then,' continued Kathy, 'we'll have a long theological discussion about how to avoid hurting the saintly kitchen's feelings, followed by some sort of attempt to mend our fractured domestic situation. Next we'll clean the house up – that should only take about four hours, then we'll do the things we shall have undoubtedly forgotten about, and then, assuming that our dear sons will be generous enough to accompany us, we'll set off, intending to go to the airport, but knowing in our hearts that, in fact, we are heading for a pre-ordained spot in the middle of nowhere, miles from a garage, where our sad vehicle will lie down and die. And that,' concluded Kathy, releasing her hair and bringing her fists down on the table with a thump, 'apart from my intention to inflict serious injury on the deaf imbecilic duck if and when it returns, completes the itinerary for today.'

'Kath finds going away a bit difficult,' said Mike, rather unnecessarily. 'You haven't started your coffee yet, Dip. Is it okay?'

I shrugged noncommittally. 'It's err … it's still a tiny bit strong for me, Mike. Nice, but strong. Look won't you let me help you?' I laid a hand on Kathy's arm. 'I would really and truly love to stay behind after you've gone, and sort the kitchen and the rest of the house out. I like being in other people's houses – I honestly do.'

Kathy gave a weary little whimper as hope battled with politeness. 'Oh, Dip, you don't want …'

'Apart from anything else,' I went on persuasively, 'it'll give me a chance to look through all your private papers and poke my nose into things that don't concern me. Please don't deprive me of that opportunity. People in the church would love to hear a few iffy things about you – just in confidence and for prayer, of course.'

Kathy's changes of mood always reminded me of the weather in Melbourne, where I lived when I was training. Suddenly the sun came out as she threw her head back and laughed. 'You're on! Make sure you put Mike's pornography back where you find it, though, won't you?'

'Kath!' Mike was very nearly annoyed. 'I *never* look at that sort of magazine at all – I wouldn't dream of having anything like that in my house. I can't remember ever looking at – well, I suppose if I'm absolutely honest, when I was young ...' Mike's fresh complexion turned a deep, rich, red colour, 'I might have glanced occasionally at – well ... some picture that a friend had, or something, but certainly not err ... now. Certainly not.'

'You don't have to do your giant radish impression, Mike. Dip knows I was only joking, don't you, Dip?'

'Well, yes,' I replied, 'but I was just thinking that I've got plenty of pornography of my own.'

They stared at me in surprise. 'You have?' said Mike.

'Certainly – up here.' I tapped my head. 'Lots of it up there. You don't flick all the switches to "off" just because you've gone past fifty, you know. It's a bit of a nuisance sometimes. Anyway, never mind me – the point is, you're going to let me stay behind and clean up for you, aren't you? That'll leave you free to sort the packing out and do anything else that needs doing.'

Mike was obviously still wrestling with the idea that single middle-aged ladies might sometimes battle with pornographic fantasies, but his face was almost its normal colour again. 'Well, if you're sure, Dip ...'

'I'm sure.'

'She's sure,' said Kathy, standing up decisively. 'Let's get on with the packing.'

Mike got to his feet as well, but as they faced each other across the table I sensed that a new tension had introduced itself. Could it be that the essential Packing Argument mentioned by Felicity was about to get under way?

It was. Mike launched it.

'Darling, let's be really systematic this time. We've got five large suitcases altogether, haven't we?'

Kathy's jaw moved soundlessly for a moment. Her fingers drummed quietly on the edge of the table. 'What was wrong with the way we did it last time?'

Mike moved away towards the window, one hand raised in silent pre-emphasis as he mustered his arguments. I don't know if you've met people like Mike. If you have, you'll know that, whilst generally mild and non-confrontational, they can become quite feverishly obsessional about the most trivial things. Even now, at this early stage in the forthcoming debate, Mike was quivering with restrained passion. Strange, but true.

'Well, come on,' repeated Kathy irritably, 'tell me what was wrong with the way we did it when we went to France.'

Mike turned to face his wife, gripping the front edge of the window sill behind him with both hands, as if frightened that, inflated by his passion, he might ascend slowly to the ceiling and hang there like a helium balloon.

'Nothing much – it's just that I can't get involved when you organize it. We end up in a sea of clothes and shoes and books and bits and pieces, with the cases buried somewhere underneath, and I wade dismally through it all with a teacloth in my hand wondering where it fits into your master plan.'

Mike was really motoring now, bobbing up and down on his heels very rapidly, and sounding like a man who has been brought face to face with some dreaded, ultimate emotional crisis.

'I don't know where anything is!' he continued wildly, 'I don't know where anything goes – I don't know what's going on, and I – '

Kathy finished her husband's sentence acidly. 'And you start shaking your head and hissing through your teeth and talking about how your wonderfully organized childhood makes it very difficult for you to cope with chaos.'

In the short silence that followed, Kathy slumped back into her seat, put her elbows on the table, and rested her chin wearily in her hands.

'I *don't* do that,' said Mike, his eyes wide with outrage.

Kathy didn't even look at him, 'You're almost doing it now, and we haven't even started yet.'

Mike turned stiffly and stared out of the window, exercising what must have seemed to him heroic self-control. 'Look, all I'm saying is that we could try it my way and see how we get on – just try it, for goodness' sake. That's all I'm saying.'

'Your way being what, exactly?'

Pleased with the opportunity to explain, Mike swung round and began to pace the length of the kitchen, addressing Kathy as though she was an infant class.

'We take all five cases out into the garden, right? And – '

'And we put them in a nice neat row – ' Kathy seemed to know what was coming.

'We put them in a row with the lids open, and we number them from one to five, and agree about what sort of luggage is going into each one, then we bring stuff out from the house bit by bit and fill the cases until there's nothing left in the house that should be in the cases. Apart from anything else it would be so much more fun doing it this way. You'd say to me, "Here's a shirt, Mike, it goes in number three", and I go out and put it in number three. Then you might say, "Here's a pair of shoes, Mike, they go in number five", so I put them in number five and come back for the next thing, and so on. Then we could swop round and I'd say, "Here's a blouse, Kath, it goes in number four", and you'd go out and put it in number four, then you'd come back for the next thing, and so on.'

Kathy groaned, as if she was in pain.

'Then, when everything's in, we shut the cases and that's that. The packing's done, everything's ready and we haven't had to hack our way through forests of overcoats and underwear just to find the floor.'

Emboldened by what he obviously felt to be the overwhelming force of his own logical argument, Mike ceased his pacing, sat down opposite Kathy again and invited her to submit to reason.

'How can you say that doesn't make sense, Kath? How can it possibly *not* make sense? How? Well, how can it? Come on – tell me how it can possibly not make sense. It seems so obvious. Surely you can see that, can't you?'

Folding her arms and leaning back in her chair, Kathy looked into her husband's imploring eyes and spoke with implacable calm.

'Michael, I wish to make the following observations. First of all, let us consider the difference between your method and mine. Your system may be neat and logical, but it would take about a year to get everything packed. In fact, it would become more of an ongoing hobby than a functional task. My method, on the other hand, may appear wild and unfathomable and cause you unspeakable anguish, but it would mean the packing gets done *before* we leave for America – an attractive little feature of my approach, wouldn't you say? Furthermore, touched though I am by the picture of you and me trotting happily and eternally to and fro with shirts and blouses and pairs of shoes, I have no intention of playing "Jane And John Go On Their Holidays" out in the garden just to pander to your completion neurosis. You may not know what's going on when I pack, but I do. And as it's always me that ends up doing it anyway, that's all that really matters, isn't it? Why don't you give Dip a hand with the kitchen and leave me to do the packing, then you won't have to worry about it at all, will you? How does that sound?'

'So you don't want me to help?'

Something told me that we had reached the real point of the discussion at last.

'Of course I'd like you to help – if you really mean it. What I can't stand is having you huffing and puffing around getting upset about not being able to do anything while I'm busy *doing* it.'

'Oh, well ...,' said Mike, sounding hurt, but not very convincingly so, 'I might just as well stay here and help Dip, then, if that's how you feel about it. By the way, Dip, what do *you* think of my way of doing it?'

I wanted to make real friends with the Robinsons.

'Ridiculous,' I smiled, 'charming, but ridiculous. Leave it to Kathy.'

I loved the way they both laughed.

Later, as Mike and I tackled the sink section of the 'infernal pit' side by side, I talked to him about the Packing Argument.

'It was almost,' I said, 'as though you had to go through all that just so that you'd arrive at a place where you knew you'd end up anyway. I don't think there was ever any question of you helping with the packing – not, I hasten to add, that you didn't mean what you said, of course, Mike. You've obviously got very strong views on how to fill suitcases. I'm very unformed in that area. I have none at all.'

Mike chuckled. He was back to his cheery, unruffled self again.

'We are a bit silly sometimes, I suppose. Kath worries that we haven't got one of those perfect Christian marriages that you read about in books, but, well ... we do love each other. That's pretty important, isn't it?' He suddenly gave a little embarrassed cough, and put down the plate he was polishing. 'It must be very hard for you sometimes, Dip – I mean, you must get sick of people going on about their wives and husbands and all that, when you ...'

'When I've never married? Yes, it is a bit difficult sometimes, but I love being with families, and I don't find single living quite so bad nowadays, actually. Not being married isn't an illness, you know. To be honest, Mike, I don't know if I could stand sharing – you know – intimate space with someone else after all these years.'

Through the window I could see Felicity spinning round and round very fast on the yellow plastic swing that hung from one of the apple trees. Little girl dreams came back suddenly.

'I tell you what, though, there are times when I long for there to be someone waiting for me when I get home – someone to ask how things have gone at work, make me a cup of tea – that sort

24

of thing. And sometimes, when I'm out at a place where there are lots of people, I wish … you're going to think this sounds extremely silly.'

'No,' said Mike, 'go on, I'm interested.'

I glanced quickly at his face and carried on.

'Well, I wish there was an eye to catch across the room, above the heads of the others – just for a moment – one of those small smiles that tells you someone understands exactly what you're thinking, and then you go back to chatting or whatever it is you're doing, but you know you're not on your own. Being special to someone, number one in their lives – I know it's silly, but I still cry for that every now and then.'

For a few moments the dribble of tap-water into the sink and the clink of dishes was the only sound to be heard in the Robinson kitchen, but it was not an awkward pause.

'There's one thing,' said Mike at last, 'at least you don't have to go through convoluted arguments before anything gets done, like we just did.'

'Well, no, but …' I paused, suddenly a little afraid. This was very solid coin I was passing across the counter of our still developing friendship. Not the sort you can ever take back again. 'No, but we single people play our own silly little games, you know. At least – I do.'

'Such as?'

I peeled the rubber gloves from my hands and dropped them into the sink.

'Dry tea-towel?'

'In the drawer under where the stick-insects are. Acres of tea-towels. We're good at having dry tea-towels. Carry on about your little games.'

'Sometimes,' I said, reaching for a handful of wet cutlery, 'I lose confidence in people.' I checked myself. 'Actually, that's not fair. I guess what I really mean is that I lose confidence in myself. Maybe it's a family – like yours – and I've been visiting a lot and everything seems fine, then all of a sudden I get this cold feeling in my stomach, and I think – what if they've just been putting up with me? What if they're being *kind* to me? Then I panic. And that's when the games start.'

Outside, Felicity had abandoned her swing, and was squatting down by the small flower bed that was specially her own, poking the earth with a stick. Happening to look up at that moment, she caught my eye and grinned. Why did Felicity's smile produce these spasms of choking tearfulness in me sometimes?

'I dive back into my little house like a frightened rabbit, and I shut the door behind me – lock it, bolt it, put a chair against it – anything to shut the world out so they can't see my embarrassment about being an interfering old bore who shoves herself in where she's not wanted. Then I might walk round the house with my fists clenched for a bit – have a little swear at myself, that sort of thing.'

Poor Mike had to say something, of course. 'But, Dip, you don't really think – '

'I'm not talking about what I think, Mike. I'm talking about what I *feel*. On those days I *feel* like a shapeless piece of rubbish, and I know that no one really likes me. They're just pretending, and I never want to see any of them ever again.'

'So the game is . . . ?'

'The game is – oh, I do feel a twit, Mike! The game – one of the games – is that I don't make contact with anyone for days and days, or even weeks, just to see how long it will be before they get round to remembering that I exist and write or phone or something. I know it's childish and silly, but – I suppose I just reach the bottom of myself every now and then and turn into a blob.'

'You've dried that last knife five times, Dip. Does it work?'

'Does what work? The not-making-contact, you mean? No, not really. I cuddle a load of burning resentment to myself for a bit, then I start missing people, so I go and see them and they're usually so pleased to see me, and I'm so pleased to see them that I forget all about being deeply hurt and everything gets back to normal.' I laughed. 'It backfired badly once. There was this couple in my last church but one who reckoned they had a "Ministry To Single Folk", and got very stroppy when I didn't go round for a while. They turned up at the door one evening with their mouths looking like bits of frayed string, and told me that because I had not been attending their gatherings – oh, Mike, I'd have had more fun being buried alive – they felt led to draw apart from me for a season, whatever that is. Then off they went, leaving me feeling very relieved and a bit guilty – only a bit, though.'

Mike threw the bottle-opener into its place, and closed the cutlery drawer with a triumphant bang.

'That's the washing-up done. Now we'll tackle the floor. Let's be syst – , I mean, you sweep, Dip, and I'll put the chairs up because I know how to arrange them, then you can talk to me from the hall while I mop. Okay?'

Leaning against the doorway with my arms folded a few minutes later, I felt a touch uneasy watching Mike as he worked slowly and methodically back towards me with the mop. A question was taking shape in the concentrated rhythm of his movements. If I hadn't known that the forthcoming holiday was about to create a natural gap, I might have done my rabbit act there and then. What price was I to pay for my vulnerability?

'Can I ask you something, Dip?'

'No.'

'Can I?'

I sighed. 'Yes.'

'Well – why did you tell me all that? I mean, you've blown the whatsit, haven't you? How can you go off and play games about not contacting us when we'll know exactly what you're doing, and turn up at your door with huge bunches of flowers and declarations of everlasting friendship as soon as we don't see you for more than a day or two? D'you see what I mean?'

I was determined not to cry. I took a deep breath.

'The thing is, Mike, I don't want to play games with you and Kathy and the others. I'm nearly fifty-one years old, and I don't think there's much chance of me hitching up with someone special now – not if I'm realistic. I meant it just now when I said that I couldn't imagine being that close to anyone in that way nowadays. But recently I've begun ...'

Sensing my need to know he was with me, Mike turned round, leaned on his mop, and nodded. 'Go on, I'm listening.

'Recently I've begun to feel lonely in a way that's different – there's a sort of panic in it, a fear that I'm going to become old without giving away – ' I struggled for a moment ' – without giving away *me* to anyone, me without the games and the unnecessary holding back and the staying calm and dependable and all that. I don't want to be a block of concrete round anyone's neck, but I would like to belong somewhere.' I stared hard at the tumble-dryer. 'You and Kathy and the kids have – how can I describe it? – you've let me be part of what's going on without tidying up your Christian act before I see it. You've let me in to where you really are, and, well, I've never really known what that feels like before. I want it to go on happening. I want that very much. Have I embarrassed you?'

Mike shifted his weight on the mop handle. 'Last night, after everyone had gone,' he said slowly and seriously, 'Kath and I were in bed, having a rather familiar end-of-the-day conversation. This particular one never changes much. She despairs about her terrible mothering and her looks and the decay of her writing talent and her ingratitude to God for what he's given her in all those areas, and I say things like, "Come on now, Kath, you know things aren't really that bad." Then she tells me what's wrong with me, and I listen but don't say anything – used to, but not any more – until she's said whatever's on her mind, then she usually cries, and we have a cuddle and everything's more or less all right. Well, we went through all that, and then, just as we were settling down to go to sleep, Kath suddenly said, "Mike, I wish Dip would come and live with us and be part of it all. I feel safe and warm when she's here." Those were the words she used – "safe and warm." '

He paused, searching for a way to convey the sincerity of what he was saying.

'Dip, we're a chaotic family – I don't have to tell you that. We seem to spend an awful lot of time pretending that we're more organized or more holy or more together than we really are. A waste of time, I'm sure, but I'm afraid it's the way we're made. You're the first person we haven't minded seeing us just as we are.' He smiled. 'Whether you like it or not, Miss Reynolds, you've got this warmth and acceptance about you that Kath and I just – well – just love. We both said exactly the same thing the other day. When you come in to the house everything lights up a bit.'

He turned abruptly and attacked the floor with even more vigour than before.

'This is a big old house, Dip,' he said over his shoulder, 'plenty of room for a bedsitter on the top floor. Think about it while we're in America, will you?'

'But Kathy – '

'Just now, you said that you wanted to be number one in someone's life, right? Well, I can't guarantee that, but I *can* tell you that you come an easy sixth as far as Kath's concerned – in fact, the way things are going with Mark at the moment, I should think you've been promoted to fifth. Think about it while we're away, will you? Promise?'

'I promise.'

The kitchen clock was showing exactly twenty-five minutes past two when Kathy, Mike, Jack, Felicity and I sat down at the table to a late lunch of fish and chips fetched from the High Street by Jack, whose room now looked (according to his mother) as though something sad and terrible had been poorly concealed. There was still no sign of Mark. Kathy's method must have worked pretty well because the packing was all done, but she looked very tired and grumpy.

'We won't bother having plates or anything,' said Mike slightly tensely, as he unwrapped the food, 'there's no point in cleaning everything up and then using it again. We might as well use our fingers and eat off the wrapping paper, then we can just screw the paper up and wash our hands, can't we?'

'I don't know why we *ever* bother to use plates,' commented Jack, 'it's just another way of complicating life, isn't it? As far as I'm concerned food's just a fuel. You put it in and it makes the engine work.'

He placed a large piece of fried fuel into his mouth and chewed it with visible relish.

'I like eating with my fingers,' said Felicity serenely. 'Why don't we say grace when it's just us? We never say grace unless someone's here – a *visitor*.' She pronounced the last word as though it was a dangerous disease.

'Dip is here, Felicity,' said Mike, 'doesn't she count?'

'No, silly,' replied Felicity scornfully, 'Dip *is* us. Mummy, why don't we say grace when it's just us? Do you think God only wants us to thank him for our food when someone important comes to dinner? At Emily's house they say grace before breakfast and tea and *everything*, even if there's only Emily and her mummy and me there. At Emily's house they – '

'Felicity, shut *up* about Emily's house,' interrupted Kathy irritably, 'I couldn't care less what they do at Emily's house. They're obviously much more wonderful at Emily's house than they are at Felicity's house, but I'm afraid you're stuck with living here with your own useless mother, so eat your fish and be quiet!'

In the silence that followed two huge tears welled up in Felicity's eyes and trickled slowly down her face. Mike had stopped eating and was staring at Kathy, perhaps waiting for her to repair the damage she'd done before someone else had to. Jack broke the silence. He wasn't going to stop the fuel transportation process for anything, but he had time between two mouthfuls to express a view.

'That's a bit unfair, Mum. Flitty was only pointing out how hypocritical it is to put on a show for some people and not bother with others.'

A huge forkful of fish and chips postponed Jack's developing defence of his little sister, but he wouldn't have been allowed to continue anyway. Whatever was heating up in Kathy came to the boil at that moment. Leaning across the table, she raised a rigid forefinger and jabbed it in the direction of her oldest son.

'Don't you *ever* lecture me on the subject of hypocrisy. I am an expert in that area after living with you for the last year or so. You sit there stuffing your face with chips and telling me that plates complicate life – well, let me add to your vast store of information by telling you that milk bottles complicate life as well, especially when I find five of them in that pit you call a bedroom, each with at least a quarter of a pint of rancid milk stinking the place out. When you've started clearing up your own messes and stopped wasting our money, I might be willing to listen to your views on the way we conduct our spiritual lives and bring up the rest of our children.'

There was a miserable pause. Jack put his non-fuel-injecting arm round Felicity, who was still sniffing, and Mike opened his mouth to say something. The blast was turned in his direction.

'If you're about to tell me that I've dropped a bit of fish or something on your nice, clean, blasted kitchen, Mike, I think I shall walk out of this house – I really think I will. I seem to be surrounded by neurotics and idiots who haven't got the wit to sort anything out for themselves, and I've had enough!'

Kathy placed her hands flat against her face and started to sob noiselessly, the top half of her body shaking with emotion. Felicity, red-eyed, looked at her mother in puzzlement.

'Daddy,' she said in a small, bruised voice, 'why's Mummy crying? Is she cross or upset?'

Mike spread his hands, bewildered and unhappy. 'I'm not sure, darling. Don't worry, though. Mummy didn't mean to get so – she didn't mean what she said. She's just got a bit upset.

'It was only four milk bottles,' offered Jack tentatively and perhaps rather empty-headedly, as though he felt it might make all the difference to the situation.

I felt terribly sorry for them all, but at the same time, inside my own head, the memory of something Felicity had said was singing like a bird – the same song over and over again: 'Dip *is* us, Dip *is* us, Dip *is* us ...' I was certainly the happiest person in the Robinson kitchen at that moment. I longed to help.

Something about the way Kathy was behaving brought to mind all those occasions in the past, mostly in the evenings, when a wave of panic-stricken loneliness had come crashing in to engulf whatever peace I'd achieved, leaving me gasping for air

31

and crying for the same reason that a baby does, out of pure need. You never shared that. What you did was – you waited until the tears had stopped, then you went upstairs and washed your face and brushed your hair, and when you looked reasonably all right you went down again, sat by the phone, and thought through a list of the people you knew. When you finally got round to calling somebody you sounded bright and casual. You said you'd thought of popping round a bit later (because you'd be passing anyway) to sort something out, or make some arrangement, or pick up something you'd left there. It wasn't urgent, you'd insist. It could wait – just a thought …

Then, if they said it was a good idea, you listened hard to discover if they really wanted you. If they did – or if they acted it convincingly enough – you went round. When you got there they'd ask you how you were, and you'd tell them you were fine and do a little light laugh, but inside you'd be screaming silently for them to put their arms round you and love you and look after you.

I'm quite sure other people cope much better with living on their own than I used to. But experiences like mine make you very sensitive to the proposition that people might *mean* something they're not saying. I knew that Kathy's problem was nothing to do with anybody sitting in the kitchen. I leaned across and gently took one hand away from her face.

'It's Mark, isn't it?'

At that moment we all heard the sound of someone opening the front door. The absence of any corresponding sound of the front door shutting suggested that Mark had returned at last. Two seconds later he walked into the kitchen and stared at the food on the table.

'Couldn't wait for me, then?' he said indignantly.

Chapter 3

Plenty here for you, Mark, sit down and I'll sort yours out for you.'

Mike's brave attempt to carry on as if nothing was really wrong failed almost immediately. Kathy had stopped crying. Now she was white and still with anger. Pushing her seat back she stood up and moved round until she was directly behind the chair into which Mark had casually dropped. He had already started to chomp noisily. Kathy's voice was tight with fury.

'Your father may think there's no problem, young man, but I happen to think there is.' She paused. 'Are you listening to me?'

Mark went on eating as though his mother didn't exist.

'I *said* – are you listening to me?' Another pause. 'If you don't say something to me I'm going to drag you out of that chair and *make* you answer.'

'I can hear your voice, if that's what you mean.'

The ghostly premonition of a clout round the back of the head had forced a response from the boy, but his words were just about as graceless and provocative as he could make them.

'Well, if you can hear my voice, you can hear me saying this, then, can't you? In my opinion – not that you give a monkey's about my opinion, I'm well aware of that – your behaviour has made a very difficult day almost impossible. Let's just go through it, shall we? You started at eight o'clock in the morning with this extraordinary claim of yours that you didn't know we were going to America today. I'm sorry, Mark, but that means you're either terminally dense, or just not interested enough in your own family to register any information that isn't directly connected with hanging around the precinct with your dismal friends. You *must* have known we were going today – I think you *chose* not to know. And then, after coming out with all that rubbish, you disappear – goodness knows where – for hours and hours, leaving us to do all the work, then you stroll back in leaving the front door open – '

'*I* left the front door open this morning, Mummy,' said Felicity in a frightened, trying-to-make-things-better sort of voice.

'Ah, yes,' gritted Kathy, still addressing the back of Mark's head, 'but, you see, Felicity, when your dear brother does it, it's yet another symptom of the fact that anything that might benefit anyone else isn't even worth considering – totally irrelevant as far as you're concerned, isn't it, Mark?'

Mike leaned forward. 'Kath, don't you think you're going a bit over the – '

'Over the top? Is that what you were going to say?' Kathy was almost breathless with anger now. 'Yes, I am going over the top. I'm going over the top for good and sufficient reasons. I'm going over the top quite rationally, thank you very much, and if you must know I'm sick of the way you regard any attempt I make to discipline this – this *child* as some kind of neurotic outburst.'

Bending down and resting her forearms on the table, she spoke right into the side of Mark's face. He twitched his head slightly away from hers and went on eating. 'I find it utterly inconceivable that you can walk back into this house and sound put out because the rest of the family have decided to eat, instead of waiting for you to grace us with your presence at whatever time you see fit to come in.' She breathed deeply for a moment or two. 'Now, I'm going to tell you what I want. I want to know what you think about all the things I've just said – unless, of course, *you* think that I'm being unreasonable as well. *Is* that what you think?'

To my ears, the washing-machine-like noise of Mark's eating was amplified in the pause that followed, until it seemed to fill the kitchen and the house and the whole world. Seeing that he was lifting another mouthful to replace the one that was on the point of being swallowed, Kathy took hold of his wrist and repeated her question.

'*Do* you think I'm being unreasonable?'

I suppose that if a committee had been appointed at this stage in the proceedings, with the express purpose of devising the worst possible response for Mark to make to his mother, it might, after some weeks, or even months, of deliberation, have come up with something less politic than what he actually said, but I doubt it.

'Why can't I stay here and look after myself while you all go to America?'

That was what he actually said, and it was the straw that well and truly broke the camel's back. Kathy snatched the laden fork from Mark's hand and threw it across the table, where it landed in front of her oldest son, who had just finished his own lunch. Jack stretched an absent-minded hand out and then withdrew it again quickly, suddenly aware, I suppose, that such crude opportunism was inappropriate, to say the least.

'You stupid little …!' Kathy was almost beyond words now. Pulling Mark to his feet, she held him and shook him by both wrists, pushing her face right into his as she shouted. 'How can you say such stupid things? You stupid, stupid …! Do you know how much this holiday is costing us? Do you know how long it's taken to plan? What the hell do you mean by asking if you can stay at home? I can't believe you could do this to us – the amount of money we've spent on you lately – you just don't care, do you? When you needed a lift to town yesterday to get your precious trainers the whole household screeched to a halt so that you could have what you wanted. But that means nothing, does it? The fact is you just don't care. You don't care! You don't care!'

Anger became tears again. Kathy was crying out from a place in her that had nothing to do with the present conflict. Some wound from the past had been opened, and it was hurting her. The trouble was, it was hurting Mark as well, in ways that confused and frightened him. With his face set hard against the torrent of emotion, he wrenched himself from his mother's grasp and spat words back at her in a strangely pitched pseudo-adult voice.

'Why do you say nasty things about my friends, then? An' why do you always talk about what you've done for me and how much money you've spent on me when you think I've done something wrong. *You're* the one who doesn't care!'

Turning abruptly, he stomped away along the hall and we heard his footsteps pounding up the stairs above our heads towards his bedroom. A door slammed violently and then there was silence.

Felicity said, 'Why is everything so horrible on our holiday day?' and burst into tears. Jack lifted her carefully onto his lap and put his arms round her.

Kathy didn't seem to be conscious of anything but her own response to Mark's parting shot. '*I'm* the one who doesn't care – I'm the one who doesn't care – I'm the one . . .' Rage flowed in and out of her as if she was breathing it. 'I'll teach the little rat to slam doors!'

As she set off at a near sprint towards the stairs, Mike rose to his feet and called out nervously, 'Kath, don't you think you ought to wait until . . . ?' He subsided. Kathy wasn't about to take suggestions from anyone, let alone feebly expressed advice from her husband.

We waited and listened. Kathy's feet on the stairs sounded heavily above us just as Mark's had done, but then, unaccountably, there was complete silence – no crashes, no shouts, no screams, no explosions of any kind. Straining our ears for the slightest sound, we sat and said nothing for what seemed like a very long time, although it was probably only a couple of minutes.

'She's killed him,' said Jack.

I found this remark less than amusing in the circumstances, but, despite the fact that tears still stood in her eyes, Felicity was obviously greatly relieved by what she saw as the total absurdity of Jack's comment. She giggled as though she'd been tickled. Mike expelled the breath he had been holding and let his chin drop to his chest like a weight suddenly released. 'I think,' he said, studying his interlocked fingers on the table as he spoke, 'it's probably going to be all right – for a while, anyway.' He stood up. 'I'll put some of this food in the oven for when Kath and Mark come down. I expect we all feel a bit – bruised at the moment, but it'll all be okay later on.'

'What time have you got to be at Heathrow, Mike?' I asked.

He closed the oven door and glanced over his shoulder at the clock. 'We need to check in by six, so if we're away from here by four-thirty we should be okay. Plenty of time if you really meant what you said about clearing up after us, Dip.'

'Oh, I meant what *I* said, Mike. How about you? Did you mean what you said?'

'Did I mean ...? Ah, well, all things being equal – and that's by no means guaranteed in this household, as you were well aware long before this last little domestic interlude – you're going to hear a bit more about that just before we leave, and I think you'll be surprised how much – '

Mike broke off as Kathy appeared in the doorway. Tears, anger and tension had all disappeared. She looked quite happy, though somewhat sheepish.

'Hello, everybody,' she said, 'I've come to make huge acts of contrition. Felicity, darling, come and give Mummy a cuddle. I didn't mean to get cross with you like that.'

The little girl's unhesitating, scrambling descent from Jack's lap was a wonderful display of that unconditional, joy-filled forgiveness with which some children freshen the world. She ran across the kitchen, threw herself into her mother's arms, and, after a long swinging hug, asked (as I rather thought she might) the question whose repetition proved that Felicity really did believe in her mother's apology.

'Mummy, why *don't* we say grace when it's just us, like they do at Emily's house?'

We all burst into laughter, including Kathy, who said, 'I'm afraid the answer's exactly the same even when I'm not cross, sweetheart. You're stuck with your silly old Mummy – '

'And your silly old Daddy,' contributed Mike.

'Whereas lucky old Emily has a mummy and daddy who are nice and calm and organized and do all the right things at the right times, *even when no one's looking*! And good for them, I say. I wish I was like it, but I'm not.'

Felicity squeezed Kathy's cheeks with the thumb and forefinger of each hand, then drew back her head and chortled at her mother's distorted face. 'I *want* to be stuck with you and Daddy,' she said, putting on a very little girl's voice. 'I wouldn't want to be stuck with Emily's mummy.'

'Nor would I!' said Mike with unexpected passion, and everyone except Felicity laughed again.

'Did you kill Mark?' enquired Jack pleasantly.

'No, I didn't kill him, Jack – not this time. Please forgive me for sounding off at you the way I did just now. It wasn't you, although the milk bottles do make me cross. I shouldn't have gone on like that. I really am sorry.' She lowered Felicity to the floor and addressed Jack again. 'Would you mind making a start on taking the cases out to the van, love? And there are quite a lot of small bags as well, so Felicity can come and give you a hand. You'd like to do that for Mummy, wouldn't you, Felicity?'

Felicity looked at her mother with the narrowed eyes of an expert decoder. 'I want to stay and hear what happened with Mark as well,' she said.

'Come on, Flitty.' Jack uncoiled himself from his chair and held out a hand. 'You know they won't talk about it while you're here, anyway, so we might as well go and do the bags. Tell you what – you can have a chocolate drop for every bag you take out. How's that?'

'You haven't got any chocolate drops,' said Felicity, looking hopefully up into her brother's face.

'Oh, haven't I? How do you know I haven't got a packet hidden away in my room?'

''Cause I'd have found them by now if there were any.'

'Oh, you would, would you? Right – you've had it now!'

Frowning with mock severity Jack hoisted his giggling sister up onto his shoulder and marched away with her, closing the door between the kitchen and the rest of the house behind him with his foot. Squeals of anguish and ecstatic laughter floated back from the hall as the pair headed for the front sitting room.

'Is Mark coming down to finish his lunch?' asked Mike quietly.

Kathy nodded as she pulled a chair up to the table. 'Yes, he'll be here in a minute. I shan't want any food – not after eating all those words. I just wanted to tell you what happened upstairs.'

I was suddenly embarrassed. 'Would you like me to go and give Jack a hand? I don't mind at all ...' Feeling hot and heavy I made a movement as if to leave, but Kathy reached across and laid a restraining hand on my shoulder.

'You are joking, aren't you, Dip? If I'm not bothered about you seeing the worst of my dirty washing I'm certainly not going to mind you seeing one of the rare occasions when a scrap of underwear actually gets laundered, am I? In fact – I insist. Incidentally, that reminds me. We were going to suggest something for you to think about while we're in – '

'I've already mentioned it to Dip,' interrupted Mike, 'we'll say some more about that just before we go. Tell us what happened with Mark.'

'Oh, right ... you've mentioned it, right.' Momentarily, Kathy searched my face for a response, but found none. The Robinsons may be good at having clean tea-towels, but I am very good at closing my face. Kathy knitted her brows in thought for a second, then spoke. 'About Mark – okay, well, I set off up the stairs with the deliberate intention of doing him some kind of serious physical damage. You probably guessed that, right?'

'We had an inkling,' replied Mike solemnly.

'I went up there like an express train, and I wasn't thinking at all. I could only feel all these emotions crashing around inside me.' She waved a hand in the direction of her husband. 'Mike's seen it all many times, of course – been on the receiving end of it more than once as well, I'm afraid. I just get filled up with this wild, storming fear.'

'Fear of what, Kathy?'

'I'm not quite sure. The night, the end, everything falling apart, not being loved, some kind of looming final disaster – I don't really know. I've never been able to pin it down. It's always been there under the surface, waiting for something like this Mark business to open the cellar door and let it out. Don't get me wrong – Mark *has* been a pain in the neck, and he does need sorting out. He can be a little devil. The trouble is that after these dreadful feelings have been going on in me for a while they stop having anything to do with the thing or person that set them off. But it's too late by then – the express is going at full speed and someone usually gets hurt. You see, the problem is, Dip, I ain't got no brakes on my train.'

'But something stopped you this time.'

Kathy placed the palms of her hands together like a child in prayer, resting her face on the tips of her fingers as she considered. She looked up. 'Yes, it did. It was something I read this morning in the blighted fox-hole that we risibly refer to as our Quiet Time. It was the bit about loving our enemies. Jesus said we have to love our enemies. Mike and I decided we had one person each we'd describe as real "Enemies", didn't we, Mike?'

Mike frowned guiltily. 'Yes, we were going to pray for them, but unfortunately we got a bit err ... distracted by thinking up all sorts of tortures we'd like to put them through – '

'You mean *I* did. Non-stop Scottish music in a confined space whilst playing Monopoly with our three children – that sort of thing.' Kathy grinned, enjoying the memory. 'Anyway, just now when I arrived upstairs and I was about to push the door in like an American detective and pull Mark's head off, I remembered those three words – Love Your Enemies. And I suddenly realized that – oh, Mike, it was awful – I realized that, in that moment, I was thinking of my *own son* as my enemy. I still wanted to kill him, you understand, but I was brought up short by ...' She brushed the hair back from her forehead. 'I was brought up short by the knowledge that I could either obey by loving him, whatever that might involve, or disobey by giving in to my own feelings. Standing outside that door, still seething away, it seemed as simple as that.'

'The Lord was speaking to you,' said Mike, his eyes shining. 'That's what you've always wanted, Kath. Always happens to other people, but never to you – that's what you've said so many times.'

Exasperation shadowed Kathy's face. 'I wish you'd resist the temptation to turn the whole of life into an infant classroom, Mike. You can go around sticking helpful little labels on all your experiences if you like, but I'd like mine left as they are, thank you very much. Maybe God *was* talking to me. I don't know. All I know for sure is that I thought and felt certain things, and that, as a result, I did things differently – that's all.'

'Sorry, Kath,' said Mike. His tone was repentant, but his eyes were still shining.

'What did you do in the end, Kathy?'

'In the end, Dip, I turned the handle of the door very, very slowly with that intensive muscular control you use when you're in a temper but you don't want it to show, and walked in. Mark had actually got into bed in his clothes – he knows I hate him doing that during the day – and he was sitting up reading a comic. He was obviously waiting for the explosion, as I'm sure you all were down here. I sat down on his bed without saying anything and he looked at me a bit puzzled before pretending to go back to his comic. Then I put my arms out and said, "I love you, Mark – whatever happens in the next five minutes, I'll always love you – whatever happens." He lowered the comic and looked at me for a second, then he put his arms out and we had a cuddle. He said something like "Sorry I've been a bit off, Mum" and I said "I'm sorry I've been a bit off as well", and that was it really. He's coming down to have his lunch in a minute, so . . .' She broke off and then gave a little laugh.

'What were you thinking then, Kath?' said Mike.

'Just – how pathetic I am,' replied Kathy, 'a bit of affection – that's all I need to chase the cold away. A good hug, and the sun comes out. I'm such a child. All my troubles seem to resolve themselves into one big question. Do you still love me? I tell you what, though,' she added with a smile, 'it's a good job he did respond, because if he hadn't – I'd have thrown him through the window.'

Peace reigned for some time after that. Mark duly appeared, apparently unaffected by the recent trauma, ate his own and his mother's share of the remaining food, and talked to me with transparently genuine happiness about the family adventure that was about to begin. When I asked him if he had really not known that the holiday was to start today he insisted that he had thought it was next Saturday, and went on to explain at some length that he had only been upset because he and his friends had planned to go fishing on the Monday, and he'd been 'well looking forward to that' because they were going to take sandwiches and drinks and (quite inexplicably to me) a football, and they were coming back to Mark's house in the evening to cook and eat all the fish that would have been caught during the day, and it had to be Mark's house because none of his friends' mothers liked a mess in their kitchens. I stored up this last, slightly backhanded, compliment to pass on to Kathy at an appropriate time in the future.

By four-fifteen the Robinsons were ready to go. Felicity, full of excitement and chocolate drops, skipped up and down the hall singing, 'We're going to America!' over and over again, until, together with her two brothers, she was summoned by her father for a last-minute family conference around the kitchen table. Mike sat at the end nearest the window, looking a little nervous as he waited for the hubbub to subside. I was feeling nervous too. I suddenly regretted my earlier move into self-revelation and wished that everything could stay exactly the way it had always been, for ever.

'Isn't it funny,' said Kathy, when the general chatter had died down, 'how you feel just before you go off on a trip like this? You've been looking forward to it for ages, you've been ever so excited about going, it's what you really want, and yet – I can't describe it exactly – at this precise moment I'd like to settle down amongst all these nice familiar, safe things and just be at home. Does that sound very silly?'

'Yes,' said Felicity simply, 'very silly indeed, Mummy.' She gave a little rippling laugh at the thought of such foolishness. 'Of course we don't want to stay here. We want to go to America.' She turned to her father. 'Is America in England, Daddy?'

'No, darling,' replied Mike, sounding slightly shocked at this vast gap in his daughter's geographical comprehension, 'you *know* it isn't. I've explained to you that we have to go in a big aeroplane across an enormous sea called the Atlantic Ocean because America is a completely different country. I showed you on the map, remember?'

'It's where the cowboys and Indians come from, Flitty,' added Jack, 'like on telly.'

'I thought it was where Disneyland is.' There was a trace of anxiety in Felicity voice as she tried to make sense of her six-year-old store of information. 'We're going there, aren't we, Mummy?'

'Of course we are,' said Kathy reassuringly, 'it's going to be such fun.'

'There aren't any cowboys and Indians any more, Flit,' explained Mark, 'they all dress like us in America now and they don't wear guns.'

'Joke!' Jack leaned his chair back on two legs and guffawed loudly.

Mark's face hardened angrily. 'Why is what I say a joke? Why wasn't what you said a joke?'

'There may not be any cowboys and Indians any more, but to say that Americans don't have guns nowadays is plain ridiculous. There are more guns per person in the United States of America than in any other – '

'I never said they don't have guns any more. I said they don't *wear* them like they used to. You never listen to what anyone else says, that's your trouble. You're too busy pretending to be grown-up, and listening to music that nobody else understands because it's so bad that they can't be bothered.'

'Oh, get lost!' Jack turned his face away from Mark. 'I hope he's not going to be like this for the next three weeks. I don't know if I can stand it.'

Jack's languid dismissiveness detonated something in Mark.

'Why don't you shut up, Jack! You make me sick! You make me – '

'Mummy, there *are* still cowboys and Indians in America.' Something had risen to the surface of Felicity's memory. 'I've seen them in a thing on television about Disneyland. They've *got* them at Disneyland. Jack and Mark both said that there aren't any any more, but there are, aren't there?'

Mark had folded his arms as if to contain the furies that occupied him. He spoke in terse, clipped tones. 'Dad, can I not sit next to Jack on the plane, please?'

'Suits me,' drawled Jack, 'I don't want to sit next to a silly little boy for hours and hours.'

Kathy put both hands over her ears. 'If you two don't – '

'Mummy, tell Mark and Jack that there are still cowboys and Indians in America. They both said – '

'Stop.' Mike didn't raise his voice at all, but there was something about the firmness of intention behind his one word that secured everyone's attention. 'I'm afraid we're all being rather selfish. This last little bit was supposed to be for Dip. It wasn't supposed to be an opportunity for Jack and Mark to see how unpleasant they could be to each other. I'd like you both to say sorry to her, please.'

There are few things more excruciating than having to receive apologies from people who have been instructed to offer them, but I couldn't help smiling as both of the boys mumbled their penitence.

So difficult, I thought, for Jack, poised between childhood and growing-up, to find the stability to cope with older *and* younger folk. Felicity was too little to present a problem – indeed, I sensed that she made him feel more like an adult, but Mark must be a significant image in the juvenile picture of himself that Jack didn't want to acknowledge any more. Scorn and dismissiveness seemed to be the only weapons he had found to use in the battle to prevent his younger brother dragging him back into a world that he yearned to leave behind.

Perhaps it was even more difficult for Mark to understand

why the big brother who had probably been closer to him than anyone else for the last few years, was becoming so treacherously distant in manner and lifestyle. I felt such sympathy for both of them.

'Did I do anything wrong, Daddy?' asked Felicity interestedly.

'Not quite,' said Mike, smiling despite himself, 'but you can apologize to Dip as well if you like. That'll count for the next time you do something naughty.'

This idea appealed enormously to Felicity. Kneeling on her chair she draped her arms around my neck and rested her head on my shoulder. 'Oh, Dip,' she cried theatrically, 'please forgive me for the next naughty thing I do. I can't tell you how sorry I shall be!'

I patted Felicity's back. 'Thank you very much, Felicity, I shall look forward to that. Actually – I think Mike's the only member of this family who hasn't apologized to me today. I'm beginning to wish I could do something bad myself, then I'd be able to apologize to one of you.'

Mike clapped his hands briskly three times. 'Right! No more messing about. No more arguing. Let's show Dip what we've done. Can you get out that certain something we made yesterday, please, Mark?'

'Oh, yeah!' Mark's eyes came alight with anticipation as he stood up and reached into the lower cupboard of the kitchen dresser that stood beside the back door. Releasing me from her embrace, Felicity bounced her bottom up and down on her ankles and flapped her hands with excitement.

'This is the surprise, Dip!' she squealed, 'I did some of it. You look!'

'Take the other end, Jack,' said Kathy, 'he can't manage it on his own. You two may not agree about most things, but I know you feel the same about this.'

'Okay, Mum. Close your eyes until we tell you, Dip.' Jack rose amicably to his feet and took one end of the long, concertinaed strip of paper that Mark had been carefully unfolding.

I closed my eyes.

When the chorus of 'Look now!' came, I opened my eyes to see an eight-foot paper banner, decorated with stars and trees and people and all sorts of less identifiable shapes in every colour of the felt-pen rainbow. It was a beautiful piece of work, but most beautiful of all was the message spelt out in capital letters that had been cut from coloured paper and stuck on separately:

WE LOVE YOU DIP – COME AND LIVE WITH US

When I was a young girl at school in Adelaide I wrote a story which included the immortal words – 'Two pairs of eyes stared at him open-mouthed ...' I seem to remember that my English teacher was not at all impressed by this unintentional flight of anatomical fantasy. She spent some time trying to explain that eyes don't have mouths and therefore cannot open them, but, perhaps because we focused on it for so long, that incorrect phrase has stuck in my mind ever since. Every time someone looks at me in a certain way I say to myself, 'That pair of eyes is looking at me open-mouthed'. That's how it was in the kitchen now. Five pairs of Robinson eyes were staring at me open-mouthed, and I knew that five pairs of Robinson ears were waiting for me to respond in the most obvious way, by simply saying, 'Yes, of course I'll come and live with you'.

It would have been so easy to say exactly that – not immediately, because my eyes filled with tears and I had to hunt for a tissue in my sleeves – but once I'd recovered I could have said the words, and that would have been that. I'm very grateful to God for that little pause, because I think it saved me from making a serious mistake.

'Dip,' I felt Felicity's arm creep around my shoulders, 'if you come to live with us, you'll be able to tell me lots more stories about crocodiles and jellyfish and things, and you could take turns with Mummy and Daddy putting me to bed.'

This ingenuous assessment of the major benefits likely to accrue to me if I moved in with the Robinsons made me laugh but also set the tears flowing again for some reason.

'We all mean it,' said Mark gruffly. 'Flit an' me did the colouring an' Jack did the letters. We spent ages on it.'

'Please forgive me, everybody,' I said damply, dabbing my eyes as I spoke, 'it was such a lovely surprise that it made me cry. I'm sorry to be so silly – it really is the most beautiful thing I've ever seen, and you must have worked so hard on it.' I gave Felicity a quick squeeze. 'Thank you, darling – and Mark and Jack. When you've gone I'm going to have a really good look at all those pictures. I can't tell you what it means to know that you took all that trouble, and that you – you love me enough to want me living in your house. It makes me feel very special.'

Kathy slid the palms of her hands from side to side across the table-top, as if sweeping away invisible obstacles. 'So, what's the answer, Dip? Yes or no?'

'No, Kath, don't bully – we said we'd leave Dip to think about it while we're in America, and that's what we're going to do.' Mike turned to me. 'Kath and I didn't do any of the banner, Dip, but we mean it just as much as the others. We'd love you to live here, but it's up to you. Let us know what you've decided when we come back. It's not something you can decide on the spot. Now!' He peered at the clock. 'If we don't go in the next few minutes we're going to be in trouble. You boys fold the banner up and leave it on the table. You know about the keys and the switches and everything, don't you Dip? It's all yours till we get back.' He looked from face to face. 'Anything else?'

Felicity prodded an accusing finger into my chest. 'You've been saying for ages and ages that you'd tell me why you're called "Dip" before we went to America. Now you've got to. Why are you?'

I have never really understood why I desperately hang on to secrets that would seem foolish and trivial to anyone else. Perhaps it's something to do with living alone in your own little world for so long. I had put Felicity off again and again, without knowing quite why, but now the deadline I had so rashly specified was upon me and there was no escape.

'I'll tell you very quickly,' I replied, 'because you've got to go, so listen carefully.'

Felicity nodded, eyes huge with interest. I took a deep breath.

'When I was a little girl I used to play with my cousin called James, who was a bit older than me, but very nice.'

'I've got three cousins,' said Felicity proudly, 'and they're called Paul, Rachel and Amy. They're very perfect and they live in West Wickham.'

'Well, I only had this one called James, who wasn't perfect, and he lived in a place called Glenelg, which was near the sea.'

'In Australia?'

'In Australia, yes. My mummy and I used to travel on a funny old thing that was a bit like a train and a bit like a tram – I loved going on it – from Adelaide, which was the big city where we lived when I was small, to Glenelg, where James lived with his mummy and daddy and a much older brother. One morning we went to see them when it had been raining through the night, and we all went shopping together. The sun had come out and it was very hot, but there were puddles everywhere, and because my mummy had made me wear my rubber boots I was allowed to jump around in them as much as I liked. James wasn't, because he had his best shoes on – I don't think he was very pleased really. Anyway, when we stopped somewhere for the grown-ups to have a cup of tea and us to have an ice-cream, James told me that he'd been reading a book about red Indians – '

'Like I'll see in Disneyland?'

'Yes, that's right, and this book said that little Red Indian children were given their names when they were older than children in Australia or England, because their mummies and daddies wanted to see what they were like, and call them something that really suited them. So, for example, let's say you liked to practise a lot with a toy bow and arrow, well, your name might end up as "Hunts With Arrows", or if your favourite game was pretending to be a galloping pony you might be called "Running Horse". James said that if I was a little Red Indian girl who hadn't got a name yet my mummy would have to call me "Dances In Puddles". I was very cross with James for saying that, but my mummy, and James' mummy and daddy and big brother laughed and laughed and laughed, and when we were back in Adelaide my mummy told the story to lots of people we knew. Then someone noticed that the first letters of "Dances In Puddles" made DIP, and they said that's what I should be called. So "Dip" has been my name ever since.'

There is no history of anyone except Felicity expressing any great enthusiasm for my narrative talents, so I was a little taken aback to discover, on looking around the table, that every member of the Robinson clan appeared totally transfixed by the true story I had just told.

'Go on,' I said, breaking the spell. 'Go! You'll miss your plane. Go to America!'

Two minutes later they were all packed into the van ready to leave, and I was leaning on Felicity's pillar, waiting to wave goodbye. Through an open side-window I distinctly heard Mark making the provocative suggestion that, if Jack had been a Red Indian, he would have been known as 'Listens To Rubbish'. I wondered how harmonious the journey was likely to be. Finally, with much wild hand-waving and loud shouts of farewell, the Robinsons were gone.

I watched the van disappear over the brow of Maiden Hill, then I lingered for a moment, enjoying the afternoon sunshine, and talked very quietly to God about the Robinsons.

'Father,' I said, 'you gave me a wonderful gift today, and I'm really grateful. Ever since we first met I've been asking you for someone special to love me. You've given me a whole family, and I'm really pleased. Don't cancel the order for the Paul Newman look-alike, I'm still in the market for that, whatever I might say about personal space – but I'm so pleased they want me.' Tears filled my eyes again suddenly. 'Look after those Robinsons, Lord, and help them not to be too disappointed when I tell them I can't come and live with them, because I don't think I can – not yet.'

Chapter 4

I did enjoy being left in charge of the Robinsons' home, not so much because of the chance to sift through everyone's private papers and Mike's fabled pornography, but because there simply is something very 'tasty' about roaming freely in somebody else's house when there's absolutely no chance of them coming back.

As I finished my prayer by the gate-post and walked back inside I felt oddly light-headed, as though I'd had just the right amount to drink. The front door shut behind me with one of those very satisfactory locked-on-the-inside sounds, and I paused in the hall for a moment, savouring the very particular hush that falls over a newly de-familied house.

In the kitchen I made myself a coffee exactly the way *I* liked it for once – weak, with just a suggestion of sugar – and sat on a stool by the open window overlooking the garden.

I knew that I was going to have to work through my feelings about the invitation I'd just had, and I also wanted to be very clear in my own mind about the best way to tell the family that I didn't yet feel able to move in with them, but I couldn't face all that just now. Maybe it would be easier just to forget my reservations and do what they wanted. The cowardly way out was very tempting at that moment. I sighed. Such heavy considerations would have to be postponed while I had a little board meeting with myself concerning my immediate responsibilities as guardian of the Robinson castle.

These meetings with myself tend to be fairly lively, because when I'm on my own I chatter to myself, a habit which, if I'm not careful, can sometimes leak out into places where other people are likely to be. More than once I've turned the corner of a street, haranguing myself quite loudly and sternly on some topic, only to be confronted by an alarmed member of the public coming in the other direction who, quite reasonably, was expecting to encounter at least two people, if not a large public meeting. There is only one feeble thing that I have ever been able to think of doing in that situation – I sing, and try to give the impression that that's what I was doing all along. Pathetic, isn't it?

I felt I was quite safe in the Robinsons' kitchen.

'Right,' I said out loud to myself, 'living creatures first. Just the two stick-insects to be fed and tickled. Thank goodness Stan is no more.'

Until recently, Felicity had owned an obnoxiously bad-tempered hamster, christened 'Stan' by Kathy, because the expression on his beady-eyed little face as he sniffed with incredulous disdain at food, people, the air and everything else, bore an uncanny resemblance to the expression habitually worn by one of our older church members. Every attempt to handle him and establish friendly relations – with the hamster, that is, not the church member – had been met with such energetically relentless biting and weeing, that even Felicity's enthusiasm waned after a time, and Stan, presumably enraged at being deprived of the opportunity to inflict pain and dampness, became a sort of Houdini of the hamster world. Despite being confined in an extravaganza of purpose-built, brightly coloured plastic tubes and living spaces, described in true American style on the side of the box it came in as a 'Small Animal Module', he discovered that, given time, he could always find a way to nibble himself to freedom. He would make triumphant appearances on the kitchen work-surface or the window-sill, sniffing smugly and daring his human jailers to re-incarcerate him. The queue for this task was never a very long one and it trickled away to nothing as the weeks went by. Whenever the cry went up 'Stan's out!' all Robinsons (and one Reynolds if I was visiting at the time) would suddenly discover pressing engagements elsewhere, and Stan would be left to feel, with some justification, that he had possessed the land – well, the kitchen anyway.

It was usually Kathy who ended up sacrificing flesh and dryness to get the animal back into its cage, although truth compels me to admit that she generally performed this task with a conspicuous lack of Christian grace and goodwill – not that anyone blamed her for that. We were too relieved that she was doing it to worry much about the spirit in which it was done. Mike attempted to intervene only once. I recall the occasion well.

There had been such a sound of crashing, and such a torrent of swearing, snarling abuse issuing from the kitchen where Kathy was dealing with Stan, that it seemed to those of us crouched in hiding (Felicity and I) as if she must be rolling over and over on the floor with the creature, locked in mortal combat. Mike, who simply cannot leave well alone at times, abandoned the television programme he'd been watching in the sitting room, and took up a position in the kitchen doorway from which he remonstrated mildly but firmly with his wife over the language she was using.

I don't know if Kathy actually threw Stan at Mike, or what happened at the end of that particular row, because, at this juncture, Felicity and I folded our tents and stole quietly away to play on the swings at the recreation ground, but I do know that (to my knowledge) Mike never criticized any aspect of Kathy's Stan-handling again. A few weeks after that incident God had mercy on the afflicted. He caused Stan to escape captivity in the middle of the night, and the small but powerful creature was never seen again by any of us. Felicity was encouraged to believe that he was well and happy in some Promised Land behind the wainscoting, but I think the rest of us felt fairly sure that biting, weeing Stan had gone to that great Small Animal Module in the sky, and, to be honest, we were glad – although we felt very sorry for the angel who would have to look after him.

Stan's departure meant that my sole living charges for the next few weeks were the stick-insects, which belonged to Mark, nominally at any rate, and they had certainly never caused any direct harm to anyone. Being of a type that is native to Australia, they had originally (and terribly unoriginally) been given the names Bruce and Sheila, but at my suggestion had been rechristened

Rowan and Kimberley, names that were equally Australian in flavour but a little less crudely predictable. Now, as I sipped my coffee and leaned down to tickle Kimberley's tummy with my thumbnail, I couldn't help smiling as I recalled the events surrounding their arrival in the Robinson household.

Mark had brought them home one Friday evening after a school trip which included a visit to a nature centre on the South Downs. He demonstrated a certain gruff pride in relaying the information he had been given by the person who had sold him the insects. Mike and Kathy were obviously (and understandably) more than happy to cancel their statutorily annoyed response to the fact that Mark had spent some of his emergency outing money without permission. In Mark's case enthusiasm and voluntary communication were too rare to be squandered on recrimination.

'She said they're an Australian sort,' he explained, 'and one's male and one's female, and they'll get really big, and one'll have wings but I can't remember if it's the male or the female, and they only eat bramble leaves, and you have to spray 'em with water instead of giving 'em it in a pot or something, and if we want to know anything else it's all right to phone them at the place, because they always like to know what's happened to their stick-insects.'

The next day, inspired by the interest that Mark had shown in his new pets, Mike decided to construct a specially designed home for Rowan and Kimberley out of an old bedside-unit drawer while the boy was out. I must say, speaking as a total incompetent in the field of 'making things', that I was very impressed.

First of all he cut a piece out of the bottom of the drawer and made it into a removable hatch, held on by a groove at one end and a piece of wood that rotated on a nail at the other. Then he carefully shaped another, larger piece of wood so that it would hold a small glass bottle which could be filled with water and used to keep the bramble leaves fresh. This piece of wood was glued and nailed into place so that the bottle would be vertical when the drawer was standing up on end. Finally, he pinned a sheet of fine gauze across the top of the drawer, and stood the whole thing upright so that the original handle of the drawer was on top, and could be used to lift Rowan and Kimberley's new world from one place to another. It was brilliant!

People who can do that sort of thing have difficulty understanding people who can't. As Mike worked methodically away on a table out in the sunny little brick-paved yard at the back of the house, I sat on the doorstep watching the whole process, and was quite fascinated. I found myself wishing yet again that I was able to use practical skills with such confidence.

'How do you know what to do next?' I asked Mike when the thing was finished. 'I mean – an hour ago you didn't have a stick-insect cage, and now you have got one. You just *did* it, as though you'd got grade one at "A" level in making stick-insect cages. Who told you how to do it? What made you think of using the drawer in the first place? And then there's this little thing you've made to put the bottle in – I mean, it's so clever. Why can't I do things like that? I would have made some holes in a cardboard box, dropped a few leaves in, and that would have been that. But this – well, it's a mansion!'

Mike laughed at the escalating mania that I deliberately injected into my speech, but, like nearly all the practical people I've ever known, he didn't really understand what I was talking about. He shrugged and gestured with his competent hands.

'I just think about what's needed and then – well, I just do it I suppose. Bit by bit, stage by stage, that's the way my mind works. You could have done this, Dip. You must do all sorts of things on the wards. It's only a couple of bits of wood and a scrap of gauze. Anyone could have done it – honestly.'

Mmmm ...

The cage was duly presented to Mark when he came in later, and he was just as impressed as I had been.

'Thanks Dad, that's great!' he enthused. 'Shall I put 'em in now?'

The rest of the family gathered in the yard and watched as Mark removed Rowan and Kimberley from the small plastic pot covered in perforated cling-film that had been their home since yesterday, and installed them in their smart new residence, freshly stocked with the best bramble leaves that my, now slightly scratched, hands had been able to pick a little earlier. I couldn't honestly say that my two fellow antipodeans registered any discernible joy or amazement at this unexpected move from bed-sitter to Buckingham Palace, but I have no doubt that, on some deep entomological level, they knew the good times had come. Felicity put her face up close to the gauze and peered with intent excitement at the motionless inhabitants of the cage.

'I'm going to watch them till they move,' she said, more to herself than anyone else.

'Have we got the spray for the water yet?'

That was Mark's question, and it turned this pleasant little occasion into a typically Robinsonian family argument. It was one of the first ones that I'd witnessed, and it was an absolute classic, demonstrating the way in which full-blown conflict could begin with an issue so trivial that, later, no one was able to remember what it had been.

'Oh, I don't think we need to specially buy a spray,' replied Mike mildly, 'just stick your hand under the cold tap and then sort of shake it in their direction, that's all they'll need.'

Like many people who respond negatively towards authority in one arena, Mark could be extraordinarily literal when it came to carrying out the instructions and recommendations of anyone whose authority he *had* decided to accept.

'No, the lady at the place said it had to be a spray so it goes over them fine, and not splashing big drops.'

Mike scratched his head. 'I take your point, Mark, but there isn't really going to be any difference, is there? You don't have to drown them just because you do it with your hand. Just make sure you do it from a distance and it'll be exactly the same as using a spray. After all, the stick-insects won't know whether it's a spray or not, will they?'

'I don't care – she said use a spray,' said Mark sullenly, his mouth tightening with determination. 'They're my stick-insects an' I'll do what I like.'

'The stick-insects *might* know the difference, you know, Dad,' contributed Jack in his best provocative manner. 'Kimberley will say, "Rowan, old chap, are you altogether happy with the way in which our water is being served at the moment? I mean – does this Mark Thingummybob honestly think we're prepared to be fobbed off with random-sized globules of water that he just happens to fling in our direction? Why, yesterday I was hit by what I can only describe as a Big Drop. I don't know about you, but I positively refuse to drink any more water unless it comes out of a spray. After all, this Mark person must have heard what The Lady said." '

Mark turned on Jack. 'Why don't you mind your own business, beanpole features? I never asked you to come an' watch anyway. Why don't you go an' pretend to read something clever or something. No one wants you here!'

Kathy, inflammable as ever, turned on Mark. 'Excuse me, Mark, but I *do* want Jack here if it's all the same to you, and I also want to point out that when you say these animals belong to you, you are in fact completely wrong.' She rested a knuckle on the corner of the table and placed her other hand on her hip. 'They were bought, if you'll just cast your mind back, with money that belonged to your father and me, money that you were supposed to bring home with you unless an emergency happened. We didn't say anything because we didn't want to make you unhappy ...'

Kathy!

'Well, you have 'em, then,' grumped Mark, backing away until he was stopped short by the wall of the house, 'I don't want them any more. You have 'em if you're that worried about the stupid money!'

Jack put both hands flat on top of his head and swivelled the upper part of his body from side to side in disbelief. '*Why* do you have to be so childish, Mark? Do you realize Dad's spent most of the morning putting this thing together for you? Doesn't that count for – '

'Oh, come on now, everyone,' said Mike coaxingly, 'let's not get this whole thing out of perspective. The money's not really important, and it actually only took about an hour to do the cage. It would be a shame if – '

Kathy rotated ominously on her knuckle in Mike's direction. 'Oh, thanks! Thanks a bundle for supporting me, I *don't* think. I point out that he shouldn't have spent the money in the first place, and you tell him that the money's not important.' She swung both arms as if conducting a piece of music that she hated. 'I wish you didn't find it necessary to just dismiss what I say as if it can't possibly mean anything. If you think you can bring him up properly by apologizing to him every time *he* does something wrong, well – good luck to you, that's all I can say.'

Jack was sulking slightly under his tented hands. 'I was only trying to help, Dad. I just meant that you'd spent a long time making a house for his stick-insects, and it didn't seem fair – '

'Yeah, very helpful of you takin' the mickey out of me. Thanks a lot, Jack!'

Mike nodded. 'Well, I happen to think Mark is quite right this time, Jack. I'm grateful for your support, but – '

Kathy jumped on that. 'And I'd be grateful for yours if ever there was any – '

'Could I make a suggestion?'

There was a blessed hush as all eyes turned to me – all eyes, that is, except Felicity's. Seemingly unmoved by this particular pitched battle, she was still leaning on the table, concentrating hard on Rowan and Kimberley, apparently determined that when they did make their first move she would be the one to see it.

'Do forgive us, Dip,' said Kathy eventually, 'it's terribly bad manners to bite great lumps out of each other in front of visitors.'

There was a general, vaguely apologetic mumble.

'No, no, please don't apologize, and *please* whatever you do, don't sentence me to your good manners for the rest of my life, I really couldn't stand it. No, what I was going to say was – I mean, it's none of my business – '

Jack interrupted, sternly admonitory. 'Now, now, Dip, it's very bad manners to tell people that you don't want their good manners after they've just demonstrated their bad manners, and then to use good manners yourself when they'd rather you used bad manners with them. Don't you agree?'

I laughed. 'Sorry, forgive my politeness, and my bad manners – what I was going to ask was whether I could make a suggestion that might help.'

There was a pause.

'Well – yes,' Mike glanced around a little uncertainly at the other members of his family, 'I'm sure we'd all be glad to try anything that might make things more peaceful, wouldn't we, everybody?'

Jack and Kathy nodded, Felicity didn't hear and Mark grunted something monosyllabic that might possibly have meant he would be glad to try anything that might make things more peaceful, but might quite easily have meant the exact opposite.

I ploughed ahead. 'Well, you remember how the argument started, don't you?'

They looked blankly at each other. I looked at them and said nothing for a moment. It was hard to believe that the origins of such a pungent exchange could be so easily forgotten. Surprisingly, it was Mark who hazarded the first guess.

'Was it about me spendin' the money on the stick-insects when I wasn't s'posed to?'

'Nnno,' I answered, sounding like a junior teacher who's just asked her class one of those very focused questions, 'no, that was mentioned, but it wasn't what actually started the row, was it?'

'Wait a minute,' said Mike, a little exasperated with himself, 'let's just work backwards. Mark said something about Jack taking the mickey out of him, because Jack had just said that I'd worked on the cage all morning and it wasn't fair because – ' Mike held his head with both hands and screwed his eyes tight shut – 'What was it that wasn't fair? It wasn't fair because ...?' He opened his eyes and extended both arms with open palms, inviting someone to fill in the missing information.

'Because Mark said he didn't want the stick-insects any more?' suggested Jack.

Mike clicked his fingers. 'That's right! Because he didn't want the stick-insects any more.' His face cleared. 'That's it!' His brow furrowed again. 'But why didn't he want the stick-insects any more?'

Everyone looked at Mark, who stared, open-mouthed with concentration, for several seconds before saying, 'Can't remember.'

Mike turned to Kathy, looking more perplexed than ever. 'And there was that bit in the middle somewhere, when you said something about me dismissing everything you say because it doesn't mean anything. What was that all about?'

Kathy's lips twitched silently as she thought. 'I think,' she said doubtfully, 'it was about the money that Mark spent – '

'Ah!' exclaimed Mike, 'so Mark was right. It *did* begin with the money.'

Kathy shook her head slowly. 'No, because I wasn't going to say anything about the money. There must have been some reason why I suddenly brought it up.'

'Because I told Jack no one wanted him here?' volunteered Mark.

It was becoming like a party game.

'That's it!' cried Kathy excitedly. 'And the reason you said that was because you didn't like Jack taking the mickey out of you about, err ... something or other.'

They all exchanged blank looks again. Nobody seemed able to identify the mysterious Something Or Other.

'How to put the water in,' said Felicity calmly and unexpectedly, without taking her eyes from the inside of the cage.

There was an instant of silent paralysis followed by hubbub.

'Of course!'

'Oh, yes!'

'About the water spray ... '

'That was it!'

The commotion died away at last, and in the quiet that followed a single voice was heard. It was Mark's voice, and it said, 'When are we getting the spray for the water?'

I intervened hurriedly. 'Just before you have exactly the same argument all over again, here's what I was going to suggest. Mark, have you got the number of the place where you bought Rowan and Kimberley?'

'What, you mean the nature place?'

'Yes, the lady said you could phone whenever you need to know anything, didn't she?'

'How'd you know that?' Mark looked at me as if I'd done some amazing mind-reading trick.

I laughed. 'You told us when you first got them, you ninny. Doesn't anyone in this family ever remember anything they've said? Listen, why don't you give her a ring and just ask if it has to be a spray or not? Then you'll know.'

Mark fished in his pocket and drew out a crumpled leaflet. He studied it for a moment.

'This is it,' he said, 'it's on the bottom at the back.' He looked up at me. 'You mean phone now?'

'Yes, go on.'

'All right – will you come with me, Jack?'

'Come on, then, I'll phone and you listen on the extension.'

The most sacred moments are miniscule and easily missed, are they not? Mark's request for help from his older brother in this ostensibly trivial little matter, and Jack's immediately positive response was a case in point. The two brothers were in continuous conflict mode at present, but something in Mark's vulnerability had drawn instinctive care from Jack, and in that small incident it was perhaps possible to see that the relationship they had once had was alive and well – if postponed – and would probably reassert itself in the future, when both boys had sorted out who and what they were.

To nobody's surprise, Mark and Jack returned a few minutes later with the news that it was not necessary to use a spray, as long as some moistness was introduced into the living environment from time to time.

'She said I could use a wet cloth,' said Mark, 'and sort of shake it over 'em.'

'Well, that's what I said in the first place,' replied Mike, clapping his hand to his forehead, 'just wet your hand under the tap.'

'No, it has to be a cloth. She said – '

'They're moving, Mark!' squealed Felicity suddenly, 'Rowan and Kimberley are moving! I saw it first, didn't I?'

It was true. Six human heads crowded around the cage to watch as, very slowly, like two little pieces of mobile hay, Rowan and Kimberley began to investigate their bramble leaves, hoping, no doubt, that in due course, when the discussion had finished, some moistness would be introduced into their living environment. Whether this was to be effected by a specially bought spray, by a hand that had been held under a running tap, or by the shaking of a sacred wet cloth was not, I suspected, an issue that occupied a great deal of their time or attention.

I finished my coffee and put the mug in the sink to wash up later. Getting down from the stool I knelt and put my face up close to the front of the converted drawer, just as Felicity had done all those months ago, marvelling, as I did so, at the change in Rowan and Kimberley since the day when they arrived.

Mark's information about the stick-insects becoming really big had turned out to be quite accurate. The wispy little things from the plastic pot had grown to three or four inches in length and were about half an inch wide at the thickest part of their bodies. You could actually see their jaws moving nowadays when they consumed their beloved bramble leaves, and the larger one especially seemed to greatly enjoy being gently tickled as it clung to the gauze on the front of its cage. Some visitors found them repulsive, reckoning that the female in particular looked like a cross between a scorpion and a praying mantis, but I was rather fond of them, and perpetually intrigued by the fact that they were *made* of leaves.

'Don't worry,' I said to them, 'I'll make sure the grub keeps coming – after all, we ozzies have got to stick together, right?'

Having unearthed a pair of scissors from the drawer of the dresser, I wandered out into the garden to hunt for bramble leaves in the little wilderness area down behind the shed. Still in a rather lightheaded mood, I paused dreamily in the centre of the lawn, enjoying an unusually warm April sun on my face, and reflected on the fact that one of my most persistent fantasies takes place in a garden, a garden, however, that boasts a little more style than the Robinsons' rather unmanicured third of an acre.

My dream garden, which fronts a magnificent mansion, is huge and ornate, featuring trim lawns, an occasional peacock (not the sandwich stealing variety), fountains and lakes, weather-beaten statues of shy maidens and chubby little boys, and, crucially, one of those really well-maintained mazes with the thick box hedges, with a sundial ringed by seats at the very centre.

In my fantasy I am wandering slowly (but fascinatingly) through this Chatsworth-type garden on a glitteringly dew-bedecked morning. I am afflicted with some deep and dramatic sadness, the sort that makes your eyes look bigger and more beautiful because they sparkle with unshed tears, and definitely not the sort where they look red and puffy and awful because you've been bawling like a baby. I think I'm usually wearing one of those full-length, old-fashioned dresses that has at least half a chance of disguising the matronly figure against which I have battled unsuccessfully for many years. My hair has grown mysteriously longer and more lustrous, and is firmly in the 'can't-stop-myself-from-running-my-hands-through-it' sort of bracket.

Eventually, after a decent period of wandering fascinatingly about, I become aware that I am being watched from the terrace of the mansion by a man who, oddly enough, combines every attractive feature that has ever appealed to me in the opposite sex. He is in his mid-thirties, tall and slim – but not thin – with well-set shoulders and a general air of physical alertness and strength. His hair is dark (or light if he looks like Paul Newman) and quite straight with a little curl at the point where it touches the collar. His face is mobile and sensitive, the large, honest eyes glimmering softly like deep pools in the moonlight (I would imagine), with just a hint of something wild and untamable beneath the surface. The blatantly expensive, tailor-made thirties-style suit is worn with casual elegance, and is obviously just one of many that he might select to throw on each morning.

Eventually this wonderful man detaches himself from the terrace wall he has been leaning on, descends the steps to the lawn and walks (with the obligatory lithe grace of a panther) slowly across the grass towards me. When we meet nothing is said. As I gaze into his eyes I sense that he too is suffering the pain of some terrible loss or tragedy (this is pretty good sensing on my part, when you consider that I still haven't got the faintest idea what's the matter with me, let alone him). We turn and, in silent communion, walk side by side through the nearby entrance to the maze (assuming it's wide enough) agreeing, without the need for mere vulgar words, that, in a very real sense, we shall be happier if we can be together in the midst of the puzzle that is life. (Occasionally I wonder if I ought to make this chap blind. After all, a man who looks like that could pick anyone he likes to go and do symbolic things with, but the trouble is, he wouldn't be able to see me from the terrace then, would he?) Anyway, he takes my hand as we pass between the tall hedges, and a jolt of electricity seems to shoot through my body. Suddenly the rules I have tried to live by mean nothing, because on this day, at this time, in this place, I know that there can be no other law but the law of passion.

We reach the centre of the maze and he turns to me, his smouldering eyes ablaze with passion (actually, I suppose if they're smouldering, they can't really be ablaze as well, can they? Still, never mind – you know what I mean) and my whole being is filled with urgent awareness that the *moment* has come.

The fantasy does tend to break down a little at this point. One option is that we make wild, passionate love there in the centre of the maze, but the practicalities make this a little tricky. How quickly, for instance, would I be able to remove my matronly figure from the full-length old-fashioned dress that I had forced it into earlier (I never have been able to fantasise a better figure for myself convincingly), and if I did manage to get it off, what then? Assuming that he wasn't put off by my matronly figure or the time it took to unwrap it, where would the passion take place? Seats at the centre of mazes are notoriously short and hard – made of wrought-iron usually, I seem to recall. I certainly wouldn't fancy that. The grass would be softer, I suppose, but you can't have glitteringly dew-bedecked lawns at one point in your fantasy and expect them conveniently to dry up a few minutes later just because it suits you. I do like to be consistent in these matters. Nor is it likely that Smouldering Eyes would have brought something to lie on – you just don't carry a spare tarpaulin under your arm in stylish fantasies like mine.

The other option, and to be honest, this is the only one which I find in any way satisfying, is that he and I sit quietly down on one of the seats to talk about the lives to which we must soon return. He senses in me a sympathy and beauty of spirit that makes him long to be with me always (matronly figure notwithstanding), and I yearn to reach towards the helpless child that until now has cried out in vain from within his manly exterior, but we both know that it can never be. At last he stands to leave. We part bravely. There is one, sweet, never-to-be-forgotten kiss, and then he is gone, turning his face away quickly so that I shall not see the tears that already blur his vision.

I sit motionless for a few minutes, mourning the fact that something so fragile and so fleeting has disappeared for ever from my life. He has gone, and I am left alone at the centre, suddenly wondering how on earth I'm going to find my way out of this blinking maze.

I chuckled out loud at this point in my reflections, causing the Robinsons' neighbour, Mrs Van Geeting, to glance up from the flowerbed that she was prodding with a neat little garden fork. Mrs Van Geeting was a long-widowed, white-haired, but very sharp old lady in her late seventies, who, despite her alleged addiction to a large daily intake of white rum, was amazingly fit for her age. I had met her several times since she moved in a couple of years ago, to be a few roads away from her son and his family, and we got on well, especially as I had been able to help sort out a little misunderstanding between her and Mike when she first arrived. She got on well with the Robinsons too, seeming quite entertained by the roller-coaster style of their family life. The ghost of a smile appeared on her face as she looked at me now.

'You know, Miss Reynolds,' she said, 'people who stand in the middle of the lawn laughing at nothing at all with scissors in their hands tend to get taken away eventually.'

I looked down at my hands and laughed again. 'Do you know, I'd completely forgotten what I came out here for. I was just on my way to get some brambles for the stick-insects, but the sun was so nice, and I got thinking about – this and that. I was in another place, miles away.'

Her eyes twinkled. 'Well, from the way you laughed just now, I wouldn't mind going on holiday there, wherever it was. Looking after the house, are you?'

I waved my scissors vaguely. 'Yes, sort of. Keeping an eye on things, you know.'

'I've always thought you might end up moving in with them,' said the old lady in her forthright manner. 'You'd do them good. They think the world of you, you know.'

Embarrassed, I made a feeble protesting sound, and was about to say something else when the ringing of the telephone sounded clearly through the open kitchen door.

'You'd better answer that,' said Mrs Van Geeting, 'they might have got the wrong airline or the wrong day or the wrong planet or something.'

The slim, track-suited figure bent to her gardening again as I turned and hurried in to take the call. Shutting the kitchen door behind me I lifted the receiver from its wall-mounting.

'Hello – Dip Reynolds here, can I help you?'

'Oh, yes, err, hello, Dip, it's Daniel Wigley here. I just wanted to check with you and the family about tonight. Do you like steak, and is Mike there?'

Chapter 5

Because of Mrs Van Geeting's final words I was strongly antic-
ipating that it would be the Robinsons who were phoning,
so it took me a while to focus on the fact that the man's voice
on the other end of the line was not Mike's. It was in fact a
slightly odd man called Daniel Wigley, who attended our sister
church, St Paul's, a man whom Jack said should have been shot
long ago for not having already changed his name in case he ever
got married and produced children who would have to endure
the horrors of school life as little Wigleys. He was one of those
square-shaped friendless men who need to shave twice a day but
don't. He had recently confided in Mike, Kathy and me that he
felt unjustly treated by certain members of his church, and was
secretly convinced that no one really cared for him. For Daniel,
taking offence seemed to be practically a hobby, and this, God
help me, was the man who now wanted to check with Mike and
me about something involving all of us that was supposed to happen tonight while Mike and the others were in an aeroplane over
the Atlantic. Why had he asked me if I liked steak?

'Mike's not here just now, Daniel. The whole family is – out
at the moment. Can I help at all?'

Daniel's deep, slightly fussy voice sounded again.

'Well, I simply wanted to make sure that I hadn't made a silly
assumption.'

'Yes, what – ?'

'I felt that, as this is such a very important occasion, I should
be a little more expansive than usual, and so I've decided that we'll
be having rump-steak for our main course. I've been marinading
all the steaks for the last twenty-four hours, but it occurred to

me just now that some members of Mike's family, or yourself, of course, might not enjoy steak, or perhaps even be vegetarian, in which case – '

'Rump-steak!' My voice was filled with delight, my mind with unspeakable horror. I had interrupted in a desperate attempt to establish the actual dimensions of the impending disaster. 'My goodness, that *is* pushing the boat out. Tell me – I can't quite work it out – how many steaks is that altogether?'

'Oh, well, let me see, there's myself, five members of the Robinson family, and yourself, of course, so that's seven in all. I've also made a choice of three puddings, one of which,' he laughed rustily, 'is my own favourite – marmalade tart, and there's a box of red wine,' another rusty laugh, 'so I think we need have no fear of being understocked in that department.' He paused. 'You think steak will be all right with everybody?'

'Oh, yes,' I responded enthusiastically, my mind racing, 'especially on an occasion like this. How, err, how would you actually describe the occasion, Daniel?'

'Well, I think,' he replied, sounding a little surprised, 'I would simply describe it as a fiftieth birthday party, wouldn't you?'

Thank you, God!

I cackled hysterically, as though he'd said something terribly witty. 'I know *that*, I meant ...'

Yes, what did you mean?

'I meant – how would you describe what this special day means to you personally?'

'Ah, yes, sorry, I see what you mean – well, of course, it is a significant milestone in my life, a happy life generally, although, as I think you know, I've felt let down from time to time by folks one should perhaps be able to trust. Our curate's wife has done her best to reassure me, but ... Anyway, none of that matters today, because today is a time to celebrate with good friends, and I look forward to seeing you all at seven-thirty.'

Here was my last chance to blurt out the truth – and I couldn't. I wanted to, but I just couldn't do it.

'See you at seven-thirty,' I trilled brightly. 'Byee!'

As I slowly replaced the receiver on its hook and leaned my forehead against the coolness of the kitchen wall, I was filled with a strange sense of calm. The situation I had been placed in was so appallingly, mind-blowingly awful, that its very awfulness had a kind of sedating effect. I sat like a statue on the nearest chair and reviewed the situation.

'Seven steaks sizzling.' I giggled hysterically suddenly as if I was tipsy. 'Three puddings doing something beginning with P. A world of wine wasted. Oh, dear, what am I going to do?'

Isn't it amazing how inventive the human brain can be when it comes to covering tracks or saving face? My own experience is that a sort of creative adrenalin begins pumping ideas up at a furious rate, much more so than when the same sort of mental energy is required for the benefit of someone else. It was true that in this particular case the fault was not really mine – it was Mike who had made this arrangement and not only forgotten it himself but forgotten to tell everybody else who was concerned as well – but I was, at the very least, almost a Robinson, and from the moment I had failed to be honest with Daniel I was as implicated as anyone else.

The first idea that occurred to me was the obvious one of illness. I could say that two or three of the family had been struck down by Ukrainian flu or something, and I and the others had to stay at home and look after them. Entirely adequate as an excuse, but, as a moment's reflection showed, useless in fact, because if Daniel met any friend of the Robinsons over the next few days and enquired about their health, he was likely to learn, not only that they were not ill, but that they were on holiday in America, and had been since the day when we were all supposed to go to dinner. No, it needed something much more radical than simple illness.

Suddenly remembering that I still hadn't collected lunch for Rowan and Kimberley, I picked up my scissors and wandered back out into the garden, pondering as I went. Another idea. What if I rang Daniel and told him that a phone-call had come just after he and I had spoken, to say that the Robinsons' flight to

America, which was originally scheduled for tomorrow, had been unexpectedly moved forward to today because of an error by the airline? Mike and the others were devastated, I could say, about missing Daniel's birthday celebrations, but they had just had to get everything together in a tearing hurry and go. Of course, I'd add, I would still love to come to dinner this evening if that was all right.

I nodded with satisfaction. That should work very well – as long as I grabbed Mike as soon as they got back and made sure he knew about the 'rescheduled' flight before he ran into Daniel. Yes, that solution would cover just about all the angles. Confusion over flights was an area that could be fudged to a point of total confusion, and the real beauty of this particular idea was that, apart from some anonymous (and imaginary) official buried deep in the bowels of airline administration, it was nobody's fault. I felt a touch of the wobblies at the thought of the actual phone-call to Daniel, but once that was done all would be well, and I might even get out of going myself.

I felt quite pleased and proud. An impossible problem solved by a little thought and ingenuity. As I bent to snip off a length of bramble that would undoubtedly be the equivalent of a large steak and chips followed by apple pie and custard, as seen through Rowan and Kimberley's eyes, yet another idea suggested itself to my fertile brain. I was drunk on my own cleverness. What about if I contacted some people from Daniel's church, threw myself on their mercy, and implored them to arrange a surprise party to which Daniel would be lured later in the day, before the hour at which the ill-fated birthday celebration was due to begin? At the moment when Daniel, like some *This is Your Life* victim, learned with delight that he was, after all, cared for by his church community, I would make sure I was close to the Robinsons' phone, ready to graciously insist that neither the Robinsons nor I would mind in the least if the steaks went into the freezer and our dinner engagement was postponed to a later date.

A good plan, I thought to myself, as I crossed the lawn towards the house, trailing my bramble behind me, but there wasn't enough time left really, and – I stopped as a fatal flaw suggested itself to me. Aloud, I said, 'Why didn't they ask the Robinsons?'

'I've always wanted to be in an Agatha Christie book,' said a voice dryly from the other side of the fence.

I'd forgotten about Mrs Van Geeting, who was still working at her flowerbed a few feet away from me. The Robinsons' equivalent strip of cultivated ground was way overdue for weeding and thinning out, the narrow bed crammed with coarsely foliaged, yobbish weeds and plants, fighting and pushing and shoving as they battled for every cubic inch of soil and air. By contrast, the Van Geeting garden was inhabited by beautifully shaped, well-behaved plants who kept a suitable distance from each other and displayed their attractions in a proud but quietly civilized sort of way. Mrs Van Geeting was dropping a little handful of what looked like purple crystals into each weed-free space between her plants – some kind of nutrient, I supposed.

'I'm sorry,' I said, 'I was thinking aloud. I'm not even sure what I said.'

She chuckled. 'If you get murdered when you go back indoors and no one knows who did it, I shall have to tell the police that the last thing I heard you say, standing in the middle of the lawn with scissors and bramble leaves in your hand, was, "Why didn't they ask the Robinsons?" I just thought it sounded like something Monsieur Poirot might have tackled with those little green cells of his.'

I frowned. 'Grey cells, you mean, don't you? Wasn't it his eyes that glowed green when he suddenly knew who'd done it?'

'Whatever,' replied Mrs Van Geeting unconcernedly, 'colourful sort of chap, wasn't he? Fancy a cup of tea in the garden?'

Blessed postponement!

'Yes please, but it'll have to be a quick one. I've got a rather tricky phone-call to make in a moment. I'll tell you all about it. Give me a second to serve Rowan and Kimberley with their steak and chips and I'll be right with you.'

I enjoyed sitting in the next-door garden describing my

problem and its possible solutions as I drank Earl Grey tea from a proper cup in a proper saucer. Mrs Van Geeting and I had enjoyed a very comfortable, occasional relationship since the day when I had saved Mike from the awe-inspiring wrath of his recently installed neighbour by managing to interpret one of his unfortunate attempts at making a joke. Actually, Mike's attempts to make jokes were never anything but unfortunate in the sense that they were never even remotely humorous, but like many people who joke very rarely, he sometimes fancied he'd hit upon a retort or comment so side-splittingly hilarious that other people were bound to roll around in hysterics when they heard it.

On this occasion, responding to a gentle tap at the front door, Mike had discovered a nervous-looking small boy perched on the front step. The child, who subsequently proved to be Mrs Van Geeting's grandson, Luke, bravely delivered this tremulous speech:

'Please may I get my boomerang back from your garden, please?'

It was at this point that Mike saw an opportunity to exercise his flashing wit. How a man with his long experience of working with small children could have been so lacking in good judgement is impossible to say. Just about everybody else in the universe could have told Mike that making obscure jokes to nervous four-year-old children whom you've never met before is unwise, to say the least. I was sitting in the lounge next to the front door at the time, balanced on the edge of my chair in not-very-well-known-guest-on-her-best-behaviour mode, so I heard every word of the dialogue between Mike and Luke. As far as I can remember it went as follows:

Luke: Please may I get my boomerang back from your garden, please?

Mike: (HERE COMES THE JOKE, IN CASE IT'S NOT IMMEDIATELY OBVIOUS) What I'd like to know is what you were doing in my garden in the first place.

Luke: (WITH LOWER-LIP TREMOR) I didn't come in your garden. I only been in Gran's garden.

71

Mike: (REALIZING THAT, INCREDIBLY, THIS CHILD HAS NOT UNDERSTOOD HIS BRILLIANT JOKE) Yes, I know, I meant that because it was a boomerang you wanted to get, you must have been in my garden in order to –

Luke: (BEGINNING TO CRY BUT PHYSICALLY PARALYSED BY FEAR OF BIG BULLYING MAN) I n-n-n-never went in your g-g-g-garden. I only been in G-G-G-Gran's garden.

Mike: (PANICKING SLIGHTLY) I know you haven't been in my garden – I didn't mean you'd really been in my garden. What I meant was that boomerangs are supposed to come back when you throw them so you must have been in my garden to –

At this point Luke burst into floods of tears and Mrs Van Geeting appeared on the scene demanding that Mr Robinson provide an explanation for the little boy's obvious distress. So overwhelming was the force of the elderly lady's grandmotherly defence of her charge that Mike became less and less convincing in his attempts to explain what had happened. Yes, he admitted, he had said that the boy had been in his garden, but he hadn't meant it. It had been a joke. Mrs Van Geeting begged to know what was even slightly funny about accusing a child of something he hadn't done and making the child cry. Mike said that the joke hadn't been that the boy had been in the garden when he actually hadn't, but it was to do with the fact that it was a boomerang he wanted back and not something like a ball. When Mrs Van Geeting replied to this statement she still sounded very cross, but an element of wariness had crept into her voice, and I decided to intervene before men in white coats were summoned to take Mike away to a place with nice soft walls where he could rave about jokes and balls and boomerangs to his heart's content. After I had joined the little group on the doorstep and quietly explained Mike's pathetic joke, all was well. In the end Mrs Van Geeting was highly amused, and as soon as little Luke finally understood that the big man was not a nasty man but a nice man who made silly jokes, his tears gave way to that watery rainbow chuckling which seems to be a common feature in very small people who are mightily relieved. He fetched his boomerang from the garden and we all had a drink together. From that day onwards Luke referred to Mike as 'The nice man who makes silly jokes', a title which greatly amused the rest of the Robinson family.

'So you're planning to tell this Wigley fellow a thumping great lie, are you?'

I was a little taken aback by Mrs Van Geeting's summary of my intentions. I hadn't really thought of it in terms of lying exactly, more as a kind of protection for Mike – and for Daniel, of course.

'Well, he'd be terribly hurt if I told him what's really happened, wouldn't he? He's already convinced that nobody cares about him – this would just about be the last straw for the poor chap.'

The old lady sipped tea and said nothing. Over the top of her cup the shrewd eyes, surrounded by hundreds of tiny wrinkles, held mine. I babbled on as though I was answering some fresh argument.

'It's all very well saying that people ought to be told the truth, but when it's hurtful I can't see the point. Mind you, I don't actually know what Mike would want me to do, and I suppose it's his problem in the end. He might want to be quite open about the fact that he's forgotten the dinner, and I don't want to put him in a position where he has to ... '

My voice trailed away as I lost my grip on something that had seemed quite straightforward. This uncompromising person was absolutely right. I was planning to tell Daniel a thumping great lie.

'Tell me something.' Mrs Van Geeting placed her cup down on its saucer and leaned back in her chair. 'Why do you think Mike forgot about this Wigley man's dinner? I mean – what was the *real* reason?'

Dismissing immediate responses, I tried to make my mind into a still pond. It was a few moments before the truth bobbed up to the surface.

'Because he doesn't really care about him.'

'Why doesn't he really care about him?'

'Because he's a tense, not very attractive person who's always complaining about the way other people treat him.'

'Does anyone ever tell him that?'

I thought about the people I knew at St Paul's and in my own church. No, we didn't do confrontational things like that. We kept the peace. We were Christians – or cowards, or both.

'I shouldn't think so, no.'

'Perhaps someone should. I don't follow your bloke, but I should think that's what he'd have done. I don't know how he would have put it, but I bet he wouldn't have told Wigley a thumping great lie.'

I thanked Mrs Van Geeting for the tea and the chat, and I meant it. I really was grateful, but I went back to the house feeling very chastened. It had taken someone who didn't follow my 'bloke' to show me where I was going wrong. I picked up my car keys, hunted out the Robinsons' disreputable address book in order to check where Daniel lived, took a few deep breaths to calm myself, and was about to leave when someone rang the front door bell. I nearly crept out through the back to avoid whoever it was. I'm glad I didn't, because when I opened the door, there on the step, looking very excited and very embarrassed, stood Daniel Wigley.

The shock of seeing Daniel really did take my breath away. People use that expression in books and it doesn't always sound very convincing, but that's exactly what happened to me. For a moment I thought I was going to faint. Fortunately, Daniel had so much to say himself that it didn't really matter.

'Oh, Dip,' he said, his eyes full of the strangest mixture of anguish and ecstasy, 'are the others here? Mike and the others, I mean? Are they in?'

All I could do was shake my head dumbly. My lungs still felt like two stale kippers.

'Dip, I have to ask you all the most enormous favour, and I feel dreadful – awful about it, but, you see ... ' He gestured towards a large expensive car parked in front of the house. I could make out the vague shapes of two people, probably a man and a woman, one in the driving seat and one in the back, peering in our direction. 'My brother and his wife – my only family – such a surprise to see them. Come to take me out for my birthday.' He waggled his hands with the passion of apology and joyful anticipation. 'Please – *please* would you forgive me if we were to arrange a different date for our evening together, only, you see ...'

Daniel was one big knot. My breath had returned, so I untied him.

'Daniel,' I said (no dishonesty required here at all), 'I know without a shadow of a doubt that Mike and Kathy and the boys would want me to say that you must forget all about the evening we'd arranged and go and have a good time with your family. We'll get together some other time – don't worry. Just go.'

Throwing profuse thanks, humble apologies and promises for the future over his shoulder, Daniel went. He was relief personified. A final wave from the front passenger seat as his brother's posh car purred away up the hill, and he was gone. I stood in the doorway for a little while shaking my head. I felt perfectly calm but profoundly bewildered.

'You know,' I said very quietly to God, 'I'm beginning to learn never to trust you.'

I glanced up at the front wall of the house as a light breeze set the leaves of the Virginia Creeper rustling. The noise they made sounded like a round of applause on the radio with the volume turned down, or perhaps a little like someone laughing a long way away.

Chapter 6

The business of Daniel's birthday and that brief conversation with Mrs Van Geeting helped to clear my mind about what to say to the Robinsons when they came home. I decided that I would simply tell the truth, and, in the end, that's exactly what I did.

The family arrived back three weeks after they'd left, in a state of jet-lagged weariness, but, as far as I could tell, they had enjoyed their epic holiday. It was the variety of separate comments that fascinated and amused me more than anything when I went round on Sunday, the day after they returned. Mike, for instance, said that it had been 'absolutely marvellous from beginning to end!', while Kathy's summary was 'Mostly good with one or two hell-on-earth family rows thrown in'.

Jack silently (and discreetly) showed me a photograph of a very attractive young lady leaning against an airport luggage trolley and looking slightly weepy. To him I said, 'What a *lovely* girl.' To myself I said, 'What Large Phone Bills.'

When I asked Mark what he thought of America he said that he'd enjoyed going to see a real baseball match, and the food – particularly the beefburgers – had been 'well excellent', but apart from that, it was just like England really, and he didn't think he'd bother going again.

Felicity – oh, how I enjoyed seeing Felicity again – was, of course, enthusiastic about everything she'd seen and done, but especially about something she said she'd brought back to make up for me not going to America. After annoying her mother with five minutes of insistent rummaging through the Robinsons' typically depressing rubble of half-unpacked luggage (nobody seemed to have any philosophy at all about *un*packing) she finally produced a nice little decorated box about an inch and a half square, and placed it into my hand with quivering excitement.

'I bought the box for you when we got off the plane back in England yesterday, Dip,' she said, bouncing impatiently on her toes, 'but that's not the really important thing. The really important thing's inside. Open it! Go on!'

I admired the prettiness of the box for a short time and then carefully prised the lid off. Inside was a very ordinary, irregularly shaped piece of grey stone. I took it out and held it between thumb and forefinger, trying to look as fascinated as Felicity obviously thought I was bound to be.

'It's a bit of America, Dip,' breathed my small friend, 'I brought you back a bit of America!'

Kathy, who was watching, smiled. 'Well, all I can say is – thank goodness that stone is in your hand at last. All we've heard for a fortnight is how pleased Dip's going to be when she gets her bit of America. We've lost it two or three times, and it was no use saying any other piece of stone would do. That's the one she found for you, and that's the one you had to have, and now you've got it.'

All the Robinsons brought back gifts for me, some of them quite expensive, and I genuinely appreciated every one of them, but there was something very special about that small coloured box containing such concrete evidence of love. I put it on my mantelpiece, so that every time a curious visitor looked inside and seemed to be wondering what the value of such a commonplace fragment of stone could possibly be, but didn't like to ask, I could take enormous pleasure in saying, 'Oh, that's one of my favourite things. It's a bit of America.'

I had decided to wait until the following day before giving the family my decision about moving in to live with them, but before leaving I took Mike into a quiet corner to describe the amazing saga of Daniel Wigley. The effect on poor Mike of suddenly remembering the arrangement he'd made for Daniel's birthday party was quite alarming. He clapped a hand to his forehead and seemed to shrink physically before my eyes, rather like an over-inflated, man-shaped balloon that has suddenly had its bung pulled out. He recovered a little as I went on to describe my wonderful hypothetical solutions, the significant chat that I'd had with his neighbour, and the heart-stopping appearance of Daniel himself just as I'd steeled myself to the prospect of driving over to tell him the whole truth.

'It all seemed terribly neat at the time, Mike,' I concluded, 'like one of those Christian books that make you feel useless because there's a miracle on every page. But when I think about it, I actually let poor old Daniel go off with his family thinking that it was him who had to apologize, and that's not neat – that's awful.'

Mike said nothing for a while when I'd finished, then he hugged me and kissed me on the cheek – hardly garden, maze and mansion stuff, but more real and very nice.

'I'm so sorry you had to go through all that, Dip,' he said dismally. 'I felt sorry for him, that's what it was. Worst of all it was me who actually suggested to Daniel that one or two of us could pop round on his birthday because he sounded so fed up, and he got very excited and said we must all come to dinner, you as well, and I said yes, thinking that we could just – just go, and make him feel a bit happier, and then – well, it went completely out of my head. So much for me and my efficiency. Thank goodness for the brother and his wife coming along to be the cavalry for you.' He nodded soberly. 'I'm afraid dear old Mrs V.G. is absolutely right. Deep down I guess I didn't care enough to remember. But I'm really glad you didn't tell him a – what did she call it?'

'A thumping great lie.'

'Yes, one of them. Don't worry, I'll put it right. I'll go round and see Daniel later in the week and tell him what really happened. I'll do my best to be dead straight with him. Not easy, but I will try.'

Before leaving that afternoon I arranged to go round on the Monday evening, and asked that everyone could be there together for not more than about twenty minutes so that I could tell them what I'd decided to do. I felt quite frightened.

Some memories stay like photographs in your mind for ever, don't they? I can still see the assembled Robinsons on that Monday evening – Mike and Kathy like two bookends on the sofa, with Jack, their first edition, squeezed between them, Mark sitting stiffly in the armchair by the bookcase, and Felicity lying on her tummy on the hearth-rug, elbows on the floor, her chin cupped in her hands, gazing with untroubled expectancy into my face as everyone waited for me to say something.

'Before the holiday,' I began, 'you did something very beautiful for me. I don't just mean the banner that some of you worked so hard on, although that was *such* a good idea, and I've looked at it ever so many times since then – I've got it in my wardrobe now, hanging up at the back so that I see at least a little bit of it every time I go to get some clothes to wear.'

'Or when you go to put away the ones you've been wearing,' added Felicity helpfully.

'Or to put away clothes, that's quite right, Felicity. It gives me so much pleasure to see it there, because every picture and shape tells me that I'm important to you. Much more important, though, is the fact that you actually asked me to come and live right here, and be with you all the time. I've spent the last four weeks thinking about that, and I've decided that my answer is yes – but not yet.'

Pause.

'When, then?' from the armchair.

How strange, I thought, that it should be Mark who reacted so immediately, and whose face clouded more quickly than any of the others.

'I don't know,' I answered, 'but when the right time comes I will know, and I do hope you'll still want me then.' Time for the most difficult and most important piece of truth now. 'I'm rather nervous, you see, that if I came and lived here all the time, you might find I wasn't quite what you think I am. When you live on your own for a long time you forget all sorts of things. You forget what it feels like to have little arguments or even big rows with people without them really meaning anything at the end of the day. You forget how to get up in the morning and be grumpy and not feel you've got to hide it and look as if everything's okay. It's such a long time since I had any practice at being in a family – being part of a family. I'm worried that I wouldn't be very good at it. I've got so used to being the one who listens and tries to help and stays calm and gets leant on. And I'm not like that at all really. I take all my upset and crossness and worry home to my little house and stuff it into cupboards and drawers because it isn't any use to anyone.'

This produced a little giggle of laughter from Felicity, who, I feared, had probably not understood a word I'd said so far.

'Coo, I wouldn't like to open your drawers, Dip,' she said, 'and have all that crossness and stuff jumping out at me like a lion. Do you like The Beatles, Dip?'

Seeing a mild rebuke hanging on Mike's lips I hastened to answer Felicity's question.

'Well, yes, I think I'd just stopped being a teenager when they became famous in Australia, and my friends and I used to listen to them all the time. Why do you ask?'

'Well, when we were in school the other day we had a student called Miss Barfield teaching us, and Miss Jarman said we had to be good because Miss Barfield's teacher from her college was coming in to watch her teaching us and – '

'Felicity!' interrupted Kathy rather testily, 'I hope this story isn't going on for too long because Dip's trying – '

'And it was easy being good,' continued Felicity, ignoring her mother completely, 'because Miss Barfield played some music to us, and one of the things was The Beatles singing a song about a lady called – something to do with football ...'

The rest of us exchanged mystified glances.

'Rugby!' cried Felicity, sitting up and pointing a finger to the ceiling in triumph, 'That was it – Eleanor Rugby!'

A shadow of troubled embarrassment appeared in the little girl's eyes as we all laughed involuntarily. She swivelled her head, looking from face to face, trying to locate the source of our amusement. Jack slid down onto the floor and sat behind his sister with his legs on either side of her.

'It's all right, Flitty,' he said, putting his cheek next to hers and wrapping his arms round her chest, 'we weren't really laughing at you – it's just that you got it a bit wrong. It's Eleanor Rigby, not Rugby. You almost got it right. It just sounded funny.'

'Oh ... ' Felicity trilled in a relieved sort of way, her eyes at peace again. 'Eleanor Rigby – that's right. Anyway, after we'd listened to it on the thingy, Miss Barfield said she was going to read the words out to us and we were going to say what we thought they meant. And when we got to the bit about Eleanor – '

'Rigby,' whispered Jack.

'When we got to the bit about Eleanor *Rigby* keeping her face in a jar by the door, Jeremy Philips wouldn't stop laughing and Miss Barfield got cross and red and had to send him to sit outside Mr Wooldridge's office in the end, and then she asked us what we thought it meant, and I said p'raps she was a clown and wore a mask. But Miss Barfield said she wasn't a clown, but it was a *sort* of mask. She said that Eleanor – '

'Rigby,' supplied Jack kindly once more.

'She said that when Eleanor Rigby got home she started to be who she really was and she stopped being how other people liked her being, and took her sort of mask off and put it in a jar next to the door ready for when she had to go out again. Is it like that, Dip?'

Nobody spoke for what seemed quite a long time.

I said, 'Just call me Eleanor,' and then, foolishly, started to cry.

It all ended very well really. I felt a bit of a soft lump because they all crowded round and comforted me at the same time – even Mark patted my shoulder rather awkwardly. Later, over one of those miraculously reinvigorating pots of tea, Mike and Kathy suggested that I should have a key to their house, come in and go out whenever I wanted, and spend as much or as little time as I liked with the family until, as Kathy put it, I felt free to be 'as ratty and moody as everyone else'. I extended the same invitation to all of them, but I realized, even as I said it, that I didn't actually want people – not even the Robinsons – to walk into the place that was specially my own without any warning at all. I still needed a moment to dip into old Eleanor's jar. That awareness, and the fact that I kept my mouth shut about it, made me feel a little bit guilty, but it also made me feel a great sense of relief that I hadn't been too hasty in accepting the family's invitation. One day I would – probably – but until then I was happy to accept the title bestowed upon me that day by Jack.

'From now on, Dip,' he said, just as I was leaving, 'you are entitled to put DHR after your name.'

'Which stands for ...?'

'Detached Honorary Robinson.'

Chapter 7

'Shall I tell you one of the most depressing things about being a parent?' said Kathy one blowy morning a few weeks later, as we hung clothes out in the garden together.

I replied through a mouthful of pegs. 'Only if you tell me one of the nicest things about being a parent first.'

Kathy threw back her dark head and laughed into the newly washed blue of the sky. 'I see. Another stage in the "Encouraging Katherine To Be More Positive Campaign", is it? You're all so subtle – I don't think. I can just hear dear old Mike's voice. "The thing is, Dip, that Kath does tend to get a little big negative about things from time to time, so if you get the chance to – you know – steer her into counting her blessings a bit more, it would be jolly helpful." Is that more or less the way it went?'

Kathy's impression of Mike's occasional parsonical style of speaking was such an accurate caricature that I dropped a towel into the flowerbed and nearly swallowed my pegs trying to catch it.

'Come on,' I said firmly, when I'd gathered myself and everything else together again, 'I refuse to be deflected. I want to hear at least one nice thing before you indulge yourself by wallowing in the most depressing one.' I pointed. 'Sit down there for a minute while I peg these socks up, and tell me what you've enjoyed about being the mother of three lovely children.'

Kathy flopped obediently onto the dilapidated wooden bench that constituted the Robinsons' 'Garden Furniture'. Leaning back against the trunk of the ancient apple tree that supported one end of our washing line, she closed her eyes and thought for a moment.

'Well, I made a good start – I enjoyed conceiving them.'

I pegged another three socks up.

Kathy raised a finger. 'Here's a good one! They've made me laugh as much as they've made me cry, and that's saying something.' She opened an eye and grimaced questioningly in my direction. 'That do?'

'Hmmm, sounds a bit backhanded to me, but I'll let you off. Go on, then – what is one of the most depressing things about being a parent?'

She linked her fingers behind her head, and closed both eyes again. 'On a day like this, when the wind's whipping those sheets blindly around, and everything's coloured like a Ladybird book, I get sort of excited. I almost begin to believe that I might have a present – a now – of my own. Just for a second or two I get these tantalizing little nibbles and tastes of memory about how it felt to be me without constant reference to a houseful of other people. Tell you what, Dip, most of the time I feel as if I'm living in my children's pasts. I've indefinitely postponed being myself in order to serve them. I'm out of the current of my own life, if you see what I mean. I'm not even getting wet. I might as well – '

'Cold drink, Mum?'

Jack's unexpected arrival in the garden with two tall glasses of iced orange juice and lemonade stemmed the flow temporarily. I sat down on the bench beside Kathy, who sipped ecstatically from the glass in her hand. For a few moments we watched Jack as he strolled amiably back towards the house, banging the drinks tray rhythmically against his leg as he went.

'What was I saying?'

I cleared my throat and peered up through the leafy branches, seeking inspiration. 'Err, let me see, I think you were saying something to the effect that you have indefinitely postponed being yourself in order to serve your children. That's right – then Jack brought you a drink and you stopped.'

Kathy extended her hand, palm upwards, in mock emphasis. 'Yes, well, doesn't that just prove my point? I'm not even allowed to feel sorry for myself without one of them deliberately doing something completely out of character and spoiling everything.' She threw me a rueful glance. 'You must think I'm a perfect idiot, Dip, rabbiting on like that. I wish I hadn't said anything now.'

'Carry on with what you were saying,' I murmured, 'get to the end of your furrow.'

She smiled. 'Thank you for that interestingly agricultural image, Dip. Not terribly appropriate for one as delicate and prettily feminine as me, but never mind. No, seriously, I know I tend to exaggerate a bit, but there was some truth in what I said. You'll think this sounds horribly selfish, but sometimes I get razor-blade close to resenting the fact that I mother around like crazy in my children's early lives, making it all happen for them, trying to give them the possibility of becoming reasonably all right, happyish adults, while being fully conscious that I might well fail anyway. If Mark ever becomes famous he'll write about me in the *Sunday Times* colour supplement.'

Kathy moved her cupped hand through the air in front of her face, as though a double page was spread before her eyes.

'The beginning of my life as a genuine personality was inevitably postponed until the day when I finally escaped the cyclonic context of emotional chaos that my mother created. We were trapped by an impassable wall of flying debris. The safe space was very small and exclusively designated by her. It may have been survival, but it certainly was not nurture."

'See what I mean? Why should I change his nappies when he's going to write things like that about me?'

When I'd stopped laughing I said, 'Has it ever occurred to you, Kathy, that your children don't actually need a good mother, which is what you're frightened you'll never be, because all they really want is *you*?'

'Take this Thursday, for instance.' She hadn't heard me – this furrow was even longer than I'd thought. 'This Thursday I have to go down to Felicity's school at two-thirty for the Infant Sports afternoon. As far as my darling daughter is concerned there never has been, and never will be (Olympic events included) a more important sporting occasion than the Girls Running Backwards

Throwing A Beanbag Up And Catching It Again Race, in which contest she has immodestly high hopes of success because her nearest rival, Penny Martin, has – Praise the Lord! – twisted her ankle. I always feel horribly threatened when I'm surrounded by all those perfect mothers, but, as far as Felicity is concerned, it's absolutely vital that I'm there on Thursday, smiling and encouraging and all the rest of it. And yet, I don't suppose the child will have any recollection whatsoever of this particular sports day or my contribution to it when she's an old lady of twenty-one.'

Later that day I joined the family for supper (a meal that was indeed regularly punctuated by Felicity's excited references to the pleasure with which her mummy would witness her victory in the Girls Running Backwards Throwing A Beanbag Up And Catching It Again Race on Thursday) and sat with them afterwards in the lounge, where all of us except Mark, who had 'gone out', found ourselves watching one of those appallingly saccharine television shows in which people are publicly and tearfully reunited with long-lost loved ones. I have always claimed to loathe these emotionally voyeuristic programmes, but, as usual, I eventually became aware that a soppy grin had glued itself onto my face like a mask, entirely without permission, and that my eyes were swimming with tears. It was some consolation to discover that the same soppy grin was plastered over each of the Robinson faces as well. At least we were all mad together. I expect it was this treacly atmosphere that made Kathy's sudden explosive outburst seem all the more alarming when it came.

'Oh, no! Oh, blast! Oh, sh – '

Four sentimentally tear-bedewed pairs of eyes turned towards Kathy, whose hand was now placed flat over her mouth, as if to prevent the escape of further, perhaps even more forceful, exclamations. Felicity sat up straight on Mike's lap and took her thumb out of her mouth.

'What's the matter, Mummy?'

'Nothing, sweetheart,' replied Kathy indistinctly through her hand, her eyes bulging with some undisclosed horror. 'I – I thought I thought something, but then I realized I – I didn't think it, so it doesn't matter. It wasn't anything. It was nothing. Watch the programme....'

Nodding with childlike credulity, Felicity reinserted the damp thumb, and curled into her daddy's lap again. Mike looked at his wife, his expression saying quite clearly – 'If I pursue this, am I going to wish I hadn't?'

'Anything wrong, Kath?' he enquired mildly.

Kathy stood up, her face ashen. 'Nothing you'll be able to handle, Michael.' In unnaturally calm tones she added, 'It's going to make you very cross indeed. Dip, would you mind very much stepping out into the kitchen with me? I'd appreciate your advice on a certain matter.'

As I followed Kathy into the hall, and closed the lounge door behind me, I heard Felicity say, without a trace of concern in her voice, 'Mummy's done something wrong, hasn't she, Daddy?', and I just caught Mike's contained but ominously grim reply, 'Yes, darling, and a little bit later I'm going to find out what it is.'

Kathy already had the sherry bottle out by the time I reached the kitchen. She poured the rich brown liquid into two small glasses and put one of them into my hand with an air of doom-laden finality.

'Would you care to have a drink with me before the battle?'

I pulled a chair out and sat down.

Kathy raised her glass in ceremonial fashion. 'Those who are about to die salute you. Cheers!'

'Cheers – Kathy, what on earth have you done? Whatever it is, it can't be that bad, surely?'

She lowered herself slowly onto the chair at the end of the table, placed her glass down with concentrated precision, and heaved a very deep sigh.

The details of Kathy's face are oddly elusive. Sometimes, especially when she is very happy, or passionately angry on someone else's behalf, her face is truly beautiful, full of life and fire. At other times her features seem to lose their distinctness, the flush goes from her cheekbones, and the skin on her face turns to a parchmenty colour. The fire was certainly out now. My friend looked like someone much older and much younger than she really was.

'It is that bad, Dip. I can't believe it. It's a nightmare. I've double-booked myself for Thursday afternoon. While I was sitting in there just now watching that stupid programme, crying because one person I've never met was unexpectedly confronted with their second cousin twice removed who is another person I've never met, I suddenly realized that Felicity, whom I have met and claim to care about, is not going to have her mother there on Thursday to see her win the Girls Running Backwards Throwing A Beanbag Up And Catching It Again Race.' She took another sip of sherry and shook her head slowly from side to side. 'What am I going to do, Dip?'

Looking at Kathy's troubled face, I reflected on the fact that I never know what to say to people when they get into this sort of state. I have come to believe, however, that this 'not knowing' is a significant advance on thinking you know what to say. There was a time when I responded to other people's difficulties with a sort of bullying exasperation, probably because I secretly thought that no one could have problems as mountainous as mine. Why should I waste more energy than was absolutely necessary on the trivial little blips that interrupted their smooth-running lives? The tendency to react like that was still in me, but nowadays I tried to kick it out as soon as it appeared. I have to be honest and say that Kathy's earlier complaints about the pressures of motherhood had provoked a little '*What about me?*' cry in some back chamber of my heart, but stronger than that response was the gritty knowledge that real friendship means accepting the whole package, and not just the bits that appeal to you. Kathy was much brighter than me in many ways, but her capacity for standing in anyone's shoes but her own was very limited unless she was made to do it.

I remember, for instance, an occasion when I tried to communicate the loneliness of being single to her. 'You come home after a hard day at work,' I explained, 'and once you've shut the front door behind you, everything goes quiet and you're on your own. You hang your coat up, put the kettle on, go up and change into something comfortable, then come down and make yourself a cup of tea. After that you might plonk yourself down in front of the television or read a book, and, more often than not, that's it for the rest of the evening. You might cook something if you've got the energy, or not bother if you don't feel like it, and all that's left after that is bed – on your own.'

Kathy listened intently to every word of this sad description of solitary living, nodded solemnly for a moment, and said in almost reverential tones, 'It sounds absolutely *wonderful* – except for the sleeping on your own bit, and that would be all right most of the time....'

I tried to be quietly practical. 'Is there no chance of doing something about whatever it is you've organized for Thursday?'

Kathy's laugh had a very hollow ring to it. 'Yes, I could cancel it altogether, Dip. Then Mike would be furious with me because I'm not at his mother's house to stop her antagonizing the social worker who's coming to talk about her new bathroom, after months and months of trying to fix it up. He's going to be furious with me anyway because I didn't check the dates when I made the appointment, and Felicity's going to be in tears because I wasn't there last year either, and Jack's going to do one of his chilled disapproval numbers, and – oh, we *are* going to have a jolly time. I think I'll go and hang around outside the video shop with Mark and his mates tonight. He'll be the only one speaking to me by then.'

'But surely Mike will understand that you didn't mean to make a mistake, won't he? What about Daniel Wigley?'

Kathy leaned back in her chair and folded her arms. 'Dip, I have a feeling that, as far as Mike is concerned, I have used up my spiritual quota of forgiveness when it comes to this kind of mistake. Seventy times seven, isn't it? Well, my total must be way over four hundred and ninety by now. Daniel Wigley brings Mike's score to about three. No, any moment now he's going to come through that door with some puny excuse for being here and he's going to ask me what I've done. When I tell him what I've done he'll go puce, then he'll breathe very deeply, ask me how

I could possibly be so disorganized, release one extremely cross exclamation and suggest that we pray. Then I shall get cross with him and burst into tears. Then Felicity will come through to ask what's the matter. Then Mike will tell her that her mummy isn't going to see her win the Girls Running Backwards Throwing A Beanbag Up And Catching It Again Race after all, and she'll be heartbroken and weep loudly. Then Jack will appear to rescue his little sister from her wicked, warring parents and I shall probably get cross with *him* as well.'

'But if you know all that's going to happen, isn't it possible to – '

'Kath, I think Felicity ought to go up now, don't you?'

Mike hadn't quite come into the kitchen. He had leaned round the door and spoken with casual lightness – a brave attempt to convince himself and us that, after a quick word, he would be off again to put his daughter to bed. Kathy passed the tip of her tongue slowly over her top lip before speaking.

'The answer to your unspoken question, Mike, is as follows. I have managed to arrange an appointment about Mum's bathroom at last, and I've organized for me to be there to make sure the social worker doesn't get savaged. I'm sorry, I meant to tell you I'd fixed it.'

For a moment Mike's eyes lit up – so far the news was good. 'Well, that's great, Kath. What's wrong with that? Well done! It doesn't matter that you forgot to tell me. The important thing is that something's happening at last. Just let me get our young lady up and then we'll have a chat about it.'

'Unfortunately,' continued Kathy in a dull monotone, 'I've arranged the meeting for this Thursday afternoon, and that means that I can't go to Felicity's sports and nor can you because you've got the Calais trip, and anyway it's me she wants because I cocked it up last time and it's all she's talked about for weeks. That's about it really – oh, except that I wish I was dead.'

There was something almost comical about the way in which Mike's body became frozen into its leaning-round-the-door position as he accommodated this extra information. At last, he straightened up, came into the room, and, leaning back against the closed door, dug his hands deep into his pockets. Then, just as Kathy had predicted, he simply went a sort of maroon colour, and began to breathe heavily through his nose. Missing out the anticipated 'How can you possibly be so disorganized?' phase, he moved straight on to the 'one cross exclamation'.

'You make me so *angry* sometimes!'

As usual, Mike expressed his anger as though he'd accidentally taken a foreign body into his mouth with a forkful of food. It had to be spat out, but he would much rather it hadn't got in there in the first place.

Still breathing heavily, he turned away for a moment, his shoulders rising and falling as he wrestled for self-control. Spinning round he said, 'There's no point in getting angry and upset – I think we should pray.'

'What do you mean there's no *point* in getting upset?' Kathy somehow managed to sound guilty and scathing at the same time. 'I've done something stupid, haven't I? What's the point of diving into prayer like some frightened rabbit going down a hole just because you can't handle a bit of real emotion? Get angry, for goodness' sake – and I'll get upset and cry. Why is that such a problem? It's not a problem for me I can assure you! In any case, praying isn't going to get me to Felicity's sports. Poor little girl – she's going to be so *very* disappointed.' And then, as if to fulfil her own prophecy, she buried her head in her hands and burst into tears.

I doubt if Mike's anger has ever been able to survive someone else's tears. Visibly shaken by the whole business he sat down beside his wife and sighed in despair. 'I still think we ought to be able to pray,' he said rather defeatedly. 'We are Christians, after all.' He looked at me. 'I'm sorry about this, Dip, we seem to lurch from one crisis to another. I don't know how we manage it.'

'You mean you don't know how *I* manage it,' snuffled Kathy. 'I shovel together great piles of guilt like some sort of emotional navvy. Guilty about screwing up the arrangements, guilty about getting annoyed with you when I should have got annoyed with myself, guilty about not wanting to pray and guilty about going on and on about how guilty I feel when I should be thinking of Felicity instead of me.'

Mike reached behind Kathy and pulled off a sheet of kitchen roll. 'Here you are, Kath,' he said, putting an arm round her shoulders, 'mop yourself up, or we shall all be swimming.'

So nice.

Stop crying, Kathy Robinson, you've got a nice man.

'Say a prayer if you want to, Mike.' Kathy sniffed and sounded like a scrappy little girl. 'We've got to do something.'

'There's no need for you two to pray,' I announced, 'I've been praying since Kathy and I first left the lounge, and, what's more, my prayer has been answered, so everything's going to work out just fine.'

Silence. They stared at me as if I'd unguardedly revealed a trace of insanity. But it was true – I had been talking to God ever since that loud exclamation had interrupted the flow of treacle a few minutes ago. I was beginning to learn that it was better to get on with praying while my friends went through the dramatic patterns and processes that seemed to form a part of every minor and major crisis in their lives. It was a nice feeling, because God and I loved the Robinsons. I could almost see his smile shining in their direction, and I could feel in my own heart how warmly he received my prayers for them. If only I could feel as confident about praying for myself.

'Do you mean an answer about Felicity and the sports, Dip?'

'Yes, Mike, it's all sorted out.'

A small candle of hope began to burn in Kathy. 'What is the answer, Dip?'

'I suppose it sounds a bit conceited really, but, well … the answer to my prayer is me. *I'll* go to Felicity's sports day on Thursday.'

The candle flickered and went out. 'Oh, Dip, that's very sweet of you, but it isn't really an answer. I promised Felicity faithfully that I would make sure I was there to see her this year, and she's reminded me of it on and off for the last twelve months. I know she'd love you to come as well, but it's *me* who's got to be there.' She slapped her hands down on to the table in anguish. 'Oh, Mike, I can't bear to see her face cloud over when I tell her. I hate the way our children suss me, one by one. I'm sick of being the way they find out the world isn't as perfect as they thought. I've *got* to be at Mum's – I've just got to be, or it'll all go wrong....'

Seeing that she was about to dissolve again I interrupted hurriedly. 'Kathy, I said my prayer was answered, and it is. I know Felicity needs you to go, but if you leave me to put her to bed tonight I'll guarantee that the problem will be solved.'

Kathy didn't look very convinced, but Mike patted her shoulder encouragingly. 'Leave it to Dip, Kath, she's a bit of a wonder-worker sometimes, isn't she? You carry on, Dip, you know where everything is. We'll stay down here and beam hope up through the ceiling or something.'

Isn't it awful when you've made some grandiose claim and then have to justify it? All the optimism drains out of your body and you wonder how easy it is to emigrate to Tibet. It wasn't, in this case, because I didn't mean what I'd said. I felt quite confident that God, or some portion of the common sense of God, had spoken to me and suggested a solution to Kathy's dilemma. It was just that the gap between saying and doing has always felt an immense one to me. Two very different kinds of courage are needed. I have enough trouble with the theory, let alone the practice.

Felicity was snuggled up cosily with Jack, contentedly watching something highly unsuitable, when I went back to the lounge. She waved the four fingers of her right hand at me without taking her thumb out of her mouth.

'Bedtime, Felicity,' I smiled.

The thumb came out. 'Who's taking me?'

'I am. D'you want a piggyback?'

Children of six are generally incapable of faking their responses, and children like Felicity even less so. Please don't think it terribly strange if I say that, as usual, the child in me sighed with pleasure when my little friend rushed across to me, whooping delightedly, at the news that I was putting her to bed.

'Stand by the stool, Dip! Ready? Can I have a duck story in the bath?'

'Yes, I should think so. Say goodnight to Jack.'

"Night, Jackie!'

'Don't call me Jackie – Goodnight, darlin'.'

'What about Mummy and Daddy?'

'They'll come and say goodnight in a minute.'

'What about Mark?'

'Out, sweetheart. Hold tight, here we go, up the mountain!'

Minutes later Felicity was sitting cross-legged in the bath surrounded by bubbles, dabbing at her face with a flannel while I searched for the plastic duck that had become an essential part of bathtime routine when I was in charge.

It wasn't easy to find things in the Robinsons' bathroom. For some reason no one was bothered about taking out anything that they'd brought in. It contained a bewildering array of clothes, magazines, bath-dampened books of various kinds, forests of redundant toothbrushes, clusters of half-used bottles of hair conditioner, several shampoo containers (usually empty), the odd watch that had been removed from a wrist and then forgotten, a box of Felicity's face-paints in which the colours swam together in pools of water, plastic toothpaste dispensers caked with stripey gunge around the nozzle, sad demoted drinks beakers full of Jack's disposable razors – used but not disposed of – and an extraordinary selection of towels, varying from highly disreputable to plump, soft and newly washed. Every now and then Mike would revolt and produce complex check-lists and rotas designed to 'solve' the bathroom problem, but as no one ever made any real effort to follow them and he always broke his own rules within twenty-four hours anyway, the situation never changed much.

I found the red duck at last in the bottom of a large blue china vase that had found a home under the sink since I last excavated the bathroom contents. I held it up triumphantly.

'Hurrah!' cried Felicity, clapping her soapy hands together so that feathery wisps of froth flew around her head. 'Time for Ducky story.' Felicity's language quite often regressed to three-year-old level at bedtime.

The story about the duck had started its life on the very first occasion when I supervised bath and bed, and had been in steady demand ever since. For Felicity it was certainly a comfortably familiar ritual (she insisted that every detail should be exactly the same each time), but it had come to mean something even more significant to me. For reasons that I could hardly face myself, let alone reveal to anyone else, the telling of this very simple tale had an almost sacramentally calming effect on the most troubled part of my spirit.

As usual I started by placing the duck on top of the bathroom door, which opened against the side of the bath. Felicity gazed up at it with a dreamy little smile of happy anticipation.

'Once upon a time,' I began, 'there was a very, very lonely little duck who lived right on top of a big hill. He was ever such a nice duck really, but he didn't think anyone else could ever like him. "I'd love to have a friend all of my own," he used to say, "but I don't suppose I ever shall. Who'd want to be friends with a silly red duck who's too frightened to come down from his hill and doesn't know anything about anything? No," he sighed, "I shall never have a real friend."

'Every day the red duck would climb to the very top of the hill' – here, I always walked the duck along the top of the door until it was directly above Felicity – 'and look over the edge of a very steep cliff. Far, far below, he could see a little girl bathing in a beautiful lake, and each time he saw her he wished so much that he could be down there as well, swimming around and making friends with the little girl, who' – an invariable addition, this – 'looked almost exactly like you, Felicity.'

I walked the duck to and fro along the top of the door, tilting him over the edge each time he got to the end.

'Every single day he trudged to the top of the slope, gazed down at the swimmer below, then waddled home feeling lonelier than ever.'

This was Felicity's cue to tilt her head to one side, turn the corners of her mouth down, and wrinkle her eyes in pantomimic sympathy with the hero of my story.

'Then, one day, when the little red duck had climbed the hill yet again, and was feeling lonelier than ever, he leaned so far over the edge of the cliff to look at the little girl that ... ' (I paused so that Felicity could move slightly to one side) ' ... he lost his balance and fell all the way down into the lake beside her. Imagine that!'

The dropped duck landed in the bath with a diminutive 'splash!' This was the bit that Felicity liked best. 'Hello, little duck,' she said, 'where have you come from?'

'The duck was terrified,' I continued, 'because he thought the little girl was going to be cross with him. "I'm very sorry," he said in a flustered voice, "please don't be angry with me for landing in your lake – I know you don't want to make friends with me because you've got lots of friends already, and I'll go away right now. Oh, *please* don't be cross ..." But the little girl wasn't at all cross.'

Felicity plucked the duck from the water and gazed fondly into its eyes as I went on.

' "But, Duck, I haven't got any friends," said the little girl, "I'm a very lonely person. Every day I've seen you looking down from the top of the cliff and wished that I could be your friend, but I always thought you must have lots and lots of friends already. I was so pleased when you fell into the water beside me. Please stay and talk to me for a while." And do you know what happened after that?'

Felicity, who knew exactly what happened after that, shook her head, role-playing wide-eyed wonderment according to tradition.

'Well, they became really good friends – best friends, in fact, and they spent all their time together and they were very, very happy.'

'Good,' said Felicity contentedly, 'I'm glad. *I* wasn't very happy at school today,' she added, lobbing her duck into the toothbrush forest, and adopting an expression of fierce gloom with such suddenness that I couldn't help laughing. 'It was awful. Can I get my hair wet?'

I picked up one of the plump towels from the rack by the wash basin and spread it out wide. 'No, you can't. Out you come now – are you going to do a jump?'

Felicity hoisted her dripping, skinny form up on to the side of the bath and, after balancing precariously for a moment, threw herself into my arms and the towel with such abandon that I nearly lost my balance.

'Can I go back down when I've got my nightie on?'

'No.'

'Daddy says it's all right as long as I remember to put my pants on.'

'That's only when you're allowed to go back down, and this time you're not, and if you argue I'm going to tickle you till you squeal.'

She dug her chin into her chest and grinned. 'I'm not going to argue, Dip. Dip, it *was* awful.'

'This thing that happened at school, you mean?'

'Yeah – awful!'

By now we had arrived in the bedroom. After being set down, Felicity let her towel drop to the floor and began to execute a naked, stomping war-dance on top of it. I tried to imagine what might constitute an 'awful' experience in this child's careless, clear-eyed world.

'I'm c-c-c-cold!' she gurgled as she danced and waved her arms in the air.

'Well, dry yourself then, you silly ha'p'orth! That's what the towel's for.'

Freeze, with hands spread out like little stars, grimace, giggle – 'Oh, yeah!' – frenetic towelling.

At last she was dry, inserted into her Garfield nightdress and snuggled up in bed. 'Now,' I said, 'what was this awful thing?'

'Oh, yes, it was – Dip!' She sat bolt upright, her face full of emergency. 'I haven't done my teeth!'

Back to the bathroom. Forage in the forest. 'No, not that one, that's my old one ... No – yes, that's it, the pink one with the squiggly handle ... Have I done it long enough ...? Have I done it long enough *now* …? Mummy doesn't make me do it that long … I *must* have done it long enough now … Daddy makes me do it longer than that … Smell my teeth …'

Back in bed.

'Can I tell you about the awful thing now, Dip?'

'I wish you would. I'm getting quite worried about it. It's not a wild bear that hides in the teacher's cupboard and jumps out at children when they're sent to get something, is it?'

Felicity's eyes shone with delight. This was the kind of game she loved. 'No, worse than that – *much* worse than that.'

'Worse than that, eh? Must be pretty bad, then – wait a minute, I know what it is!'

'What?'

'There's a wicked witch working in the school kitchen, and every day she puts a spell on one of the dinners, so that whoever gets that dinner turns into a bar of chocolate on legs until going home time. Today it was you, and you had to run around under the tables all afternoon to avoid being caught and unwrapped and eaten by the other children in your class. Or was it even worse than that?'

'Oh, *yes*, Dip.' Felicity, quite an accomplished thespian at the tender age of six, shuddered with horror. 'It was more frightening than anything that's ever happened to anyone in the world before. It really was!'

I scratched my head thoughtfully for a moment, then nodded slowly and solemnly. I think I know what it was. Your teacher took the class out to see how the fish were getting on in the school pond, but when you got there there wasn't a single one to be seen. And you were all standing quietly at the edge of the pond, leaning over to look and wondering where they'd gone, when a huge crocodile with big sharp teeth leapt out of the water and swallowed your teacher and your three best friends in one big gollup!'

'Not my friends,' edited Felicity firmly, 'three of the ones I don't like.'

'Ah, right, yes, of course, three of the ones you don't like – but still quite frightening, eh?'

'Yes, Dip, but nowhere near as awful as the awful thing that really happened. Go on guessing.'

She put her thumb in her mouth and smiled a crinkly, winning smile around it. Obviously this particular game could go on for ever as far as Felicity was concerned.

'All right, one more guess, only it's not really a guess because I'm pretty sure I've got it right this time. Let me see now – it was just coming up to playtime when a huge wind started to blow outside and the whole school was lifted up into the sky and blown far away across the sea to a cannibal island – '

'What's a cannibal island?'

'A place where people who eat each other live.'

'Oh, right.' Felicity nodded calmly.

'Yes, so, in the end, the school landed on this cannibal island, and when the headmaster and all the teachers and children came out of the front door – '

'We're not allowed to go out of the front door.'

'This was a special occasion, so you were allowed to this time. Anyway, when the headmaster and teachers and children came out of the door all the cannibals were waiting for you with spears and things, and there was a giant cooking pot full of hot water on a big crackling fire, and the cannibal chief said that as it was very nearly teatime somebody would have to climb into the pot to be cooked, and who would the headmaster choose? Would he choose a scraggy old teacher, or a nice plump little infant, or a stringy junior, and in the end – '

Felicity had replaced her thumb. Now she whisked it out again so that she could interrupt. 'In the end Penny Martin ran up and jumped in the pot without anyone telling her to because she can't bear not being first at anything.'

We laughed immoderately together.

'So, was I right? Was that the awful thing that happened to you? I bet it was.'

'Dip, it was *much* more awful than that.' She reached a wheedling hand out towards mine. 'Do some more guesses.'

I pushed the hand firmly under the duvet cover. 'No more

guesses. It's your turn. If your awful thing wasn't a bear in the cupboard or a witch in the kitchen or a cannibal cooking pot – '

'You forgot the crocodile.'

' – or a giant crocodile, then what was it? And you'd better say it quietly so you don't scare me too much.'

Felicity propped herself up on one elbow and spoke in a dramatic whisper. 'This was it – I wore my new coat in the playground today, and it was too big. Whatever I did I was surrounded by bits of coat!'

'Oh, no!' I covered my face with my hands, overcome by the horror of this appalling revelation. 'When I was making all those guesses I never realized it was something as ghastly as that!' I parted my hands a little and peeped through the crack. 'Oh, Felicity, how you must have suffered.'

'Yes,' her voice wavered in true fairy-tale heroine fashion, 'it was awful. I kept wishing man-eating crocodiles would come along, or bears or something, to make me feel better, but they didn't.'

'Felicity?'

'Yes?'

'I wanted to ask you something.'

'What?' She was delighted with this new tack, unprecedentedly initiated by an adult at a point when sleep would normally be the next item on the agenda. I knelt down on the floor next to the bed so that I was nearer to her.

'The thing is,' I said rather haltingly, 'I've never had a little boy or girl of my own ...'

Oh, Dances In Puddles, how you have longed for a little boy or girl of your own.

' ... so I don't suppose I'll ever be able to do lots of things that mummies do with their children. That's why it's been so nice getting to know you and your brothers ...'

'Because you can do some of them with us,' said Felicity brightly.

'That's right, and it's been really good fun, but there is one

100

thing I'd love to do that I've never done, and – well, I just wondered if you would mind.'

Felicity's mouth was agape with curiosity. ''Course I wouldn't. What is it?'

'You're going to think I'm ever so silly ...'

'No I'm not.'

I looked down at my hands, spread flat on my knees. 'I've always wanted to go to a school sports day and be the special one who cheers for her little boy or girl and takes photographs of them as they run down the running track. I know you wouldn't mind me coming with Mummy on Thursday – '

'I'd *like* you to come,' said Felicity earnestly.

'I know you would, darling. I was really wondering if, this once, it could be just me who came, so that I could pretend I was a parent and do all the things they do.'

'Like being in the Mummies' Running Race?'

'Err ... yes, like being in the Mummies' Running Race ...' I hoped the sudden draining of blood from my face hadn't been too visible.

'The thing is ...' Felicity's brows contracted as she thought through the problem. 'The thing is that Mummy really wants to be there this time because she was so upset about not being able to come last time, and she 'ticularly wants to see me win the Girls Running Backwards Throwing A Beanbag Up And Catching It Again Race.' She sucked air in through her teeth and shook her head rapidly from side to side with excitement. 'I think I might be going to win it, Dip, because Penny Martin's the only one better than me at running and catching, and she's – '

'Been cooked and eaten.'

Felicity's peal of laughter must have filled the house.

'Would it be all right,' I said, when she'd subsided a little, 'if just I came, or would that make you very unhappy?'

'I'll have to ask Mummy if she minds,' replied Felicity with sudden gravity. 'Let's ask her now.'

I went to the door and called. Kathy came into the bedroom

looking apprehensive and guilty. She bent over to kiss her daughter.

'Hello, sweetheart, have you had a lovely time? I heard you laughing ...'

'Oh, that was about Penny Martin being cooked and eaten, Mummy. So funny! Mummy, Dip wants to come to my sports and take pictures of me and see me in the races.' The expression on Felicity's face as she continued was a remarkable approximation to the one I had seen Mike adopt when he was exhorting his children to be mature and reasonable about something that didn't appeal to them at all. 'Mummy, would you mind not coming this time, only Dip wants to be like a real parent, and' – a real clincher of an argument, this, as far as Felicity was concerned – 'she won't be able to be in the Mummies' Running Race if you're there as well, will she?'

'No,' said Kathy, with an even guiltier glance in my direction, 'no, I can see that, I really can. Well, as long as I can come next year I'm quite happy for Dip to take you this time, darling. Perhaps I'll go up and see Grandma instead, eh? That'll be fine.'

'You see, Dip,' Felicity yawned hugely, 'everything's all right. Isn't Mummy kind?'

'Yes,' I agreed, 'very generous indeed. Thank you, Kathy. Goodnight, Felicity.'

'Goodnight, Dip, thanks for my duck story. 'Night, Mummy.'

'Goodnight, my darling – sleep tight.'

When I looked in five minutes later the self-styled, odds-on favourite to win the Girls Running Backwards Throwing A Beanbag Up And Catching It Again Race was fast asleep.

Chapter 8

On Wednesday evening I asked God to give Fletton Park County Primary School some sunny weather for their Infant Sports on the following day. Honesty compels me to admit that I also asked about the possibility of a freak storm that would last just long enough to wash away any chance of the Mummies' Running Race happening as planned. Mind you, if it had to be, then I was grimly determined that, for Felicity's sake, I would stagger through the event as best I could, but my heart sank every time I thought about it.

Thursday turned out to be a suitably sun-kissed day, blessed with one of those kindly breezes that prevent the heat from becoming unpleasant. I offered a trickle of thanks for this answer to prayer, and promised an absolute deluge of additional gratitude in the event of the freak storm being granted.

The weather was perfect, but the afternoon didn't begin very well as far as I was concerned, although I certainly took a huge step towards full qualification as an Honorary Robinson.

Arriving half an hour early, at one-fifteen, I made the awesomely dreadful mistake of parking in the staff car-park directly in front of the school.

'Well done!' I congratulated myself aloud on finding a place so easily, and had just dragged a comb through my hair preparatory to leaving the car, when a loud knock on the window made me jump. Turning my head I saw, on the other side of the glass, a very efficient looking female face ringed with very efficiently controlled grey hair. Also visible was a very efficient looking finger, prodding imperiously in the direction of the ground. I wound my window down. The voice that proceeded from the face was brisk and neutral in tone, but not actually unpleasant.

'Good afternoon, I'm Mrs Palmer, the school secretary – may I ask if you are a parent?'

My car is very small, and when you're sitting in it being talked to by someone whose face is very close to yours, and you think they might be about to tell you off about something, you tend to lose your head. The simplest and most trouble-free reply might have been 'Yes', because it would have come to the same thing in the end, but when I feel threatened I have a tendency to worship a tiresome and non-existent truth-monitoring deity who will 'get me' if I stray from the path of absolute, literal veracity.

'No,' I said, 'I'm not, but – '

'Are you here to see the headmaster, then? I'm afraid he won't be available this afternoon because the Infant Sports are due to begin in – ' she glanced at a very efficient looking watch – 'less than half an hour.'

She stopped speaking, but left her face where it had been. It was my turn to say something.

'No, I haven't come to see the headmaster. I'm here for the Infant Sports as well.'

I felt about four years old. The Face still didn't move.

'I'm sorry, I thought you said you were not a parent. Perhaps I misunderstood.'

Yes, you misunderstood! Yes, you in whose eyes I hardly exist at all, I am not a parent – but I have longed to be a parent. In my dreams I have lived a promise that no waking day has ever kept. I have known the pain of yearning for motherhood but never once the joy of holding my own flesh and blood. I am not a parent – yes, you misunderstood.

Some people, I reflected, and I'm one of them, become quite remarkably good at covering up the way they really feel. One of the greatest shocks of my young life was the news that a contemporary at college in Adelaide had narrowly avoided killing herself with an overdose of some kind, having left a note to say that social and academic pressure had become too much to bear. This girl and I had always got on very well, usually meeting at least once each day over a coffee in the college canteen. The thing that had always impressed me most about Grace was her laid-back approach to life. There was usually a lazy smile on her lips, and she had a witty, relaxed way of talking about things. She seemed to have such control over areas that created chaos in me. The last person likely to attempt suicide, I would have thought. When I visited Grace in hospital, at her request, the mask was off, and I was amazed by the contrast. I remember asking her why she'd never said anything to me about how she felt, but she just shook her head and said, 'Well, you don't, do you?'

And, of course, she was absolutely right. You don't, do you? At those times in our lives when we're really suffering, someone at work or at church or in the street will ask how we are and we'll smile and nod and say, 'Okay!' or 'Bearing up!', or 'Mustn't complain!', or 'Could be worse!', and all the time we're hurting like anything inside and we know they'll never really believe it if they find out later on, because our acting was too good. At one time I had the notion that people should be completely open with everyone about their troubles, but I don't think that any more. Nowadays I know that there's no point in telling everybody we meet how we feel when we're in agony. There aren't many folk, Christian or otherwise, who can wear someone else's pain. I think I could have managed a little of Grace's, though, and she did drop me a few of her pearls after that hospital visit.

The Face was waiting.

'I'm awfully sorry. I didn't make myself clear. I'm not actually a parent, but I've come to the sports instead of Felicity Robinson's mother, who can't make it this afternoon.'

'Oh, I see, yes – Felicity.' A slight lightening.

Surely the Face would go away now, and I'd be allowed to get out of my car and go somewhere where this person was not.

Please would you be kind enough to remove your face, so that when I open my car door I shall not have the sinful satisfaction of knocking you off your efficient feet? Lord, love her for me.

'Felicity Robinson, yes.' I smiled an end-of-conversation sort of smile and made little shifting movements to signal my intention of vacating the car. The Face didn't budge.

'I'm afraid it's not possible to park here, because the spaces are all reserved for teachers, but you'll find a large space behind the builders' yard next door. They've kindly agreed that parents should be allowed to leave their vehicles there on special occasions like this.'

A little imp sitting on my dashboard urged me to point out that I had already made it clear that I was not actually a parent, and to ask what parking provisions had been made for Friends Of Children on special occasions like this.

Shut up, Imp.

'I'm sorry, I didn't realize that. Over that way, is it?'

'That's right.'

'Thanks very much.'

'Felicity's a lovely child.'

'Yes.'

Nice Face.

I drove obediently to the right place and parked my car near the entrance.

I discovered the sports venue on the other side of what turned out to be a surprisingly substantial stack of school buildings. The newly-cut grass of the playing-field had been marked out with long straight white lines to create a running track for this very special occasion. Running down one side of this six-lane strip were three neatly arranged rows of the most disturbingly minute chairs I had ever seen, while on the other side two quite big children were placing rubber gym mats end to end, presumably to accommodate the mini-athletes when they arrived. Spaced out at measured intervals behind the mats were three poles on stands, each with a bell-shaped speaker attached to its highest point. Down at one end of the track a mixed group of adults and rather self-consciously important-looking older children were attaching pieces of coloured wool to what looked like little gold safety pins, and carefully laying a length of pink ribbon across the lanes, ready, I assumed, to be used as a finishing tape for the aspiring Linford Christies and Sally Gunnells who were soon to be going for Infant Gold.

I decided to sit as near to the aforesaid finishing line as I could get, a strategic point from which to observe closely the final stages of the all-important Girls Running Backwards Throwing A Beanbag Up And Catching It Again Race. A few parents (or friends of children, perhaps?) were already stationing themselves at this end of the track, looking rather oddly near to the ground as they lowered themselves on to, and in some cases totally enveloped, the miniscule blue chairs that had been provided for them. Gingerly, I took a seat myself, hoping that the thin tubular legs would not decide to sink slowly into the ground under my weight. Thankfully, they did not so decide, and quite suddenly, Mummies' Running Race notwithstanding, I felt a wave of happiness and well-being. The scent of cut grass was, as always, a poem of past times, and the sky was extravagantly, wastefully, wonderfully blue. I leaned my head back, closed my eyes and took in a long, deep breath of sun-soaked air.

Thank you, God, *for unchangingly beautiful things.*

I opened my eyes again to find that a collection of impossibly tiny children had left the school buildings and were moving in a happy straggle towards the running track. The straggle was headed by a most elegant, meticulously hair-styled lady in a flowing ankle-length dress. She held a small hand in each of hers and appeared to have several other little figures glued to her skirts by various parts of their bodies as she and they made their tranquil way across the shining grass. Arriving at the mat directly opposite the place where I was sitting, she sank slowly to the ground, drawing children with her as if, in filmic slow motion, they were filling a vacuum created by the descent of her body. The result was unconsciously artistic, as though the class had been posed for a Victorian photograph. If this is a teacher, I thought, then teachers have certainly changed since my early schooldays. I turned to the reassuringly untidy, friendly-looking person who was balanced on the Lilliputian chair beside me.

'Who's that teacher over there?' I asked, pointing across the track.

'Oh, that's Mrs Barcombe,' said my neighbour reverentially,

'she teaches one of the reception classes. She's really wonderful. Everyone hopes their children will start with her. Two of mine have and I'm hoping the last one will. They come home all warm and soft from her.' She smiled ruefully. 'I never seem to have that effect on them, so it's a good job somebody does. I'm Mrs Elphick, by the way. I haven't seen you before, have I? Have you got a little boy or girl here?'

I was much more relaxed now. 'No, I've come instead of a friend who couldn't make it. She's Felicity Robinson's mother.'

Instant recognition. 'Oh, I know Felicity. She's in class two with Claire, my middle one. Miss Jarman's class, that is. They go to Ballet and Modern together as well. Oh, yes, Felicity's been to tea. She was at ours with another friend called Emily the other day. She's a lovely little girl, isn't she? Marvellous imagination for games and that sort of thing.'

'Yes,' I replied, trying to sound like a detached assessor of loveliness and imagination, but actually feeling a deep sense of personal pride, 'yes, I'm very fond of her.'

'That's the other reception class,' said my new friend, pointing towards a second group of children issuing from the school buildings, 'Mrs Calne's class, that is. She's very nice in her own way. Her children learn all sorts of things, and I suppose that's what they're here for really, isn't it?'

Mrs Elphick's tone said, more clearly than words, that, in her view, the Calne method, which involved learning all sorts of things, compared very unfavourably with the Barcombe method, which sent newly-schooled children home to their parents 'all warm and soft'. Certainly, the flavour of Mrs Calne's regime was visibly different from that of the other reception class. She herself was a sensibly dressed, strong looking woman in her mid-forties with short-cropped dark hair and one of those square-jawed, scrubbed faces that I have always associated, probably wrongly, with vigorous female team-games. She marched at the head of a procession (not a straggle) of children who travelled in neat, hand-holding pairs towards the second mat from the end. Not for this class the graceful dying-flower descent of the previous one.

After being arranged in a suitable pattern whilst still standing, the word of command was given, and they sat. Mrs Calne knelt tidily on one corner of the mat, and that was that. Turning her head, she flashed an unexpectedly sweet smile towards the beautiful Mrs Barcombe, who responded with a raise of the eyebrows and a friendly little shrug of the shoulders, as if to say, 'Here we go, then'.

Gazing across at the two groups of children, I was interested to note that the Calne children didn't really appear any less relaxed and happy than the Barcombe ones. They were just in a slightly different mode of behaviour, presumably because of the different types of control their teachers used.

Not for the first time I felt annoyed at life for failing to offer us nice, clear-cut heroes and villains. Why couldn't Mrs Barcombe be wholly wonderful, and Mrs Calne utterly horrible? A part of me had always wanted the world to be like that. Maybe there'd been too many story-books and not enough contact with flesh-and-blood people when I was little. People like me take years to get the real world into focus.

The rows of tiny chairs were filling up very quickly now as parents moved in a steady stream from carpark to playing field. Many wore sunglasses and carried cameras. Quite a lot had brought pre-school-aged children with them. There were babes-in-arms, wobbling glassy-eyed toddlers and sleeping tots in comfortable-looking buggies. All but the very youngest had been primed, no doubt, for that moment when an older brother or sister put in an appearance on the athletic stage. I hoped for the mothers' sakes that the sleeping ones would wake in time to enjoy the treat that had been promised to them.

The general atmosphere was one of buzzing expectancy, coupled with a rather odd air of corporate puzzlement. Because the rows of parents were stretched out over such a long distance from one end of the track to the other, it was difficult to imagine that one would ever really be able to discover what was going on until a race or event was actually under way. Most of the people around me wore encouraging, happy-to-be-here smiles in case their children happened to be looking, but while their mouths smiled their eyes peered blankly from side to side, hoping, I guessed, that someone would let them in on the secret of what had actually been planned. The three speakers on poles looked promising as far as this was concerned, but down below the finishing line a clump of worried heads bent over the microphone suggested that there could be problems in this area.

My neighbour, Mrs Elphick, told me that this was the first year they'd used a public address system (usually, someone called Mr Murray shouted) and she hoped they would get it to work, because in ten years of coming to sports days she couldn't recall ever having a clear idea of – as she put it – what had happened just now, what was happening at the moment, or what was going to happen in a minute.

Felicity's class was the last one to emerge from the school, and I must admit I felt quite nervous from the moment I spotted her relatively tall figure in the distance. Suppose she had forgotten it was I coming to her sports day instead of her mother? What if her face fell at that instant when she recognized me sitting among all the *real* parents? Like most of the other children, Felicity reached her appointed mat in a state of mingled excitement and worry. The reason for the excitement was obvious, but at first I hadn't quite understood the worry. My kindly neighbour explained.

'Most of them are checking that whoever's supposed to be here has turned up. You watch their faces when they suddenly see their special people – just watch.'

Felicity was no exception. I could see that total involvement with the thrill of the occasion had been temporarily postponed. Sitting cross-legged among her class-mates at the other end of the running-track, dressed in a white tee-shirt and little white shorts, hair neatly pigtailed, she scanned the spectators, her eyes moving from face to face with troubled concentration. I wanted to attract her attention, but all I could manage was a timid little wave of the fingers. When her eyes finally reached and met mine my heart stood still.

I needn't have worried. Seeing me flicked a switch in Felicity.

All the lights in her face came on, and she flapped her hands madly before settling down happily to chatter and giggle with her buddies.

Thank you.

'That's Mr Murray,' said my new friend, pointing to a figure that had just detached itself from the group of folk who had been worriedly examining the microphone, 'the one who usually shouts. The children really like him – he makes them laugh with his jokes. He's a good teacher too.' She giggled suddenly. 'Not what you'd call self-conscious about how he dresses, though, is he?'

It was a fair comment. Mr Murray, a tall, nicely built man, who might have been in his mid-thirties, was wearing what he obviously considered suitable garb for an outdoor sporting occasion. This outfit consisted of a pair of ludicrously long khaki shorts, two ancient black army boots surmounted by the merest glimpse of flimsy light-blue socks, and a violently orange, short-sleeved tee-shirt that just failed to meet the top of his shorts. The whole effect was topped off with a battered white floppy hat of the cricketing variety. Beneath the hat, Mr Murray's rather good-looking, pleasantly studious face was adorned by a pair of spectacles whose thick black rims seemed somehow to add an intensity of purpose to everything he did. Mrs Elphick was absolutely right. Mr Murray did not appear remotely self-conscious about his eccentric appearance, and, because he was so relaxed, he didn't really look funny at all. I have always rather envied people like that.

He strolled along the edge of the running-track past the long lines of parents, trailing the microphone lead behind him, his progress, punctuated by little flurries of conversation and laughter as he paused to exchange a joke or greeting. He seemed to know nearly all the mothers, and even some of the little pre-school children.

'He looks like a nice man,' I said mildly, as if I was commenting on a fairly agreeable piece of curtain fabric.

'Oh, he's *lovely*,' replied my neighbour, her voice echoing

111

the fourteen-year-old response that I had contained so carefully within myself. 'He can wear whatever he likes, as far as I'm concerned. Don't you think he's dishy?'

'Mmm, very nice.' I now sounded as though I might be talking about a *very* agreeable piece of curtain fabric. I had never described anyone (silently or out loud) as being 'dishy' in my life.

'Well, *I* think he's lovely,' said Mrs Elphick, her tone signalling a little disappointment at my lukewarm response. 'Oh, look, he's going to use the sound thing – the what-do-you-call-it? – the microphone.'

And indeed, the oddly dressed, dishy Mr Murray, now about two-thirds of the way up the track, having stopped and raised the microphone to his lips, was twitching his eyebrows and silently mouthing words as he prepared to speak to us all through the public address system.

'It'll be much better than other years,' declared Mrs Elphick with comfortable optimism.

I have no doubt that it would have been better than other years – if it had worked properly. It wasn't that Mr Murray's words were not amplified, because they certainly were – three times in fact: once through each loudspeaker, at intervals of approximately half a second. The result was the sort of thunderously loud, cosmically-echoing, cloud-cracking voice that you'd expect to hear at the commencement of Armageddon, and all he had said was 'Good afternoon, everybody'.

A shocked silence fell, followed immediately by a ripple of laughter as the assembled parents realized they were not about to be judged by God, but addressed by Mr Murray.

'It was better when he shouted,' commented Mrs Elphick.

Minutes passed as one or two practical looking staff members joined Mr Murray for prolonged and anxious discussion about various aspects of the sound system. Soon, we were being treated to further shatteringly dramatic attempts to impart information through the three speakers. The ranks of parents fixed their happy-to-be-here smiles yet more firmly on their faces lest their offspring should lose heart, and awaited further developments.

Finally, from the loudspeakers came an unnaturally slow, sepulchral voice speaking in a low monotone, the sort of voice you would expect to hear if a major tragedy had to be announced from the stage of the Albert Hall.

'WE ... ARE ... HAVING ... A ... LITTLE ... TROUBLE ... WITH ... THE ... SOUND ... SYSTEM ... BUT ... IF ... I ... SPEAK ... VERY ... VERY ... SLOWLY ... AND ... CLEARLY ... YOU ... SHOULD ... BE ... ABLE ... TO ... HEAR ... ME ...'

A round of applause from the parents, and a chorus of near-hysterical laughter from the older children on the mats greeted this extraordinary Vincent Price impersonation.

'WE ... WELCOME ... YOU ... ALL ... VERY ... WARMLY ...,' continued the voice in terrifyingly ominous tones, 'AND ... OUR ... FIRST ... EVENT ... WILL ... BE ... A ... PRE-SCHOOL ... RUNNING ... RACE ....'

Six twitchily excited, but plainly bewildered, small children were steered firmly to their places on the starting line, and pointed in the right direction. Then came the command, 'Ready, steady, go!'

This first event was not an unqualified success. The six athletes concerned seemed to have absorbed the fact that 'Go!' meant they were supposed to be somewhere else, but only two of them had cottoned on to the fact that everyone was supposed to end up in the same place. The rest didn't so much run as scatter in various unrelated directions. One plump little girl dashed straight back into the arms of her mother, who was seated near the start line, while the little boy next to her turned around and ran as fast as his legs would carry him in a direction diametrically opposite to the finishing line. He stopped at the end of the field by the hedge and started to practise roly-polies in the long grass. Another decided to settle down for a little sleep as nothing of great interest seemed to be happening, and a fourth made her way to the nearest speaker on a pole, where she stood gazing upwards in fascination as Mr Murray's doom-laden voice announced, 'I ... THINK ... WE ... SHALL ... HAVE ... TO ... BEGIN ... THAT ... EVENT ... AGAIN ....'

Expert child catchers were despatched to round up the six participants, including the two who had already finished the race. This pair returned looking a little puzzled, but they seemed quite happy to do it all over again. Soon, after some strenuous eye-level pointing and careful repetition of earlier instructions, the race was under way once more. This time, with the assistance of Mrs Calne, who, crouching low with her arms outspread, performed a sort of sheepdog role at the back, they all reached the finishing line to the accompaniment of wild parental applause.

Things seemed to go reasonably smoothly after that. Event followed event, each preceded by Mr Murray's sombre declarations. There really was something very strange about hearing the boys' obstacle race, for instance, announced as though something sick and sadly dreadful was about to be perpetrated.

Many things made me laugh, but I had a secret cry as well. In the girls' egg and spoon race (introduced by Mr Murray as if we were being invited to witness a mass burial), five of the competitors finished more or less at the same time, but the sixth, a skinny little thing with thick spectacles, had been seriously delayed by her tendency to lunge wildly all over the track as she alternately lost and regained control of her egg and spoon. It was as if some invisible, irresistible force took hold of the spoon every now and then and tried to drag it from her hand. The result was that she could only manage to travel in an average straight line. But she didn't give up. That was what brought the tears to my eyes. Long after the others had crossed the finishing line this heroine was putting as much effort in as she had done since the race started. When she did finally approach the end of the track her face was set in a mask of fierce determination. 'Who knows,' that face seemed to say, 'if I go on trying really hard right up to the end, even though the others have finished, I might still win! Who knows?'

I dried my eyes surreptitiously, and mourned the death of hope and innocence in all of us.

The moment for which Felicity had been waiting so long arrived at last. Like some Old Testament prophet foretelling the misery of Babylonian captivity, Mr Murray's voice echoed eerily across the field once more.

'OUR ... NEXT ... EVENT ... WILL ... BE ... THE ... GIRLS ... RUNNING ... BACKWARDS ... THROWING ... UP ... A ... BEANBAG ... AND ... CATCHING ... IT ... AGAIN ... RACE.... WOULD ... COMPETITORS ... PLEASE ... TAKE ... THEIR ... PLACES ... ON ... THE ... STARTING ... LINE ....'

Felicity bared her teeth at me in a grin of intense excitement and gestured wildly towards the starting line. I nodded and waved enthusiastically to show that I'd understood. The great event was about to take place, but inside I suddenly felt sick. For some reason I had taken Felicity's chances of winning at her own valuation. She was unswervingly confident of success, but what if she was wrong? She could easily be wrong. Suddenly, the last thing I wanted was responsibility for dealing with a negative outcome to this race. I swallowed hard and waited.

The first part of the race seemed to bear out Felicity's self-assessment. By the time all the competitors had passed the half-way point, she was several yards in front and looking unbeatable. The difference between Felicity and the other girls was quite simple. Felicity could run backwards *and* throw a beanbag up and catch it. The others could only run backwards *or* throw a beanbag up and catch it. The result seemed inevitable, and the sensation of nausea in my stomach was just beginning to lift, when disaster struck.

As if he had been fired from a giant catapult, a toddler shot out onto the track and stopped abruptly, right in the path of Felicity, who, because of running backwards and concentrating on her beanbag, was completely unaware of the unscheduled obstacle. In a flurry of arms and legs, the two bodies collided heavily and fell to the grass in a heap. The toddler remained prostrate on the ground, roaring loudly for his mother, while Felicity sat up, rubbing her leg and looking dazed.

Even then, all might have been well. Grasping the situation quickly, Felicity jumped to her feet, beanbag still in hand, and having stepped round the small bawling figure, set off backwards once more in the direction of the finishing line. Unfortunately, she chose the wrong side of the toddler to continue her run, and immediately got tangled up with the child's mother who was intent on rescuing her son before he suffered more damage. By the time Felicity got going again and reached the tape she had been overtaken by all but one of the other runners. Instead of winning the Girls Running Backwards Throwing A Beanbag Up And Catching It Again Race, she had come fifth.

A great choking lump rose into my throat as I watched Felicity make her dismal way back to the other end of the track. Chin on chest, stiff-legged with containment of her grief, she was the embodiment of misery.

I shiver with horror when I think how close I came to making an absolute fool of myself and her. Everything in me wanted to get hold of whoever was in charge of this so-called Sports Day and insist that the race be run again so that a more just result could be achieved. Why, I would ask, should Felicity's dream be spoiled just because some silly toddler decided to run out on to the track? Perhaps, I would suggest, if the whole event had been a little better organized, with railings or something, it wouldn't have happened, and Felicity would be happy and smiling now instead of sitting on that mat over there, keeping her eyes tight shut to stop the tears from coming out. Thank God, I didn't do anything so awful. Instead, I found myself tidying my handbag with feverish intensity, as though the removal of chaos in one little world might help to unscramble the unfairness in another.

'Wasn't that a shame?' said Mrs Elphick with real compassion in her voice. I think she knew why I was tidying my handbag. 'You feel for them so much when it's like that, don't you?'

'Yes,' I said shortly, close to tears, 'you do.'

Even the dreaded Mummies' Running Race had lost its terrors now. As I panted down the track behind the lycra-clad figures of these very modern mothers a few minutes later, all I was conscious of was the glimpse I'd had of Felicity's eyes, large and shining with contained grief when I'd lined up for the start, and the crumpled little smile forced on to her face for my benefit just before the race began.

I came solidly last, of course, but apart from ending up in a state of near physical collapse, that didn't trouble me at all. The thing that troubled me was the prospect of driving home in the car with Felicity and coping with the weight of her unhappiness.

'THAT ... CONCLUDES ... THE INFANT ... SPORTS ... AND ... WE ... WOULD ... JUST ... LIKE ... TO ... THANK ... CHILDREN ... STAFF ... AND ... PARENTS ... FOR ... HELPING ... TO ... MAKE ... THIS ... AFTERNOON ... SUCH ... AN ... ENJOYABLE ... OCCASION .... IT ... WOULD ... BE ... VERY ... HELPFUL ... IF ... EVERY ... PARENT ... COULD ... TAKE ... ONE ... CHAIR ... INTO ... THE ... SCHOOL ... AS ... THEY ... LEAVE ... AND ... PLEASE ... TAKE ... YOUR ... CHILDREN ... HOME ... WITH ... YOU ... AFTER ... THEY ... HAVE ... CHANGED .... THANK YOU ... AGAIN ....'

Mr Murray's final message from the Pit Of Hades provoked a little patter of applause from the parents, and was followed by a general buzz and clatter of departure and clearing up. I thanked the friendly Mrs Elphick for her company, then picking up my miniature chair, walked slowly towards the school buildings. As Felicity's class passed me on the way back to their classroom I called out, 'See you in the car-park, darling – no hurry, take your time.' She flapped a sad hand and nodded in mute agreement.

Sitting and waiting in Daffodil a few minutes later I mentally rehearsed a variety of potentially comforting comments.

You did your best, that's all that really matters.

You'll have another chance next year, and you're so much better than the others that you're bound to win.

Your class did well in the team games, and you were involved in all of them.

It doesn't do you any good to get upset – try to think of something nice that's going to happen soon.

Cheer up! It's not the end of the world.

Pull yourself ...

... together. I really can't believe you're getting yourself in such a state over a stupid mouse, Elizabeth. Anyone would think you'd never had anything else that meant anything to you. We'll get you another one if it's that important to you. You've got a party coming up on Thursday – think about that instead. All right, well if you can't stop crying you'll just have to go and sit in your room until you can stop.... Getting angry and being rude won't help either, Elizabeth Reynolds. We don't want to see your temper – or hear it. Go on, off you go, up to your room! When you've learned to control your feelings you can come back down and be with us. No, I don't want to see you again until you can smile at me – and mean it. We seem to have been through this so many times....

The sound of the passenger door opening took me by surprise. My thoughts had been far away in space and time. Clutching her lunch box and reading folder in one hand, Felicity climbed in and clunked the door shut behind her. We looked each other in the eyes momentarily, a forlorn little girl and an anxiously perplexed middle-aged woman.

'I didn't win, Dip.'

'I know.'

'I came next to last.'

'Yes, I saw.'

Felicity's bottom lip started to tremble. 'I really, really thought I was going to win, Dip. I really thought I was.'

I don't want to see you again until you can smile at me....

My bottom lip started to tremble as well. 'Darling Felicity, it must have been the most awful, awful feeling in the world, and I'm so sorry you didn't win. I bet you want to cry and cry.'

That was what she wanted. Dropping her lunch box and her reading folder on to the floor of the car, my small friend stretched her arms out to be held, and sobbed on my shoulder for at least a minute. I had a bit of a weep as well – mostly for Felicity, but partly for another little girl.

By the time we arrived home the tears had all gone, and Felicity was smiling at me again – and meaning it.

'Did you feel like a real parent today, Dip?' she asked brightly, as we walked from the car to the front door.

'Yes, Felicity,' I nodded with heartfelt sincerity, 'yes, I think I probably did.'

Chapter 9

'Why do you keep a tube of bubbles by your bed Dip?'
My sandwich making was arrested in mid-spread by Mark's casual question. It takes a moment to focus on details of your life that have been around for so long that you never really think about them any more. They're simply there, aren't they? Besides – I felt a little embarrassed.

'Do you want me to make something up, or shall I tell you the real reason? I think I'd rather invent something.'

Glancing over my shoulder I saw that Mark's habitual expression of glowering resentment had been replaced by one of his dazzling, infrequent smiles. It was, typically, a quite startling transformation, and it revealed more than a hint of the very good-looking young man who would undoubtedly emerge eventually from the grumpy chrysalis that continually drove Kathy to such extremes of rage and impatience.

'Go on, then,' he said, slumping down on one of my creaky kitchen chairs, 'tell us the real reason.'

It was Friday, a couple of weeks after the school sports, and Mark had dropped in to visit me on his way home from school, just as he'd done a few times in the past, and rather more frequently since my announcement that I wasn't yet ready to move in with the family. Very early on I had learned that effusive greetings and bright chit-chat about his school-day were exactly what he didn't want on these occasions. Indeed, we were positively in competition over which of us could be the more laid-back and breezily nonchalant during the half hour or so that he stayed. The truth, though, as I soon came to realize, was that there was always a specific reason for these after-school visits, but the unwritten

120

rules were quite clear. I was never to ask why he'd come, and he was allowed to choose his own moment to communicate whatever was on his mind. Once or twice he'd been unable to open up at all, and had left with an expression of baffled frustration on his dark features, furious with himself for not saying what he'd come to say. I feared for the peace of the Robinson household when that happened.

This time there was one thing I had known for sure as soon as he walked into the kitchen. He was hungry. Kathy had told me, and I had seen for myself, that Mark preferred what his mother called 'grazing', to eating. This graphic term perfectly described his habit of strolling around the kitchen picking bits off the edge of cakes, scooping stuff from containers in the fridge with his finger, tearing ragged wodges from the loaf in the bread-bin, and drinking straight out of milk and lemonade bottles without bothering to use a glass. All in all, this grazing was yet another of the annoying habits that was likely to produce almost instant aggro when he was at home. I was amused to observe, on this particular Friday, that Mark was cruising slowly around my kitchen, extending his hand in the direction of the food cupboard, then the fridge, then a chocolate cake with white icing on top that I'd left out, then the fruit bowl, and in each case suddenly withdrawing it at the last moment, as though the demands of politeness were just – but only just – managing to overcome the power of his appetite. It would have taken a harder heart than mine to ignore such plaintive, blatant need. I was bonelessly casual.

'You wouldn't fancy something to eat, would you, Mark?'

'Err, yeah – thanks.' How on earth could I have known? Desire emboldened him. 'Can I have a bit of that cake?'

'Of course, I'll cut you a slice. Will that be enough, though?'

Mark licked his lips. 'Any chance of a Sizzler?'

'Well, there might be if I knew what it was.'

I cut a large piece of cake as he explained.

'It's a special sort of sandwich thing I make sometimes when Dad's out. Mum dun't really mind me making 'em, but Dad throws a wobbly when there's a mess, and I always leave a mess. Let's make two, Dip, then you can have one.'

Irresistible enthusiasm. I put his cake on a plate and handed it to him.

'Tell you what, Mark – if I happen to have got whatever sizzlers are made of, and it doesn't take more than about ten minutes to make them, and you tell me how to do it, I'll make us one each. How about that?'

'Great! First of all you need a slice of bread.'

I patted the bread-bin. 'Got that.'

'Then you need some Marmite.'

I stroked my chin. 'Mmm, I might have to delve a bit deeper for that.' Opening the larder, I burrowed among jams and pastes and tins of this and that on the bottom shelf until, at last, my efforts were rewarded with a sighting of the familiar yellow lid. I held the marmite jar aloft in triumph. 'Got it!' I examined the jar more closely. 'Not much left, I'm afraid.'

'It's all right, you don't need much. Now we need an onion.'

'A whole onion?'

'No, you know – slices of one. You slice it up.'

'Right, no problem. Here's one in the vegetable rack. Looks a bit black and vile on the outside but it'll all peel off. Anything else?'

'Cheese.' The word elbowed its way out through a mouthful of chocolate cake.

'Cheese, did you say?'

'Yeah.'

'Any special kind of cheese?'

'Just ordinary.'

'Cheddar, you mean?'

'Yellow – ordinary. I think it is Cheddar, yeah.'

I opened the fridge and took out a block of cheese. 'There we are.' I unwrapped it and put it on the table with the onion and the Marmite. 'Let's get the bread out ready as well. How many slices are we going to need for both of us?'

'Just two.'

'Is that everything now?'

'Yeah.'

I studied the ingredients of our forthcoming snack. 'So, we've got Marmite, onion and cheese. Mark, are you sure you're not doing some undercover work for Rennie's?'

He didn't even notice my feeble joke. 'What you do now is – you toast the bread on one side, right?'

'Right.'

'Then you spread the Marmite – but not too much – on the other side, right?'

'Yes, got it.'

'And then you cut slices of onion off the – well, off the onion, only they've gotta be thin, right?'

I nodded.

'And you put the onion on top of the Marmite, and then you do the last thing, and that's putting slices of cheese on top so you can't see any of the stuff underneath – '

'Thick slices of cheese?'

'Not too thick or it goes bubbly on top too fast – and then you put it under the grill and wait till the cheese all melts together in one lot and then you take it out and eat it.' He smacked his lips and sucked air and saliva through his teeth. 'Can't wait!'

'It does sound pretty good,' I agreed. 'Okay, then, you sit down and read the paper or something, and I'll see if I can produce a pair of perfect sizzlers.'

As I began to peel and slice my bruised onion I wondered how often Mark felt relaxed enough to communicate with such enthusiasm and proprietorial confidence. It may have been just the making of a humble toasted sandwich that had inspired him, but it was good to see so much animation.

'Can I look round your house, Dip? I can't get into reading the *Times*. I only really like the *Express* and *Mail* and all those.'

I didn't stop what I was doing, but this innocent enquiry sent my imagination sprinting around the various rooms of my house checking bedroom and bathroom floors for underwear or general mess or anything else that might offer embarrassing revelations about my personal life. My imagination returned, puffing and panting, to report that all was clear. I had a very stern word with my imagination later about its failure to notice the bubble mixture.

'Yes, you carry on and have a look round, Mark. After all, I've seen all round yours. I don't think you'll find it very interesting, though.'

I had just reached the Marmite-spreading phase when Mark returned with his casually expressed question. Ludicrously, I felt as if I'd been caught out in some dreadful fetish or perversion, and it was quite true that I had been on the verge of pretending that the bubbles were for Felicity, or were left over from a children's party or something like that.

'Okay, well, the real reason I keep that tube of bubble mixture by my bed is that it helps me when I start to feel tense.'

Something in the quality of the silence behind me suggested that I had struck an unexpected chord. I started to lay slices of onion neatly on to the Marmite as I continued.

'Every now and then I get – I don't know how to describe it really – I get sort of panicky and my chest goes tight and I feel as if I'm in one of those horrible little tiny prison cells where they used to cram people in the old days. Does it matter if the cheese goes over the edge, or not?'

'No, you don't want to do that or it melts all down on the grill. You mean the ones where you couldn't stand up or stretch out or anything?'

'That's right. So, when I start feeling like that I reach for the bubbles, and that really helps me.'

'How does it help you?'

My two carefully constructed sizzlers were ready for toasting now. I placed them carefully under the grill and turned the heat up to just above halfway.

'There! Two or three minutes, do you reckon?'

'Till the cheese melts sort of neatly over everything else. I usually put it on too high.'

'Okay – I think I'll sit down for a moment.' I sat next to him at the table. 'The thing is, Mark, it's just not possible to blow bubbles in a hurry. There's no such thing as urgent bubble-making. You have to blow very gently and really concentrate if you want decent bubbles. And it's just the same if you do it by waving the wand thing through the air. You have to make smooth, graceful movements with your arm' – I mimed the action – 'so that the bubbles come out in a nice regular stream.' I shrugged, feeling rather pink and silly all of a sudden. 'I s'pose it's just that after a few minutes of playing with my bubbles I – well, I settle down a little bit. Does that make sense to you, or are you beginning to think you're dealing with an absolute loony?'

'Yeah.' Mark nodded gravely, then suddenly grinned as he realized the implication of his agreement.

'I mean – yeah, it does make sense, not you're a loony. D'you like going to church, Dip?'

I haven't learned many things in my life, but one thing I have begun to understand is that when B follows A it is quite often disguised as W or even Z. In Mark's case this was particularly true. You simply had to accept that there was a sort of sub-conversational logic going on inside him, and that apparent *non sequiturs* were quite often directly linked to what had just been said. I knew that if I simply answered the question and expressed no surprise at what sounded like a complete change of subject, all would be revealed in the end.

At the same time I was very aware that this was perilous ground. I knew for a fact that Mike and Kathy were feeling very tender and guilty about what they saw as their failure to bring Jack and Mark up as enthusiastic followers of Jesus. Felicity believed everything she was told without question at the moment, but there was little evidence that either of the boys felt any real interest in the Christian faith – not, at any rate, as it was expressed and practised in our own church community.

'I have to be honest, Dip,' Kathy had said to me only a week or two previously, 'despite the fact that I've always said I'd like them to be their own people making their own decisions and all that, when it comes to the crunch I panic, and none of that seems to matter. All I want is for them to be nice, uncomplicated, incurious, card-carrying members of a chorus-singing, sausage-sizzling, sex-avoiding, Bible-studying, evangelical church youth group. I can't bear the thought that it might be me who's put them off the whole thing. Jack was converted about five times when he was little, and he used to be quite involved, but he doesn't come with us at all any more, and I'm afraid to ask him what he thinks about God in case he announces that he's an atheist. I can't bear the thought of him smiling that annoying little young-old smile of his and pitying me for my middle-aged naïvety. As for Mark – well, as you know, taking Mark to church is rather like taking a small but intense rain cloud to some sunshine holiday resort. He sends out great waves of gloom and misery and boredom, and I get horribly embarrassed because of the impression he must give to other people, and then I get furious with myself for caring what other people think, and then I get wild with him afterwards for spoiling my enjoyment of the service, and he says, "Well, why do you make me come, then?", and I can't think of an answer, and Sunday goes gurgling down the plughole yet again. It's getting me down, Dip, but I'm not giving in. I *refuse* to give in – he's coming with us whether he likes it or not, and that's that!'

It was the recollection of these comments of Kathy's that caused me to pause rather lengthily before attempting to answer Mark's question. Being an honorary family member is all very well, but it doesn't give you the right to undermine decisions that are being stuck to like grim death – even if you don't altogether agree with them.

'Well,' I replied warily at last, 'it depends what – '

'I mean, what about last Sunday?' An expression of mingled anger and resentment darkened Mark's face as he spoke. 'Well bad, that was!'

I thought back to the previous Sunday. Yes, I was forced to admit to myself, much as I loved many things about my church, it had indeed been *well* bad on a number of levels, but, for me personally, that particular day had been a lot more complicated than that. Last Sunday had been ...

'The worse thing was,' said Mark, interrupting my musings, 'a kid in my class called Bradley Jenkins was there 'cause it was his cousin. He's been taking the .... He's been laughing at me about it all week. I reckon the sizzlers are done.'

They were done, and they smelled absolutely wonderful.

'Get a couple of plates out of the carousel under the corner, Mark, and a knife and fork for me out of the drawer – I don't suppose you're too bothered about cutlery, are you?'

'Tastes better with your hands,' said Mark.

The sizzlers tasted as good as they smelled, and for a few moments we chewed in companionable silence.

'Tell me what you really thought about last Sunday, Dip.'

'All right, Mark, I will. I'll tell you what I really thought about it.'

It had been one of those Sundays when a christening had to be inserted into the middle of the family service. I was sitting somewhere around the middle of the church, and the Robinsons were on the back row because, consistent as ever, they had arrived late.

The inclusion of a christening in the service had its normal quota of predictable effects, the most inevitable being the transformation of Stanley Vetchley, our resident reluctant Anglican, into an even darker little cloud than Mark, if that was possible.

Two years earlier Stanley, a widower of past retirement age, had felt called to leave the small non-conformist chapel at the other end of town, a place where he and his beloved wife, Ethel, had worshipped for decades, and to become an attender at St George's instead. It was a brave piece of obedience because Stanley clearly found most Church of England practices quite abominable. Generally speaking he was able to control his negative responses to the liturgy and the communion ('Coming to the Lord's table' Stanley called it) and the 'fancy dress' worn by our vicar – indeed, we were often able to laugh with him about his reaction to these things, but when it came to infant baptism the laughter had to stop. Stanley just *knew* that was wrong, but unfortunately he didn't stay away. He turned up to signal his disapproval on each occasion in exactly the same way. Sitting bolt upright at the back of the church in his smart, double-breasted, obsolete Sunday suit, arms folded and jaw set grimly, he would refuse to communicate in anything but a graceless grunt from the beginning of the service to the end. It was like having an extra pillar in the church, one that, in its own way, was even more obstructive to some people than the ones that were made of stone.

Another common feature of christening services was the sudden increase in the number of human bodies present, particularly, for some reason, when members of the family in question were not usually church attenders. It had been like that last Sunday. More than twenty people filed self-consciously into St George's to witness the baptism of baby Samantha, and they all dressed up more smartly than most of the people who came regularly.

Particularly self-conscious on this occasion were a couple of young men in their very early twenties who had the unmistakable aura of those who have been encased into their best suits and behaviour by determined wives, mothers or sisters. They sat on the pew just in front of me, bent forward with their heads together, rather as they might have sat on one of the features at Disneyland, waiting for the ride to start in that submissively non-connected way that people do. Flicking an occasional nervous glance sideways at their unfamiliar surroundings, they comforted each other with whispered funny comments, hiding their laughter behind their hands as though they believed that jokes might be as unacceptable in church as cigarettes. Above their heads, in a phantom thought bubble, I seemed to read the words: 'If we can just sit this one out – the booze will come.'

There's quite a lot of talk in our church from time to time about the great opportunities that are presented by baptism services. People who would never normally come into a church have a chance to be exposed to the Gospel – that's the theory. In fact, we don't actually adapt what we're doing very much to suit these occasional visitors. Maybe we shouldn't change anything. Maybe we should just be what we are. I'm not sure. Sitting behind these two fellows really made me think, though.

The vicar wasn't conducting the early part of the service on this particular day. Instead, it was led by a man called Roy Tap-house who lived with his wife and two grown-up children in the same road as the Robinsons, but much farther down the hill towards the recreation ground. Roy looked rather like the film actor, Christopher Lee, but there was nothing of the vampire in him. Always kind and considerate, he was one of those people who put an awful lot of hard work into following and obeying God. Much as I liked and respected Roy, though, I found the fact that he invariably led services in a light, bright, totally optimistic, ever-cheerful sort of way a little irksome – not that I would ever have said that to him or anyone else. Lots of people loved the service to be conducted in that way, and why, I dutifully asked myself, shouldn't they have what suited them?

On this occasion Roy started with a prayer from the green service books – much flurry, page-turning and puzzlement from the uninitiated christening-attached ones – and continued with an announcement that we were going to learn a new and exciting chorus from the yellow song-books.

'I'm pretty sure we haven't tried this chorus in the past,' he enthused, 'but I heard the music group playing it through before the service, and' – he beamed roguishly – 'I have a feeling we shall be singing this one all through the week.'

Nervously, the members of the music group launched them-selves severally into the beginning of the exciting new chorus, and, having regrouped a little further along the tune, led us halt-ingly through three attempts at one of those strangely insubstan-tial, fiercely celebratory songs that cause congregations to bare their teeth in determined joy. The exhausted silence that followed reminded me of a hush that descended at one of my birthday par-ties once, when a lot of very noisy things had cascaded from the top of a kitchen cupboard and we were all waiting to hear if one more was going to fall after a moment's pause.

It was in the middle of this silence that I overheard one of the fellows in front of me make a dispassionate comment to his friend.

'Oh, yeah, I'll be singin' that all through the week, won't I?

Can't wait to get in to work down the garage tomorrow – teach all my mates that one, eh? They'll love that, won't they? We'll *all* sing it all week. That's a great song....'

Prayer time followed shortly after that, conducted by Amy Bennison, an impossibly vague middle-aged lady who smiled constantly through thick, round-framed glasses and would do absolutely anything for anybody. Amy and her husband Derek, a similarly good natured, jockey-like little man, had never had children of their own, but they adored everyone else's offspring unequivocally and indiscriminately. Amy was always volunteering to help with children's groups, but had to be deflected most of the time because her enthusiasm was just not matched by her ability to maintain control. Not that the chaos she engendered caused her any personal alarm or discomfort. As far as Amy was concerned, children were simply wonderful – whatever they did. I suppose the vicar had reckoned that prayer-time was a pretty safe bet, as no little ones would be involved. He was wrong.

'I think it would be so nice,' said Amy sweetly, 'if some of the little children could come up and help me with the prayers this morning.'

A breeze of dismay ruffled the still heads of the congregation. I'm sure many of us prayed that the children would stay in their seats. But children are contrary little persons, aren't they? On those occasions when you really want them to go up to the front they suddenly turn shy or even tearful, and cling, poultice-like, to their coaxing, slightly embarrassed, vaguely annoyed parents. Not this time. This time our silent prayers of entreaty were not answered. Several small children clambered excitedly from whichever laps had been accommodating them and toddled up to cluster around dear Amy, who patted their heads delightedly, and smiled broadly at Roy Taphouse, as if to say, 'Aren't they sweet – isn't it wonderful!' Roy, who had retreated to a chair at the side, smiled back nervously. Even his eternal optimism wasn't proof against the potential disaster of any situation that involved Amy and small children.

'Now,' said Amy, addressing the congregation, 'I thought it

would be so nice if our little friends here could suggest some topics for prayer, because I'm sure the things they think of will be just as important as anything that we grown-ups talk to God about. So, come along, children, what shall we pray about in our service today?'

There was silence for a moment. Most of the congregation watched and waited in a considerable state of tension. I felt like a close relative of some amateur juggler who has found himself performing at the Palladium.

Annabelle Short was the first child to make a suggestion. She spoke in a thin, squeaky voice, but with crystal-clear enunciation.

'Could we pray about the wind?'

Amy's fond smile froze for just a second as she accommodated this novel proposal for prayer. A sharp intake of breath from the row behind me suggested that Renee Short, Annabelle's elegant mother, was desperately willing Amy not to embark on a plea for the healing of flatulence in the church worldwide.

Amy's accommodation process was complete.

'Of course we can, Annabelle. Do you want to say a little prayer for us about the wind, dear?'

An even sharper intake of breath from behind.

'No,' said Annabelle simply.

'Fine, then I'll say one. Let's all close our eyes and talk to God about the wind.'

Amy closed her eyes, her smile moving inwards and upwards as she addressed the creator of the universe.

'Dear God, we come before you now to pray about the wind. We thank you for the wonderful way in which it err ... blows, and we remember all those mechanical things that go round to produce – is it water or electricity? I think it's one of those. Without the wind that you send, dear God, those things wouldn't go round and people wouldn't be able to have the water – actually I think it *is* electricity – err, they wouldn't be able to have the electricity that is produced when they do go round, so we do thank you on their behalf for the wind that you send, in all its many, err ... facets. Amen.'

We regulars murmured a relieved 'Amen', but the two young men in front of me were bent over double, their faces buried in their hands, producing little explosive noises as they tried to control their laughter. Next to them, on the same pew, an aggressively well-behaved and hatted female, presumably a connection of theirs, glared and nudged threateningly.

'Is the wind something you're specially interested in, Annabelle?' asked Amy, her voice full of kindly interest.

'No,' said Annabelle comfortably, 'it's not.'

'I *see*,' said Amy brightly, as if she'd said it was. 'Now, who else has got something for us to pray about?'

'I have.' The chunky infant voice came from a little boy whose name I didn't know, on the other side of Amy.

'What would you like us to talk to Jesus about?'

'Drizzle,' said the little boy,

'Drizzle?' said Amy.

'Yes.'

'Oh, drizzle, yes – well, that's the same as rain, isn't it, dear?'

''Snot.'

'It's not?'

The infant opened his mouth wide and, in a husky monotone, delivered one of those mechanically abrupt, computer-like emissions of newly acquired knowledge that small children specialize in.

'Rain-is-when-you'd-get-really-wet-if-you-went-out-to-play-and-drizzle-is-when-you-might-be-able-to-go-out-and-play-soon-'cause-it-prob'ly-won't-last-long-so-just-be-patient.'

'Well, I think we'll pray about rain for now, dear, because I think they really are the same, you know.' Amy shut her eyes. 'Dear God, we thank you for the rain that – '

The infant burst into tears. 'Don't wanna talk to Jesus 'bout r-r-r-rain! Wanna talk to Jesus 'bout d-d-d-drizzle!'

'All right, dear,' said Amy hastily, 'we'll say a prayer about drizzle. No more crying now.'

The infant's crying shuddered to a gasping halt. He passed the back of a small hand across his tear-streaked face and gazed expectantly up into Amy's face.

'Dear God,' prayed Amy, still smiling, but with just a hint of desperation in her voice, 'we thank you for the drizzle that falls down on us from the sky....'

The pattern was set. There was no going back now. Those children were determined that every meteorological condition they had ever encountered or heard about should be presented before the throne of the Most High. We thanked God for the snow, the hail, the thunder and the sunshine. We also thanked him that none of us had been killed in earthquakes or drowned in floods. The whole episode was like something out of a comic novel, especially as it became increasingly clear that Amy didn't know how to stop. As the children gained confidence their eyes gleamed with the knowledge that an adult was dancing to their tune. They grew much more competitive and deluged her with weather-related subjects for prayer. Fortunately, just after we had prayed that the little clouds wouldn't get hurt when they bumped into each other, Roy had the sense to intervene at last, and the children returned to their parents' laps in a state of extreme excitability. Amy went back to her place beside Derek, still beaming, clearly convinced that it had all gone very well indeed. I noticed that Derek smilingly nodded approval and laid a hand over his wife's as she sat down. I felt a little pang of jealousy. Amy had someone who would always tell her she'd done well. What did it matter if she was a bit vague and deluded? I felt depressed suddenly.

'I wish they'd pray for a job for me.'

It was one of the young men in front who had addressed these words to his companion. He spoke quite quietly, and had obviously not meant anyone to overhear what he said, but I was taken aback by the passion in his voice. My depression increased as I asked myself what this man must think of the service he had been corralled into attending today, a service in which nothing that had happened so far had any identifiable relevance to the life he led or the people he knew or the things that were important to him. I wished, as I had wished so many times in the past, that Jesus could be here in the flesh, sitting among us, answering questions, healing those of us who were sick, telling us off when we were silly or wrong or presumptuous, praying for a job for this young man ...

I wish they'd pray for a job for me.

I couldn't get those words out of my head as the service went on, led now by the vicar. All through the christening section, while the parents and godparents mumbled miserably that, yes, they *did indeed* turn to Christ, they *did* repent of their sins, they *did* renounce evil and they *did* believe and trust in, not just one, but all three persons of the trinity, that one sentence returned to me again and again. By the time the final blessing was being said I had descended into an all too familiar morass of self-pity and judgementalism. Why should I go on coming to this useless church where no one seemed to understand how to relate to a real world full of real needs? Why did we let Stanley Vetchley get away with sitting there in a big sulk just because he didn't happen to like what was happening? Why did the vicar allow people like Roy Taphouse and Amy Bennison, sweet-natured though they were, to be a public expression of what we claimed to believe? What was the use of it all? Why couldn't Jesus be here with us to sort it all out?

It was while that final blessing was being said that a few words from the New Testament slipped in through the merest fissure in my self-absorption. I certainly wouldn't have let them come in and spoil my sulk if I could have prevented it. They consisted of a few words from the end of Matthew's gospel, and a verse from that wonderful section at the end of John where Jesus is talking so passionately to the disciples before his arrest.

Behold I am with you always....

But I tell you the truth, it is for your good that I am going away. Unless I go away, The Counsellor will not come to you, but if I go, I will send him to you.

When I opened my eyes the vicar was inviting everybody to stay to coffee in the hall attached to the church, and the two chaps who had been sitting in front of me were standing up with a purposeful, 'Let's get out of here' look about them.

I came so close to chickening out. Everything in me wanted to go and get a coffee and a biscuit and chat comfortably to someone who would make no demands on me, but I had said that I wanted Jesus to be here to pray for a genuine, practical need, and he was – in me.

Come on, Reynolds, put up or shut up.

I found them just outside the church. The rest of their party were still inside, presumably drinking coffee and eating biscuits and showing off baby Samantha, but these two were standing happily in the sunshine with newly-lit cigarettes, deeply inhaling the smoke, like drowning men who have found an air supply just in time. I cannot tell you how difficult I found it to begin my conversation with them.

'Err, excuse me, you don't know me,' I began breathlessly, 'but I was sitting behind you in church just now during the service, and there was something I just wanted to say to you ... err, if that's all right?'

'What, did we leave something behind?' said the slightly more affluent-looking one who had mentioned the garage he worked in.

'Oh, no no, nothing like that, it was just that ... well, I couldn't help overhearing something.' I looked into the eyes of the tall, skinny, large-featured young man with the spiky haircut who was responsible for my present embarrassment. 'It was something *you* said.'

'D'I say something wrong?' he asked, glancing over his shoulder with a trace of alarm at the church doorway through which those who policed his life might pass at any moment.

'Good heavens, no! Of course not. No, it was after the children had said all those silly prayers about weather, remember?'

'Oh, yeah.' He looked down, grinning, avoiding his friend's eye and stirred the gravel with the toe of his boot.

'It's all right, I thought it was very funny as well – for a while, anyway.'

He glanced up into my face, focusing with sudden wariness on the strangeness of my approach to him. 'What'd I say then?'

I took a deep breath. 'You said something like "I wish they'd pray for a job for me". In fact, I think that's exactly what you said – "I wish they'd pray for a job for me". You did say that, didn't you?'

His face turned a dull brick-red colour. 'Might've said something like that. What about it?'

'Well, I wanted to offer to pray with you now – if you'd like me to, that is. We could ask God to find you a job.'

He waved an arm towards the church. 'I'm only here for Sammy's whatsit. I don't belong – '

'You don't have to belong to the church. We can just talk to God here and ask him.'

He looked helplessly at his friend, desperate for guidance in this highly specialized area of acceptable ways in which to respond to strange females who invite you to pray with them outside churches. The friend rolled his eyes, shook his head, and shrugged with equal helplessness.

'Might as well have a go,' he said doubtfully. 'You might get one.' Then to me, 'Put our fags out, shall we?'

A little bubble of hysteria rose in me and popped into a chuckle.

'No, it doesn't matter about your cigarettes. God won't mind that. We'll just talk to him now. What's your name?' I asked the brick-red one.

'Err, Michael Edward Simmonds – Mick.'

'Mick, right. Let's pray, then.'

Awkwardly, the two men bowed their heads and clasped their hands in front of them like footballers preparing to block a free kick in front of goal. Smoke curled up in two grey columns from the cigarettes held between their fingers, adding an oddly ceremonial atmosphere to the triangular proceedings.

'Father,' I began, straining to believe in miracles, but woefully conscious that my faith seemed to be draining out through my feet, 'we want to ask you about a job for Mick. We know there aren't many jobs around nowadays, but if there's something that would really suit him – '

'Dun't matter what it is,' qualified Mick gruffly, and rather surprisingly. He was obviously anxious for God to be quite clear, that, far from being fussy, he was in the market for anything that was going.

'If there is something he could do, Father – anything at all – he'd be really grateful, and so would I, and so would his friend here.'

'Steve,' mumbled the friend informatively into his tie.

'So would Steve. Thank you for what you're going to do. Amen.'

After that we shook hands solemnly, and I went back into the church, leaving Mick and Steve highly relieved and lighting up fresh cigarettes to replace the ones whose smoke had carried our prayers up to heaven. As soon as I was back inside I became aware that my legs had turned to jelly, and I had to sit down for a while to recover. I had done it, though! Feeble, faithless, fearful and judgemental I certainly was, but I was so glad that I had done it!

'Well embarrassing!' exclaimed Mark, who had listened to my account of last Sunday's service with rapt attention. 'Glad I wasn't them.'

'Glad you wasn't who?'

'The two blokes – Mick and the other one. Praying out in the street where everyone can see – *well* embarrassing! D'you think he'll get one?'

'A job, you mean?'

'Yeah.'

'I think God can do anything he wants. I just hope he wants to give Mick a job. I can't bear the thought of running into the poor fellow in the High Street over and over again if nothing happens. *Well* embarrassing for both of us, wouldn't you say? Anyway, that's what I thought about church last Sunday. It was pretty terrible, but I was part of the terribleness, so I can't really criticize.'

'You know you said you have the bubbles because of getting tense?'

'Mmm.'

I sensed that we had arrived at the reason for Mark's visit.

'I get tense.' Mark's eyes dropped. He began to draw on the tablecloth with his finger.

'What about?'

'Lots of things. Mum getting cross and saying I don't listen, and her not listening when I try to say things. And she says I ought to be nice but I can't when it happens – the words don't come out. I have to wait till I can do it differently.'

I leaned back in my chair – people like Mark are drawn, not pushed. 'Do you mean that you feel all the things she thinks you ought to say, but you can only show it in ways that are more doing than speaking? I haven't put that very well, but is that more or less what you mean?'

Mark nodded and a huge tear plopped on to the plate that had managed to catch a few of the crumbs from his sizzler. He jammed the heels of both hands into his eyes and rubbed hard until they were reddened and tearless.

'I want Mum to let me stop going to church, Dip. It's boring an' embarrassing an' it goes on for ever. Jack's allowed to stay at home. None of my friends have to go, an' they all think I'm stupid for going. It ruins all the week for me thinking about it coming an' messing up the weekend, an' then it comes an' it's awful. I know Mum wants me to look as if I'm liking it, but I can't. I hate church. I hate Sunday! I really *hate* it!' He paused. It wasn't difficult to guess what was coming next. 'Will you talk to Mum an' ask her if I can stop going? She won't get cross with you.'

'Hmm …' I found myself puffing my cheeks out and drumming with my fingertips on the tabletop – a clear sign that I was out of my depth. 'Mark, I can't simply ask her to let you stop going – not just like that. I'm sure that wouldn't be right. Anyway, it's not just your mum. Your dad's got to agree as well, hasn't he?' I did a bit more puffing and drumming and shot silent, panic-stricken prayers into the ether as I tried to decide what to do for the best. 'What I can do, if you want me to, is talk to your mum and dad about what you've said, and tell them you're really, genuinely upset about going, and not just making a fuss, and then I'm afraid I'd have to leave it to them to decide what to do.'

Mark stretched his arms up straight above his head, linked his fingers and yawned as if he was in the last stages of exhaustion. Then he dropped his arms into a folded position on the table, shivered abruptly from head to foot, and sniffed loudly.

'Could you talk to them soon, Dip, please?'

'I'll pop round and have a chat tonight if you like. Are you all right, Mark? Is there anything I can get you?'

That smile again. 'Wouldn't mind another bit of chocolate cake.'

Chapter 10

I spent a couple of hours at the Robinsons' later that evening. We talked in the kitchen while Jack was watching television in the lounge. Mark was out with his mates and Felicity was staying the night with her friend Claire Elphick.

I described to Kathy and Mike how Mark had dropped in, I talked about the success of our culinary adventure, and I went on to convey – or to try to convey – the passion with which he had expressed his negative attitude to church services in general and last week's in particular. I was careful to mention Mark's single tear, hoping that even that tiny amount of liquid would be enough to dampen the fire of what was likely to be an automatically angry reaction from Kathy. In conclusion, I made it clear that I was not taking an advocate's role, but simply passing on a message, as it were. When I'd finished they were both still and silent for a while. Finally, Mike leaned back sighing deeply and ran both hands through his thinning hair.

'Thank you, Dip,' he said quietly, 'you're a good friend.' He looked worriedly at Kathy whose gaze, wide-eyed and trance-like, was fixed on a little red wooden top of Felicity's that she was twirling endlessly between thumb and forefinger. 'I don't think there's any doubt that we have to respond to this, Kath, wouldn't you say?'

'Have to respond,' echoed Kathy dully, her eyes still fixed on the object in her hand. 'What a very splendid idea – yes, we shall certainly have to respond to this, shan't we? We shall devise a suitable response, and then we shall – well, we shall respond with it, and everything will be all right. All quite simple, really.'

'I didn't say it would be simple.' Mike's voice had become

even more hushed, but it was not the hush of peace. His tone was muted by apprehension and growing annoyance. 'I just meant that we can't pretend we don't have a problem. We have to do something about it, and whatever we do has to be thought through properly. I really hope that, just for once, we can take a short cut and avoid all the emotional stuff so that we come up with something that's right for Mark and within God's will. I don't see how the logic of that can be faulted.'

Kathy thrust her left hand up in the air and, with her right, spun the top into whizzing life on the table. It shot across the pine surface, bounced against the edge of an uncleared supper plate and twizzled drunkenly back towards her. She caught it and set it spinning again.

'Please, sir,' she said, speaking in a little girl voice and flapping her raised hand as if to attract attention, 'please, sir, can I have permission to tell you how the logic of that can be faulted?'

The muscles in Mike's jaw tightened. He laid an arm across the base of his chest, rested his right elbow on his left wrist and scrubbed wearily at his face with his free hand. Meanwhile, the red top, having bypassed the plate this time, flew across the table and fell to the floor at Mike's feet. Kathy pushed her chair back with her bottom and ducked under the table-top to retrieve it. Mike clenched his teeth and burst in a contained sort of way.

'Could you *please* stop playing with that stupid thing when we're supposed to be discussing something as serious as – as our children's church attendance! *Please!*'

Delighted with such signal success in making Mike play schoolmaster to her naughty child, Kathy scrambled back into her chair in simulated panic, and placed the recaptured top down beside her with exaggerated, finger-tip care before sitting up nice and straight with her arms folded. An infant 'being good'.

'Sorry, sir – won't do it again, sir. Don't hit me, sir!' Didn't mean it, sir. Permission *to* tell you now why I can't take a short cut and avoid the emotional stuff, sir?'

Nobody said anything for a moment. Boringly, I had yet another of my 'should I be somewhere else?' hot flushes, but I couldn't bring myself to say anything. No lines had been written for a third character in this particular sketch. But Kathy, whose perceptions, like most agonizers, can sometimes be very dulled but occasionally are very keen indeed, must have registered some twitch or change of colour or involuntary sound on my part. She dropped out of role for a moment, but she didn't look at me.

'Please don't go away, Dip. Part of me – not a very nice part, I'm afraid – wants to kill you for being someone Mark says things to because he thinks he can't say them to me without me boiling over and not really listening. But another part of me is glad he did.' She paused and swallowed. 'I honestly am. I'm glad. I just wish – I just wish I'd done it all better....'

Kathy's eyes looked so sad and lost that both Mike and I extended a hand towards her involuntarily. She took Mike's.

She took Mike's – one flesh.

'We don't have to go through any more of this, Kath,' said Mike gently, 'I'm sorry – say whatever you want to say.' He smiled ruefully. 'We'll do it my way next time we get married.'

'I'm always saying you should have married that Miss Rendell from your school office,' said Kathy, blinking away some unshed tears, 'she'd have recorded details of her wedding night in triplicate and sent a copy to all close relatives – very efficient and unemotional. Item number five – consummation satisfactorily completed at eleven forty-nine precisely.'

'Kath!'

'I'm sorry too, Mike. We waste an awful lot of time playing our rubbishy little games, don't we? But I can't just coolly discuss things like this as though they don't affect me – you know I can't.' She shook her head slowly as if in disbelief at what she found within herself. 'The pain is so awful – so *bad*. It cuts into me and makes me feel I'm going to fall over or something, not physically, but in some other unspeakable way, some fundamentally collapsing, nightmare-come-true sort of way. And there's nothing I can do about it, there's nothing to rub on it, nothing powerful enough to distract me from it. Even Boots hasn't got anything to make it better – except sometimes in the music section, I suppose, and that medicine's expensive nowadays.' She looked at the ceiling, fighting back fresh tears, and spoke very slowly and clearly. 'It really does hurt very much indeed, Mike. I know you find it extremely irksome when I give in to these feelings – '

Mike made a noise that seemed compounded of apology, impatience, slight embarrassment and sympathy. 'Kath, it's not that I don't – '

'And I don't blame you,' continued Kathy, adding for the sake of absolute veracity, 'well, I know I *do* blame you, but I shouldn't – I really shouldn't. Because it's not your problem, Mike. It's nobody's problem.' She swung a hand towards me. 'It's not Dip's problem, it's not Jack's problem, it's not Felicity's problem, and it's certainly not Mark's problem. It's mine. It belongs to me, and I ought to keep it in a sock under the bed.' She smiled a watery smile. 'Can you keep psychological pain in socks under beds, do you think, Dip?'

'No space left under my bed,' I replied. 'Care to have a look sometime?'

Care enough to have a look?

Kathy smiled again. 'All right, fair exchange. We'll swop problems. In fact, why not go a step further? Why shouldn't we be the very first people to introduce the concept of neighbourhood Neurosis Parties – make a change from Tupper-ware, wouldn't it? We could all sit around oohing and aahing over each other's obsessions and manias, and pass the latest "Knit Your Own Delusion" kit round while we're sipping our coffee and nibbling our thin slices of Valium Gateau. The sky's the limit after that. How about a mail order catalogue called *ANGST*, offering easy terms on the very latest straitjackets in pretty pastel shades of powder-blue, leaf-green and salmon-pink? We could make a fortune. We could – '

She broke off as Jack, humming idly, came into the kitchen with an empty glass in his hand. He studied our three faces calmly as he took a bottle of milk from the fridge and filled his glass, then he took a gulp, swallowed it down and nodded knowingly.

'Heaveeee, right?'

143

'Enjoy your milk, Solomon.' There was no offence in Kathy's tone.

Jack must have read something in his mother's face, or perhaps he just saw the tears in her eyes. He leaned down and planted a milky kiss in the middle of her forehead.

'Take it easy, Mumsy,' he drawled, in a broad American accent, 'I'll be next door ready to come in with both guns blazin'' if these here varmints start any trouble.'

He winked at Mike and me as he went out, closing the door quietly behind him.

'I'd say it was you varmints who need the protection,' said Kathy, dabbing her eyes and her forehead with the tea-towel that Mike passed her. 'What is a varmint? I've often wondered.'

'I think it's wonderful that Jack feels free enough to give you a kiss like that in front of other people, Kathy. A lot of parents would give their eye-teeth to have that kind of relationship with a son of his age. You must have done a few things right.'

Mike murmured agreement with me, but I sensed that they had been over this ground many times before.

'Oh, I'm pathetic, Dip.' Kathy threw the tea-towel in the direction of the rack and missed. Mike got up and hung it neatly back where it belonged. 'Suddenly I feel all right again because one of my children did something warm and nice. It's ridiculous to keep swinging from one mood to another – absolutely ridiculous. As you're standing up, Mike, can we have a glass of sherry now that I don't need one?'

Mike busied himself with glasses and crisps and nuts and bowls. I wanted to know more about how my friend became so tender in the first place.

'Kathy, what exactly is the pain you were talking about? Why does Mark and church and him not being able to say things to you make it quite as bad as it was just now?'

There was a long pause before she answered. Mike put the drinks and nibbles before us, then sat back down in his chair without saying anything. Kathy sipped her drink and gazed across the top of her glass into the distance.

'I got injured, Dip. A long time ago, when I was little, I got injured. Believe it or not, I can hardly remember how. I just know that life was a blur of uncertainty and tension and things going wrong whenever you got excited about them going right. I used to have the same dream – well, nightmare really – over and over again when I was a small child. I would be at a party or a film-show or a picnic or something really nice, but I would know that just as I was beginning to really enjoy myself the *voice* would whisper in my ear.'

'The voice?'

'A sad, disgusted sort of voice – not disgusted with me, I don't mean, but with life, with everything. I hated it.'

'What did it say?'

'It always said the same thing – the same words every single time in this horrible hoarse whisper. "Black curtain time", that's what it said, and in the dream my heart would sink like a stone and I'd be filled with terror and try to move towards the other people but my legs wouldn't move, and then a thick, black, vel-vety curtain would fall with a flapping, swishing, cynical thud between me and all the light and noise and life, and I'd try to get through it but I never could, and I'd scream in the dark and wake up sweating and gasping for air as if I was suffocating.' She peered at her hand, curled round the stem of the sherry glass. 'You know – I haven't told you this, Mike – but I realized the other day that every time I think about that part of my life my teeth clench and my hands curl into fists, and all the feelings and memories come back as though it was yesterday instead of years and years ago.'

'What sort of memories?'

'Well, I suppose the ones that come back most are all those evenings I spent sitting on the landing wrapped in my bedspread listening to Mum and Dad arguing and shouting downstairs. I used to follow every word they said, straining with all my might to *make* the power of my wanting affect what they were doing to each other. That's the trouble with being little, you see. You believe what grown-ups say, so when you hear your mother screaming that she's going to walk out and never come back, you don't understand that it's just another move in a sort of wild game of emotional chess. You believe it. Every single time – you believe it. I came down from my room once, after she'd said that, because I'd heard the front door open and slam, then it all went very quiet and I thought she really had gone. I could hardly breathe with the fear and panic inside me as I went down the stairs. I was going to tell my father that he had to go after her and get her back and promise her there wouldn't be any more rows.'

Mike asked quietly, 'What happened when you got downstairs, Kath?' I felt a moment of surprise that he had never heard this story before.

'Well, nothing really, that's what was so awful. Mum was doing something to the washing machine in the kitchen, and Dad was in the sitting-room watching *What's My Line?* on television. I still have this mental snapshot in my memory of grumpy old Gilbert Harding in a brown box spouting off about something or other. I was so taken aback by my mother being there and not having gone after all that I didn't know what to say. This little engine of fear inside me was suddenly roaring away without actually engaging with anything. It was a most odd feeling, and part of it was a totally uncomprehending childish anger towards my mother for creating such panic in me and then not doing what she said she was going to do, even though I didn't want her to do it. *Well* rational, eh?'

'So what happened in the end?'

'Oh, this is a real multi-Kleenex-job, Dip. I ended up getting told off for being rude, would you believe? When Mum spotted me palely loitering out in the hall she said, "What are you doing down here at this time of night?", and there was just no way I could turn all those feelings into words, so I let the anger in me talk. And *it* said, "I'll come downstairs whenever I want and you can't stop me." Of course, the roof fell on my head after that. Mum told Dad what I'd said, and they suddenly found – surprise, surprise – that they did have something in common after all. They were both very cross with me, and I was shot back to bed and told I was a very naughty little girl. I lay and raged in the dark for ages – but I was glad my mum hadn't gone.

'I understand a lot better now, of course. My parents had their problems just as we've got ours, even if most of them are completely different ones. But the things you learn when you're a kid are facts, even if they're not facts. And the constant, gut-twisting uncertainty of those times, the feeling that everything's bound to end in disappointment or conflict or disaster of one kind or another – that's what the kid in me still knows for sure is the way the world really goes. That's the injury I was talking about and it's never had a chance to heal properly. Any sort of failure with the children just opens it up again and it hurts as if it had only just happened.'

Kathy drank the last drop of her sherry and placed the empty glass suggestively beside the bottle on the table. Mike did pour more sherry for us all, but, rather to my private annoyance, only a very little into each glass. One day I shall murder someone who takes it upon him- or herself to monitor my alcohol intake.

'When I became a Christian,' continued Kathy, 'I thought somehow that everything would work out okay in the end. Because God was on my side my marriage would be successful, and the kids would grow up believing the same as we do – whatever that is – and the past wouldn't be allowed to keep reaching out and grabbing me by the throat and spoiling everything. I wasn't quite sure how all that would happen – I just assumed that it would. I really was quite naïvely optimistic about the future, but I think now that I got it wrong. God hasn't got rid of the problems – he hasn't scrubbed out the inside of my life with a divine abrasive cloth and left it shiny and germ-free. Right deep down I think I'm glad he hasn't. I want to be me, and I want him to be *in it* with this ragged, turbulent me. I just wish – ' She sighed wistfully. 'I just wish he could have stretched a point and made the kids want to go to church with us. Just now, when you passed on what Mark had said, Dip, it was Black Curtain Time again and I couldn't handle it. Silly really, isn't it? So!' She bounced the palms of her hands on the table. There we are. That's why we can't take a short cut and avoid the emotional stuff, Mike. There's too much of it to find a way round. I have to burrow right through the middle. And if you ever pour me a third of a glass of sherry again I shall go on to meths, and so will Dip, won't you, Dip?'

'Yes,' I said solemnly, 'I probably will. Kathy, I was just thinking – thanks, Mike – I was just thinking, bearing in mind all that you've just said, that you must find it difficult sometimes to work out whether you're an amazing success as a mother, or a miserable failure.'

She blinked. 'What do you mean?'

'Well, you've got this bag full of weights that you drag around with you everywhere you go, and it's invisible, so no one really knows how much effort is involved in just keeping going. But you have kept going, and considering the size of that handicap – '

'You make me sound like something not worth backing in the three-thirty at Haydock Park.' Kathy is hopeless at handling any kind of compliment.

I pressed on doggedly. 'Considering the size of that handicap you've done an amazing job, and I think you should be proud of yourself.'

And so should I, shouldn't I?

'It is an interesting thought,' responded Kathy, driven by embarrassment into whimsy as usual, 'that the time will come when God will press the Show All Characters button on that great computer in the sky and every one of us will be revealed for exactly what we are. There'll be me staggering around with my ton of garbage wrapped up in a big black curtain, and there'll be Mike tripping along with a small neat attaché case, containing small neat problems inserted tidily into appropriate compartments.'

'If you think being married to you is a small neat problem that can be inserted tidily into an appropriate compartment you can jolly well think again!'

Mike's indignant explosion was so comical that we both burst into laughter. He looked a little offended for a moment, then laid his head on his shoulder and smiled sheepishly, like a small boy.

'What you say about Kath is quite true, Dip,' he said, 'she does do a great job with the kids – I've been trying to tell her that for years. I know I get annoyed and fed-up sometimes, but that's because I honestly do find it very difficult to identify with all this burdens-from-the-past stuff. I know it's all quite real,' he added hastily, raising both hands as if to ward off attack, 'but, you see, I had a genuinely happy, well-organized childhood with Christian parents – my mother can be a bit fierce, as you know, but very kind and loving – and I guess I'm always trying to make it like that here. I get just as upset about the boys' attitude to church as Kath does, but I'd rather take the problem straight to Jesus, and then make some practical decisions. I guess we're just made very differently.'

Vive la difference!

'What are we going to do, Mike?'

'You say a prayer, Kath.'

'Me?'

'Yes, you. Put all your care for them into a prayer.'

Kathy showed her teeth and widened her eyes in pretend horror. 'Now? Out loud? I think you or Dip would be much better at praying about this than me. You're both calmer – more rational, you had happy childhoods....'

Did we?

'Oh, all right, Mike. You don't have to look at me under your brows like that any longer. I'll pray.'

In the silence that fell just before Kathy began her prayer I experienced one of those strange moments of almost complete peace. The other two had closed their eyes and bent their heads, but I kept my eyes open as I usually did nowadays, and gradually became conscious that something unusual was happening. Familiar objects and surfaces in the kitchen had acquired something that I can only describe as a luminosity – a greater, shining reality, and the warmth of – what can I call it? – of sheer Presence, was rippling gently through the air and through my own body, producing the kind of unearthly intoxication that seems to inflame the spirit rather than the mind. So rare, those times, and so valuable.

'Father, it's me, Katherine – Kathy, I mean. We want to talk to you about our children, Jack and Mark and Felicity. You know how much' – Kathy's voice broke a little,' – you know how much we adore them, and how much we want to do the right things for them, and you know how we – I – keep on failing because I get so upset and those horrible jagged feelings get in the way of what I know I ought to do and say. Please – oh, please don't let it be held against them if they move away from you because of me. Forgive me for the times when I give in to the feelings inside me, and help me to be stronger and – and more obedient. You know what it's like to have a son, and watch him going through difficult, terrible times and not be able to do much about it, don't you? Oh, Father, doesn't it hurt to be a mum or a dad....' Mike retrieved the tea-towel and put it into Kathy's hands again. She mopped and sniffed and recovered. 'We've got to decide what to do about church now, Father, and we don't really know what to do for the best, so we just want to ask you to be with us and help us and guide us, because we're a bit lost at the moment – well, I am anyway. Look after them, love them, be real to all of them one day. Thank you very much – goodbye.'

For some reason, Kathy's involuntary and slightly confused substitution of 'goodbye' for the more traditional 'amen' brought the tears to *my* eyes. It was so plaintive somehow. For what must have been a full minute after that we sat and savoured the atmosphere that had been created by Kathy's prayer. Then Mike spoke at last.

'You all right, Kath?'

She took a deep breath and blew it out again loudly. 'Fine – thanks for the tea-towel, Mike. I'm beginning to feel rather fond of this square of cloth. If we ever come across a home for broken-down tea-cloths this faithful old friend shall spend the autumn of its life there, instead of being torn into strips and used for unmentionable things. What do we do now?'

'Well, I'm no more certain about anything than you, but I suggest we get Jack and Mark together before Sunday – '

'Not Felicity?'

'No, I wouldn't have thought so, would you?'

'No.'

'Would you have thought so, Dip?'

'No.'

'And we'll ask them quite quietly and openly what they think about it all. We'll make it quite clear that they can say whatever they like.'

Kathy nodded sombrely, then leaned forward and glanced around the kitchen as if to check for eavesdroppers. 'All right,' she whispered, 'but we won't mean it, will we?'

Chapter 11

The planned meeting took place on the next day, Saturday. I met the Robinsons by arrangement at their house when they returned from a whole-family walk up on the 'bosomy hills' as Kathy termed the gentle chalk range that lay a few miles to the south of our town. I knew that Mark was always keen to get up into the hills, mainly because he loved to fly his kite, one of those big, manoeuvrable ones with two control lines attached to plastic handles. He had let me have a go now and then in the past, and I must admit it had bubbles beaten into a cocked hat – it's a bit tricky flying a kite in your bedroom, though....

The sky had been piled high with heavily laden clouds all day, and rain was just beginning to spatter against the windows when the clang of van doors shutting, thumps, clatters, flapping noises, one high-pitched voice and mutual recriminations on a slightly lower register announced the family's arrival at their front door.

The 'plan', carefully worked out by Mike, Kathy and me, was that I would have a really nice tea prepared and laid out in the sitting room, and that in this convivial, post-ramble, familial setting it would be much easier for the boys to speak openly and freely about church-related matters. The problem of Felicity had been solved, in theory, by hiring a video of *Three Men and a Little Lady*, her favourite film of all time ('all time' being six years, of course) which she was to watch on Jack's portable set upstairs, with her own special tea laid out on a tray. Felicity received the news of this arrangement with hand-clapping delight, switching abruptly to deep suspicion.

'What are you all going to be doing in the sitting room when I'm upstairs, then?' she asked, after I'd described what was happening.

'We're going to be saying things we don't want you to hear,' I replied, 'but not about you.'

The frankness of this explanation made her giggle, and she was soon settled in front of the television, a corned-beef sandwich in one hand, a glass of orange squash with one of those twisting, coiling plastic straws in the other, her eyes fixed adoringly on the screen as those three wonderful men appeared.

Meanwhile, in the sitting room, the warm, familial setting was obviously turning out to be rather less convivial than Mike and Kathy had hoped. I arrived at the bottom of the stairs to find Mark at the front door explaining grumpily to two of his friends that he wasn't able to come out because his parents were making him stay in to have tea when he didn't even want any tea, but that he'd come out as soon as he was allowed to, so why didn't they wait just outside the front door until then. At this juncture Kathy appeared at the sitting-room door, furious but icily polite.

'There's no point in asking your friends to wait,' she announced, 'because we don't know how long we shall be, do we?'

'Don't wait.'

The friends drifted off into the rain, and Mark stomped back to the sitting room. I closed the front door and followed him.

'Well, this is nice,' said Mike a few minutes later, though it palpably wasn't. Everyone was drinking tea and eating, including Mark, who had miraculously regained his appetite, but the general atmosphere was strained, to say the least.

Jack was sitting on the floor with his back against a glass-fronted bookcase containing one or two books and several stuffed-in, unclassifiable piles of papers and magazines. He finished a mouthful of sausage-roll, brushed a few flakes of puff-pastry from his pullover onto the carpet, and addressed his father.

'Come on then, Dad, let's have it.'

'It?'

Jack gestured widely with one arm. 'All this. Dip's done this great tea, Flitty's been packed off upstairs, Mark's not been allowed to improve the situation by going out – '

'Nobody thinks you're funny, Jack.'

' – and you and Mum are sitting on the edge of your chairs trying to look casual and relaxed and as if you haven't got something special to say when you obviously have, and Dip's trying to look as if she doesn't know what it is – and now she can't help laughing because she knows I'm right, so you might as well get on with it.'

Mike and I were both laughing as Jack reached out a languid arm to secure another sausage roll, but Kathy wasn't. Nor was Mark. The two of them would have made very poor company for Napoleon on those long Elba evenings. Mike laid his plate gently down on the occasional table beside him.

'You're quite right, Jack,' he said, 'we do want to talk to you both about something, or rather we're hoping that you might say a little bit to us. It's about church and what we – you believe about God and Jesus and all those things. Those things have always been important to us, as you know, but we'd like to know what you think. Jack doesn't come to church with us at the moment and we don't try to make him – well, we wouldn't want to at your age, Jack. But we've never really spoken about it, have we? It's one of the faults Mum and I have got – just letting things drift more than we should, I mean. And Mark still comes, and obviously doesn't really like it, and that's not much good, is it? So – ' Mike drummed a rhythm on his knees with the flat of his hands in a slightly nervous fashion ' – we just wanted to clear the air a bit, that's all. You can say whatever you want – anything. And we won't, you know, get upset or anything.' He glanced at Kathy for confirmation. 'We won't, will we, Kath?'

'No,' said Kathy, shaking her head over-vigorously and looking very upset, 'no, we won't.'

Mark, who had quite deliberately perched himself on a hard, uncomfortable wooden-backed chair near the door, threw an urgent question at me with his eyes, but I just smiled back as noncommittally as I could, and hoped that he wouldn't ruin his own chances of getting what he wanted by making some typically ill-considered comment at this early stage of the proceedings.

'So,' continued Mike, 'who's going to be first?'

Something told me that Jack was extremely unlikely to open up in front of his brother. In fact, during the seemingly eternal silence that followed Mike's speech I seriously doubted that either of the boys was going to say anything at all. A glance around the room did not reassure me. Mark had stopped eating and was leaning forward with his elbows on his knees, his face scrunched between his fists, Jack was well into his second sausage roll, apparently quite relaxed, but with little lines of thought wrinkling the space between his eyebrows, and Kathy had flopped back into the corner of the sofa, one bent arm resting high on the back of the seat, her hand covering her eyes. Only Mike looked comparatively serene, now that his first little attack of nerves had passed. Sitting on the other end of the sofa from Kathy with his legs neatly crossed, his eyes moved expectantly but calmly from Jack to Mark and back again, like a teacher who is quietly confident of his ability to control. Surprisingly, it was Mark who broke the silence in the end.

'I don't mind God but church is crap.'

This ungracious but obviously sincere comment had a near-disastrous effect on me, particularly as I had a mouthful of vanilla slice at the time. I don't know why I found it quite so funny, except that as soon as Mark had spoken I formed a mental picture of Almighty God seated majestically upon his throne, receiving that harassed angel whose task it is to monitor the progress of the Robinsons. 'What news of the boy Mark?' the creator of the universe would enquire impressively, and, as the mighty hosts of heaven leaned forward in solemn expectation, the angel would reply, 'He says he doesn't mind God but he thinks church is crap'. Perhaps my view of God's nature is a mistaken one, but I suspect that, far from dipping automatically into the thunderbolt box, he might have smiled a little to himself on hearing this, and said, 'Well, first of all, it is, of course, immensely flattering to hear that Mark doesn't mind me, and, as for the second point, well, I wouldn't have put it quite like that myself, but the lad has a point – he certainly has a point.'

Fortunately, I managed to prevent the involuntary distribution of my vanilla slice and to keep a straight face, which was just as well, because neither Kathy nor Mike had found anything amusing about Mark's comment. Kathy whipped her hand away from her eyes as soon as the word 'crap' issued from her youngest son's mouth, but, presumably not trusting herself to speak, simply turned to Mike with a 'Get The Thunderbolts Out' expression on her face.

'I hear what you say, Mark,' said Mike, adding the restrained rebuke, 'but I don't think you needed to use that word to say it.'

Don't you just hate it when people tell you they hear what you say? For one fleeting moment I really wanted to hit Mike, but then, I'm not a parent.

'It's not as bad as what Mum's said to me sometimes, an' anyway, you said we could say anything we wanted,' protested Mark. Then, after a moment of fierce concentration, 'All right, then, church is boring and goes on for ever and I hate it. I mean, I hope that bloke gets a job an' that, but that was outside church, and inside's *well* grim.'

I made a mental note to explain Mark's obscure reference to 'that bloke' to Mike and Kathy afterwards.

'If I was God I wouldn't go,' continued Mark. 'Mum, *please* let me stop going.' His tone had switched suddenly from aggression to supplication, and I sensed that this was far from being a mere strategic move. He was actually offering, as a kind of hostage, the vulnerable part of himself that he knew his mother yearned to have access to. 'I can't stand it any longer. I feel all big and red and ugly when I'm sittin' there. Don't make me go any more – I'll do the dinner washing-up every Sunday instead.'

This implicit equating of church attendance with household chores brought a smile to Mike's face, but all of Kathy's spirit was gone. She seemed to have sagged into complete defeat. When she spoke to Mark it was with the weak submission of one who sights inevitable surrender. She barely had the energy to speak.

'You're quite right, Mark,' she said faintly, 'I have used some awful words when I've been angry with you, and I'm really sorry

156

about that – I always said I'd never do that with my children. Please forgive me for doing that, and for shaking you and smacking you sometimes when I run out of words. . . .'

Mark moved uncomfortably on his chair and mumbled something that, although quite unintelligible, carried with it faint nuances of both apology and forgiveness.

'I hope you know, Mark,' went on Kathy in the same energyless tone, 'that God is very important to me. I think Jesus died for me so that God could be my Father, and I've been trying to understand what that means ever since I – well, since I became part of it. I mess things up all the time in all sorts of ways, but right deep down inside I think I know I love God, and he loves me – although I lose my way a bit with that sometimes. So, what I'm saying is that, however it might seem, even if the church blew up tomorrow morning and I couldn't go any more, there'd still be God and Jesus and me. It isn't just how it looks to other people – although I'm afraid that seems to really matter to me sometimes – it's about me hoping you'll know God as well one day. That's the only thing that matters in the end.' She looked at Mike. 'I think we ought to let Mark stop coming to church for the moment, except for Christmas and things – only if you agree, of course, Mike.'

The cessation of breathing from the chair by the door was louder than the breathing had been.

Mike nodded judicially. I stuck an invisible plaster on the place where I had wanted to hit him earlier. 'I'm happy to go along with that,' he said, 'as long as Mark is quite clear that this is a decision made by us, and that we shall expect there to be no argument on those occasions when we do require him to attend church with us.'

Despite being addressed by his father as if he was an applicant at some land tribunal, there was no doubt that Mark understood what was being said. It was lovely to watch. He sat bolt upright in his chair and stared open-mouthed at his mother, hardly able to take in the fact that his weekly torture was over.

'So I don't have to go tomorrow?'

'You don't have to go tomorrow,' she confirmed, in the same weak voice that she had used before.

Mark, driven to an excessive show of emotion by sheer relief and excitement, crossed the room at a most un-Marklike speed and threw his arms round his mother's neck. 'Oh, thanks, Mum!' Those were, I think, the words that emerged in a rather muffled state from this unexpected embrace. The miraculous effect on Kathy, though predictable to anyone who knew her, still amazed me. It was as if she had been instantaneously and totally healed, like one of those New Testament sufferers who encountered Jesus. One sudden, substantial dose of physical and verbal affection, when she had thought the medicine bottle might be empty, and her whole being was transformed. As Mark disengaged himself I saw that her eyes were shining and her body had ceased to sag. When she spoke her voice had regained its strength and vibrancy.

'You can probably catch your friends up if you hurry,' she said, pretending to push him away. 'It's no use expecting Jack to say anything while there's any food left, so you might as well go and spread the joyous news.'

'All right.' Mark, grabbing the shining moment, headed for the door, pausing only to say, 'Thanks, Mum – thanks, Dad.' Just before disappearing he flashed one of his film-star smiles at me – a real sizzler it was. After that we heard hurried coat-flapping noises as he got ready to go out in the rain, and then there was a short silence during which I believe (and I would bet quite a lot of money on this) that, in the solitude of the hall, Mark raised his eyes, bent his arm, and shook a triumphant fist towards the ceiling, this being the gesture that traditionally accompanies the universal victory cry of the fourteen-year-old.

'Yes-s-s!' we heard him cry exultantly. 'Yes-s-s!'

Then the front door opened and didn't close again, and he was gone.

'I'm glad you let Mark go.' Jack was speaking to his mother as I came back in after shutting the rain out. 'I couldn't have said what I really thought if he was here. I'm afraid I can't stand him at the moment – he makes me feel about thirteen, and I start saying childish, stupid things that I'd never say to anyone else.'

Kathy shook her head and sighed wistfully, failing to register, perhaps, that Jack's analysis of his relationship with Mark almost exactly described her own. 'Such a shame. The two of you used to be such good friends. He called you Jackypot when he was a very little boy – '

'Thanks for remembering that, Mum. Cheers!'

' – and he thought you were the most wonderful person in the whole world. You and he spent hours together in the garden making up stories and building dens down behind the shed.' She smiled as a particular memory surfaced. 'And I'll never forget once in the summer, when we were on holiday in Dorset, down in that very quiet place beginning with "K" that was difficult to get to because we hadn't got a car then, remember? One day we went down to one of the beaches you could get to by walking through a cornfield from our cottage. A lovely twisty walk. There was no sand or anything like that when you got down to the seafront, but there were loads of rock-pools. You loved it, Jack. You always loved rock-pools.'

'Still do,' murmured Jack.

'There you were as usual, picking your way between the rocks, turning over stones in the water, and every now and then you'd look up and shout that you'd found a crab, or a little fish or a prawn or something, and we'd be really impressed, wouldn't we, Mike?'

Mike smiled and nodded. Jack took the last vanilla slice and bit into it with a resigned air.

'And just behind you,' Kathy was totally immersed in the past now, 'little Mark was toddling along as best he could, turning over much smaller stones because he wasn't as strong as you, and peering into the water as hard as his little eyes could manage, desperately wanting to find something that he could call out about just like you'd been doing, and he wasn't having any luck at all.'

'That's right,' interrupted Mike, leaning back and signalling sudden recall with a wagging finger, 'and he got so fed up with not coming across anything real that he decided to inject a little creativity into his research, so – '

'He turned over yet another rock,' interposed Kathy, who hates to be deprived of a punch-line, 'and he looked up to where we were sitting at the base of the cliff, and he shouted, "Mum! Dad! I've found somefink!" And I shouted back, "Oh, good, darling – what is the somefink you've found?" And he shouted back, "It's a camel! I've found a camel! Look, Jackypot, I've found a camel!"'

Jack chewed and nodded, remembering. He swallowed and said, 'Well, I suppose from Mark's point of view it seemed just as reasonable that he might find a camel as any of the other things I'd been shouting about. After all, he couldn't have known what most of them were anyway.'

'And you started clambering over the rocks towards him,' continued Kathy, 'then all of a sudden I saw that wonderful proud smile fade away from Marky's face, because he'd realized that when you got to his pool there wasn't going to be any camel to see, and he said in this small, troubled voice, "Well, I tort I saw a camel". I got all frantic, remember, Mike? I flapped my arms about trying to attract your attention, Jack, and I couldn't because you were too busy making sure you didn't slip on the rocks. But the lovely thing was that it was all right anyway because when you reached him you looked down into the pool and then you shouted up to us, "Heh, Marky's right! There *is* a camel in his pool, but it's gone under a rock now, so you won't be able to see it." Oh, Dip, you should've seen that little boy's face when he knew his big brother was backing him up. So happy and pleased! That was so typical of Jack, Dip – such a kind little boy. I remember, just before we moved down from London, we had two cats, and Jack was really worried that – '

'Mum!' Jack rolled his shoulders against the bookcase in embarrassment. 'We're not going through every event in my entire childhood, are we? I don't like that kid I used to be. If I'm honest, he makes me shudder. I've been trying to get rid of him for some time now. I don't need reminding about the little twit, and especially not about all his clear-eyed, piping heroics. Can't we throttle him once and for all?'

People are funny, aren't they? Mark only had to twitch an eyebrow for Kathy to react strongly in one direction or another, but this speech of Jack's, devastating as it sounded, just made her laugh. By contrast, Mike, who could handle anything that Mark threw at him without becoming unduly troubled, looked deeply distressed and puzzled by what he had just heard.

'I don't follow you, Jack,' he said, leaning forward and frowning, 'why on earth should you mind about having been that sort of child? I really don't understand.'

Jack had the look of one who having started down some perilously steep cliff-side, wishes he hadn't but discovers that there is no possibility of going back. He screwed his face up, trying to find words to express what he was feeling.

'Don't get me wrong. It's not that you haven't been good parents,' he said.

Oh, dear....

'It's just that I think you wanted me to be a sort of – I dunno, a sort of Enid Blyton boy, an honourable, manly little chap who isn't afraid to look the world in the face, and, apart from a few rather endearing little naughtinesses, always does the right thing, whatever that is. You taught me to think that being like that was the best way for a person to be.'

'Something of a caricature, Jack?' suggested Mike very quietly. 'And I'm afraid I still don't understand how the qualities you just mentioned could be regarded as some sort of handicap – rather the opposite, I should have thought.'

'But that's just it! That's just the word. A handicap, that's *exactly* what it was.' Jack accompanied this uncharacteristically vehement speech with a series of rhythmic punches, one fist upon another. 'What you don't understand, you see, is that Enid Blyton boys have a very tough time when they find themselves in the middle of real life, especially if real life turns out to be the kind of secondary school I went to. You get crushed and bashed and laughed at, and at first you can't work out why it's happening to you. Your mum and dad, who are the people you trust most, have told you that if you're good and kind you'll be happy. It turns out to be not true. If you stand up for what you believe in people are going to respect you. Not true. If you try hard with your school-work you'll feel happy about yourself. It's not true. Everything will be all right in the end, because everything can be fixed by Mummy or Daddy or God, but it can't. It isn't true. It may be true if you're not an Enid Blyton boy. If you were a sort of King David boy who's faced a lion or two you might manage to cope with the odd giant, because you'd know from early on that things *do* get difficult, and you'd be a bit more ready for them. Well, I wasn't ready, and I didn't cope.'

Mike's face looked grey. 'I know you had some difficult times at school, Jack, particularly in the fourth and fifth years, but most children – '

'Dad, you're not hearing me. I'm not saying I had a terrible childhood. I didn't. We had lots of fun and good times, and I know you and Mum love me, and I love you both very much.'

'So what's the – '

'It's just that – ' Jack spread both hands wide and closed his eyes' – it's just that I think, in a funny sort of way, you used me as a little museum – a place where you could keep your ideals, and your moral values and your religion all shined up and care-fully placed and untainted by the mess and untidiness that sur-rounds them in your lives – in *real* life, I mean. But the trouble is, they're yours, not mine, and I have to throw some of them out and smash a few others and keep one or two, and get some you never thought of, and make a bit of a mess of my own, and gener-ally – well, make it all real for me.'

Vibrations of feeling double-bassed through the air.

'Yes, the trouble is, Jack,' replied Mike, his voice very care-fully controlled but heavily laced with pain, 'that when you talk about wanting to – what is it? – throttle the child you used to be, you're talking about one of the most wonderful, magical periods of my life.' Mike's words fell on our ears with the softness of cotton wool being dabbed on a grazed knee. 'It really does hurt me that you want to dismiss it – just chuck it away, as though it's worth nothing. It *can't* have been worth nothing, can it?' He shifted his weight on the sofa. 'You know, I used to think that the way you are, all the good qualities in you – and they are there, Jack, even if we got lots of it wrong – I used to think it was, well, it sounds so silly when I say it out loud, I used to think it was the best thing I'd ever done.' He stared into the distance for a moment. 'I wish I hadn't said that now, it does sound very foolish indeed. I'm sorry.'

'No, I'm sorry,' said Jack, looking rather pale, 'I wasn't going to say all that – ' He checked himself ' – not because it isn't true, but because it's only one part of the truth. And I overdid it a bit trying to be clever. I promise you I wouldn't have wanted any other parents, and I'm very happy to be me. Dad – '

Drawing his feet in, he levered himself up from the floor with one hand, and moved across to his father, who was still staring into the distance as if stunned by the discovery that some fundamental law of the universe was not immutable after all. Jack leaned down and put his arms around Mike, who jumped slightly, but responded straight away, patting his son's back with one hand as if he was trying to bring up wind.

I think that silent cuddle poured a measure of reassurance into Mike. As he watched his son return to his seat on the floor, he blinked a little and wiped his glasses on a soft green cloth that he produced like a conjuror from his top jacket pocket. Kathy shoved along the sofa and linked her arm in her husband's. Kathy has two main modes, whatever she's really feeling, one is tragedy and the other is flippancy.

'Well, we are having a torrid time, aren't we?' she said to no one in particular. Then looking at me, 'What do you think of the story so far, Dip? "Stress Family Robinson". Better than *East-Enders* or *Coronation Street* any day, wouldn't you say?'

I shook my head. 'I'm just so impressed with you all. I mean – Kathy, you worry about not having the perfect Christian family, but you're way ahead of the one I grew up in. I know you argue and get cross with each other and go through all sorts of problems, but you really love each other as well, and every now and then you even *say* so! The nearest my father ever got to telling me he loved me was those rare occasions when he didn't actually tell me to clear off.'

Don't let them home in on that – this is not the time.

I laughed lightly. 'But don't get too sad, that was pretty much par for the course in the part of the world where I grew up – and my dad was one of the more demonstrative ones. The nearest some of my friends got to being told they were loved was not being belted.'

Okay.

'I was supposed to be telling you what I thought about Christianity and all that,' said Jack. 'Do you still want me to?'

Kathy groaned wearily and laid her head on Mike's shoulder. 'Oh, Jack, I don't know if I can handle any more true-life revelations at the moment. You're not going to tell us you're a closet satanist, are you? I couldn't stand it.'

'No, Mother,' replied Jack patiently, 'I am not a closet satanist. In fact – if anything, I suppose I'm more of a closet Christian than anything else. Do you want to hear about it?'

Mike's eyebrows had shot up at Jack's use of the phrase 'closet Christian'. He nodded briskly, very interested. 'Yes, of course we do. Tell us what you mean, Jack. We'd really like to know where you stand nowadays.' (Mike did plunge from time to time, but he was always happiest hopping from one little island of cliché to another.)

'Well, I won't go on and on about it,' said Jack, 'but what I was going to say before all this childhood stuff came up was that I guess I stopped going to church every week for three reasons, one that really meant something, or I thought it meant something, anyway, and two very bad ones. I won't bother to tell you the bad ones – '

'Oh, yes you will, Jack Robinson,' interrupted Kathy with some asperity, 'you don't get to make us feel inadequate and deeply impressed at the same time with your deep philosophical arguments until we've heard the miserable, shameful little confessions that are probably the real reason you stopped going. Come on – give!'

Jack giggled embarrassedly, and I thought how much he looked like Felicity. 'Oh, all right, Mum. If you must know, the first one was that – '

'You didn't like getting up on Sunday mornings?' suggested Mike shrewdly.

'The first one was, as you so rightly say, that I didn't like getting up on Sunday mornings,' agreed Jack, 'and the second was to do with the quality of the coffee they used to serve – and presumably still do – through that little hatch in the hall after church. Do they still do that?'

'Yes, they do,' said Kathy. 'Do I take it that we're coming on to the reason that really meant something now? Something deep and significant to do with the coffee?'

'No, Mother, we are coming on to the second of the very silly reasons, as you well know. Because I always found it so difficult getting out of bed on a Sunday morning, I was almost invariably up just in time to get to church only if I ran *very* fast. This meant that I missed out on the first cup of coffee of the morning, the one that turns me into a human being. So I'd sit through the service, trying to banish all these lurid fantasies about steaming hot mugs of strong, sweet coffee, and failing miserably, and then when the service was over we all went through to the hall to actually *have* a coffee, didn't we?'

'We did.'

'And every single time I tried to convince myself that for once they would use decent coffee granules, and that said cup would be just a tiny bit more than half-filled with water that might have actually boiled at some point in its history.'

'Water boiled – coffee spoiled,' quoted Mike boringly, but he added, 'well, you're right really, the church coffee is pretty awful.'

'Yes,' said Jack, 'especially for someone like me, who's been brought up by his misguided parents to believe that the only coffee worth drinking looks like something dredged out of the Black Lagoon, has half a field of sugar-cane dissolved in it, and comes in a container the size of a chamber pot.'

'Hear, hear!' I said, with deep feeling.

'Thank you, Dip. As I was saying, for a long time I was a believer. Every Sunday I had faith for change.' Jack gestured with his hand towards heaven like an old-style preacher and raised his voice to evangelizing pitch. 'Friends, I knew in my *heart* that the coffee would be good, and I refused to believe the voice of the deceiver telling me that no good thing would ever come out of that hatch. Hallelujah! I *refused* to believe the evil one! However,' Jack switched abruptly to his normal voice, 'it soon became clear that on this occasion the evil one was absolutely right. The coffee was uniformly and unfailingly vile. I went through a period of dark, yearning agnosticism as I tried to make sense of my shattered faith, but in the end I just couldn't stand the hypocrisy of it all – going through to that hatch every week, mixing with all those bright-eyed others who still believed, knowing in my heart of hearts that they were deluded, that good coffee was just a pleasant illusion that gave people a reason to keep going through the hardship and drudgery of the church service. In the end I – ' Jack pretended to choke on his words ' – I had to stop going, and now,' he looked up with an expression on his face that was, I think, supposed to approximate a brave smile, 'I have found a kind of peace.'

There was a short pause.

'You know, Jack,' said Kathy, dispassionately reflective, 'I really, really wish I hadn't insisted on you telling us about your two bad reasons for giving up church. How long is it going to take to tell us about the good reason?'

'Not long, Mum, I promise. Right, the good reason was that I had to have a break from being a Crimean Christian.' He raised a hand slightly in Kathy's direction. 'I am going to explain, Mum, just give me a chance. I've thought about this. You know how in the old days the army used to dress up for battle in just about the most unsuitable gear you could possibly imagine? Most of it was much more decorative than practical, and those poor old foot soldiers in particular must have got so hot and uncomfortable when they were supposed to run and dodge and fight and do whatever soldiers have to do. They were trapped, really, in a load of traditional stuff that had no connection at all with what was going on, or the job that actually had to be done. But I don't suppose it occurred to many of them to complain about it, because that was just the way things were, and you'd have needed to be a real lateral thinker to picture it any differently. Well, I began to feel a bit like that in our church. It wasn't that I stopped believing in God or Jesus. I know you're always joking that I was converted five times when I was little, Mum, but one of them must have stuck, because I've never stopped believing that I – I'm afraid I don't find it all that easy to talk about – I've never stopped believing that I belong to him, if you know what I mean.'

Mike nodded, his face suddenly full of happiness.

'I just needed some time,' went on Jack, 'to see what would happen if I took the old traditional uniform off and wore something more comfortable – more suitable, if you like. After all, the British army did that a long time ago – changed the gear, I mean. I'd hate to think the Church hasn't caught up with the army! Dad, I know this must all sound a bit self-centred, but it's not just about me. We've got to be able to wear camouflage sometimes, so we can fit in with the world. We've got to be able to adapt and be flexible even though the reason for joining up in the first place stays exactly the same.'

I wish they'd pray for me....

'And what have you found out about life without the uniform, Jack?' asked Mike.

'He's there,' said Jack quietly, 'he's there whatever you wear, wherever you go. He's always there – church or no church – he's simply there. And I think he's beginning to teach me that I'm here as well.' He smiled at his father. 'He's my God now, Dad, just as much as he's yours. The Enid Blyton boy and the Crimean uniform, both chucked out, so that I can be me, and that's what he wants, thank goodness. Oh, and since we started talking this evening I've got an idea there's something else he might want as well.'

Kathy and Mike looked at each other, and prepared for the best or the worst. 'Yes?' breathed Kathy.

'Well, I don't mean I've had any voices in my head or anything like that, but I just have a feeling it would be right for me to start coming to church again, at least now and then, in any uniform I want, as long as I'm there – but I still don't have to pretend that I like the coffee.'

Kathy stared. 'Are you telling me that you're coming with us tomorrow?' She sounded exactly as Mark had done when he learned that he didn't have to go.

Jack nodded brightly. 'That could be possible, Mumsy.'

I don't know if Jack's decision was motivated by conviction or kindness, but it didn't really matter. Kathy was *so* pleased. She passed a hand across her brow.

'Glory be, we've lost one and gained one back! The mathematics of it are beyond me. I feel a bit giddy, Mike. Pour me a small, full glass of sherry, will you?'

Beaming all over his face, Mike headed for the kitchen. He didn't pause in crossing the room, but as he passed the bookcase his hand rested for the merest fraction of a second on the top of his son's head.

Chapter 12

Let history record that Jack Michael Robinson did indeed attend church with his parents on the day following that conversation, but let it also record that on the following Sunday he did not so attend, for reasons more self-indulgent than philosophical. Kathy didn't really mind, though. Her oldest son was back in the fold – had never actually left the fold – and even his occasional appearances in the visible portion of the fold were to be a source of great pleasure to her.

Mark began to enjoy Sundays as well, although he kept a very low profile on Sunday mornings, fearing, probably quite rightly, that his mother's generous gesture could be eclipsed in an instant by fury at the sight of her youngest son settling down with toast and orange juice in front of the television just as the rest of the family were setting out for church.

I joined the Robinsons for lunch on that second Sunday, a day in which, for an hour or more in the middle of the day, the sun shone brightly through the merest crack in a leaden sky. I loved the lighting effects that resulted. Brightly coloured things like Daffodil, my Mini, seemed artificially vivid against the slate-grey, and the hundred-year-old brickwork of Mike and Kathy's house glowed richly red, possessing an almost edible texture. It felt like a day when something exciting ought to happen. And, I'm pleased to say, it did. It rained.

Just after two o'clock, when Mark and Felicity were dealing with the dirty dishes – having Felicity's assistance with the washing-up was generally reckoned to be the short straw of short straws – and the rest of us were hopefully awaiting reluctantly promised coffee in the sitting room, heaven opened and rain flung itself to the earth as though it frantically needed to escape from the sky. So abruptly did the deluge begin, and so loud was the sound it made, that Mike, Kathy and I all stood up, more or less involuntarily, and moved across to the window that overlooks the back garden. Through the cascading downpour only the vaguest outlines of trees, bushes and neighbouring houses were visible.

'God's putting the house through a giant car-wash,' murmured Jack, 'isn't it wonderful!'

It was at this moment that Mark and Felicity appeared in the doorway, their faces alive with excitement and anticipation.

'Rain walk!' exclaimed Mark.

The dynamics of family life are very strange, but they can be very precise, can't they? Instead of looking at each other, Mike and Kathy looked at Jack, and I knew somehow that, though none of them would have recognized it, the decision about whether to accept Mark's suggestion or not depended entirely on how the older boy reacted to the idea. Rain walks, I guessed, were some kind of lapsed family tradition. Jack would have to 'bend' towards his temporarily estranged younger brother if the tradition was to be resurrected.

'Great!' said Jack. 'Let's get the stuff!'

As I followed the general stampede towards the kitchen, Mike explained that when the boys had been younger the whole family had discovered the delights of not only accepting rainy weather, but actively setting out to enjoy being in the middle of it.

'You watch them when they get out there,' he said happily, 'they go completely mad.'

First of all, though, the hunt was on for wellingtons, waterproof coats and umbrellas. If the Robinsons' bathroom was chaos, the cupboard under the stairs where these things were theoretically kept was chaos cubed. Anxious to get out before the rain eased off, the family attacked the jumbled mass of footwear and clothing as if their lives depended on it, sending up a veritable fountain of discarded items behind them as they burrowed. Assuming, correctly, that I would want to come along, Kathy, flushed with the hunt, produced a pair of green wellies that fitted me at a (literal) pinch, together with one of those old-fashioned thin plastic macs that button right up to the neck and come down as far as your ankles. Topped off with a fisherman's sou'wester held on by a strap under the chin, my outfit was not the stuff of fantasies, but it was just right for the weather.

Leaving the rejected things outside the cupboard where they'd landed, the washing-up half done, and two or three lights on, we piled out of the front door into the teeming rain, to the accompaniment of loud war-whoops from Mark and Jack who, within seconds of being outside, threw off such headwear as they'd found, tilted their heads back and ran along the footpath, allowing the water to soak their faces and drench their hair. Felicity watched her brothers with amazed delight, and looked a question at her mother. Failing to see anything like a negative reaction, she pushed back her red waterproof hat so that it hung by its strap around her neck, and ran as fast as her rubber-booted feet would carry her after the two boys, shouting at the top of her voice, 'I'm doing it too! Jack! Mark! I'm doing it too! Look – I'm wet too!'

'I used to try to stop them,' said Kathy, moving closer so that her umbrella augmented my sou'wester, 'but they never took any notice, so I gave up. And it never seemed to do them any harm anyway. In fact, the hot bath together when they got back was one of the bits they liked best. Nowadays, of course, it'll be an argument about who gets to use the bath first.' She sighed. 'I loved it when they were little. More fun.'

'Doesn't look much different to me,' said Mike, who was walking on the other side of me beneath a huge, highly coloured golfing umbrella, 'they're still going as loopy as they always did. And look at Felicity – talk about a drowned rat.'

The rain had lessened a little by the time we reached the bottom of the road, but it was still beating an urgent rhythm on our umbrellas as we followed the three revellers through a small metal gate into the recreation ground, and watched Jack lead a flight of different sized human aeroplanes in big wheeling circles around the grassy expanse. There was, by now, no greater wetness than their wetness, and they were ecstatic. The wheeling stopped, there was a brief confabulation between the three aircraft, then Mark ran across to us, his face washed and lightened by rain and joy.

'We're goin' over to play on the kids' things,' he announced breathlessly, 'but we've all got to go on 'em. Come on!'

Without waiting for a response he dashed off to catch up the other two, who were running hand-in-hand towards the enclosed children's playground at the far end of the recreation ground, a place that Felicity and I knew very well. We followed Mark at a more sedate pace.

'Jack and Mark are technically too old to go on playground equipment,' said Mike stolidly, his voice sounding oddly hollow in the rain-free space under his umbrella.

Kathy shrieked with laughter. 'Oh, Mike, you'll be the death of me!' she spluttered. 'We're probably the only people in the universe who are out of doors at the moment. The police might have chosen today to launch a massive operation for the arrest of over-aged playground users – is that what you're worried about? "Ah," they'll have said, up at the local nick, "a monsoon. Just what we've been waitin' for. Should catch a fair few this afternoon – come on lads!" I expect there's loads of them there now, crouched under the slide, hiding inside the roundabout, disguised as climbing frames – they're all trained to do that, you know – and there'll be loads more just squatting in the long grass at the edge, waiting for whoever's in charge to blow a whistle so they can rush out and warn Mark and Jack that anything they say will be taken down, wrung out, and used in evidence. You crack me up sometimes, you really do.'

'It was only a comment,' said Mike mildly, 'anyway ....' He stopped and looked at Kathy with a new light in his eyes. 'Are you prepared to put your money where your mouth is?'

Kathy and I came to a halt as well. 'Always,' replied Kathy untruthfully.

'All right, then.' Mike slowly and deliberately lowered his umbrella, passed it to me, and let the rain fail on his bare head until it was streaming down his face. 'Last one on the roundabout's a cissy!'

He galloped off in the direction of the playground at a wellington-hampered sprint, watched by a momentarily amazed Kathy, who, half a second later, thrust her umbrella into my hand as well and set off in giggling pursuit. By the time I reached the wooden fence that surrounded the playground area the whole family had abandoned themselves to shouting, splashing, squealing, rain-soaked enjoyment of the weather, the equipment and each other. Mike, bedraggled and happy as I had never seen him, stopped halfway up one side of the climbing frame, and shouted in my direction.

'Come on, Dip – join us!'

They looked so complete.

'Where do you hide a leaf?' Father Brown once asked his friend, Flambeau. 'In a forest', was the answer. Where do you hide a tear? In a rainstorm ....

Too much standing outside fences holding things for other people. Far too much, for far too long. I stuck both umbrellas into the ground, threw off my absurd sou'wester, and joined them.

Book 2:

The Birthday Party

one

Saturday

1

'Kathy Robinson,' I muttered to myself, 'you seem to have arrived in hell a little before your time.'

It was just after seven o'clock, the beginning of one of those long, bad days when everything smells of fish. Mind you, it followed a Friday night that had smelled even worse of failure. I woke at least four times, always with the same negative thought rolling uselessly round and round in my brain like the proverbial marble in a cake-tin. The last one had been at about three thirty in the morning, when such an oppressive weight of despair pressed on me in the darkness of the bedroom that in the end I had to slip out of bed and escape, leaving Mike, my husband, fast asleep.

Resonant nasal sounds issued reassuringly from behind the closed door of our older son Jack's room as I tiptoed along the landing trying not to wake the rest of the household, and it would have been a waste of energy worrying about his brother Mark, who slept in the big room right up on the second floor. Mark, recently turned eighteen, had consistently demonstrated a capacity bordering on the supernatural for remaining asleep in the face of any and every disturbance.

At the angle of the stairs I paused by the open doorway of my daughter's room. No problem there either. Felicity was sleeping at a friend's house for the night. She was ten, as wide open as that door of hers, and still quite convinced that she lived in the best of all possible worlds. In the light filtering through the curtains from a streetlamp outside, I could see her favourite old teddy sitting patiently on the pillow waiting for his mistress to return. Felicity had phoned the evening before to say what a good time she was having. She would be fast asleep now. I sighed, glad for her, but sorry for myself.

Downstairs in the strange, alien world of the early hours I made a cup of tea and tuned in to one of those Sky channels that American evangelists buy slots on at that time of the morning, hoping to comfort myself with the knowledge that there were one or two people in the world who might be even loonier than me. I eventually got back to sleep just before five.

Continually waking at night is bad for me, but not half as bad as it's likely to be for those who are favoured with my presence the next day. I may have slightly miscounted, but, as far as my blessedly selective memory can recall, I went on to offend or upset at least five people before teatime on Saturday. Those who love me have been kind and helpful enough to explain that I have an abrasive quality at the best of times, but this must have been a record, even for me.

The person who headed this queue of applicants for verbal abuse was brave or foolish enough to present herself on the telephone shortly after the alarm went at seven o'clock, a time when I am only embryonically human at best. I desire no companion then, other than strong, sweet coffee, made by me, just the way I like it. It was my turn to get up first to make sure that Mark was stirring in his lair, and although Mike would have understood if I'd prodded him awake and begged for a swop, I simply had not been able to face that infernal negative revolution again, so I got up. Slumped at the kitchen table after giving my son a call and receiving the statutory moan of irrational resentment and understandable agony in reply, I had just spooned the second sugar into my mug, and was on the point of stirring it before taking my first sip of the morning, when the telephone rang.

That was the moment when I thought I might have entered eternal torment without realizing it.

Those of you who have read about our exploits of a few years ago will be aware that we Robinsons have raised the art of confusion and absurdity to new, rarefied heights. What followed on this occasion was quite up to our normal standard. I waited for half a minute or so, then, uttering an oath of pagan pungency, I put my mug down and huffed into the hall to answer the infuriatingly insistent ringing. As I picked up the receiver and barked 'Hello!' into it, Mike did exactly the same (well, he did more of a polite little 'woof' than a bark) on the extension phone that lives in a small alcove next to my side of our double bed. Hearing Mike answer I grunted with relief, dropped the phone back on its thingy, and returned to my coffee, which was still just about hot enough to get the revival process going again.

This would have been fine if Mike hadn't done exactly the same thing upstairs. For a minute and a half we both enjoyed the satisfaction of believing that our early-morning caller was being dealt with by the other person, then the silence was shattered once more by the ringing of the telephone. I could hardly believe it! Who was calling now? Once again I waited for it to stop. Once again it didn't. Once again there was a spooky synchronicity about the way in which Mike and I picked up our receivers and replied at exactly the same time. Once again we both replaced the phone and returned to our respective dozing and coffee-drinking.

Two minutes later, when the phone went for a third time, I felt cross to the point of snarling. Why had everybody in the entire world elected, one by one, to call at some unearthly hour of the morning, inflicting telephonic Chinese water torture on two innocent people? Just how stupid was it possible for the entire world to be? I decided that it would be far better to let Mike answer the call this time as I would find it very difficult to avoid being openly aggressive.

Isn't it interesting how immediately identifiable a certain amalgam of sounds can be? 'Getting out of bed in an infuriated state to come and give someone a piece of your mind' is one good example. First, there's a sort of 'Hurrumph!' of annoyance followed by a flapping and a slapping of bedclothes, then the thumping sound of a pair of feet landing with unnecessary force on the bedroom floor before they stomp irritably across the room and along the landing towards the top of the stairs. There might be a slammed door thrown in as well, according to choice.

'It is your turn to get up, isn't it, Kath?'

Mike almost always stops short of really expressing his anger. He screeches to a halt on the edge of rage, like someone nearly driving a Volvo estate over Beachy Head. I think it frightens him. That's why, on this bad-fish morning, the flapping and stomping actually culminated in a question of such reedy restraint from the top of the stairs. If it had been me I would have come flying downstairs like a loosely tied bag of laundry and burst indiscriminately over everyone in sight. Mike's question was a coded statement, an all too familiar attempt on his part to insert a skeleton of order into the flabby, chaotic flesh of what was actually happening. He went on to expand his point with that very particular brand of school-masterish heavy patience of his that maddens me more than almost anything else he does. It wouldn't have been so bad if he had come downstairs and spoken to me on the same physical level. Being addressed sternly from the top of the stairs by a junior headmaster makes you feel like the school assembly hearing that a few of us are letting the rest of us down, or perhaps like a failed pilgrim being told off by God in a morality play.

'Kathy, we have an arrangement, have we not, that we'll take it in turns to be the first to get up in the morning, and this morning it was your turn, so I stayed in bed. In the half hour or so between you getting up and me getting up, you know that if anything happens it's your concern. I happily take that responsibility when it's my turn, so why can't you? My only responsibility this morning is to make the bed when I *do* get up. Each time the phone has gone this morning, I have optimistically hung on to the tail-end of my dream and gritted my teeth waiting for you to answer it. You know full well that the phone is just beyond leaning reach from my side, so to get to it I have to support myself with one hand on the floor, and pick up the phone with the other. I don't *like* doing that. Each time it's rung, you've delayed answering just long enough for me to give up waiting and feel like screaming and have to throw my body across to your side of the bed and answer it myself. Then you put the phone down as soon as you hear me speak, presumably not realizing that I have put mine down as well. Dreams don't survive all that, Kathy. Whoever has been trying to call is now ringing for the *third* time.' His voice rose to a strangled pitch. 'Please, *please* will you answer it, so I can go back to bed for the tiny little bit of time that's left? I hope you don't think I'm being too unreasonable.'

Stomp, stomp, stomp, slam, boing, flap!

The process by which my mind roots around to find logical justification for my misdeeds is a shamefully industrious one. I can't believe that I am capable of putting so much mental effort into being right at times when I know perfectly well I'm wrong. As I picked up the still-ringing phone from the hall table and put it to my ear, I was busy constructing arguments with which to slay Mike over the marmalade a little later.

'Yes?'

My Basil Fawlty-like tone of voice can hardly have sounded very welcoming, but some people are pretty well immune to tones of voice.

'Oh, Kathy, is that you? Joscelyn here – I had a bit of trouble getting through just now. Listen, I know it's early, dear, but I just had to ring you to pass on the good news. I was sure you'd want to hear.'

I knew the deep, female voice well. Joscelyn Wayne was a member of our church, one of those people who make the very joints of your body ache because it's virtually impossible to react honestly to them. At least, that was the problem I had with her.

She was a large, handsome woman with, in the best cartoon tradition, a small submissive husband called John. When they were first introduced to Mike and me as a couple I suffered one of those embarrassingly explicit nasal extrusions on hearing that I was in the presence of a cottage-sized John Wayne.

I remember the same thing happening once when I was introduced to an elderly man who happened to have his back to me at the time. When he turned round the first thing I noticed was his nose. I couldn't help it. No-one could have helped it. He was wearing a large, shiny, blatantly obvious plastic nose. Trapped helplessly between the only two feasible options, that it was this person's idea of a practical joke or that he was undergoing some kind of nasal treatment that demanded a temporary replacement, I fell to pieces and produced a similar snorting explosion – through my *nose*, of course. Our chat was a trifle strained after that, I seem to recall.

Poor John Wayne was obviously used to this kind of childish reaction, because he just smiled with his eyes, offered me a tissue that he fished out from somewhere, and said mildly, 'Don't worry, it is funny. Don't quite match up, do I? The hell I do!'

I felt terrible after that, but as time went by I discovered that little John really was very nice, and quite dryly funny when his wife wasn't filling the horizon. They really were an extraordinary contrast in size. He was neatly dressed and nicely made, as far as one could see, whereas she was one of those women who wear their hair long a bit too late in life, and you can't quite tell where their flowing clothes end and their flowing bodies begin. I suppose you shouldn't conjecture about other people's sex lives, but – no, well, I've already said it, haven't I – you shouldn't, should you?

Joscelyn was a seeker after spiritual adventure, one who, as my son Jack once graphically put it, runs frantically round pushing an open wheely-bin, trying to work out exactly where the blessing is going to fall. A strange mixture of self-assurance and neediness, Joscelyn wrote exhortational articles for Christian magazines, and was in demand as a speaker at ladies' meetings in various parts of the country. I drove her to one of these once and was amazed at the confidence with which she offered hands-on ministry to a large group of poshish women. Many of them moved from chintzy, tea-sipping ordinariness to tearful, crumpled collapse and back again, and they did it in a bewilderingly seamless manner. One of the problems I had with our relationship from that day onward was the assumption in Joscelyn that I had been deeply awed and moved by what I had seen at that meeting. In fact, my overwhelming response had been troubled puzzlement.

In her writing, and in the one example of her public speaking that I had witnessed, Joscelyn projected a bright-eyed definiteness about the presence and power and closeness of God that must have been inspiring to many of her readers and listeners. The trouble was, I didn't really believe that what came out of her had ever been *in* her, if you see what I mean. It seemed to me that the person she was actually trying to convince about the reality of God was herself. Perhaps that was all right. I didn't know. What I did know was that, in her case, you didn't have to be deeply insightful to detect the fundamental panic that fuelled this constant outpouring of spiritual optimism and confidence.

Every few weeks Joscelyn would announce with great excitement that somewhere she had been or something she had done had enabled God to do a completely new thing in her, and that, as a result, her entire life was changed for the better. I should have reacted more honestly in the early days, when she first said these sorts of things to me and all I felt was a gnawing scepticism. Now, hampered by my long history of chickening out, all I could do each time was squeeze little bleating noises of approval out of my mouth, indulging the child inside Joscelyn who needed such huge dollops of self-deception in order to survive. And that, as my dear husband will tell you – and he certainly would tell you if you were to ask him – is the trouble with people like me. We only seem to have two modes of response in situations like that, rudeness or collusion.

There is, however, nothing like chronic fatigue and disgust with oneself for provoking rudeness to others. I sensed that I was about to change modes in my interaction with Joscelyn.

'What news would that be then, Joscelyn?'

'Oh, Kathy, I have had *the* most amazing time at Falston Manor over the weekend. God really did – look, you don't mind me ringing you this early, do you? John said I ought to leave it an hour or so, but I said you'd be dying to hear how it went.'

'John was right, Joscelyn.'

'Oh, good,' said the voice on the other end of the line, 'I told him you wouldn't mind.'

I was fairly used to Joscelyn not appearing to actually hear what I said, but on this fishy morning it infuriated me beyond measure. What on earth was the matter with the woman that she didn't even register the words I spoke? I had often had the feeling that I was superfluous to our conversations. I might as well have been a stuffed dummy equipped with a tape-loop and loudspeakers for all the genuine interest that she showed in my responses. Joscelyn knew exactly what she expected my reaction to be, and never bothered to stop and check whether she was up the creek or not. Well – okay! Right! This was where things were going to start changing.

'I don't think you can have heard what I said, Joscelyn. I said that – '

'They had the most marvellous speaker for the weekend, someone called Brian Wills from somewhere in the Leicester area, although he goes all over the place, apparently. Have you come across him? He's written two books. I bought them while I was there and I *must* lend you the first one and a tape of the Saturday evening session from this weekend. He writes just like he speaks, which is quite unusual, isn't it?'

I decided to try again.

'Joscelyn, this is not the – '

Like a panzer division with its periscopes misted up, she rolled blindly on.

'Kathy, this man has a ministry to leaders that is truly anointed – *truly* anointed. I have never, *ever* felt the sheer power of God as I felt it on that Saturday night in the session before the entertainment. The very air crackled with – with, well, with the sheer power of God. At the end Brian asked all those who wanted prayer to come up to the front and form a line, and then he prayed and prophesied over each of us, one by one. People were going down and getting filled with the Spirit and being healed, and Kathy, he said things to me that went right down deep inside and were literally life-changing. I tell you what, God has totally transformed me over this weekend in the most *amazing* way, and – '

'Joscelyn, Joscelyn, what *are* you talking about?'

This time I got through, probably because I had projected the words down the telephone line with as much vim as I could muster, and then some. Joscelyn, arrested at last, sounded puzzled by my question.

'Sorry – what do you mean? What are you – why are you asking me what I'm talking about? I'm telling you what happened at the weekend.'

'I mean, Joscelyn, that just about every month or so since I first met you, you've rung me up or come round to tell me about your life being *totally* changed by someone or something in the most *amazing* way. But you always appear to me to be exactly the same as you were before it happened. I mean, let's face it, if you really had been radically altered and transformed by God as many times as you reckon you have been, then there can't be much of the original you left, can there? You must be Elmat Zog from the planet Vorgan by now.'

'But I – '

'What you probably really mean,' I continued mercilessly, 'what you almost certainly are actually saying is that you've simply moved another small but important step towards understanding that you're a sinner like the rest of us and that God forgives you.'

Suddenly the things I'd thought but never said during those other conversations welled up inside me and poured out. I had said it all in my head so many times. It was like reading a finely-honed script.

'Why you have to dress it up in all this "totally transformed" rubbish is beyond me. Do you not realize that what you're actually talking about all the time is *you*? That's what Christians do, Joscelyn. We all do it. *I* do it. I'm just the same. I go on and on and on about myself and *my* standing with God, and how *I'm* doing, and how far *I've* got, and all the time God is trying to get a word in edgeways so that he can say, "Look, it's not about you – it's about me and what I've done for you. Stop navel-gazing and look in my direction because I've already saved your blinking navel, just as I've saved every other part of you. That's the good news. The bad news is that you're never going to be this wonderful person you seem to think you have to be before I notice that you exist." What you need, Joscelyn, if you don't mind me saying so, is to learn how to relax.'

With this final, grotesquely hypocritical piece of advice from me, the least relaxed person in the universe, I terminated my sermon, and a profound silence fell at both ends of the line. It was broken at my end by the sound of the doorbell ringing. I was more than relieved to have such a genuine exit presented to me.

'Look, Joscelyn, I'm going to have to go, there's someone at the door. You're not upset by what I said, are you?'

'No, no ...'

'Well, look, I'll give you a call later, all right?'

'All right ...'

A tiny voice. I had never heard Joscelyn sounding so deflated and defeated. I replaced the receiver on its hook with agonized deliberateness. What had I done? Who did I think I was? What would Mike say when he heard that I'd tried to snuff out Joscelyn's spiritual confidence as though it was a cheap candle? I sighed as I suddenly remembered that my friend, Dip Reynolds, was coming round for coffee later that morning because she had something important to tell me. Another potential victim? Perhaps I'd be more human by then. Dip always had a good effect on me.

When I opened the door our new milk-delivery girl was standing with a crate on the step by her feet, holding a little sheaf of bits of thin paper in her hand. She was a young, skinny, almost very pretty girl with large trusting eyes, an oval face and a coil of black hair dangling on to each cheek. There was a very earnest expression on her face. Since taking over the franchise for our round a few weeks ago, she had developed a new method of giving out bills and collecting money which was supposed to make the paying-for-milk side of our lives much easier for her and for all of us, her customers. I was absolutely open to the proposition that it might have made life much easier if we had ever managed to understand it, but neither Mike nor I had been able to grasp the new system at all, despite having invited the girl in one Saturday morning to sit down in the kitchen and explain it to us.

Mind you, this was as much to do with us as her – more, probably. Mike has quite a clear head for most things, but, thank God, we share a chronic inability to understand what people are talking about when they address us at any speed above a crawl on subjects that involve money.

This had certainly been the case several years ago, when we were in the middle of buying the tall, thin, three-storey Victorian house within which we now scuttled up and down from trough to sleeping areas and back again like a family of neurotic hamsters.

The man who dealt with our mortgage might as well have spoken the language of a lost South American tribe as far as the gaping, dull-brained Robinsons were concerned. Every few minutes, when our broker stopped to take a breath, Mike, optimistically armed with a pad of paper and a biro and trying to sound like a grown-up, would say rather plaintively, 'So, what's likely to be the total we pay each month?' Then the man would reluctantly name a figure, which Mike would write down, and after an immaculately timed pause the man would casually add that, of course, this didn't include two or three other expensive but vitally essential items that he would mention later, and Mike would cross out the amount he had just written down on his pad and run his hand wildly through his hair, and look as if he was going to ask another question, but by then the man would have started talking again, and it would be another few minutes before it became possible to go through the whole routine once more. We ended up feeling like lobotomized chimpanzees in a ballet class.

There was an up-side to our encounters with this obscurantism, by the way. Smart as this young man presumably was, he had, in the course of his professional encounters with customers, unconsciously acquired the habit of beginning every other sentence with the phrase, 'Quite honestly'. As the time for our third meeting with him approached, we agreed, like a couple of naughty children, that, as we had not the faintest idea what he was talking about anyway, we might as well while away the hour or so spent in his company by counting the number of times he used this suspicious verbal ploy. (Mike can do this sort of mildly wicked thing when he tries, and I really love it when he does.) It must have been very gratifying for our broker that day to observe the way in which we hung on to his every word without once interrupting. I think the score had reached twenty-four by the time the meeting was about to draw to a close, and it was then that I decided to try an experiment.

'I hope you don't mind me asking,' I said innocently, 'it's pure curiosity on my part, but I was wondering if you actually come from around here?'

He cast a worried look in my direction, disconcerted, of course, by the near impossibility of coming up with a reply to my question that would either cost us money or be impossible to understand. He did manage to twist his features into more of a now-we're-talking-on-a-personal-level, relaxed sort of expression, but there was nothing he could do about the words that came out of his mouth. His mouth knew no other formula.

'Quite honestly,' he said, as though confessing to some sick and miserable vice, 'I live in Brighton.'

Inexplicable collapse of Robinsons. What, he must have wondered, is so very amusing about living in Brighton? Quite honestly, nothing ...

In the case of our new milkgirl and her system, it was just the same. The more she talked, the less we seemed to grasp what she was getting at, until, in the end, lying was the only remaining option. So we did. We sat back and flapped the air with our hands, saying things like, 'Aaah, with you – right! *Now* I see what you're saying. Yes, that is a *much* better way of doing it! Gosh, that will make a difference!' and she went away pleased. Mike and I had laughed a great deal about this at the time, but I wasn't in the mood for humour or humouring right now. This girl was number two in the victim queue, or number three if you counted Mike as number one.

I snapped, 'You want me to pay for the milk?'

'Not all of it,' she said, brushing one of the dangling coils away from eyes that gleamed with the joy of seeing her master-plan in action. 'If you remember, Mrs Robinson, I said the best thing would be if people where I collect on Saturdays go from Tuesday to Tuesday in retrospect, so as you were away until last Monday you only owe me for one day, unless you want to add it on to what you'll owe up to next Wednesday, in which case I won't take anything until the end of next week.'

I stared at her. Incredible! The remarkable thing about this modern deliverer of milk was that she obviously understood what she was saying. There was a logical pattern hidden away in there somewhere, forever inaccessible to a brain such as mine, but perfectly meaningful to her. I was quite awed in a way. The poor girl might have suffered only a morose dismissal if it hadn't been for Mark, who selected that very moment to bring his newly showered, dripping form stumbling comatosely down the stairs behind me, wrapped insubstantially in a stupidly small towel and clutching one of those horrible, floppy, unfunny joke-books that get progressively soggier in the bathroom until they finally con-geal and die. Pausing unselfconsciously in the hall, in full view of those in the world outside our open front door, he read aloud from his cornucopia of rubbish.

'Did you hear about the constipated footballer who squeezed one through in stoppage time?'

Throwing his head back, Mark guffawed with such energy over this terrible so-called joke that he lost his one-handed grip on the towel and it dropped around his feet. This is pure conjecture, but my guess would be that for one eternal moment our milk-deliverer forgot even her new system as she stared open-mouthed at my naked son. Then, the towel was scooped up and the great comedian beat a hasty retreat to the safety of the kitchen. An all too familiar, Mark-related tide of hot fury rose in me as I turned once more to the embarrassed girl on the step.

'I'm afraid you've completely confused me about the money. Why don't you just come back next Saturday and tell us what we owe you and we'll pay it. I think we can all understand that. All right?'

And I shut the door on her. I hate myself sometimes.

At this moment, however, reflection was not the order of the day. Just now, I hated Mark much more than I hated myself, and I was determined that he was shortly going to hear about it in graphic detail. With my hand still resting on the closed door I screwed my eyes tight shut and took three or four deep breaths through my nose in an effort to dull the near berserk edge of my fury. One of my secret fears was that wild anger would one day cause me to totally wreck a room or a relationship or perhaps even a person, in the attempt to clearly communicate *just how cross I was!*

A voice from the kitchen called out in cheerful unawareness of Hurricane Kathy's imminent approach.

'Mum, could you bring us a bottle of that milk through for my cereal? Cheers!'

Could I bring ... ? Right!

When I arrived in the kitchen Mark's inadequately betowelled figure was seated at the end of the table nearest the hall, in front of a large glass mixing bowl containing a miniature mountain range of five Shredded Wheat, surmounted by an additional Everest-like peak of sugar. He was tapping the table rhythmically and happily with a huge serving-spoon as he waited for me to arrive with supplies of the missing ingredient. For some reason the sight of the wrong kind of bowl with too much in it and that ludicrously large spoon had the effect of racking my annoyance up yet another notch. I leaned against the sink and folded my arms.

'Why are you using a mixing bowl and that spoon when we've got plenty of things the right size?'

'They're all in the dishwasher. Where's the milk?'

'So why didn't you take them out of the dishwasher?'

Silent pause.

'Come on! Why didn't you take everything out of the

190

dishwasher and put it all away like I do just about every morning of my life? Why do you take that stupid great serving thing out of the drawer instead of getting one everybody else would use? No, don't wear yourself out answering. I'll tell you why – it's because you can't be bothered, that's why. It's too much like hard work, isn't it? And besides that, it might benefit other people, and the last thing we'd want to do is anything that might be useful to anybody else, isn't it? Silly of me to even think of it.'

Mark had stopped tapping with his spoon and was staring fixedly at the far end of the table. Eventually, taking a deep breath and expelling it loudly through pursed lips, he rose to his feet, still hanging on to his towel, and turned towards the hall.

'I'll get the milk myself,' he mumbled.

'You will not get the milk yourself. Don't you think the world has seen enough of you already this morning? No, you're going to sit back down on that chair and listen to me!'

Mark debated inwardly for a moment then, slumping heavily back into his seat, he leaned his elbows on the table and rested his chin in his cupped hands.

'What's going on?'

Mike, presumably drawn by the rumblings of imminent conflict, appeared in the kitchen wearing my dressing-gown and his very own aggrieved-but-ready-to-listen expression.

I struggled to find appropriate words. I was so tired! For an annoying second or two I found that I had completely forgotten everything that had gone on just before coming into the kitchen. That's often a problem when you get as het up as I do. You lose track of your original, excellent reasons for being so angry, then all that gets talked about is the last thing you said and it sounds pathetic. That was exactly what happened now. Mark leaned back in his chair and spoke to his father in the sort of wearily ironic tone that a guard in an institution might use with a colleague to describe the boringly predictable irrationality of one of their long-term resident lunatics.

'Mum is really, really, really cross with me for using the wrong size of spoon with my cereal, so she won't let me get any milk for some reason.'

The common expression about people or events making your blood boil is horribly accurate. When, as Mark had just done, someone manages to scrabble all the loose ends of everything that's happened into a knot, and you know that, because you're so full of outrage, trying to explain will only pull it tighter, it does feel as if steam might well come shooting out of the top of your head. And I don't care if string and steam don't fit together, because that's how it feels.

'I have never heard anything quite so absurdly ridiculous in my life! You know perfectly well that I got cross with you because you told a stupid, vulgar joke in front of a strange girl standing on the step with no clothes on.'

'What! When was this?'

Mike's face was a picture of shock and bewilderment.

'Just now, at the bottom of the stairs.'

'Who was the strange girl?'

'The milkgirl – person, whatever you're supposed to call them nowadays. The girl with the impenetrable system who delivers our milk.'

'But she's not strange. We know her.'

'Oh, you know perfectly *well* what I mean! She's not – you know – one of the family.'

'But why was she standing on the step naked?'

'*What?*'

'Why was the girl naked?'

'She wasn't.'

'But you just said she was.'

I did not!' I almost screamed, 'I said that Mark was naked. Mark! Your son! Watch my lips – MARK WAS NAKED IN THE HALL!'

'No I wasn't,' protested Mark indignantly, 'well, only when I hadn't got anything on.'

'Oh, sorry! I stupidly assumed that we might all agree on that as a reasonably accurate definition of nakedness.'

'No, I mean it was only for about half a second because my towel slipped off, and I didn't know she was there anyway, and in any case, it was an accident. And I wasn't telling *her* that joke, I was reading it to myself.'

'Ah, yes, but it's always an accident with you, isn't it, Mark? You never actually *mean* to do anything, do you?'

Why do I always feel as if I'm being bullied myself when I have a row with Mark? I proceeded to recite the list of his sins, chopping the edge of my right hand into the palm of my left to emphasize each one as I ground it through clenched teeth.

'You cause chaos, you embarrass me, you push me into being rude to someone who hasn't done anything wrong, and then you tell me that none of it's your fault because it was all an accident. Well, I'll tell you what *is* your fault. You don't *think*! That's your fault, isn't it? You're not aware of anybody else. If there's no chance of you gaining something personally from a situation then it's of no interest to you. It just doesn't exist!'

'That's nice – so that's what you think of me, is it?'

'Kathy, don't you think – '

I swung a warning finger in the direction of my husband.

'Just for once, Mike, *please*, just for *once*, could you let me have my say without interrupting and taking Mark's side?'

I turned back to my son, who was sitting very still now and studying the end of the table again.

'Would you like me to tell you, just as a matter of interest, how I always manage to find the comb that you have to borrow from me every morning because you lose every single one you ever have within about three minutes of getting it? *Would* you like me to do that?'

Silence.

'Well, would you?'

'Not partic'ly.'

'It is always in exactly the same place, Mark. In the middle of the hall carpet just under the place where the mirror's hanging, that's where I find my comb. And it's there because when you've finished doing your hair you just – drop it! I've stood and watched you lots of times. As soon as you think your hair looks okay, your fingers just open involuntarily and the comb drops out

193

of them on to the floor. It doesn't exist any more, you see, because you've got no use for it. I'm very much afraid that's the way you tend to treat people as well, Mark, and you're going to have to do something about it, because when you leave here no-one's going to put up with it the way we do.'

'You always do this!' The words seemed to burst out of Mark. 'You always start saying things about my whole life when I do one thing wrong. You're always on about what I never do an' what I always do. You don't know me like you think you do. I only read a joke out and used the wrong spoon – that's all I did! You just look for reasons to say things to me, you do. I don't want any cereal now.'

Suddenly his lower lip started to tremble, just as it had done so often when he was a little boy. As his eyes filled with tears, he sent his huge bowl sliding down the table away from him and ran from the room, still clutching that ridiculous handkerchief of a towel around him.

Darkness filled me. I had made my son cry. Why? For what?

2

Mike sat down weakly on the chair that Mark had just vacated, shaking his head slowly in puzzlement. I turned round to the sink and loudly began the process of emptying the dishwasher and refilling it with last night's unwashed dinner things. I felt so ashamed and angry with myself. In recent weeks I had struggled more or less successfully to swallow the breathtaking fury that was periodically generated in me by Mark's behaviour, and now, in a few indulgent moments, I had blown it all completely and gone back to square one – no, probably the bit before square one, where you have to throw a compensatory six before you're allowed to get back on the board, let alone start moving again.

'Kath, have you decided what you're going to do about you and Felicity flying out to Pete and Dawn's later this year?'

I do so hate it when people try to *manage* me. I knew exactly what Mike was doing. Knowing full well that I was almost certainly inaccessible to reason and calm debate on the subject of what had just happened, he was making a wide conversational circle, a bit like those clever sheepdogs on television, with a view to penning me up good and tight when the right moment came. And he had chosen his route with care.

My older brother, Pete, adored by me since before time began, had emigrated to Australia with his wife fifteen years ago. I didn't think about my tall, dark, laughing, younger-sister-loving Pete all the time, of course, but every now and then a spasm of real pain would pass through me at the thought that I might never see him in the flesh again, and that my two attractive nieces were growing up in distant Brisbane without ever meeting an aunt whose ability to put people's backs up on a daily basis made a show like *Neighbours* look even blander than it actually was. I had always intended to use some of the money my mother left me to go out and see them, but you know how it is with money. It gets spent. This year, a week from now, in fact, I was to celebrate my fiftieth birthday, and, to my surprise Mike had suggested that a couple of thousand pounds, sitting in a building society account that Jack had shrewdly suggested we open a few years ago in readiness for when most of them went public and sprayed money around like a dung-spreader at planting time, should be used to fly Felicity and me off to the Antipodes for a family reunion.

Wonderful, eh? Yes, of course, but have you noticed the strange things that can happen when you're actually offered something you've always wanted? I've seen it on a much smaller scale the other way round, on those rare occasions when my sense of drama has fuelled an attempt to give substance to somebody else's casually expressed dream. At the moment when fantasy and reality touch there can sometimes be an effect like an electric shock. People don't like having their dreams messed with, perhaps because they offer a useful way to deal with reality.

In this connection I remember, a year or so ago, getting into trouble with Mike and our housegroup leader and just about everyone else except my friend Dip, when I asked someone a question on this very subject.

In our Bible study group we had a youngish couple (since moved on to pastures a little more explosively charismatic) called Bernard and Julie, who had been married for five or six years. Bernard, the husband, was a pleasant, laid-back sort of guy who drove a van around doing inexplicable things for the water board, and she was all right, I suppose, if a bit giggly and immature (not that I'm judging the foolish little person, of course). I think she had a job as a dental receptionist in one of the surgeries in our town, so perhaps having to witness all that fear and pain had affected her somehow.

Julie seemed to be wholly obsessed with Ralph Fiennes, about whom I knew only that he was a popular film actor. Whenever she talked about him, which was often and at length, she would go all droopy and languid and say how much she fancied him and dreamed about him and goodness knows what else. It really irritated me, I must admit, and her husband looked a bit browned off with it as well, although he never said anything in front of us. One evening, when we were all drinking coffee and stuff after the Bible study and Julie had somehow managed to wrench the conversation round from a discussion about which point in the service the notices should be given out to whether 'Ralph's' hair or mouth was his best feature, I asked her a perfectly innocent question – well, this is supposed to be a truthful account, so I confess that it wasn't that innocent, although I claimed it was at the time.

'Julie,' I said, 'can I ask you something about Ralph Fiennes?'

'Ooh, yes,' she dribbled, obviously a little surprised at my interest.

'You really fancy him, don't you?'

'Ooh, yes!'

'Well, suppose you had a phone call from him – from Ralph Fiennes, I mean – tomorrow morning, right?'

'Ooh, yes?'

'And he said, "Hi, there, Julie, I'll be round to your house at half past three to have wild sex with you," well, my question is – would you?'

The silence that followed this purely technical query was so profound that I began to think none of us would ever speak or move again. I wondered if we would just go on sitting there like actors in some frozen theatrical scene for the rest of time. It wasn't a very Bible-studyish question. Julie had turned bright scarlet, Mike had his I-thought-you'd-stopped-doing-things-like-that expression on his face, and most of the others just looked embarrassed. The only two who didn't were my dear friend Dip, who leaned her head right back so that she could study the ceiling, pressing her lips together to avoid smiling, and Bernard, who cocked his head in the direction of his wife as if keenly interested in hearing her answer to my question.

Mike was very chilly about it afterwards, and Simon Davenport, our housegroup leader, rang me up the following day to ask me how I felt about what I'd said. Translated, this was the crinkly-eyed, non-confrontational way of communicating the message, 'You shouldn't have said it', and I agreed with him in order to keep the peace.

Funny things, dreams.

And the Australian dream was a really tricky one. Part of me wanted nothing more than to jet off with Felicity to visit my brother and his family, but there was another cringingly immature part of me that was terrified of the actual meeting after all these years. What if I messed it up? What if the towering significance of the encounter shut down some part of my emotional confidence and made the whole thing uneasy and tense? I couldn't bear the thought of all my golden memories being transmuted into one leaden weight of failure. I found myself wishing that I was the sort of person who didn't think and ponder everything out of proportion so much, someone like Mike, who, when I made an attempt to explain my fears, looked utterly mystified, but nodded like a good counsellor and said, 'Just be yourself and I'm sure it'll all go fine.' I wanted to scream that it was 'myself' I was worried about.

'The answer to your question, Mike,' I replied, without turning round or ceasing my dishwasher operations, 'is that I intend to faff around, changing my mind repeatedly, until I'm faced with having to decide something, and then I shall make a random decision that will turn out to be wrong. I would have thought you knew that without having to ask. You know how consistent I am.'

There was a sigh from the other end of the kitchen. I felt sure that if I listened very hard it would be possible to hear Mike's brain thinking that there was no getting through to me when I was in this frame of mind. He tried again, though.

'So who was that on the phone earlier after all our messing about?'

Oh, God ...

'Oh, yes, it was, err – it was Joscelyn. She wanted to tell me about her weekend away at that manor place, how much it ...'

'How it revolutionized her life in every particular, no doubt.'

There was a little chuckle in Mike's voice. He felt himself to be on safe ground here. The business of Joscelyn's need for epic spiritual adventures had frequently been a topic of mild amusement and genuine sympathy between us until now. He continued with greater confidence.

'Well, that explains the earliness of the call. The only reason I got fed up just now was that it was your turn to look after everything and you kept putting the phone down when I picked it up – didn't you, you naughty person?'

Oh, no. Not the playful voice. Please, Mike, don't start using the playful voice because you think everything's sorting itself out. I always hate it at the best of times, and especially now. Please, I beg you, don't try to be playful ...

Running out of things to do with the washing-up, I turned heavily to face my husband. I could tell that he was feeling it wouldn't be very long before we could safely move on to the subject of Mark. A word more about Joscelyn first, though, no doubt, just to round off that pleasant little chat.

'Hey, Kath, it's fortunate we know old Joss so well, isn't it? If anyone else had phoned at that time of the morning to talk about their spiritual condition I think you'd have told them where to go in no uncertain terms, wouldn't you?'

It was impossible not to detect the extra question in his voice. Finding a hardened blob of some ex-edible substance on the work-surface beside me, I began to scratch at it with my thumbnail.

'I did.'

The light little laugh with which Mike had concluded his last speech died an abrupt death at the back of his throat. Feeling suddenly rather weak at the knees I pulled out the chair at the other end of the table and sat down. I waited for him to run his hand through his hair and shake his head as if to clear it. Having done both of those things he spoke.

'What do you mean, you *did*?'

'I mean that I *did* tell Joscelyn where to go in no uncertain terms – well, not exactly that, but, err ...' I cleared my throat and looked up before going on. 'You see, she was saying all the normal stuff about – you know – everything changing, and I was about to trot out all the usual affirming crap – Mike, why do you always do that shooting-a-guilty-look-towards-the-door thing when I say a word you don't approve of? We're not smoking in the toilets, you know. Or did you think there might be an undercover Ofsted inspector hovering in the hall, gathering evidence about the unsuitability of your private life?'

'You know, you can be most unpleasant when you're on the defensive,' said Mike in a very quiet voice. 'I was just concerned that Felicity might have come down and heard you talking like that, that's all.'

'Well, she'd have had a job, seeing as she was at Caroline Burton's sleep-over last night and hasn't come home yet. Presumably this deep concern of yours for your ten-year-old daughter doesn't extend to a passing interest in where she might have spent the night.'

'What did you say to Joscelyn?'

'I can't believe that you'd really forgotten Felicity wasn't here. That seems extraordinary to me.'

Mike physically stretched himself back and away from my pathetic attempt to change the subject.

'Don't be silly. *What* did you say to Joscelyn?'

I steepled my fingers together and hid my face behind them.

'I told her that she never seems any different to me after these big God-binges of hers and that all she's really doing is getting nearer to finding out she's a sinner who's been saved.'

'Uh ...'

Waves of irritated disapproval broke over my bowed head.

'And I, err – I told her that all her stuff about being completely transformed was a load of rubbish, and that what it boiled down to was her talking on and on about herself.'

'You said all that in those words?'

'No – yes – well, worse than that probably. I did say that I do it as well ...'

I risked a glance over the palisade of my fingers. Judging by the expression on Mike's face I was about to be sent out into the corridor to do sums at a little table all day as an example to the other children. I remembered something else.

'Oh, and I finished by telling her that she needed to learn how to relax. Mmm, that's right, I did say that as well.'

'*You* criticized *her* for not being able to relax?'

'Yes.'

'I just don't know what to say ...'

At these not infrequent moments when I openly confessed the enormity of my crimes I always had the feeling that Mike was silently and frustratedly urging me to tell *myself* off so that he wouldn't have to do it – smack my own face, as it were, and call myself names until I wept uncontrollably – and a little judicious comfort from him would be only right and proper. It maddened him that I spoke in a flattened voice and never automatically volunteered to scrub the latrines with a toothbrush or cut the lawn with nail-scissors as penance for my sins. Observing that, as usual, the hoped-for implosion of remorse was not on the cards, he moved on.

'And the girl at the door – the milkgirl – what did you say to her?'

'More or less told her to clear off because I didn't know what she was talking about and shut the door in her face.'

Mike was shaking his head again.

'Kath, I don't know how you can just sit there and say that so calmly as though it doesn't matter, I really don't.'

We are supposed to be Christians, you know.

'We are supposed to be Christians, you know.'

We sat in silence, Mike wondering why I didn't get on with the job of beating myself up, me knowing wretchedly that we were about to move on to the subject that probably *would* make me cry.

'So, where does Mark come into all this, then? What did he do?'

I leaned back and slapped the palms of my hands down on my thighs, trying to remain brisk.

'I don't know.'

'You don't know what he did? Then why – '

'I know what I felt. I sort of know what he did. He didn't think.'

'About what?'

'Oh, Mike, you've heard me say it all before. You've heard me say it all before, before and before that. If I have to go through it all again I shall just end up sounding like a congenital idiot. The whole thing sounds so stupid. He wore a towel that was too small, he read a joke that wasn't funny, his towel fell off for half a nano-second, he was about to eat too many Shredded Wheat with too much sugar in the wrong-sized bowl using a giant spoon and, most reprehensible of all, he picked the wrong stupid mother. That's what happened.'

'And what was it about him dropping his – sorry, I mean *your* – comb on the hall carpet when he's finished with it? You seemed to feel that was a vitally important point.'

'Sarcasm doesn't become you, Mike. Why don't you just stick to being boring?'

Aaagh ...!

I wanted to reach out with both hands and catch those last eight words I'd said before they could reach his ears. I couldn't, of course. You never can, can you? They were said. They were gone. They were doing whatever they would do. Unable to stand the hurt and puzzlement in Mike's eyes, I pushed my chair back and walked round behind him so that I could put my face next to his and wrap my arms around his chest.

'Look, don't take any notice of what I say, Mike. I know I've been horrible. I hardly slept last night. I should have asked you to get up this morning instead of inflicting myself on everybody. I woke up so many times, worrying and trying to make sense of things ...'

'Trying to make sense of what?'

His voice was horribly cold.

'Oh, just *things* – stupid things. It's always the same, everything seems so much more intense and serious in the middle of the night, doesn't it? I just got it all out of perspective. You know what I'm like when I don't sleep – the wife and mother from hell.'

My heart sank. There was something rigid and unyielding about the feel of my husband's upper body. Mike was a very kind man. Usually, any mention of lack of sleep or a bad night was good for a pat on the hand at the very least. Not now, though. Carefully unwrapping my arms, he leaned forward with his elbows on the table and spoke without looking at me.

'One of the things you were trying to make sense of all through the night was why you've ended up married to someone as tedious as me, was it, Kathy?'

I decided I owed him the truth.

'Mike, I don't want to be ...'

'What?'

'I'll tell you in a minute. Just – just let me do something first.'

Retrieving Mark's Brobdingnagian breakfast from the other end of the table, I carried it along the hall, opened the front door and baptized it in nearly a whole pint of the milk left by our recently extinguished lactic entrepreneur. When I presented this peace offering to Mark in his room a few moments later, he was somewhat taken aback, but very pleased and willing to accept it. A vast bowl of cereal in the hand is worth any amount of justified lingering resentments in the bush.

'Sorry about just now, Mum,' floated down the stairs after me as I descended.

'So am I.'

Same old pattern. Someone throws an apology into the ring, and someone else picks it up. Doesn't much matter who does which.

I got back to the kitchen to find Mike sitting exactly as I had left him, staring into space with an expression so sad and serious that it cut into me like a sharp knife. I sat next to him.

'Don't want to be what?' he asked very quietly, as if I'd never left the room.

'I don't want to be fifty,' I said, and burst into tears.

3

'So whose idea was this party?'

'It was Mike's idea, amazingly, Dip. He said we couldn't bring the old days back, but we might as well remind ourselves of what they were like by having a sixties party. I think it's a really good idea. And then he said he thought we ought to have it next Saturday, actually on my birthday, and I said a week's such short notice that people won't be able to come, but he said try them. So I got our little book out and phoned loads of people one after the other on the spot, and so far they've all said yes. And the following week's half-term, so we'll have a whole week to recover in. So, there we are – it's on! Exciting, eh?'

'What did you mean about it being amazing that it's Mike's idea?'

'Oh, well, what I mean is – it's amazing considering how he pretends to loathe big untidy things that make a mess. You know what he's like as well as I do.'

'I think it's a good idea, too,' chipped in Felicity, aged ten, taking her pen from between her teeth to speak. 'You'll be a twentieth of a thousand years old Mummy. How many of my friends can I ask? Can we move the big telly up to Mark's room and have videos?'

It was early afternoon, and a sort of peace had once more descended on the Robinson household. One of the strange things about our lives is the way in which high drama and twiddly ordinariness seem to alternate quite naturally. At ten o'clock we could all be in deepest, darkest despair, but by eleven o'clock we might easily be laughing like drains, or shelling peas and discussing the price of kitchen-rolls. By the time Dip arrived at eleven o'clock, Felicity was back from Caroline's with a ludicrously excessive party-bag full of vile-looking sweets and colouring pens (Caroline's mother, Sally Burton, was having difficulty in understanding that her little girl was no longer six, and she had always been very competitive in this area, in any case), and Mark had gone off to his weekend job at the stationer's in the high street. Incredibly, Mike and I had progressed from near divorce to gooey cuddliness in about half an hour flat, and he had now driven off to eat a large lunch, play uncommonly guiltless golf and look forward to a little mild marital flirting with his repentant wife when he got back.

'What sort of things will you do at your party, Mummy? Food and talking and selling things nobody wants and that, all in a circle?'

We both sat in silence for a second, inwardly digesting Felicity's picture of the sort of party adults might enjoy.

'Certainly not, totally wrong, small and silly person,' I replied eventually. 'Your mummy is going to have the sort of party we had back in the sixties. The house will be jammed – stuffed with hordes of people who love me very much, all swirling around the house, listening to David Bowie records turned up too loud, and talking complete nonsense to each other about the meaning of life – that will be compulsory. And we're going to have a room where people pile their coats when they arrive and have trouble finding them at the end. What else, Dip?'

Dip looked at me slightly oddly for a moment, then dropped her eyes and rubbed the top of her head with the tips of her fingers as she spoke.

'Well, I suppose there'll have to be a place by the kitchen door where I can be trapped for the whole evening by a man with bad breath telling me in gory detail about all the awful things that are making his life miserable. It wouldn't be the sort of sixties party I remember if that didn't happen.'

'You're all weird,' pronounced Felicity. 'Can I go and ring Caroline?'

'You've been with her solidly since the beginning of yesterday evening. Which vitally important thing did you forget to say in the course of the last fourteen hours? Why do you need to ring her now?'

Eyes wide with concentration, Felicity tapped the end of her pen against her teeth as she tried to think of an answer.

'Tell her about the party, of course.'

'All right, clear your pens and paper up first, then.'

'I'm going to carry on afterwards, Mummy. There's no point putting it all away, is there?'

'All right, but if you don't carry on you will be severely punished. Go!'

'Can I do it from your room?'

'Go, will you!'

Dip laughed affectionately as my slim, golden-haired daughter twirled her way out through the door, pulling a silly face as she went.

'She's so lovely, isn't she? I used to wish she'd stay little, but I'm glad she hasn't.'

My heart was warmed all over again by the fond expression on my friend's face. Dip (real name Elizabeth Reynolds) had known Felicity since she was a baby, and probably loved her as much as we did. She was also my best friend, and very popular with the rest of the family, especially Mark, who seemed to find things he needed in her (acceptance being one trivial example) that he was seldom able to find in me. I confess that I had had to battle hard with resentment of that fact from time to time, but the better part of me was glad that she had been there for him over the last few years. She and I were very different in a number of ways. I was wild, she was mild. Everything about Dip was comfortable and comforting. No-one has ever described me as comfortable. I was dark, like my younger son, and a little over average height. She was a few years older than me, quite tall with short fair hair, gorgeous blue eyes and a slight but unmistakable Australian accent left over from her early life in Adelaide. She worked part-time as a nurse in the local hospital and belonged to the same church and housegroup as us. The areas we did have in common included an extremely silly sense of humour, a shameless attachment to the best sherry in the world, and a real passion for God. These three seemed to get us through most things.

A few years earlier we had decided as a family that we would all love to have Dip living with us. Just before flying off on holiday to America, we issued a ceremonial and absolutely definite invitation, then left her to look after our house and our two stick-insects, Rowan and Kimberley (long since departed to the great bramble-patch in the sky), while she attempted to make a decision about whether to move in permanently or not when we came back. We were all quite surprised when she announced that she'd decided to stay in her little terraced house on the other side of Standham, but when I saw later what she'd written about – well, about being *her*, I think I understood. Funny, isn't it? You really think you know people. (If you want to know where her nickname came from, by the way, I won't bother telling you now, because she's written all about that as well.)

'So, what started all this off, then, Kathy?'

Dip was continuing a conversation that had been interrupted and radically adjusted as a result of Felicity arriving in the living-room to commence her third unfinished activity of the morning since getting back from the Burtons' house.

'Well ...'

'Suddenly realizing fifty is coming towards you like an express train and getting into a bit of a panic because evil, moustachio-twirling life has tied you to the tracks? That's more or less how it felt to me.'

'Yes, I think it's been – did you just make up that "moustachio-twirling life" bit, Dip, or did you have it all prepared? I bet you've been waiting ages for an opportunity to casually trot that out, haven't you?'

She threw her head back and laughed.

'I'm sorry. Is my conversation usually so boring that a sudden pathetic burst of metaphor calls for special celebration? If so, I'll have a small sherry.'

'I thought you'd never ask. As you know, we have a small bottle specially set aside for celebration of metaphor, in the grammatical section of the Brinks cabinet.'

Two minutes later we both had a glass of Bristol Cream in our hands. I took a lovingly reverent sip and decided to answer Dip's question truthfully.

'Mike and I were invited out to dinner a few weeks ago by the Handleys, who live in one of those really huge Victorian houses in Swan Road, the ones with the long drives and lovely big sash windows that still work. You know the Handleys, don't you? I think she works up at the charity shop in the precinct most mornings, and Frank was something terribly important to do with the House of Commons before he retired, but not a member of parliament or anything. They used to go to our church, if you remember, then they retired and stopped coming for some reason, and Mike ran into Frank on a committee a couple of months ago and – '

Dip raised a hand in surrender.

'I know who you mean. I never knew them very well, but I *do* know who you mean.'

'Well, it doesn't really matter, actually. We never knew them very well either, that was the trouble. So we were both a bit stiff and nervous. Their *house*!' I lowered my voice as though the Handleys might be crouching behind the sofa listening to us. 'Dip, I've never seen anything like it. Huge place, all leather and polished wood and antiques and things made out of elephants' feet, and a lady who comes to "do" for them, you know the sort of thing I mean. I think Mike's just the tiniest bit susceptible to your genuine poshness – '

'Oh, me too, I'm afraid,' sighed Dip.

'And he goes into this funny sort of falsely relaxed mode, specially after a couple of drinks. It's difficult to describe – somewhere between sentimentalism and spurious worldly wisdom. Drives me mad, because he usually calls on me to support his attempted witticisms or tinny little scraps of homespun philosophy and all I want to do is tell him to shut up.'

'But you don't?'

'No, of course I don't, not if I can help it, but with the Handleys I came very close to it. After dinner we got on to the subject of "marriage in this day and age", and you know how it is at dinner parties with people you don't know very well. Somehow you get carried away on a wave of enthusiastic agreement about absolutely everything in the universe because it's too much like hard work if you don't, and after a while you hear yourself talking absolute piffle or saying things you don't actually go along with at all, and your brain goes all numb and dead and you just want to go home and die of shame. Anyway, we'd all solemnly agreed that young couples nowadays don't have the moral fibre that young couples used to have, and that "commitment" was a word people don't seem to understand nowadays, by Jove, and that in our day (their day was considerably before our day, I might point out, but we were good enough or cowardly enough not to remind them of that) you made your promises and *damn well stuck to them* through thick and thin, and all that stuff, and then Frank whatever-his-name-is said what he thought the real trouble was. The *real* trouble, he declared, was that the youngsters of today expected fireworks (meaningful nod to indicate that he was speaking of "marital unpleasantness", as that character of Harry Enfield's calls it) all the way in their marriages, and gave up when it didn't happen. Surely, he inquired confidently, Mike would agree with him that such expectations were ridiculous.

'That was when Mike embarked on one of those little speeches of his that sceptics like us might suspect are designed to snuggle up to the good opinion of people he feels inferior to. They make my bones ache! Dip, it wouldn't have mattered if he'd just nodded and grunted something or other that sounded like a vague agreement – I mean, I don't really care what the posh Handleys think about our sex-life – but he didn't.

' "No," said the style-king of the junior teaching world, the Oscar Wilde of Standham, swirling the brandy round in his glass and sipping with judicious consideration. "I don't think you could describe what happens in a mature relationship as fireworks. No, Frank, I would say that long-term marriage is more like one of those wonderful, heavy old Aga cookers – wouldn't you agree, Kathy? They last for years if you look after them properly, it's possible to get a really excellent glow going, and they produce really good meals as long as you give 'em a stoke every now and then." Dip, this sherry is very expensive. If you're going to spit it all over the room I shan't give you any next time.'

'I'm sorry!' spluttered Dip, 'I really am. Give me some more. Gosh, I bet he wished he hadn't said that afterwards.'

'Oh, yes, afterwards, you may bet your best cami-knickers on it. At the time, though, he just sat back and lapped up all the expensive, throaty sounds of merriment from Frank and Thingy Pooey Poshperson. Then, in the car on the way home, he said it had really gone well, didn't I think? And I said, using my famous impression of a cucumber served after twenty-four hours in the freezer, "I regret to announce that the heavy old Aga has gone out through consistent neglect and will require a complete service before it becomes functional again. Because of this there will certainly be no glowing tonight, and you need not expect any really good meals in the foreseeable future, stoke every now and then though you may," and it was then that he began to realize I wasn't too impressed with his little flash of wit. Actually, we did laugh about it next morning, but ...'

'But it set you thinking.'

'It was a sort of trigger, I suppose, Dip. I started to feel very sad, and worried and panicky about getting old and everything winding down and feeling flat. I don't *want* to be a heavy old Aga that glows sometimes. I'm not interested in being one of those highly respected Christian women in suits, with kind-sad eyes, who resisted temptation once for all the very best reasons and are in a sensible long-term relationship with no fireworks and have written a Lent book about it. I want some sparklers and some bangers and some rockets and some – some things you have to be very careful with because they could be dangerous. There's got to be at least an outside chance of getting your fingers burned, hasn't there?' I paused, sipping my sherry again and wondering how much more to say. 'I started to feel as if there was a really big decision to be made.'

'About what?'

'Well, at the risk of you thinking I've finally looped the loop, it was – well, I saw it like this. It was the decision about whether to burst like an exploding star, or shape myself like a comfortable armchair. I didn't feel ready to get old and spend my time shaping myself into whatever other people wanted me to be. I really didn't want that. I wanted lots of other things. I wanted to go through those first stages of falling in love again, Dip, when you go for a walk and ordinary things like trees and buses and brick walls look shiny and vivid and textured and full of meaning. Do you remember that glorious, half-witted feeling?'

'I remember – '

'I wanted to turn up in some cafe on Saturday morning at ten thirty with everything in me buzzing and tingling because I was going to meet someone I'd been dreaming about all night and dressing and making-up for since getting up. I wanted to walk along a river-bank under weeping willows in the autumn like Mike and I used to when we first discovered each other up at Durham, finding to our amazement, like all couples falling in love since the beginning of time, that we felt exactly the same about absolutely everything under the sun, wondering when it would be right to hold hands for the first time, and whether he would kiss me when we got back to the halls, and worrying about not being able to do it properly and – and all those warm and fruity things. I sat up really late in the kitchen one hot summer night this year with all the doors open, feeling one of those magical warm breezes running right through the length of the house from front to back, just gently brushing my face. It was sad and lovely, and it filled me full of aching and longing for – for something or other. Do you know – ?'

I looked at my friend for a moment. How safe is it to say some things?

'Go on,' said Dip, 'you might as well spit it out.'

'In case it's infected, you mean? Sorry. Sorry, it's just that I was embarrassed for a moment. It seems so ridiculous to be saying this sitting at home on a Saturday morning at eleven o'clock – but there've been times when I wanted to sneak off down to a pub in the next town and sit at the bar and have a couple of drinks and see if I got chatted up.'

'That doesn't sound much like the "wondering when it would be right to hold hands" sort of stuff that you were talking about.'

Putting my glass down on the small table beside me, I clasped my hands tightly together as I tried to find the words to explain.

'Oh Dip, it wasn't that I really did want some sordid encounter with a fifth-rate gigolo from Milton Keynes – always assuming there might be a fifth-rate gigolo in Milton Keynes who specializes in travelling down this way for sordid encounters with forty-nine-year-old mothers of three. And I'm not one for getting crushes on film stars, like that droopy girl we used to have in our group.' I couldn't help laughing suddenly. 'Honestly, Dip, can you imagine me taking on the role of resident *femme fatale* in the Dog and Duck on Friday nights? It isn't just about sex, you see, Mike and I have always got on pretty well in that area – well, most of the time, anyway – it's more about feeling special and sparkly and – and fancied. Do you know what I mean?'

'Well, I ...'

I think I did actually notice out of the corner of my mind, as it were, that Dip was looking a trifle strained or strange or something by this point, but I ploughed on without waiting for a reply, as I'm afraid I so often do with my close friends, and especially this one, oblivious to any universe but the one existing solely for the benefit of Kathy Robinson.

'So, after I'd accused Mike of being boring this morning, and then admitted that my real fear was getting old and him thinking

I was boring, it was like a boil bursting – no, that's horrible, it wasn't like that. It was like a bubble popping – no, as you were, it was definitely a boil. Anyway, whatever it was, bubble or boil, it burst, and after that we got more glutinously lovey-dovey than we've managed to be at that passionless time of the morning for ages. And Mike said why don't we celebrate the beginning of me being old by having a real old-fashioned sixties party with the right music and silly dancing in tiny spaces because the room is too crowded and all the other things we were talking about just now. And he has promised, a little worriedly, him being stuck with being who he is, that he will do his best to ensure that romance will blossom once again in our relationship. In the meantime, I have to repair the damage I've done to our friendship with Joscelyn, apologize to the girl who delivers the milk, and be pro-actively nice to Mark to make up for this morning. I must say, you know, Dip, with the best will in the world, there is nothing like three children for killing the prospect of careless and spontaneous passion in a marriage. Sometimes I wish they would all clear off somewhere and be happy. So, there we are! That's my day so far. What do you think?'

I didn't know what Dip was going to reply to this, but whatever it was had no chance of being heard, because Felicity reappeared at that moment clutching a sheet of paper in her hand. Smiling a funny little frowning smile and signalling that she was just popping out to the hall for a moment, Dip slipped through the open door.

'Mummy, I've got a question for you. Which is the most frightening prehistoric monster of all, more frightening than tyrannosaurus rex or raptors, or any of those in the film you wouldn't let me see and Daddy did? Jack just wrote it down for me.'

Felicity was indeed once more among us, bright with her interest in whatever it was she wanted to communicate. Jack was her oldest brother, just back from his final term at university and working through one of the local job agencies during the week, while he considered the little matter of what to do with the rest of his life. Jack never seemed to get out of his bed unless there was some exceptionally good reason for doing so. Today was Saturday and there was not even a bad reason for surfacing. No doubt his little sister had jumped on him, ignored his groans and demanded entertainment. Their relationship was a constant joy to me. I had been so afraid that when Jack went away Felicity would lose touch with the feeling of closeness there had been between them for the first few years of her life. Not a sign of it.

'Go on, then,' I said, 'let's hear it.'

'Okay.' She cleared her throat and read from her piece of paper. ' "The most frightening dinosaur of all is one that has not become extinct like all the other dinosaurs, but can still be found in this present age, lurking in libraries, studies and bookshops all over England. It is called the Thesaurus, and it is huge, massive, very large, enormous, gar – gargantuan, colossal, king-size, monstrous, immense, titanic and vast. Because of this, anyone who sees, observes, spots, notices, views, perceives, regards, witnesses or looks at it, is likely to be terrified, aghast, petrified, scared, shocked, alarmed and windy." *Windy*!' she repeated with a peal of laughter, 'I think I'd be windy if I saw a dinosaur. Maybe that would put it off eating me.'

'Well, it would me. Just as a matter of interest, darling daughter,' I said, 'do you know what a thesaurus really is?'

'Yes, Mummy,' she replied calmly, referring once more to her sheet of paper, 'it is a collection of concepts or words arranged according to sense. What did you think it was?' She grinned. 'Jack said you'd ask me that.'

'I shall come up those stairs in a minute and make your lazy big brother swallow Mr Roget's entire collection of concepts or words arranged according to whatever you said in a minute. You go and tell him that, and tell him to get up and come down and say hello to Dip.'

'I think Dip's gone, Mummy,' said Felicity. 'I just heard the front door go.'

'What? What are you talking about? No she hasn't, she's just gone out to the – the toilet or something.'

I got up quickly and went into the hall. No sign of anyone

there. Calling up the stairs brought no response either. Opening the front door I walked as far as the gate and, leaning over, looked up and down our road, expecting to be met with the familiar sight of Dip's elderly but beloved Mini, Daffodil. There were lots of places available for cars to be left, including the space under the tree directly outside our house where she usually parked, but the Mini simply wasn't there. Felicity was right. Dip had gone.

4

That sort of thing has an odd effect on the pit of your stomach, doesn't it? I may be wrong to think this applies to lots of people, but I have always supposed that one of the security blankets most of us cling to is the knowledge that, in nearly all respects, we are battling through the same things together in this wild world. And, if you're anything like me, it tends to be the common understanding and close identification possible through truly close friendships that are the most secure things of all. If you like, you and your friend are facing the same way to withstand the onslaught, shoulder to shoulder, which, in my view, is the most matey configuration of all.

I'm really beginning to wish I hadn't vowed to be totally truthful in this account. You're going to think I'm hopelessly egocentric – well, I expect you do already, but even more so, I mean – when I tell you that Dip's disappearance left me feeling almost breathlessly lost and hurt. It was as though she and I had escaped from a sinking ship by clambering on to the same little life raft, and suddenly, after a long experience of clinging together in order to survive, she had unaccountably slipped away into the water and left me on my own. Ridiculous! She'd only gone out of the house – once! – without saying goodbye. It was hardly on a par with the *Titanic* tragedy.

But why? *Why*? Why had she? I went back to the kitchen and sank into a chair, head in hands, trying to make sense of what had happened. Why had Dip gone? She just didn't *do* that sort of thing. She simply did not get up from her seat, walk out of the front door, and drive away without looking back or saying goodbye, or telling anyone, or – or anything. I cast my mind back as best I could over the conversation we had just had, searching for a clue that might help to solve the mystery of such unusual behaviour. I had certainly talked a lot and not done much listening, but that was hardly unusual. And anyway, Dip was never backward about telling me what she thought about that aspect of my personality.

There had been the time, for instance, when a family court found me guilty of continually trying to control everybody and everything around me. They cited such family events as Chinese meals when, according to them, the tedious process of individual decision-making made me so irritable that I always attempted to whip or bludgeon everyone into ordering one of the set meals for five so that we and they could 'get on with it'. Somewhat bruised by them painting this picture of me as a sort of impatient bully, I had appealed to Dip when she joined us a little later.

'Dip,' I said, 'they're all accusing me of being controlling over things like meals and trips and that sort of thing. Would you say I was the kind of person who tried to control other people? Don't be polite, be honest.'

'Oh, yes,' replied Dip pleasantly and casually, 'that's exactly how you are.'

I hesitate to record yet more evidence of my need to be confined in a place with nice soft walls where I can't easily hurt myself, but as the reality of Dip's abrupt departure started to sink in, I even began to feel a faint shadow of dread that was a little bit similar to the sort of fear I had known as a slightly younger child than Felicity was now, when a visiting preacher at my parents' church had talked with loud and cheap-suited authority about 'The Rapture'. This harbinger of peace and joy had described how two people would be working in a field and one would be snatched up and go off to be with God, while the other would be left on his or her own. He claimed that one airline in the state of California had instituted a rule that, of the pilot and co-pilot who crewed their planes, at least one must not be a born-again

Christian, in case both were taken by God and the plane crashed. I listened goggle-eyed and was terrified! I remember reef-knotting myself to my mother's arm on the way home, hoping that, if this rapture business happened before we reached the solidly roofed safety of our house, I would be hooked up into the sky on her arm, and God would let me stick around because it was so obvious how much my mother loved and would miss me if I stayed on earth and she lived in heaven. It took me a long time to get over that sermon.

I comforted myself with the reflection that yellow Minis were unlikely to be included in God's rapturous removal plans.

Nevertheless, by the time Jack made his yawning entrance into the kitchen a few minutes later, I had managed to get myself into a bit of a state. He stopped on his well-worn path to the kettle and studied me expertly for a moment.

'Coffee and counselling, Mumsy?'

'Hello, Jack, darling. Yes, I'll have a coffee, thanks. No counselling needed, though. I don't suffer from a mysterious and unaccountable reluctance to walk out in front of moving buses, nor am I trying to control an unnatural urge to attack Labour politicians with cactuses wrapped in cling-film.'

'Oh, dear, bad as that, eh? Where's Dad? It's cact*i*, by the way.'

'I don't care what it is – incorrect plurals are the least of my problems at the moment. Golf. What do you mean – bad as that?'

'Well,' said Jack calmly, filling the kettle from the tap and plugging it in as he spoke, 'as I've explained to you before at some length, ever since I was a small boy you've set out to entertain me when something's wrong, instead of simply telling me what's up. It's supposed to put me off, and it used to, but now that I'm incredibly mature I see through it immediately, so it's a waste of time.' He perched himself on the stool by the sink and held out a tin towards me. 'Biscuit?'

'No thanks, but, err, I would like to have that coffee you've offered me. Is there any chance that the full power of your incredible maturity could be focused on to the need to actually switch the kettle *on* so that the water has a chance to become hot enough to make it? What's Felicity doing? She needs to do a violin practice today.'

'Oh, yeah! Sorry, it's on now. Writing out a news bulletin for later, that I suggested. She's all right. What's happened? You're upset. Tell Uncle Jack.'

It said a lot for the way things had changed that I proceeded to do exactly that.

One day, at about the age of nineteen, Jack had favoured Mike and me with what you might call a comprehensive rundown on ways in which the 'Enid Blyton' boy he accused us of trying to create had run into great difficulties when faced with the grittily real world of teenage life in general and secondary education specifically. He also said some gratifyingly nice things about us, thank God, and this highly emotional encounter turned out to be most constructive in the long run. One crucial item in Jack's complaint package had been his feeling that we tried to shield him from family issues and problems that might worry or upset him. He made it abundantly clear that he would rather unite with us in facing trouble, whatever it might be, than hear about it by accident and be more upset than if he'd heard about it in the first place. Being a simple soul in some ways, it had been quite hard for poor old Mike to hear any of the things that his oldest son so needed to express, and especially difficult to make this particular adjustment. You will not be surprised to hear that it was relatively easy for me, since running off at the mouth happens to be a bit of a speciality of mine.

Nevertheless, as I looked at the tall, lean figure of my son, draped on the stool in front of me, I found it difficult to believe that he was very nearly twenty-four, and quite definitely an adult who happened to live in the same house as us.

As Jack finished making our coffee I explained about everything that had happened that morning, with just a little judicious editing of the comments I had made about myself (for my own benefit rather than his), finishing with an expression of my real puzzlement about Dip's vanishing so unexpectedly and completely.

'The thing is,' I said, 'it's such a very definite – oh, what's the word? You know – what's the very definite thing that people make in books? Something vaguely unpleasant to do with banks, is it?'

'A definite statement?' suggested Jack.

'Yes, that's it – such a very definite statement. "I have removed myself without any reference to you." What's a person saying when they do something as unusual and total as that? It reminds me of when my mother – when Nanna died.'

There was a pause, then Jack spoke.

'Look, Mum, there's a couch in the next room where you can lie down, and I've got a false beard and a notebook and pencil and an old pair of horn-rimmed glasses upstairs. We might as well do this thing properly.'

Why does Jack's mickey-taking draw me in a way that sympathy pure and simple rarely does?

'No, I mean it. Mixed up in all the upsetness and crying and missing her there was quite a lot of hurt and bewilderment about her being able to just go so completely when she was supposed to love me so much. Please don't bother to tell me that's not rational. I know it doesn't make any sense – but then, what does?'

I stopped and thought for a moment.

'You know, I had a dream about my mother a couple of years after she died that I never told anyone about, not even Dad. It really upset me at the time.'

Sigmund Robinson detached himself from his stool and sat at the opposite end of the table. He took the elastic band from his pony-tail and, keeping his eyes fixed on me, began to readjust it.

'Go on, then, Mumsy. Hit me with the bad dream.'

'Well, I was in Grantley – you know, her village – walking along the high street with the shops and houses and all that as normal. It wasn't in the past – I mean, in my dream she'd died and everything, and I was just there, feeling sad. And then, quite suddenly, *there she was*, crossing the road in front of me. I could only see her back, but – you remember Nanna's shape, don't you, the sort of triangle her back made – it couldn't have been anyone else. I was so excited and pleased. I hurried to overtake her but when I caught her up and turned to look her in the face, she – oh, Jack, her eyes were a long, long way away, and they were – bruised with deadness. I so wanted her to give up being dead and come back and make everything how it used to be. Then, in my dream, I looked down and saw that her big, old-fashioned knickers had fallen down round her feet, so I told her and she started to bend down as though she was going to pull them up, but she stopped almost immediately and looked at me, all sad and helpless, and – and somehow I knew she'd stopped because there's no point in pulling your knickers up when you're dead. I felt like crying. I wanted to beg her to pull her pants up, just as a little sign that if she could have chosen she would have wanted to stay alive and walk along to the house I grew up in and have a cup of tea in the warm world with me, but her eyes were – so, so far away. Then I woke up, thank God.'

I shivered suddenly in the warm kitchen. Jack wiped his eyes with the knuckles of one hand, then looked up.

'Dip's not dead, Mum.'

'No, I know. I'm being silly. What happened with her was just like a kind of echo, I suppose. I can't believe I'm so feeble.' I stood up. 'Perhaps if I give her a ring it'll turn out to be some really ordinary thing that she suddenly remembered and rushed off to do, and we'll both have a good laugh and it'll be all right.'

'Mum, why did Dip come round this morning?'

I sat down again.

'Why did she come round?' I gazed blankly at him for a moment. 'Why does she ever come round? To see us – have a cup of coffee, glass of sherry, bit of a chat. What are you getting at?'

'This morning in particular – I just wondered if there was anything special about her coming.'

I put my hand to my mouth like a child caught telling fibs.

'Actually, I think she did say yesterday she wanted to come and talk about something important, and I did rather go on and on and on about the trials and tribulations of being me and – and fifty and everything. But that still doesn't really explain – does it? Surely not.'

Jack shrugged. 'Depends what the important thing was, I suppose. Why don't you ring her?'

I stood up again.

'I will, I'll ring her now.'

I collided with Felicity in the doorway. She put her arms lovingly around me and looked soulfully into my face.

'Mummy, you and Daddy owe me two pounds, thirty-nine pence.'

I looked soulfully back at her.

'Felicity, for ten years we have clothed you, fed you, paid for your outings, furnished and equipped your room, taken you on holiday and financed your vast range of after-school activities. Help me to understand how *we* can possibly have ended up owing *you* two pounds, thirty-nine pence.'

'You just do,' said my daughter sweetly, quite unmoved by this very cogent argument. 'Daddy said yesterday. Why did Dip go?'

'I don't know, but I'm going to find out. Take it out of my purse on the dresser. I'm just going to make a call from upstairs. Jack, can you make sure I'm not interrupted, please?'

'Do you want to hear our news bulletin, Mummy?'

'I'd love to later, sweetheart, but I must phone Dip to make sure she's all right. Okay?'

'Don't worry, Mummy, I'm going round the corner to the shop. Give Dip my love. Coming, Jack?'

Jack pushed himself out of his chair and drained his mug.

'Okay, Flitty, good idea. We might meet some of your friends and I can sing to them.'

'Promise you won't.'

'I might dance as well.'

'I don't want you to come now.'

'Oh, I'm coming all right'.

The sound of good-natured banter drifted away as I went up the stairs and they set off for the shops. I sat on the edge of the bed, watching through the window of our room for a minute or two as they dawdled and danced their way along the pavement.

Those were two of my children there. My children. They looked all right, didn't they? Fit – laughing, *I*'d brought them up – well, helped to bring them up.

I tried to summon up the nerve to ring Dip. The fluttery feeling in my stomach took a little while to calm down, but at last I picked up the receiver and dialled the familiar six-figure number. After five rings the cowardly part of me began to hope there would be no reply. I decided to let it ring another four times before hanging up. At least then I wouldn't have to feel guilty about not having tried hard enough. It wasn't, I told myself, that I didn't want to make contact with Dip, it was just that I had no idea what to expect, and I have always feared black surprises like other people fear spiders.

On the fourth ring there was a crackling and clicking at the other end, as though someone had done something, but still there was no voice to be heard. My own voice sounded husky and strained with tension as I spoke.

'Hello, could I speak to Dip, please?'

It was an absurd thing to say. I don't know who I thought I might be speaking to if it wasn't Dip. She lived on her own, and I could imagine nothing but the most extreme circumstance in which anyone else would answer her phone. There was a pause of a few seconds, then Dip's voice, slow, slightly blurred, but unmistakably hers, spoke dully and as if from a distance.

'Something you forgot to moan about, was there?'

'Dip, you sound funny, I can hardly hear you.'

'I'm speaking on the – when you don't – you know – you don't have to pick it up. Did you say you can hardly hear me? Oh – well, that's fine then, isn't it? That's fine, *I* can hear *you*, so that's fine. No change there, eh? That is ab-so-bloody-lute-ly fine!'

'Dip, you're – you're a bit drunk. You don't get drunk. You've got drunk without me.'

'Oh, Miss Marple strikes again! Do I remind you of some sad old single biddy in the village who overdosed on cough medicine? Yes, Katherine, I am somewhat intoxicated. I am – I am an intoxicated Anglican of Antipodean extract – actually, perhaps I'm not, 'cause I can say that – but, look – I really cannot listen to *any* more of your incessant *moaning*, Katherine, I really cannot listen to …'

'Dip, I was very selfish this morning. I never even asked you what it was you wanted to talk to me about. I'm sorry, I honestly am.'

'Huh! You honestly am, am I?'

'No, *I* am. *I* am very sorry, Dip. Dip, you sound like a stage drunk. What have you been drinking?'

'Damnation to myself – and some Scotch, and a few tablets.'

Oh, sweet Jesus, hold her until I can …

'Dip, what did you want to talk to me about this morning? Please, *please* tell me. I really do want to know. I know I went on and on and on without listening, but this time I'm not going to. Take your time and just tell me. I'm listening. I *am* listening now. Give me another chance.'

Silence.

'I was so very young, you know – silly and young, I was.'

Pause.

'Kathy?'

'Yes, I'm here.'

'Kathy, I was only sixteen – that's all I was. I didn't even know …'

'What?'

'You know – who, what, how, when – nothing! I knew nothing!'

'Dip, are you talking about sex?'

'Huh! That may be what you call it. That may be what *you* call it, Mrs "Mike and I have always got on very well in that area" Robinson. D'you want to know what I call it? I call it something ugly happening in the dark among some smelly coats like you're going to have at your party when I was too drunk to know what was happening because some – some *man* had made me drink vodka or something and I'd never drunk anything like that before.'

222

Suddenly Dip's voice rose into a wail of sheer anguish. I gripped the phone tightly with both hands, my own eyes wet with tears, wanting so much to be there with her.

'I call it not even remembering it and never doing it again because I felt so sick and mucky and *bad*! Oh, Kathy ...!'

Lord Jesus, please sit beside me on this bed and put your arm round my shoulders and whisper in my ear the words I should say to my friend. Forgive me for being so grumpy and rotten this morning and thank you for all my family and all the other things I'm so lucky to have. I expect I'll make all the same mistakes again tomorrow, but I'll try not to. I really will try ...

'Dip, do you want me to come round? I can come straight away. Felicity's with Jack, so – '

Dip interrupted, her voice more under control now, but wobbly and faint with crying, more strongly Australian than I could remember ever hearing it before.

'Every single time I see her, Kathy – just about every single time I see that lovely, lovely girl of yours – it crashes against my chest. Boom! It crashes against my chest every single time I see your Fli – Fli – Felicity. It hurts so much, Kathy, and it won't go away.'

I covered my eyes with my left hand, looking for the least spot of light in the darkness. What on earth was she talking about? Crashes against ... I asked the question as gently as I could.

'What is it that's hurting you, Dip? Just that – that it happened, or – '

'It's this heavy weight, Kathy, the one that got hung round my neck, the one I hung round my neck – so heavy – it hurts so much. I can't get rid of it, Kathy.'

She was pregnant. She had an abortion.

'Did you have to have it terminated, Dip?'

'No, not terminated – wrong word altogether. Don't say that. Killed. Killed is the word. That's the word. *Killed*. Had to have it done. My dad said it was the only way. Mum cried and flibbered about a bit, but she always did what he said. Our house wouldn't stop being shivery and dark because his – his bloody

223

shame went roaming and roaring round and round outside like a monster, blocking out the light. It was huge, Kathy, so much bigger than – than what they killed. The thing they killed wasn't much bigger than a – a grain of rice, a little tiny grain of rice. Little tiny ...'

She gave it a name.

'Dip, darling, did you give the – the baby a name?'

Silence. A small voice.

'How did you know?'

'Err, I didn't – really. What – what was the name?'

'Kathy, I've never said it out loud before. I've never dared.'

As I waited, Jack and Felicity came back into view up the road at the corner of the street. She was holding a bulging paper bag, probably filled with the familiar assortment of cheap sweets that I'd always said I'd never let my children eat. A cherry boot-lace hung from her mouth, the sort that gets shorter and shorter as you walk and chew. Felicity's face was tilted up towards her brother in rapt attention, her features splitting continually into a wide grin at the things he said. I pictured Mark, fortified by the Shredded Wheat swamp he had carted into his system earlier, joking with customers up at the shop as he dispensed newspapers, stationery and postage stamps in his own inimitable style. He was very good with people, a darn sight better than me. I suddenly wanted to rush up there and throw my arms round him and tell him I loved him. He'd hate that. Jack, Mark and Felicity. Three names, and three whole people to go with them. Riches. Treasure.

'He – he's called David. I mean – I don't know whether he would have been a boy or a girl, but – but I've always called him David.'

Dip didn't sound quite so drunk any more, just tired and burdened and sad.

'The guilt's been terrible, Kathy – terrible, like a great lump of concrete or something, always there, always reminding me that he could have grown up, he could have learned to walk, and he could have run and jumped and fallen over and grazed his knee and cried and I could have kissed it and put something on it to make it better. But I didn't make it better – all I did was kill him, Kathy. I killed my little David.'

Dip started to cry again, but in a different way. When I told Mike about it later I said that the sound of that weeping seemed to me like a lake or sea of grief that had at last found a way to escape and flow evenly out of the place where it had been trapped for all those hard years.

We could have a communion service.

'Dip, I wonder if we should – look, if I put the phone down right now and drive round to you, are you going to be okay until I get there?'

'Yes.' Sniff. 'Yes, come round – don't worry, I'm not going to do anything silly. Just cry.'

'Sure?'

'Sure.'

'Felicity sends her love, by the way. See you in a jiff.'

5

The story that Dip haltingly related to me after a quite lengthy recovery period, as we sat drinking black coffee together in her little kitchen, was far from being an uncommon one, but no less tragic for all that. As a naive and inexperienced sixteen-year-old she had gone with a schoolfriend to a party in a different suburb of Adelaide from her own and been offered alcohol for the first time in her rather sheltered life. The fumbling act of procreation that followed was conducted in a panic-stricken haze among jackets and coats and scarves on one of the beds upstairs, and it had left Dip trembling with disgust and self-loathing which, over the following weeks, was transmuted into terror as she realized that she was almost certainly pregnant. A reasonably happy if tentative life was turned overnight into the traditional bad dream, made worse by the fact that she never woke up from it (except when she was asleep, as it were), and that her mother and father were solidly present in the nightmare with her. The moment when she told them of her pregnancy had closely rivalled that dismally loveless encounter at the party as the most appalling experience of her life.

'After I'd said this awful set of words I'd been dreading to hear coming out of my own mouth, my father just – I don't know how to put it – he sort of ejected out of his chair as though he'd been shot, or as if something had stung him really hard, and I remember the momentum of it carried him over to the window, and he just stood there stiffly with his back to me staring out at the traffic going past and saying nothing. Mum turned pale and went into one of her pronoun frenzies. "Who? What? Where? Why? When?" Then she started to cry. It was such a weird feeling, Kathy. I remember thinking to myself, "This is real life, but like a film. In a minute, Dad's going to turn around and ask me if I'm sure, and I'm going to tell him that I am, and then he's going to ask who the father is, and I'm going to have to say that I don't know, I don't remember, and he's going to be disgusted and appalled." He was always either disgusted or appalled, or, on special occasions like this, disgusted and appalled at all sorts of things. When I was a little girl I used to believe that the two words must have very specifically different definitions. Do you know what I mean?'

I nodded energetically.

'Yes, as a matter of fact, Jack and Mike and I were talking about that the other evening. We were saying that it's like when some great global disaster happens, and world leaders have to issue statements, but there's a problem because they all like to say something different, and there's only a few suitable words you can use. So you get the first one being "shocked, horrified and saddened" by the tragedy, whereas the next one's "appalled, alarmed and deeply sympathetic to the victims", if there are any. Then the third leader gets greedy and says he's "stunned, outraged, scandalized, sickened, aghast *and* disgusted", so by the time the fourth one gets out of bed late on the other side of the world after oversleeping, there's not much left to choose from, and he ends up informing the world that what has happened is "very unpleasant and really not very nice at all". Sorry ... I'm blithering on as usual. So, were you right? Was your father disgusted *and* appalled?'

Dip had smiled a watery smile at my nonsense, but now she nodded sadly.

'Oh, goodness me, yes, he was. Several other things as well, I'm sure, but I can't recall what they were. I think the thing that hurt me most, although I know I wouldn't have been able to put it into words at the time, was the feeling that we were talking about something I'd brought on myself because of deciding to be "dirty" or immoral. Kathy, what happened at that party was nothing to do with sex at all, really. It was about a child – me – getting into a situation she didn't understand, and ending up being quite badly hurt. If I'd been run over by a car or something or fallen down some steps, Mum would have been all sympathy, and even Dad would have hovered uneasily around squeezing out grunts of formal compassion. That was what I needed when I told them. I felt like a six-year-old who's having a rotten time, and I just wanted to be cuddled and loved and told that everything would be all right in the end. I know it was a shock for them, and I can understand that much better nowadays, of course, but I was so scared and unhappy.'

Dip began to cry softly again. I made more coffee. After a little while she dried her eyes and went on to tell me how her father's insistence on dealing with the situation in a way 'satisfactory to all concerned' had proved too much for the fragile sixteen-year-old's instinctive belief that even an unwanted life is sacred. There was a termination. For the second time in a short while things were done to the young girl's body without the consent of her inner will, this time in the name of discretion and good sense, but from that day to this, Dip had only ever known real peace through distraction. In her mind, the hypothetical David, unborn but always sadly and accusingly present, had been waiting for forty years to hear her explain why his life had needed to end before it ever had a chance to begin.

In the preceding week, a week which included the anniversary of the abortion, Dip had reached a point of such unbearable

227

tension and anguish that she had decided to open her pain up to someone at last, the someone being me. I cringed inwardly as I thought back over the content of my prattling comments earlier that day. I had said something about wishing my children would go away and be happy somewhere. I had said how much I wanted to experience those feelings of being in love again – being fancied. I gathered from poor Dip that, apart from a life-long devotion to Paul Newman and, rather interestingly, ornate fantasies about good-looking men encountered at the centre of complicated garden mazes (takes all sorts!), she had closed the door on the prospect of actually experiencing any of these things since the age of sixteen.

'Dip,' I said sadly, 'when I ranted on and on and on about my lot not being a happy one, you must have really wanted to hit me.'

'Yes, one in the kisser would have been nice – either that, or I'd have enjoyed running off with your splendid husband so that you'd have had to spend a few Fridays down at the Dog and Duck looking for another brave volunteer from Milton Keynes to take his place. You know, I think Mike's the only man I've ever really trusted.' She shifted uneasily in her chair. 'Kathy, I really am ever so sorry about all this. I usually manage to keep this sort of stuff to myself. In fact, I've become a bit of an expert at it. I just suddenly couldn't handle it any more this morning and I had to get out. I could feel that at any minute I was going to start rushing around wringing my hands and screaming or something.' She choked very slightly on her next words. 'I – I specially didn't want Felicity to see me falling to pieces. Then, when I got back here, I opened up that bottle of Bell's that's been standing unopened in the corner of my cupboard for months, and just swigged some down.' She shuddered. 'Horrible stuff! Doesn't half work quick, though.'

'And the tablets?'

I hadn't wanted to ask, but . . .

Dip flushed.

'Yes, well, to be honest, my grand attempt at suicide was risibly similar to the times when I've had a bad headache. I had to go rooting around in my two boxes of first-aid stuff, just like I always do, hunting for enough pain-killers to end it all.' Her blush deepened. 'I don't think I was very serious about that side of it. When I said that I'd taken some tablets I was telling the literal truth, because more than one is "some", isn't it? And I'd taken three Dispirin. I'm going to need another two for my head in a minute, except that I haven't got any.'

I felt a great surge of relief.

'I'll get you some.'

It was as I stood up to go and do this that I remembered what had passed through my mind just before driving over to see Dip. Hmm ...

'Dip, nothing's actually changed, has it?'

'What do you mean?'

'Well, this morning and everything – it hasn't actually made a difference to what you went through all those years ago. I mean, the feelings of guilt and sadness and the rest of it, they're not going to go away just because you've told me what happened, are they?'

Dip shook her head slowly.

'No,' she said softly, 'the fact that someone else knows does change things a bit, and I'm really glad I told you, and I'd like you to tell Mike as well, if you don't mind, but – no, you're right, it won't make much difference.'

'You see, the other thing you said on the phone was that you'd been drinking damnation to yourself. Do you remember that?'

Dip rubbed her face with the palms of her hands and laughed.

'Oh, Kathy, how very embarrassing! I didn't really say that, did I? Another spot of over-dramatization there, I'm afraid.'

I waited without speaking. I was capable of doing that sometimes, believe it or not. Dip stopped laughing and went on seriously.

'It is true, though. I've had a sneaking suspicion all my life – well, since, you know, since I was sixteen – that on Sundays God spots me coming up towards the communion rail and shakes his head and says, "Oh, dear, here comes the Reynolds woman, that wicked girl who had the abortion. Look, there she stands, taking up some innocent person's place, eating and drinking damnation to herself. Can't stand the sight of her!" ' She held up a restraining hand. 'Please spare me comforting theology, if that's what you're tempted to come out with. I'm telling you how I feel, not what I believe at the bottom of my heart to be the case. I really think I love God, and I know deep down inside that he loves me – I never have any doubt at all that he loves you Robinsons – but, Kathy, this thing's been an open wound in me for years and years. It feels as if it would hurt just as much in the very heart of heaven, and it just will not even begin to heal.'

I found myself tapping my teeth nervously with a forefinger. The next bit was not going to be easy for me.

'Dip, I'm a bad-tempered, thoughtless person a lot of the time – I know that – and there's no reason that I can think of why God should use an idiot like me for anything at all, but when I was speaking to you on the telephone earlier, I felt sure suddenly, or – or I was sort of *filled up* with knowing for sure, that we ought to have a little communion service, quietly, just in the housegroup, so that God can do something about you and David.' The last drops of confidence drained away as I continued. 'I don't even really know why, or what might happen, but – but I just think maybe we should do it ...'

I hung my head, feeling like one of the gawkish teenage evangelicals I had been and gone around with in the sixties, some of us peddling Ouija-board Christianity for all we were worth to keep the whole thing interesting. Sensing what was going through my mind, Dip smiled reassuringly at me, already starting to settle back into the much more familiar role of unflappable friend and support.

'Kathy, I'll be frank with you, the idea of doing that frightens me rigid, but I do know how difficult it was for you to say that to me, so I think I'd better take notice. Anyway, you can't measure the value of the post by the quality of the postman, can you?'

'You can't – ? Oh, I see what you mean – no, you're right, of course.'

Pause.

'This means the other people in the group will have to know, doesn't it?'

'I suppose it does. I'm not sure. Would you be able ...?'

Dip leaned back in her chair and produced one of those sighs that starts from right down at the bottom of your boots.

'Kathy, I've lived with this for more than forty years, and I think I've been a bit of a coward. I *want* things to change. I'll do whatever it takes.'

'Right. Good. Right. Well, I'll go and get the, err, the tablets.'

'Okay.'

6

Lying cosily in bed that night, I rested my head against my husband's shoulder and held on to one of his arms with both of mine. I actually had every reason to feel sad. Mike had broken the news to me a little earlier that what we had tended to call the 'Australian money' would now have to become the 'new roof' money. I had left it too late, and now the choice had been taken away from me. After what had happened with Dip, though, this seemed relatively trivial, especially as I was able to appreciate the solid warmth of Mike's presence beside me. He was there with his library book, and he was mine. I didn't need to go to the library any more.

I had told Mike all about Dip's problem, and about the rather scary responsibility I had taken for suggesting a communion service that might help her in some way. Mike doesn't cry much, but he had shed a little tear or two for Dip, as I thought he probably would. He sounded quite worried when I mentioned the communion service, though. Now, he laid his book down and turned to me.

'Kathy, you're sure this communion thing is – you know – the right thing to do?'

'I can't talk about being sure, exactly, Mike. I only know that when the idea first came into my mind, it – well, it filled me up

231

with itself. I can't think of another way to put it. It's only happened about twice in my whole life. I know I could be wrong, but I think the most important thing is that I'm more scared of not doing it than doing it.'

He thought for a moment and then nodded.

'All right, but you do know we're quite possibly going to run into some opposition, don't you? Apart from anything else, Simon can't just agree to do something like that without giving it a lot of thought. In fact, I know jolly well he won't. Do you want me to talk to him about it, or will you?'

'Mmm ...'

For a moment or two I pictured myself having the requisite conversation with our housegroup leader. Simon Davenport was a very upright and charitable man, good-looking as well, in a dark, doe-eyed sort of way (Mike said he bore a striking resemblance to Hanse Cronje, the captain of the South African cricket team). Simon did tend, though, to travel along very straight lines in his thinking about Christian topics, greeting most of my contributions to group discussion with a shadow of slight strain on his honest face. He really did conscientiously try to accommodate the views expressed by each member of the group, but there was no doubt that my frequent excursions into the twisting byways and dark alleys of Christian living as actually experienced by human beings were fleas in the vest of desirable progress as far as he was concerned.

'Perhaps, if you mentioned it to him first, Mike, then he'll know it's not just a wild idea. I make him nervous, but he respects you, doesn't he? Then you and I could talk to him and we could meet and pray together, and meanwhile I'll ask God to fix it all for us.'

Mike looked sternly at me.

'Simon would hate to hear you talking like that, as you know full well.'

'I know,' I said drowsily, 'but he's not here, so he can't.'

'You're incorrigible.'

'No, I'm not, I'm Church of England.'

'Do you realize I've been saying you're incorrigible and you've been saying you're not, you're Church of England, ever since we first got married?'

'Well, it's good that there are some things we've gone on doing since we first got married, don't you think?'

'Did you have something particular in mind?'

'Yes, I did, actually. Have you finished your boring old library book yet?'

'Yes, I think I probably have ...'

two

Sunday

1

'Mum, when's dinner going to be ready?'

'It's ready now, Mark, but we are not having it until Felicity's done her violin practice, so speak to her, not me. I'm sick of telling her. She promised to do it last night but she watched something instead. She said it would be all right because she'd do it before church today and she didn't do it. Then she promised to do it as soon as we got back, but she still didn't do it. She can jolly well do it now or nobody's going to eat today. And you can get the glasses out.'

'Why are you speaking as if you're cross with me?'

'I'm not cross with you, I'm cross with Felicity.'

'Felicity! Come and do your – oh, it's all right, Mum, Dip's helping her.'

'Fine, but as a matter of trivial detail, I haven't heard any violin-playing yet. Call me a slave to habit, but I've rather got into the way of expecting to hear the violin being played when a practice is in progress. Get the glasses out.'

'What's Jack doing, then?'

'I can't hear you over the violin. What did you say?'

'I asked you what Jack's doing?'

'Are you eighteen or four?'

'How many?'

'Six with Dip.'

'Can I have mine on my lap? I'm going out at half past two.'

'You'll have to change your trousers if you're going to have your dinner on your lap. No, you can't.'

'No funnier than last time or the time before that, Mum. Can't we start?'

'Tell everyone to come, and we'll start as soon as Felicity's been through Vivaldi one more time, if Vivaldi can stand it.'

'DINNER, EVERYONE!'

'*I* could have done that, Mark!'

'Why did you ask me to, then?'

Sunday lunchtimes in our house had been many things over the last couple of decades. When the children were small, Mike often talked about how much he was looking forward to future years when these richly traditional occasions would be spiced with good conversation and bright convivial laughter, weekly opportunities for the cementing of good family relationships and the healing of any small rifts that might have occurred during the previous week. A ripple of mildly hysterical inner laughter passes through me when I think of those projections now. As far as I can recall, Mike's charmingly civilized scenario did not allow for such phenomena as two brothers making determined efforts to batter each other's heads in with place-mats in a vicious argument over the last roast potato, nor a wildly irrational wife and mother sending a bowl of steaming hot leeks skating down the length of the table like a curling stone after two of her family had made being-sick noises as soon as the lid was removed – these being two of the more dramatic highlights that sprang immediately to mind. Nor, to my recollection, was there any awareness, in those sweet innocent days before the children excitedly discovered God's wonderful gift of free will, that simply getting all of them to sit down at the table at the same time would so often prove to be a task of considerable magnitude.

For instance, the summer brought televised cricket, a so-called sporting entertainment inducing mystification and fury in me to about the same degree.

The mystification is easily explained. About midway through

the morning, all three male Robinsons would hang their brains up in the hall like cycling helmets, disappear to the sitting-room and peer with intense concentration at a screen showing a dozen or so men dressed in white, distributed at random around a large field, doing *absolutely nothing*. Every now and then there would be a burst of applause from the spectators as one of the men did his own little bit of nothing in what one assumes must have been a sparklingly talented way, at which point Mike, Jack and Mark would be galvanized into excited discussion about strategies by which it might have been possible for the individual concerned to have achieved inertia with even greater efficiency.

The fury usually manifested itself at about twelve forty-five, when I would have the effrontery to point out that the dinner I had prepared was ready and on the table, only to be met with groans of frustration because the cricket had reached 'a really crucial stage'.

'But you've been watching it for nearly two hours!' I would scream.

This was the cue for deep, head-shaking sighs of frustrated incredulity at the sheer scope of my idiocy, together with tut-laden groans of disbelief that I was unable to achieve even the most rudimentary grasp of this imbecile game of theirs.

'But that's the whole point!' one of them would sufferingly point out, unbearably burdened by the weight of my denseness. 'The whole morning has been leading up to this last quarter of an hour. A couple of quick dismissals between now and lunch, and by teatime we'll have polished off the tail and passed their total.'

Nonplussed by such volleys of gibberish, I tended to retire tight-lipped to the kitchen and slam things around for a minute or two. Eventually, Mike, vaguely recalling that he was supposed to be a mature adult, would ascend halfway towards the standing position from his chair in the very slowest of slow motion, and, with eyes still fixed on the screen like a rabbit hypnotized by a snake, begin to make painfully gradual progress, still maintaining his strange puppet-like, semi-sitting posture, in the direction of the kitchen. Once he was through the door, vertical again, brain re-inserted, the sight of hot food successfully broke the trance at last, and he would issue peremptory orders to the other two rabbits. He would even, on occasions, with massive unfairness, rebuke them mildly for their selfishness in not coming immediately when their hardworking mother had been to all this trouble to cook them a nice dinner. The amazing thing, on reflection, is that we seemed to go through this little drama once, at the very least, every single summer, as though it had never happened before and none of us knew what our lines or moves were supposed to be.

My only comfort was that this seemed to be the way with many other households. We human families happily (or, at least, resignedly) go through set pieces which must sometimes look quite bizarre to outsiders.

Mike and I witnessed a quite fascinating example of this as we sat on one of the old wrought-iron Victorian seats on our local common one summer afternoon.

A family of four, out for an afternoon stroll, passed us on the satisfyingly elegant tree-lined avenue that runs along the south edge of the common and the cricket-pitch. Dad was in the lead, looking faintly bored and exasperated, yet, at the same time, very responsible and Dad-like. He carried a long, whippy stick in his hand, ready to slash at brambles and beat off any bush monsters that might leap from the undergrowth to attack his wife or his little brood. Half of his little brood followed a few yards behind, a pigtailed girl of about ten, full of oldest-child confidence, leading with her chin and chest, marching along rather than walking. Next came Mum, dressed in precisely the clothes you wear for walking on the common, an exact but larger copy of her daughter, the two of them looking like a couple of those hollow dolls that fit into each other, but with two or three stages left out. The other half of the brood, obviously the youngest in the family, and certainly lowest in the pecking-order as far as this particular little familial farmyard was concerned, was a boy of around six years old, who, at this stage of the walk, had stopped to explore the invitingly accessible lower branches of a horse-chestnut. He was now dangling contentedly by both hands from the lowest branch of the tree, waiting, as small boys so healthily and enviably do, for the next thing to happen.

The next thing to happen was Dad realizing that his small son was lagging behind, and deciding it was time he caught up.

'Leave it!'

Sometimes we parents issue orders to our small children with a military sharpness and acidity that we would never dream of using with anyone else. Fortunately, the extent to which small children respond and give credence to this sort of excess tends to be in directly inverse proportion to the degree of sharpness and acidity injected into the command. Children may be inexperienced, but they're not silly. They seem to be aware at a very early age that, in the mechanics of obedience, frequency invariably outweighs vocal force. That explains why this typical specimen of a small boy continued to dangle happily from his branch despite the parental admonition. He was still a long way from having to do what he was told, and he knew it.

'Leave it!!'

This time Dad slammed the same phrase out like a man hammering a second nail into stubbornly hard wood after bending the first one, and with much greater force than he had used on the first attempt. Innocent folk who never were part of such a family might have assumed quite reasonably at this point that it was bound to do the trick. Such crashing dominance, such threateningly fierce tones, must surely result in the lad instantly dropping to the ground and rushing like the wind to catch up with his father to apologize before some dreadful punishment befell him. Touching naïveté! He continued to dangle, of course.

It was Mum's turn.

'LEAVE IT!'

The sheer venom with which the lad's mother screeched exactly the same pair of words as her mate would have been deeply alarming if Mike and I had not been so aware of the previously mentioned frequency/force equation. Mike whispered that he would have moved like a shot if she'd spoken to him like that, but the little boy we were observing with such interest was possessed of crucial, family-related information. He knew exactly what he was doing. He continued to dangle – and as he dangled, he grinned.

'Leave it!'

This fourth and, as it transpired, final command was transmitted in a lordly squeak by our little hero's sister – she who, at this stage of their lives at any rate, was probably his greatest enemy on the face of the earth. Knowing her power, she had not even bothered to turn her head as she spoke. Gloriously unhampered by the civilized restraints that might have curbed her parents in dealing with their smallest offspring, this girl would be capable, at the correct, expertly judged moment, of doing her brother surgically precise harm when she next encountered him in that unpoliced jungle of a world that is called 'When the grown-ups are not about'.

Four identical directives had been issued, culminating in the boy's worst enemy entering the fray. Clearly, he felt that it was time for the force of gravity to be strategically employed. Dropping lightly to the ground, he scampered to catch the others up – still grinning.

All families are the same, with varying degrees of sophistication. They have their own special, private sets of rules, and their own ways of playing out the same old set-pieces again and again, often in a virtually identical way, not necessarily as a result of being blinkered, but simply because they are *them*.

Ours was no exception. Sunday lunch was traditionally a rather tense occasion in our house, precisely (ludicrously, when one thought about it) because everyone was aware that Mike so wanted it to be relaxed. Five people more or less busting a gut to produce a family idyll that had never really existed in the first place is hardly conducive to relaxation. The best times had always been when Dip was there, not because the children were on their reluctant best behaviour with a visitor – as a matter of history, they weren't – but because she had that hot-water-bottle-y sort of presence that seems to so successfully combat the chilling draughts of ill grace and dispute. Even more important, perhaps, was the very special rapport that existed between her and Mark, whose usual idea of an enjoyable lunch was to get the food down his neck and clear off as soon as we acceded to his mumbled request to be allowed to 'get down'. When Dip was with us he actually seemed to want to be there.

She was with us today, saying less than usual, and a little puffy-eyed if you looked closely, but otherwise just the same.

That Sunday lunchtime, on the day after the Saturday that had been so pervaded by marine odours, was one of our less acrimonious ones – once we had all sat down, that is – but a comparatively detailed recollection of the twists and turns of comment and response during that half hour or so shows just how raggedly complex such occasions could be, and how packed with potential for disaster.

As soon as Felicity had played through her piece for a second time and been sent back to put her violin away, the six of us assembled around our long kitchen table (my favourite piece of furniture, by the way) and Mike began to carve the joint.

'Right!' he said contentedly as he carved. 'How about someone suggesting a really nice family activity for this afternoon, something we can all do together for a change?'

As he spoke the first plate was in the process of being passed to the other end of the table, where Mark distracted anyone who might have been about to answer this question by drawing back in apparent terror at the sight of the generous slices from the joint on his plate.

'This is unlucky meat!' he exclaimed, his voice trembling like one of those gloriously talent-free actors in the early horror movies.

'And why might that be?' enquired Mike calmly, continuing to saw placidly.

'Please,' groaned Jack, 'I don't think we really want to know, do we?'

Felicity wanted to know. She always wanted to know everything.

'Why is it unlucky meat, Mark?'

'Because,' replied Mark in sepulchral tones, 'this is the lamb that gambolled and lost.'

'O-o-oh, good,' said Jack Blackadderishly, apparently greatly relieved. I was only worried that it might turn out to be a bad joke, but as it's not a joke at all, that's fine.'

Felicity's frowning gaze was still fixed on Mark.

'Gambled at what?'

'Not gambled – gambolled! Gambolled sounds like betted but it means skipped about.'

Felicity looked doubtfully at the plate of meat that had by now appeared in front of her, another more troubled question framing itself on her lips.

'It's not funny when you have to explain it,' complained Mark as he passed the vegetables to his sister.

'Don't worry,' said Jack kindly, 'it's not funny when you don't have to explain it as well.'

'Violin seems to be going very well.'

Dip's bright comment was obviously designed to distract Felicity from the mental image of the collected source of our various dinners skipping happily around a field in its original state.

She nodded and Mike said, 'Yes, she's really come on lately. You're doing quite difficult pieces now, aren't you, darling?'

It was true. Felicity had begun to learn the violin a few years ago, by a Japanese method which demanded the presence of a parent at all lessons. The wretchedly unmusical but available parent in this case had been me. As the weeks went by, I had begun to feel rather like a junior school child myself in my abject fear that Mr Tyson, Felicity's violin teacher, would tell me off if I arrived late for the lesson each Wednesday morning, or if my daughter had demonstrably not practised since the last time. Early in this lengthy learning process the whole family had become accustomed to gritting their teeth and finding ways to survive endless, squeaky repetitions of 'Twinkle, twinkle, little star' in a greater variety of musical forms than it seemed possible for the mind of man or woman to devise. As time went by, though, Felicity's skill increased dramatically, and now her fingers fairly flew up and down the neck of her three-quarter-size instrument.

The trickiest aspect of it all, no-one will be surprised to hear, was getting her to practise. My arsenal in this ongoing warfare consisted of encouragement, threats, bribes, the occasional parental sulk, fury, flattery, shouting very loudly, coaxing very gently, making her cry, making her laugh and presenting her with cosmically awful, end-of-the-world-as-we-know-it alternatives. Jack's idea was the one that worked longest and best. He suggested putting a small sweet or trinket under an upturned cup in the practice area and letting Felicity have it when the session was finished. This device, one of the many ploys I would have scorned in those dear sweet days when children were purely hypothetical, really appealed to her, and got us through the most difficult patch of all. Nowadays she still had to be pressured into practising, but her music really did seem to have become part of who she was. She could actually *play* the violin, and even enjoy it. My daughter could play the *violin*! I was amazed every time I thought about it.

'Felicity, could I ask you a question about your violin music? There's something that's been puzzling me.'

Felicity looked suspiciously at her older brother as he poured gravy over the pile of food on his plate. Jack's jokes always started very seriously.

'What about it?'

'You see, I had the idea that usually at the top of a sheet of music, it says something like "Sprightly, with an air of freedom", or "Loudly, and with passion", something like that. Don't they usually say something of that sort?'

'Might do. Dunno. Why?'

'Well, your music is quite different from that, isn't it? I noticed at the top of one of them it says, "Reluctantly, and with an air of resentment", and on the other one it says, "Morosely, and with little grunting sounds of annoyance". Perhaps that's why you've found practising so difficult. You're following the instructions too closely.'

Felicity speared a piece of hot roast potato, popped it in her mouth and spoke through and round it with exaggerated, compensatory clarity.

'You and Mark should go and tell your sad jokes about skipping sheep and things at the top of music to some people who are fed up with laughing and want to have a serious time for a while.'

'Don't eat with your mouth full, Felicity,' I corrected automatically. 'What are you all laughing about? Oh – you knew what I meant.'

'Speaking of people who are fed up with laughing,' said Mike, when everyone had subsided, 'reminds me – Kathy, did you hear what Norman Davis said to me in church today?'

'No,' I replied, recalling mainly my relief that there had been no sign of Joscelyn and John in their normal places near the front that morning. 'I saw him lean over towards you, but I couldn't hear what he was saying. Now you mention it, it did strike me that he was looking almost happy. I thought there must be something wrong with him.'

We had known this Norman Davis fellow for years through the church community, and in all that time he had been about as far removed from being a twinkling little sunbeam of a person as you could imagine. On the contrary, he was what you might call a stubbed-toe of a man, hot, angry and full of some kind of throbbing misery. Norman sat through most of our services like a man being tried for murder who has just caught sight of the black cap on the judge's desk. That morning Mike and I had nodded amiably at him as we took our seats in the same row for the communion service, and we had smiled at each other when he responded with his usual negative shrug and a dark grimace hinting at untold depths of unhappiness caused by *them*, the ones who, in Norman's world, were always out to get us all. I had to confess that I was rather fond of Norman, who, like Eeyore, was a very kind and generous person despite his pessimistic outlook.

'It was just before the congregation started to go up to the altar rail for communion,' said Mike, laying down his knife and fork to tell the story. 'I just happened to glance to my right and I could feel myself doing one of those perfect double-takes they do in comedy films. And the reason was that Grumpy Norman looked transfigured. His eyes shone. There was a big broad smile on his face – I don't think those smiling muscles have had much exercise for a long time – and he was sitting up straight in his chair, more sort of buoyant than I've ever seen him in church before. Dear old Norman, he looked to me as if he might be on the verge of doing an ascension all of his own out of the chair and through the ceiling. I really thought to myself, "This man's been touched by God!" I wondered what amazing revelation had been vouchsafed to the brother on my right to account for such an unusual infilling of joy. And I think he must have noticed out of the corner of his eye that I was watching him, because just then he leaned towards me, this extraordinary light still burning in his eyes, and – well, what do you think he said?'

We all chewed in Mike's direction like a herd of super-domesticated cows and shook our heads interestedly.

'He nodded towards the vicar, and whispered ecstatically, "He's forgotten to do the Peace!"'

Felicity looked puzzled and Mark shuddered darkly, but the rest of us fell about. The 'Exchanging of the Peace', for those who are not familiar with Anglican peculiarities, was the latest attempt (that meant it had only been around for a few decades) by the good old C of E to bring a little informality into some of our services. The idea was that people would move around the church, shaking hands or hugging each other and verbally offering the Peace of the Lord to one another. Some folk, and Norman had always been one of them, dreaded and disliked this practice intensely. After years of shoving up KEEP OUT! signs at the edge of your personal space even in informal situations, I suppose it must be a kind of torture to be expected to do it artificially. Mike had been wrong in his initial diagnosis of Norman's transfiguration. There had been no spiritual revelation, just gleeful relief.

I hated that too, when I used to go,' said Mark through a mouthful of food, sounding as if he was talking about an experience of putting his foot in something unpleasant by accident. 'People I didn't know used to come up to me and act like I was their best friend suddenly. One woman kissed me once. Ugh! Glad I don't have to go now. I hate church *so* much.'

2

Silence fell around the table as everyone bent busily to their plates. It was as though an invisible person had issued a general order that no-one was to speak for a limited period. Actually, it was to do with what had just been said, and what I might be about to say. Out of the corner of my eye I saw Mike glance at me. He knew exactly what my reaction to Mark's comment was likely to be.

Some years earlier, when Mark was fourteen, he had pleaded, initially through the mediation of Dip, who was obviously far less likely to bite his head off than me, to be allowed to stop going to church because he hated and loathed it and the weekly inevitability of attending was 'spoiling the rest of his life', according to him. Mike and I had agreed, as long as he still came along on what we regarded as special times, a condition which he agreed to, but actually complied with only after considerable pressure on each occasion. This Easter, for instance, full of chocolate and ill grace, he had morosely endured the Sunday service, declaring afterwards that he would be 'well pleased' if he never had to step through the doors of a church ever again.

The agreement that Mark need not come to church any more was made with considerable reluctance on my part. It made me feel such a failure as a parent and as a Christian. Mark's tendency at that time to just disappear in the evenings and at weekends with a shadowy group of friends, characterized by their hooded eyes and mechanically strategic expressions of politeness, meant that I spent frequent sleepless nights wondering what kinds of dark villainy might be going on out there in the wild teenage world. Like many a parent before me, I had dreamed *The Waltons*, but feared I had woken up to *Trainspotting*. Telling Mark he no longer had to go to church felt like deliberately throwing him into the middle of the night. As it turned out, he seemed, by and large, to have survived whatever dark and terrible things he might have been engaged in, and he was now at the local college of further education, battling through an A level course in Communication Studies and History which seemed, to my weary perception, to have been going on for about fifteen years so far. Nowadays he spent most of his free time with two fairly mild, skinny friends with tadpole-like large heads, who were on the same college course. Jason and Richard, whose eyes were certainly not hooded, succeeded in gulping out rudimentary pleasantries at appropriate times, but generally suffered a purple paralysis of embarrassment in the presence of Mike or me.

All in all, things were certainly better with my second oldest son than I would have dared to hope a few years ago, but the business of church still hurt and troubled me on quite a deep level. It seemed to me infuriatingly insensitive of Mark to be so mindlessly, thoughtlessly scathing about such an important part of our lives, and in front of everyone else. Irrationally, it struck me as even worse that he should have done it at Sunday lunch, but then my dealings with Mark were not famous for the flow of reason which swept them to their frequently half-drowned conclusions. At Mark's words, the all too familiar wave of anger had begun to rise in me, together with the knowledge that I would either have to pursue what he had said to its bitter, lunch-disrupting end, or stuff it all back inside again, grit my teeth, and smash a cup or something later when I was on my own. Selecting the teeth-gritting option, I was still unable to restrain myself from stabbing my fork with unnecessary force against my china dinner-plate. My dear daughter noticed, of course.

'What's the matter, Mummy?'

'Just releasing a little tension, darling – nothing much. Eat up.'

'Why do people say eat up, instead of eat down? The food goes down, doesn't it, not up, except when you're ... Was it what Mark said?'

Dip tapped the table with her forefinger to attract Felicity's attention.

'Hey, can you think of an answer to your dad's question, Felicity? No-one else has.'

'Sorry, Mum,' mumbled Mark, rightly interpreting a meaningful look from his father.

If you know you've upset your mum with something you've said, for goodness' sake just say sorry, and that'll probably be the end of it.

I could almost hear Mike's voice advising his son at some quiet moment on how to deal with the resident loony when things got explosive. If I gritted my teeth much more they would begin to crumble under the pressure. I leaned an elbow on the table and rested my forehead in my hand. I didn't want to pick up Mark's used tissue of an apology on this occasion. Why should I? In my head I formed the words and sentences that would erupt from me if I decided to forget about restraint. It would be so easy and so releasing to let it all out. Why *should* I have to put up with people saying hurtful things and colluding over the best way to prevent me from reacting in whichever way I wanted? It made me so *mad* ...! I sent out imaginary bubbles containing imaginary swearwords that burst over Mark's head and showered him with my anger.

'It was about doing something together,' said Mike, firmly jolly. 'You'd like us to have a family outing this afternoon, wouldn't you, Kathy?'

'Can we go bowling and have a pizza?' asked Felicity.

'If you pay, Flitty,' teased Jack, flipping his hand across the top of her head, pretending to hit her.

'*Wouldn't* you, Kathy?'

Blow you, Mike!

'Yes,' I mumbled, 'I s'pose it would be nice to go out somewhere.'

'Can I ring a friend and ask her to come, and can she stay the night afterwards?'

'No!' chorused the rest of the family, united at least in this, their reluctance to spend an afternoon in the high-pitched, lisping presence of Caroline Burton.

'I didn't mean Caroline,' lied Felicity shamelessly, 'I meant Jenny.'

'No, darling,' said Mike firmly, 'we want to go out as a family for once. You see plenty of Jenny and Caroline without them coming today. Let's just be us for a change.'

Mark glared significantly at his father.

'Dad!'

Mike stared blankly back at his son, presumably puzzled by such unprecedented and vehement support of Felicity's right to invite a friend.

'I just meant that it would be nice for once to – '

Dip interrupted, laying a hand on Mike's arm and smiling imperturbably as she spoke.

'I think Mark was very kindly pointing out that I'm not actually a member of the family, Mike, but the very fact that you said what you said in front of me shows that you do think of me as being a sort of part of you all, so I really wouldn't worry about it.'

I look forward with interest to the day that must eventually come, when my husband will blush with such intensity and heat that he spontaneously combusts. His babblingly incoherent apologies to Dip just made us all laugh, while Felicity jumped from her chair and made a special trip round the table to lean affectionately against someone whom she certainly regarded, quite unequivocally, as an extra member of the family.

'I know exactly what we ought to do this afternoon.'

There was a hush, partly caused by surprise. It was a rather unusual thing for Mark to make such a definite statement about anything to do with the family as a whole. I think we all felt mildly excited, as though an unexpectedly special occasion had arisen.

'I thought you were going out at half-past two. That's why you wanted your dinner on your lap, according to you earlier.'

'Oh, I was, but I can phone. I'd rather do this if everyone wants to.'

'Go on, then.'

'Right! You know that big glass jar in the kitchen that we put pennies and tuppences in?'

'Ye-e-es,' said Mike suspiciously, visibly preparing himself to say no to something that would involve wasting money. 'What about it?'

The degree of animation in Mark was quite riveting in its unexpectedness.

'Well, here's what we ought to do, right? We go down to the sea and we park in one of those slanting sort of places under the grassy hill near the big hotel, right? And Felicity brings her roller-blades and Jack and I bring a tennis ball or a cricket ball, right? And we walk along towards the pier with Mum and Dip talking, and Dad sometimes catching the ball with Jack and me and sometimes talking to Mum and Dip, and Felicity roller-blading along and moaning about not having a friend with her, right?'

Mark stopped for breath.

We all said, 'Right?'

'Then, when we get to the pier, that's when we do the first really good thing, right?'

Mike was looking increasingly uneasy, but Felicity had moved slowly nearer and nearer to her brother as he spoke, until now she was standing right by his shoulder, totally concentrated on his face and on the scenario that he was developing.

'What's the first really good thing, Mark?' she asked eagerly.

'Hot doughnuts!' exclaimed Mark triumphantly. 'Just by the entrance to the pier there's a place that sells doughnuts, fresh-cooked, all hot and covered in sugar. If you get ten you only have to pay for eight. Really nice! Just think about it for a moment, and I know for a fact they're open on Sundays.'

'Well, I'm beginning to like the sound of this, even if no-one else is,' said Dip with enthusiasm.

'So,' said Mike hopefully, 'that's where the, err, the coins from the jar come in, we use just a few of them for the dough-nuts, right?'

'*Oh*, no! The coins are for the second really good thing.'

Mark glanced around the table to check that his audience was paying proper attention. He must have been gratified. Everyone was aching to know what the second really good thing might be.

'After we've had our doughnuts,' he continued, 'we take the

jar with all the coins into the amusement arcade on the pier and we all have lots and lots of goes on the thing where you put a coin in the slot and it pushes other coins over the edge in a sort of waterfall into the cup underneath, and those are the ones you win.'

Felicity clapped her hands delightedly at this idea, but I observed that the blood supply was draining away from poor Mike's face as quickly as it had suffused it a few moments ago.

'Now *that*,' commented Jack warmly, 'is what I call a very good idea. I remember when I was a kid I always wanted to have enough money to be able to have a go on one of those and have a lot of fun and not worry about using money that was supposed to be for something else. Let's do it, Dad!'

'The amusement arcade?' Mike managed to make the proposition sound as doomladen as if Mark had suggested a short excursion into the depths of Hades just to have a scout round for the afternoon to see if we might prefer it to heaven. 'I really don't think that's on, do you, Kath? Not really ...'

Looking at Mark's expression of proud initiation and the enthusiasm on the faces of Jack and Felicity, I decided that this was not an appropriate moment to offer automatic support to my husband.

'Why not, Mike?'

Pause.

'Why not? Why *not*? Well, surely that doesn't need spelling out, does it?'

Everyone nodded unhelpfully.

'Well,' began Mike, looking round at his audience of non-spellers, 'I mean, apart from anything else, it's not the sort of place that – I don't know – well, for a start, there'll probably be lots of kids from the school hanging around, and it feels sort of ...'

'There'll be hardly anyone else there around four o'clock, Dad,' offered Mark reassuringly. 'I've been down there at that time on a Sunday loads of times. It's nearly empty usually.'

Mike still looked very doubtful indeed.

'Mmm, but we did say we were going to save that change

for a rainy day. It seems an awful waste to just blow it on this machine thing you're talking about.'

Jack glanced towards the window.

'Quite a bit of cloud about, Dad. I reckon it'll qualify as a rainy day by the time we get down there. Come on, let's just *do* it. Sometimes it's good to do things you never do.'

Mike once more surveyed the ring of eager faces around the table, clearly teetering on the edge of reluctant agreement. But it was too much for him.

'No,' he said, shaking his head and looking strangely similar to the father at the head of the 'Leave it' procession. 'I can tell you three very good reasons why this is a bad idea.'

He ticked them off on his fingers as he addressed the staff group.

'First, it really is a terrible waste of the money that we've been putting into that jar for the last couple of months. Second, whatever Jack says, you can't really be a hundred per cent sure who'll be at a place like that and I do have my dignity to consider. Third, and most important in my view, betting on slot machines is not a good example for Christians to offer the rest of the world. There's something seedy and unpleasant about the idea that you set out to win money you haven't earned by gambling – not that I would expect us to win any money anyway. I'm quite sure those machines are fixed. Lastly, I know I wouldn't enjoy it at all and I'd be worried that I'd probably make everyone else feel miserable as well.'

'That's four things,' commented Mark morosely.

'The walk along the front and perhaps the – the, err, dough-nuts would be very nice,' continued Mike, 'but – ' he shook his head again ' – I think the arcade is out, I'm afraid.'

Felicity went sulkily back to her place. We sat in silence for a moment. I served pudding. Sadly for the plans Mike and I were formulating to inject a little extra romance into our marriage, my overwhelming inclination at this juncture was to empty the trifle bowl over my husband's head. I seriously contemplated doing exactly that for a moment – not violently, you understand, but with a calm, definite, downward movement that would extinguish his so-called dignity with squishy, sticky completeness. The briefest reflection suggested that, although this would be extremely satisfying for me, it was unlikely to bring us any nearer to our desired objective. Mark caught my eye and grimaced. I grimaced back in sympathy. Rare, to say the least. That was what decided me. We *were* going to take those coins and we *were* all going to use them in that machine on the pier.

'Mike?'

'Yes, Kathy? Beautiful trifle, by the way.'

He sounded nervous.

'Thank you, Mike.' I continued in what Jack calls my 'padded steel' voice. 'Mike, I think that Mark's idea is an excellent one in every respect, and I would like to say that the reasons you've put forward for not doing what he suggests are not just weak, but almost totally without form or substance.'

'We *are* going,' I heard Felicity whisper happily under her breath to Jack.

I leaned back in my chair, and laid both hands flat on the table.

'Let us take those reasons of yours in reverse order, shall we? Number one – you wouldn't enjoy it, and therefore you're deeply concerned that you might make the rest of us miserable. Have I got that right?'

'Err, yes, that's right, yes …'

'Okay, let's have a little vote, shall we? Hands up all those who will become so miserable because Daddy is standing just outside the amusement arcade *not* enjoying it, while we're inside enjoying it, that we won't want to do it? Come on, hands up, please! As I thought. Totally unanimous. No need to worry on that score, Mike. Second point – ' I waved a hand in his direction ' – no, please, no need to comment. Second point, it's a bad example for people who aren't Christians, right?'

'Yes, it's a – '

'Well, each of us has to make an individual decision about these things, according to our conscience, don't we?'

'Yes, but – '

'And as Christians we are free, are we not?'

'Yes, but only as long as – '

'So, we'll all use our freedom to go and play on the machines, while you stand outside and use yours to tell everybody that it's not a very good idea to go in.'

'That's one of the most ridiculous – '

'The third reason was something to do with your little charges seeing their noble headmaster doing something as crass and undignified as enjoying himself with his family. Well, how about if the rest of us all pretend to be a bit peculiar, and you tell any of your pupils who come along that we're a hostel outing you've volunteered to take charge of during the weekend, and that they must be very kind and nice to us, because we're just the same as everyone else really?'

'We could pretend that we're all looking after Mark,' suggested Jack. 'I think most people would find that perfectly feasible.'

'We could put a collar and lead on Mark,' added Felicity, 'and make him catch bits of doughnut in his mouth so people put money in a hat like busters. You'd like that, wouldn't you, Marky-boy?'

'I'll catch *you* in a minute,' said Mark, 'and when I do I'm going to tickle you until you scream. Anyway, it's buskers. Are we going, Dad?'

'Hold on,' I interrupted, 'I haven't come to the last point yet, the one about it being a waste of money. Just how much money do you think there is in that jar, Mike? Do you think there might be five pounds, or seven pounds, or even perhaps ten pounds? What do you reckon?'

Mike rolled his eyes helplessly and shrugged.

'I don't know – maybe seven or eight pounds, something like that, I should think.'

'Okay, let's say there's eight pounds, right? We're talking about a family outing – '

'Including Dip,' interposed Felicity with primly conscious virtue.

'You're talking about a family outing, including Dip – thank you very much, Twitty-Poos – for six people on a Sunday afternoon, that's going to cost no more than eight pounds for absolutely everything. Now, if that isn't good value and an excellent use of money, I'm a Dutch cobbler's toast-rack.'

'Gallon of petrol?'

Mike's feeble attempt to sound as if he was putting forward the one explosively crucial factor capable of dynamiting my entire counter-argument was pathetic, and he knew it. We were looking at a defeated man.

'So, can someone *please* tell us whether we're going or not?' implored Mark, hanging his head in mock exhaustion.

'What's a Dutch cobbler's toast-rack?'

'Dip,' Mike appealed to her as if she was the only other rational adult in the room, 'you agree with me, don't you? Tell us what you think we should do.'

'It's not my place to tell you what to do,' replied Dip seriously. 'I unequivocally refuse to comment on Mark's excellent suggestions, and if I happened to believe that it would do all of us in general and you more than most an awful lot of good to do something really silly for once, I would certainly not even consider putting forward such a point of view. You are the head of this family and you must make the final decision. Who's coming with me in my car?'

'Me!' Felicity shot her hand up as if she was in class.

'Very well, if you all feel as strongly as that, I suppose we'll go.' Mike spoke with conscious heroism, as one might speak who feels he has battled long and hard on the side of right and been forced to go down with colours flying. 'But let me publicly register the fact that I don't agree with wasting money on this machine thing, and let me also make it quite plain that I shall not be participating myself. Is that clear?'

We all nodded solemnly in response to this pompous little speech, except for Mark, who seemed to be miles away.

'Mark, are you listening? Is that clear?'

'What? Oh, yeah, sorry, Dad, I was just working out what we'll each get when we divide eight pounds by five instead of six.'

'What's a Dutch cobbler's toast-rack?' asked Felicity once more.

'It was just Mumsy trying to be clever,' explained Jack, 'it doesn't mean anything.'

She pondered briefly. 'What's clever about saying something that doesn't mean anything?'

'Nothing, Felicity,' I said, forestalling Jack, 'absolutely nothing at all. Finish your pudding, then we can clear the table and go out.'

3

Jack's semi-humorous prediction about the weather proved to be absolutely accurate. By the time Mike, Jack and I pulled into one of the many available diagonal parking spaces on the other side of the road from the white-painted facade of the Grand Hotel half an hour later, it really had become the rainy day that those coins had been set aside for. Far from putting us off, this kind of weather was a real bonus. Robinsons are rain freaks, and even Dip had been persuaded to join us on one lunatic but memorable occasion when we had all gone mad on the apparatus at the children's recreation ground in the middle of a cloudburst. This afternoon it was no more than a steady drizzle that was falling, but we were well equipped with three vast golfing umbrellas bought at a car boot sale a few weeks previously. As we locked the car and looked around for the other three I could almost taste the jam in the doughnut that, as Jack had put it in the car, had my name on it.

'There they are,' said Jack, pointing, 'the giant mushroom on top of the slope.'

Silhouetted against the slate-grey expanse of the southern sky, on the very crest of the hill, Dip, Mark and Felicity were gazing towards the distant horizon as they huddled beneath the hugest of our huge umbrellas. They did indeed look like a vast mushroom with a wide, misshapen stalk. As we watched, a small, irregularly shaped piece of the stalk detached itself, turned and began to wave wildly in our direction. Felicity had spotted us.

'Come on!'

Scorning the umbrella I offered him, Jack set off up the grassy slope at a brisk pace towards Felicity, who, with arms held wide and scarf flapping, came pirouetting down the hill like a sycamore seed-pod in the wind to meet her brother.

'Come on, Mike, let's catch him up – show him we're not in our dotage yet.'

'I suppose I might be permitted time to attend to the zip on my coat.'

I have never really understood why Mike ever bothers to sulk. The children, and anyone else who knows him well and happens to be around, always tease him unmercifully until he returns to normal. But then he never was what I would call a *real* sulker, certainly not an expert like me. In fact, he was as moderate in this area as he was in everything else that he did. He indulged in about one sulk a year, rather like my great-uncle Robert with his famous packet of cigars that lasted for a decade, but whenever he did decide to publicly advertise a grievance, his technique was certainly worth studying. One invariable aspect of this was that he started to sound a bit like Bertie Wooster's manservant, Jeeves, on those memorable occasions when the young master has refused to let him dispose of a violet cummerbund or a pair of yellow socks.

'Yes,' I replied in a similarly pompous tone, 'I think it might be possible to permit you that amount of time, and then perhaps we might both be permitted to join the rest of the company at the summit of this incline.'

'Why are you talking in that funny way?'

'Because *you* are.'

'I am not, I just said I needed time to do my coat up. That's perfectly reasonable, wouldn't you say? Anyway, what are they doing up there? I was under the impression that Mark's famous agenda commenced with a walk along the promenade, not an exhausting climb in the opposite direction against the wind to the coldest point on the seafront. I'm not going up there. I'll meet you down by the bathing huts in a minute.'

He began to trudge miserably away around the base of the hill, but stopped and turned after a few yards, as if something had occurred to him.

'Err, Kathy, who's got that money, by the way?'

Annoying as Mike was being, I couldn't help feeling a little sorry for him at this point. When you've got a good sulk on the brew it's always galling to have to engage in conversation of a practical nature. You know the sort of thing I mean. How do you maintain the arctic bleakness in the eyes and the voice dulled by cruel bruises to the spirit when you're only asking for the potatoes to be passed? It's jolly hard work. You have to put everything you've got into sounding as if a major battle has been fought and won against all the odds. Sympathetic though I may have felt, however, I wasn't going to let him get away with it.

'Pardon? I didn't catch that.'

Even worse than having to ask your practical question is being forced to repeat it. Mike sighed deeply, shudderingly, from the diaphragm, apparently goaded beyond endurance.

'I simply enquired as to who actually has the money.'

'What money's that, then?'

'The coins – you know, the money we saved in the jar on the side. The money that this afternoon is all – Kathy, don't be obtuse, you know perfectly well what I'm talking about. Who has actually brought the money?'

'Me. Obtuse little me. I've got it.'

I patted my leather shoulder-bag enticingly. On hearing the heavy, pleasantly horsey jingling sound, Mike took a step forward and extended a hand.

'Perhaps it would be better if I – '

'Oh, I think not,' I trilled, with ghastly playgroup-style brightness, 'because, you see, darling, if I let you take this money, we all know what's likely to happen, don't we? I think we might be sharing two doughnuts between all of us, and having one go each on the machine, mightn't we, and that wouldn't be much fun at all, would it, sweetheart? So – ' I reached into the bag and let a couple of handfuls of coins run through my fingers as audibly as possible. 'I'll just hang on to this until it's all been spent, shall I?'

Mike fumed silently. Not only had he failed to wrest control of the cash from me, but he had also lost sulking ground without gaining anything in exchange. Presumably in the hope of salvaging an inch or two of lost progress, he moved back into bleak and dulled mode.

'I'll see you down by the bathing huts,' he mumbled, turning his collar up and trudging away with little faltering steps, for all the world like some convalescent invalid out for his first tentative walk after a lengthy illness.

Meeting Mark at the crest of the hill after I had struggled breathlessly to the top to join the others was an unusually warming experience. More often than I cared to admit, the unwieldy burden of under-acknowledged and unfinished business between us meant that he and I found it difficult even to allow our eyes to meet. It was so good to be able to smile collusively at him as I indicated Mike's distant figure below us, dolefully wending its way towards the seafront.

'Dad's still sulking,' I explained, and I patted my shoulder-bag. 'He tried to get his hands on the money, but I put him straight.'

'Well done, Mum,' said Mark, slapping me vigorously on the back. 'Next stop the pier. Dad'll soon cheer up when he's got a couple of doughnuts inside him. Come on, Flit, let's catch Dad up and see if we can get him really mad by making him laugh. Beat you to the bottom of the hill!'

They raced away, followed at a more modest pace by Dip and me, sharing an umbrella, and Jack strolling a few yards behind us. There were tears in my eyes. I sometimes think that God must install a kind of automatically refuelled, hope-renewing unit in us when we first become parents. A pathetically small but positive interaction with my younger son had succeeded in flooding a dark place inside me with light, and, crazily, it was as though the darkness had never been there in the first place. Now, on this day, in this place, it was all right, and therefore, for all I knew, it might be all right for ever.

I half turned my head towards Dip, intending to tell her how I was feeling, but checked myself quickly. Normally I shared everything with my friend without even thinking about it, but now, remembering my crassness yesterday, and bearing in mind the things she had told me, I suddenly felt very unsure. Perhaps all the rules had changed. I studied the grass around my feet as we walked, and kept quiet.

We had gone only a few more steps when Dip, looking steadily out in the direction of the ocean as she spoke, said very seriously, 'Kathy, do you want to go on being my friend?'

I looked at her, filled with confusion and alarm. What could she possibly mean? How could there be the slightest shadow of a doubt in Dip's mind that I wanted to go on being her friend? I was conscious of my jaw muscles making my mouth open and shut like a dummy, as if somebody else was operating the mechanism. I couldn't make any words come out, however hard I tried.

'Do you want to go on being my friend, Kathy? Tell me you do.'

I shook my head in puzzlement. It was like those times when you nip out to make the tea during a television programme. Somewhere along the line I must have missed one whole chunk of dialogue. Or perhaps I was just too stupid to understand what she was talking about. It happened to me sometimes. My mind seemed so busy flying forwards that I missed things anyone else would have noticed along the way. Maybe that was dignifying it too much. Maybe I was just far more naive than I cared to admit.

A memory from childhood surfaced at that precise moment. I was almost physically rocked with the clarity of its images and the undiluted pungency of associated emotions that must have been tucked carefully away inside my brain for more than forty years.

I was seven, and it was the day before the junior school sports. Miss Crane, our skinny, bad-tempered teacher, had marched us up in a neat crocodile to the nearby cricket ground to practise the sack race and the three-legged race and all the other contests in which we were due to compete on the following day when our mummies and daddies would be there. I really was looking forward to the sports. For some reason I had a fixed notion that I would definitely be very talented at the sack race. I'd rehearsed it in my head over and over again every night as I lay in bed, until I was perfect. Perhaps even more important, I had a three-legged partner all lined up to shoot her hand in the air when we were asked who was going to be racing with who. That was good enough for me. The only fly in the ointment was Miss Crane. You never quite knew what Miss Crane was going to do or say. She was very strict. Once, in the classroom, she had sat down at the piano and started us off singing one of our favourite songs, then stopped us when we were halfway through the first verse, and made us write out the words of three whole songs because some of the girls in the desks at the back had sung the wrong, silly words to one of the tunes in music last week.

On arriving at the cricket ground Miss Crane had made us sit in a tidy row at the edge of the pitch so that she could tell us what to do. It was lovely being there instead of in the classroom. The sun was smiling, the sky was as blue as a hedge-sparrow's egg that my daddy had showed me earlier that year, and the shining green grass felt dry and soft to the touch. And it was sports day tomorrow! Sitting there in the bottle-green tops and little white shorts that we all wore for PT, I bent forward over my knees and rubbed the front of my legs excitedly with the palms of my hands.

'Right!' said Miss Crane crossly. 'Before we start, I don't want anyone trying to tell me how to do my job. Anybody *not* understand that?'

I didn't, but I wasn't going to let Miss Crane know that. Tell her how to do her job? Miss Crane, who went off like a volcano when someone spoke in quiet-reading time, and kept a piece of bamboo for caning naughty people's hands – tell her how to do her job? In any case, how would any of us have been able to tell her how to do her job? She was the teacher. We were the children. We didn't know how to be a teacher. Maybe, I thought, it was something to do with the lavatory. Her job. Big jobs – little jobs. For a while now I had been nursing an uneasy feeling that everything I didn't understand was probably connected in some way with going to the lavatory. I stared at Miss Crane in horror. Surely not! Could she, for some reason beyond my understanding, be saying that we mustn't tell her how to go to the lavatory? Was one of us likely to do that? A little silent scream rose and fell in me at the thought. It spoiled the sports for me, and then I forgot about it for forty-three years.

It felt a bit like that now with Dip – the same sort of panic because I didn't understand what was being said to me, and the same fear that there might be some underlying factor I wasn't going to like. Dip was talking – almost pleading, as if I'd just said something really alienating or unpleasant. Why should she be entreating me to go on being her friend when nothing I'd said or done could have remotely suggested that I would ever want to be anything else? I found my voice at last.

'Dip, you know – you *know* I want to be your friend. Why – ?'

'In that case, please do say what you were about to say just now, but didn't.'

The rain had stopped, making umbrellas more trouble than they were worth in the gusty wind. I lowered the big, brightly coloured one I had been holding over both of us, rolled it inexpertly and fastened the Velcro bits together.

'You know, Dip, my father would have been horrified to hear that our family has to buy new umbrellas more or less every twelve months. I'm pretty sure he had the same neat black brolly for thirty years, and it never wore out because he mostly only used it on days when it wasn't actually raining but there was a chance in a hundred that it might. I don't suppose the silly thing ever managed to get wet, come to think of it.' I tried to chortle merrily, and failing, swallowed hard. 'Err, I was about to say how marvellous it was to be slapped on the back by Mark and have him say "well done", instead of both of us glaring, or not even looking at each other properly.'

'And you stopped because . . . ?'

'Well, I'm not quite sure – after yesterday, you know, how much to say about the – the children. I don't want you to feel – '

'Kathy,' said Dip firmly, turning her head and looking at me at last, 'if I thought that the things I said yesterday were going to prevent you from talking openly to me about anything under God's sun, and especially your children, I would be more disappointed in our friendship than I can say.'

'Even if I'm – I'm moaning about them?'

'*Especially* if you're moaning about them. I want to be part of it, really part of it and them. I'm sorry I used that word yesterday, but it honestly isn't how I usually feel.' Her eyes shone with laughter suddenly. 'I have some of my most beautiful thoughts when you're complaining about your children.'

I pondered this. A compliment? Possibly, possibly not. It didn't really matter, because my friend was still my friend and she wanted to hear about my children – even if I moaned. I hadn't realized until just now what a gap would have been created in my life by the feeling that I had to watch my tongue when speaking to Dip.

Thank you.

'They've caught Dad up,' said Jack, drawing level with us. He watched for a moment then laughed out loud. 'Look, Dad's trying to chuck a tennis ball around without coming out of his sulk. Not easy. We'll have some fun when it comes to the doughnuts, won't we?'

4

By the time we reached the pier, having satisfactorily completed the ball-throwing, the Mum-and-Dip-talking and the Felicity-roller-blading-and-moaning-about-not-having-a-friend items on our agenda, our little party was together again, and Mark and Felicity were clamouring like three-year-olds for change from my magic bag with which to buy doughnuts.

Situated just inside the entrance to the pier, the hot doughnut emporium was a bright, crudely painted booth conceived and built for sunnier times. It was staffed on this wind-lashed day by one of those intensely miserable girls of about sixteen or seventeen who look as if they are the only one of their friends and contemporaries to have missed the last bus to happiness. This one had sixties-style hair waving down to her shoulders, making her face look the shape of a melted egg-timer, and a mouth heavily made up with dark lipstick. In its pouting unhappiness, it reminded me for some reason of the neck of an old plimsoll bag I'd had as a child, after you pulled the string tight.

One could hardly blame this girl for looking miserable, I thought. Finding yourself stranded beside a pile of unsold doughnuts at the end of a windswept pier on a grey and rainy day in a town that was virtually deserted must have fallen a long way short of her most cherished hopes and dreams. The arrival of six whole customers didn't seem to brighten her up much either, especially when Mark insisted that our ten doughnuts had to be hot ones, as advertised, and not taken from the sad little pile that we assumed she had prepared earlier to cope with an apocryphal rush. The poor girl's clear conviction that she was in some kind of outer waiting-room of hell must have been confirmed when Mark and Felicity poured a stream of one- and two-pence pieces on to the counter in front of her, and began to count out the amount she had asked for.

'There you are,' said Mark cheerfully, when they had completed their task, 'it's all there, but I expect you'll want to check it, won't you?'

We drew aside from the booth, leaving its proprietor to count coins in a pursed and acid silence. Unabashed, Mark held the two bags of doughnuts out towards us, one in each hand.

'Right, there are ten doughnuts and six of us, which is ten divided by six, which comes to-o-o-o one and four-sixths, which is the same as, err ...'

This would normally have been my husband's cue to interrupt with the solution to the sum. He always interrupted people when they were trying to work things out in their heads. Not this time, though. Standing a little apart from the rest of us, hunched against the cold like Captain Oates wishing he'd not been quite so generous, Mike bounced very slightly on his heels with frustration and just about managed to avoid breaking out of his sulk to tell us all that we could have one and two-thirds of a doughnut each.

'One and two-thirds,' announced Mark at last. 'I'll break 'em up.'

'No! I'll break them up,' shrilled Felicity, 'I know you. My third'll end up just a squashy bit.'

'Are you saying you don't trust me?'

'Yes,' said Felicity with feeling, quite unmoved by Mark's air of deep hurt and indignation, 'you did it with the chocolate bread the other day. Let Jack do it. Jack, you do mine.'

'Oh, you trust him, then?'

'Of course she does,' said Jack. 'Quite right, too. When I was at school they used to call me Abacus.'

Someone had to ask. I figured it might as well be me.

'Please tell us, Jack, why did they call you Abacus?'

'Because they could count on me.'

Dip snorted with laughter, but Felicity was only interested in one thing.

'What's happening about the doughnuts, then?'

'Well, if it's any use, I shall only be able to manage one,' offered Dip, slipping comfortably into her familiar peacekeeping role. 'Does that help?'

Mark, who had abandoned his attempt to appear desolated by Felicity's lack of trust when he saw that it wasn't going to work, tilted his face towards the flaking paintwork of the timbers way above our heads as he considered this new calculation.

'Okay, let's see now, nine divided by five goes one and four over, so Dip has one whole one, and we each get one and four-fifths. Tell you what – if I break one fifth off each doughnut, that'll make nine little fifths, which makes one and four-fifths altogether, and they'll do for you, Flit, won't they?'

'No!' screeched Felicity, biting like the dumbest of dumb fish. 'That's not fair! All I'll end up with is a load of crumbs that Mark's hands have been all over. An' anyway,' she continued, with the passionate earnestness that ten-year-olds so often bring to bear on trivia, 'it doesn't make sense to do it like that, because if you have nine separate four-fifths of a doughnut for four people to have one and four-fifths each out of, that means that the first person will have to have their four-fifths plus another four-fifths plus one-fifth out of the next person's four-fifths, which means that the second person has only got three-fifths, so they'll have to have another four-fifths plus two-fifths out of the next person's four-fifths, so the third person will only have two-fifths left and they'll have to have another four-fifths and three-fifths out of another four-fifths, and that means that the fourth person will – '

'Stop!' I covered my ears with my hands in self-defence. 'You're worse than the milkgirl.'

'But, Mummy!' Felicity was literally in tears. 'It's not fair if Mark does what he said. I always end up getting the rubbish 'cause I'm smallest.'

I felt the same wave of incredulous exasperation rising within me in response to what Felicity was saying as I had so often in reacting to Mark. It seemed to me all wrong that Felicity should get this worked up about nothing. The greatest tragedy she had ever faced in her life was the death of Mario. Blasted kids!

'Felicity, I really cannot understand you. We come out for the afternoon as a family to have a nice time, you've had a go on your blades, and you're about to have a go on the machines in the – the thingy – the arcade in a minute, and now you're crying your eyes out because you don't like the way the doughnuts are being shared out. It's all a complete mystery to me. It really is. I don't know why we bother at all.'

'Mum!' Mark, of all people, obviously felt my reaction was way over the top. 'She only meant about the doughnuts. Anyway, it was my fault – I was only joking, Flit. You can have a whole one and a nearly whole one, darlin'.'

I don't believe my children sometimes. This not only brought the sun out again on Felicity's tear-streaked face, but it also resulted in her throwing her arms around Mark and burying her face affectionately in his chest. Mad, all mad, the whole world mad except for me.

'We might as well have bought the cold ones,' commented

Jack, patently bored with these exchanges. 'Is there any danger that we might actually end up eating these doughnuts?'

'Yes,' I said briskly (and sacrificially, because I suddenly wanted to kill them all). 'I only want one as well, so that makes everything much easier, doesn't it?'

'Two each!' Felicity clapped her hands.

'I shan't be having any,' muttered the hitherto famously doughnut-loving Antarctic explorer from a few yards away.

Very well, if that was the way he wanted it.

'Good! Well, if Dad doesn't want any, that'll be – oh, never mind. Give Dip and me ours and take the rest away and fight it out among yourselves. We'll see you in the arcade in a minute.'

After the sacrament of distribution had been completed to the eagle-eyed satisfaction of all concerned, Dip and I followed Mark and Felicity as they set off happily towards the arcade. Jack dropped back to walk beside Mike in order to torture him by eating his two and two-thirds doughnuts as close to his father's face as he could decently get, and in the most explicitly jammy manner possible.

5

Mark had been absolutely right about the number of people we were likely to find using the amusement arcade at that time on a Sunday afternoon. Coloured lights flashed and winked, snatches of music blared out, buzzers buzzed, moving parts moved, whooshing sounds whooshed and disembodied voices repeated their robotic messages over and over again, but at first there appeared to be no human beings around to play on the seductively glittering machines. There were a few people there, though. Strolling slowly through the neon cacophony, we became conscious of shadowy figures moving through dark spaces between the little islands of light, like imps or devils in a portion of hell that had been taken over by the private sector.

We also saw a young man sitting in a windowed, circular booth at the very centre of the arcade. He was one of those heavily built young men who look as if they probably did weight-training with great enthusiasm for a couple of years, then stopped and took up eating as a hobby. After studying him discreetly for a moment, Dip whispered in my ear that his head reminded her of a pudding boiled in a cloth bag, with a face drawn in pencil on the cloth by someone who wasn't very good at art. Mercifully unaware of Dip's bizarrely unflattering assessment, this rare example of pudding-headed man registered our presence with the briefest of dull, unimpressed glances before returning to the limp, lurid-looking magazine that had been occupying his attention. On the counter before him little piles of coins of various values were arranged, presumably for customers who wanted to change larger coins or notes. He and the girl in the doughnut emporium would have walked away with equal first prize in any 'Most Bored Person in the Universe' competition. Idly, I wondered if they knew each other. Perhaps he picked her up every day at the end of the pier when he finished work, and they went off together to do something ever so exciting that had nothing to do with doughnuts or little piles of money. I hoped so. Did this young man know about God? Was he going to hell? Was he was already there ...?

'Come on, Mum – we need the dosh!'

Mark's stentorian voice, audible above the whizzing and dinging and mechanical chattering, shattered my holy reverie.

'Let's go, Kathy.' Dip took my arm. 'Time for Money-bags to swing into action again.'

'All right, and then after that shall we come back and win that fellow for the Kingdom with words and exhortations from the Lord?'

'Absolutely not – well, you can.'

'Hm!'

We found Jack, Mark and Felicity, their faces eerily illuminated by glaring artificial light, peering down into a squat, massively heavy-looking edifice of about chest height, with glass panels around the sides and top. Dip and I joined them. Through the glass, in each of six separate but identical cavities around the inside of the machine, a multi-layered pile of two-pence pieces could be seen teetering precipitately on the edge of a shiny metal cliff-face. It seemed impossible for at least some of the coins not to fall.

The idea of the game, as Mark and Felicity attempted to explain simultaneously, was for the person playing to put a two-pence piece through one of the slots in the top of the contraption in such a way that it fell flat in front of a sliding metal bar. This bar shunted the coin forward to a point where it made contact with the rearmost edge of the teetering mass of coins, giving the whole lot a little push which might, hopefully, be sufficient to dislodge some of the coins and send them rattling over the edge into a collection cup, which was directly underneath and accessible from outside. These 'winnings' could then be pocketed or reinvested by the successful player. Timing was crucial, we gathered. If a coin was placed in the slot at an ill-judged moment, it would lean against the front of the bar when it fell instead of lying flat, and would simply end up being deposited on top of the main pile of two-pence pieces. Also, Mark added, sometimes you had to speculate to accumulate, which smart saying meant that it might be worth sacrificing a few coins in order to gradually push the pile nearer to the edge, the theory being that when the 'avalanche' did occur, you would recoup your outlay and much more. Had we got the idea?

Yes, we had, and I also had the money. I carefully counted three lots of fifty coins into three pairs of eager, outstretched hands, then turned to Dip.

'Have a syndicate, shall we, Dip? Twenty-five coins each alternately into the same slot and share the winnings. What do you say?'

'Suits me,' said Dip. She indicated with her thumb. 'Err, what about Mike?'

Having obviously decided not to register his protest by staying out of the arcade, Mike had trailed in behind us and was parked against a fruit machine a short distance away. With hands pushed deep into his pockets, he had watched morosely while

Mark and Felicity struggled to convey the theory of the game, shaking his head in silent disapproval as I took the money out of my bag and placed it into the sweaty palms of my children.

'I don't somehow think he's quite in the mood for a flutter, Dip, but I suppose we ought to give him a chance.' I raised my voice. 'Mike, are you going to come and have a go? Come on – come and let your hair down for once.'

There is a mode of human progress whereby the person in motion manages to convey that, although his or her body is moving closer to you in geometrical terms, their assent to what is happening in your immediate vicinity has actually shifted to a greater distance than before they moved. This, I am sure you will agree, is no mean feat. Mike managed it admirably. Without removing his hands from his pockets, he levered his weight away from the fruit machine with his elbow, and crossed the distance between us with the tragic air of one about to identify the corpse of his best friend. I think he probably had some fairly impressive, doleful line all ready to deliver to us, but, if so, it must have gone right out of his head at the moment when he looked down into the depths of our devil's plaything and saw all those coins hanging over the edge in such mouth-watering profusion. I watched his eyes as they flicked over the money, the slots in the top, the moving bar and the collection cup underneath. He wanted to ask a question, but was wrestling inwardly with the enormous problem of how on earth one could manage to sound disapproving and curious at the same time. I decided to help him out – after all, he had missed out on the doughnuts. His fault entirely, of course, but, as a lifelong sulker myself, I knew what a struggle it would have been to maintain that level of voluntary stupidity. I took him by the arm and pointed.

'Look, Mike, that bar thing pushes the coin when it lands after you drop it in, and makes it push against all the other coins and then you win any that fall in the cup. Good, isn't it?'

Mike studied the set-up for several seconds without moving, then seemed to recollect with a start that he wasn't at all interested.

'I've already made it quite clear,' he said, drawing back, 'that I consider games of this sort to be a waste of – '

'Yyyess!'

A whoop of joy from the other side of the machine, followed by the clink and clatter of what sounded like many coins falling into a metal cup, prevented Mike from concluding a repetition of his earlier homily. Mark's exultant face appeared above the top for an instant, filled with more than Pentecostal ecstasy.

'Loads!' he cried, before ducking away again.

And, inevitably, somewhere lower down beside him, a higher, younger voice said, 'It's not fair!'

'Come on, Kathy,' said Dip, 'let's have a go.'

A part of what Mike had said at lunchtime was right. Something about this machine created or perhaps revealed a surprising depth of sheer old-fashioned greed in me. I found myself quite taken with the thought of all those coins cascading down and overflowing the little cup underneath. I pictured scooping them up in handfuls and filling my bag fatly to the brim. Utter nonsense, of course. Not only did the design of the thing mean that such a quantity of coins was unlikely ever to topple over the edge, but the largest possible win would certainly amount to less than we had brought with us.

Nevertheless, Dip and I had a lot of fun and laughed a great deal, which is worth a couple of quid in my view. Within a few minutes, we were down to about ten coins, despite an occasional dribbling win into our cup, and on the other side of the machine a selection of joyful squeals and shouts, outnumbered by disappointed groans and grunts, suggested that the others were faring in a similar manner. It was as I was about to put the first of those last ten coins into the slot that Mike, who had been standing just behind Dip and me as we played and whose Eeyore-like presence I had temporarily forgotten, poked his head between the two of us and seemed to burst with exasperation.

'Kathy, can't you *see* you're putting them in all wrong! You're missing it by about half a second each time. You've got to let it drop a split-second after the bar has pushed forward as far as it goes, so that by the time it gets back the coin's just slithering down in time to lie flat and get pushed forward when the bar moves again. Look, give me some of them – I'll show you what I mean.'

'But, I thought – '

'Just give me some!'

Three coins later, Mike, now fiercely, frowningly concentrated on the game that he had so recently scorned, greeted a mini-waterfall of coins into his cup with a loud 'Huh!' of satisfaction. Flushed with excitement, he turned triumphantly to Dip and me.

'You see! You see! I was right! It's all in judging the intervals. Once you've got that worked out it's only a matter of time before you're bound to win. Watch, Kath! Dip, watch!'

I glanced at Dip over the top of my husband's head as he bowed eagerly to his task once more, and made a face. Obviously our little syndicate had been well and truly taken over. Mike was really motoring now.

'There's a whole big batch over on the side just a hair's breadth from dropping,' he said tensely, sounding like a top surgeon faced with an unusually tricky piece of scalpel-work. 'If I can just make the next one land a little farther to the right, I should be able to ... No, not quite, let's just try again ... No, no, I can see where I'm going wrong. Oh, blast! That can't have been more than about a millimetre out. Blast! Blast! Now, come on ... Damn and blast! Kath, give me some more of those coins, will you. It's only a matter of time now.'

One by one, as they ran out of coins themselves, Jack, Mark and Felicity joined Dip and me to observe Mike's fascinating metamorphosis from sulky, moralizing non-participant to raving loony gambler. Every now and then he would glance over his shoulder with bright, staring eyes, comment fleetingly on how close he was to a big win, then plunge every ounce of himself and his attention back into the fray.

'Don't worry,' whispered Dip, 'he'll have lost it all in a minute and then he'll turn back into a human being again.'

It was a reasonable prediction, but wrong. Just as my stock of two-pence pieces was on the point of running out, there was a loud clattering of coins, and Mike threw his arms up with a wild yell of triumph. Unfortunately, in the excitement of the moment, one of his feet must have slipped from under him, because he fell to the side, ending up with his left hand supporting his weight on the floor, and the other clutching the collection cup, which was in the process of overflowing with his winnings. Still filled with the joy of success, he pulled himself up until, with his face not only level with the cup but very nearly in it, he was able to study the fruits of his labours with chuckling satisfaction.

At this point I became hazily aware that our small group of observers had increased by three or four persons. Looking round and focusing on the faces of the newcomers, I recognized, with a little shock of misgiving, that at least two of these short-haired, respectable-looking men were leading lights in the big House Church that met in a disused factory on the industrial estate near our home. One of them, a man who always insisted on referring to himself as Peter J. Lampert, I knew reasonably well from the monthly inter-church meetings that we'd had through the previous year. He was nice, but very holy.

'Peter J.!' I said conversationally, trying to sound as if we had met in Debenham's, or the post office queue. 'What are you doing here?'

Peter J. seemed reluctant to answer at first. He cleared his throat.

'We've been coming down every other Sunday over the last couple of months,' he said, 'to pray against the evil influence that these tools of Mammon can undoubtedly have, especially on young children. We think that, err, Christians should be very aware of the dangers of these places ...'

His words tailed off, and I followed his eyes as they fixed incredulously once more on the figure of my husband, the only one of us who had not wanted to come into the arcade in the first place, down on his knees, cackling and drooling into a sea of two-pence pieces, apparently offering grovelling worship in the presence of his family at the altar of one of those tools of Mammon that can undoubtedly exert an evil influence – especially on young children.

three

Monday

1

'Ah, there you are, come along in. Go on through and sit down, and I'll make us a drink. Coffee okay? I've only got to pour it out.'

'Oh, yes, thanks, Simon.'

'You too, Kathy?'

'Lovely, yes, thanks.'

Somewhat chastened by his fall from grace in the amusement arcade on Sunday afternoon, Mike had nevertheless remembered to phone Simon Davenport early on Monday morning to arrange for a discussion at the earliest opportunity about Dip's communion, and Simon had invited us to his house that evening.

I felt quite nervous as Mike and I set out to drive to the other side of town for this important interview. It wasn't that I didn't like or respect Simon. Over several years of belonging to his housegroup I had become quite fond of him, and I really did admire his dogged adherence to the straight and narrow as far as faith and behaviour were concerned. Simon was totally dependable. He just – well, how can I put it? He wasn't the sort of person you would want to get drunk with. Not that I do habitually get drunk with people, or on my own for that matter, it's just that I wouldn't have wanted it to be Simon I got drunk with if I did. Something like that. Oh, dear! God understands what I mean.

Simon certainly had reservations about me. A flicker of

wariness passed across his darkly handsome, oddly not quite attractive features almost every time I started to speak during group discussions. This chronic wariness probably dated from the very first housegroup that Mike and I attended. At the time I was going through yet another of my periodical bouts of soul-sickness, this time in connection with what people actually meant when they talked about experiencing God. After a Bible study on the seventh chapter of Romans, or something like that, poor unsuspecting Simon began the discussion by enthusing in statutory fashion about how wonderful it was to experience God working in our lives. As far as I can remember, the conversation that followed went roughly like this. (Doris, Stanley and Janet were also members of the group at the time.)

ME: Excuse me, could I ask a question?

SIMON: (PROBABLY PLEASED TO FIND A NEWCOMER SO KEEN TO SEEK KNOWLEDGE) Yes, of course, fire away.

ME: Well, when you say it's wonderful, what exactly do you mean?

SIMON: (AFTER A PAUSE) What do you mean – what exactly do I mean?

ME: Well, how does it feel?

SIMON: How does it feel?

ME: Yes, how does it feel?

SIMON: How does what feel?

ME: The wonderfulness of God working in your life – how does it feel?

SIMON: (SMILING AND SHRUGGING AFTER ANOTHER SHORT FROWNING PAUSE) It just feels like God working in your life. I'm sorry, I'm afraid I don't quite understand what you're asking.

ME: All right, sorry, perhaps I didn't put it very well. What I'm saying is, if it really is wonderful when God works in your life, you must perceive the wonderfulness somehow – unless you guess it or pretend it or something. Agreed?

SIMON: (WARILY – IT MUST HAVE BEGUN HERE!) Mmmm ...

ME: Well, what is that experience of perceiving actually like? What happens? Which emotions do you feel? What goes on?

SIMON: (MILDLY ANNOYED BUT STAYING REASONABLY PATIENT) Look, Kathy – it is Kathy, isn't it?

ME: Kathy, yes, that's right.

SIMON: (AFTER A LITTLE INTERNAL REGROUPING) Kathy, it's a spiritual thing. When God works in your life you appreciate the wonder of his presence and what he's doing in a spiritual way – on a spiritual level.

ME: Oh, I see.

SIMON: Good, now let's –

ME: So, how does that feel?

SIMON: (TEETH GRITTED IN A CHARITABLE SORT OF WAY) It's not a matter of feelings, it's a matter of faith.

ME: I see, so you don't feel anything when God works in your life?

MIKE: Kath, let's just –

DORIS: (REGURGITATING A CHUNK OF UNDIGESTED TEACHING) Feelings are unreliable, you see.

SIMON: (LOOKING RELIEVED) Yes, thank you, Doris. That's right – feelings can be very unreliable. We perceive what God is doing through the eyes of faith.

ME: So, we should ignore feelings? How *are* we aware of God, then?

SIMON: Look, we've got a lot to get through, Kathy, so could we just –

STANLEY: (LEANING FORWARD AND INTERRUPTING) A few years ago our car went wrong – didn't it, Janet?

JANET: Yes, it did. On a Monday.

STANLEY: And we were due to drive up to our daughter's in Stafford on the Tuesday. So, we took the car –

JANET: She was expecting the next month and feeling poorly, you see. It was her second and she'd already had trouble with –

STANLEY: So we took the car into the garage, and the man said it was going to cost a hundred and fifty pounds to put right. Well, we didn't have a hundred and fifty pounds, so we left the car there, and decided to call our daughter in the morning to say we weren't able to go. But in the morning a cheque came in the post that was a repayment of something or other, and it was for exactly a hundred and fifty pounds. (LEANING BACK TRIUMPHANTLY) So, there you are.

ME: There we are. Where are we? What do you mean?

STANLEY: Well, whenever anyone asks us why we believe in God we tell them about when he gave us the money for the car that day.

ME: Okay, so that sort of thing happening to you – the coincidence of the money coming – that's the way you see God moving in your life? But you didn't actually encounter *him* as such?

JANET: (SLIGHTLY TARTLY, AFTER A BRIEF UPROAR CAUSED BY MY USE OF THE WORD 'COINCIDENCE') It wasn't a coincidence. It was God supplying our needs. That's how we encountered him and seeing as how you're going on about feelings so much, we *felt* very grateful to him.

MIKE: Kathy, don't you think – ?

ME: (COURTING DEATH) Right – so, the times when you've urgently needed money and it *hasn't* come, you've felt just as grateful, have you, because he's wise enough to know that it would be the wrong thing for you to have and he's graciously not allowed it? (SENSING I'VE GOT A BIT CARRIED AWAY) Look, I don't mean that I don't think God gave you that money when you needed it. I'm sure he did, and I'm glad he did. All I'm asking is – what is this thing we call a relationship with Jesus based on? Do we really only experience God in the form of coincidences – sorry, occasions when our needs are met and we assume it must be God – or do we just know by faith that he's there because he says he is. Or is there something else? Is he like an absent father who loves us, but only ever sends presents in the post and never phones, or is it possible to meet him in some other way?

DORIS: (BRAVELY BUT VAGUELY) We meet him in the scriptures.

ME: Have you met him in the scriptures?

DORIS: (SLIGHTLY UNCERTAINLY) Well, yes ...

ME: And how does that feel?

DORIS: (HELPLESSLY) Errrm, sort of warmish.

ME: Aaah! (TO SIMON) So, perhaps that's what you meant when you said that it's wonderful when God works in your life. You meant it feels sort of warmish – is that what you meant?

SIMON: We've wasted enough time on this already ...

No wonder the poor bloke became wary. I certainly would have done. And how was he going to react now, when I told him that I believed God was telling us to do something quite unlike anything the group had done before? As we made our way through to the big, comfortable sitting-room where our weekly meetings were usually held, I was still mentally rehearsing my account of what had happened and sternly instructing myself to avoid being flippant at all costs. Unfortunately, something about Simon's dead straight earnestness brought out the very worst in me as far as that sort of thing was concerned, and I knew he hated it.

I was more than a little disconcerted to find another person already firmly ensconced in one of the armchairs when we entered the room, especially when I saw who it was. I could tell from the anxious glance Mike threw in my direction that he was no more thrilled than I was. He knew only too well how I was likely to react.

Eileen Carter was another member of our housegroup. Single, devout and in her early forties, she seemed to have suffered a partial arrest of development around the age of thirteen as far as clothes, hair and figure were concerned. Today she was wearing woollen stockings, a straight plaid kilt with a big ornamental safety-pin attached to one side, and one of those stiff blouses that make chain-mail look like tissue paper. Eileen had the odd habit of addressing people by their full Christian names, despite everyone else using the shortened forms. Over the years she had probably brought me as near to committing physical violence as anyone I'd met – except Mark, of course, and occasionally Mike, but then, I loved Mark and Mike, and I did *not* love Eileen Carter. I was not proud of this. An ongoing desire to inflict injury on a fellow Christian fell more than a tad short of New Testament teaching in the area of loving your brothers and sisters. Eileen had been at the top of my prayer list for a very long time, and seemed likely to remain there for the foreseeable future or until God enabled some radical change to take place in my attitude to her. I certainly never suspected for one moment that such a change was planned for this very evening.

'Eileen!' said Mike brightly, as we plumped down side by side on the sofa, 'we didn't expect to see you here. How are you?'

Eileen closed her eyes, smiled without parting her lips and inclined her head gently.

'I'm *fine*, Michael, really fine.' She sounded like a suffering nun with TB in one of those bad films they made in the fifties. I braced myself as she turned her ministering gaze on me. 'Katherine, Simon asked me to come along this evening. I gather you're having a little bit of a valley experience, and it might need some thinking and praying through.'

I drew a deep breath in through my nose and released it again before answering. I wanted to be extremely rude, but this whole thing was for Dip, not for me. I must keep a grip on myself.

'Well, actually, Eileen, it's not me who's going through the, err, valley experience.'

Eileen looked at me from under her brows with knowing eyes. I knew that look. Eileen was quite sure that it *was* me who was going through this hypothetical blasted valley, and, in any case, she would be very unwilling to admit that she had no idea what it was all about. *Why* had Simon asked her to be here? Apart from anything else, when she stared at me like that I usually overreacted and ended up sounding so cross that everyone assumed she must have touched the proverbial raw spot. I controlled myself womanfully.

'Eileen, it honestly isn't me we've come round to talk about, and it really is not a little problem. It's a very, very big one, and it's been going on for an awful long time. Simon didn't tell you why we wanted to speak to him?'

'God only deals in big solutions,' said Eileen, twinkling her eyes as she leaned forward and linked her fingers around her knees, 'not big problems.'

Simon came in with a tray of drinks and biscuits at that moment, thank heavens. I was conscious that any peace and good humour I'd arrived with was beginning to drain out at the soles of my boots.

'I hope you thought it was a good idea to ask Eileen to join us,' said our host, smiling brightly in transparent and genuine confidence that we would consider it an excellent notion, 'only she does have quite an insight into these matters, as you know. I was sure we'd all value her input.'

'Oh, yes,' fibbed Mike shamelessly, 'very good idea. Thanks for sparing the time, Eileen.'

In response to pressure from the side of Mike's foot against mine, I did make a valiant effort to express agreement with what he'd said, but the words wouldn't pass through some kind of truth-filtering block in my oesophagus. The elongated, strangled squeak that actually emerged from my mouth followed roughly the same verbal tune as Mike's sentence, but it can't have been very convincing.

'Mmmm ...'

I cleared my throat and forced a positive expression on to my face.

'All I've said to Eileen,' continued Simon, adding one small sugar to his coffee and stirring it as he spoke, 'is more or less what you've told me, that there is a serious problem with – well, you haven't yet said who it is who actually has the problem – and you feel a strong conviction that setting up some kind of special meeting would be very helpful to – to the person concerned. Is that about right, so far as it goes?'

I nodded, then hesitated, unwilling for a moment to lay Dip's inner life out for Eileen to stare at. No, I thought, get on with it, you silly idiot. If there was going to be a service Eileen was bound to be there for it anyway, so it didn't make much difference.

'Yes, that's right, Simon. And the person we're talking about is Dip.' I couldn't help noticing out of the corner of my eye that Eileen was now wearing one of those seraphic 'I knew who it was going to be all the time' smiles on her face, but I did my best to block it out. 'It began when she came round on Saturday. She'd already told me she had something important to say, but I'm afraid I was too busy talking and complaining myself to really pay attention ...'

Simon listened attentively and without interruption to my description of the phone call with Dip, and our conversation in her kitchen afterwards. When I had finished speaking there was silence for a second or two, then Eileen gathered herself together as if about to comment, but was mercifully cut off in mid-gather by Simon raising his hand in a slight but unusually authoritative gesture before breaking the silence himself.

'Thank you very much, Kathy, for passing all that on to us. I can't tell you how sad I am that Dip has had to carry such a terrible burden all on her own for so long. It was really brave of her to let you share it with the housegroup. Please tell her I said that, will you?'

The big brown eyes were moist with sincerity. Good old Simon! I warmed to him as never before. He might be a stuffy old trout some of the time, but his heart was in the right place.

'Thank you,' I said foolishly, sounding like a proud mother whose child has been awarded a good-work certificate. 'Yes – yes, of course I will.'

'And you feel, do you,' went on Simon, 'that a little communion service held here on one of our group nights might be helpful?'

'I think it's more than that, Simon,' put in Mike, bless him. 'It's not just a feeling, you see. Kathy's quite sure God is telling her that Dip would benefit enormously from something like that. She's usually right about these things, and I think we should do it. In fact, I think ideally we'd do it this Thursday.'

A warm wave of gratitude and a chill wave of uncertainty passed through me pretty well simultaneously as Mike spoke. It was very nice of him to say that, but for goodness sake! It all sounded so pompous and presumptuous and toe-curlingly embarrassing. How could God possibly be telling *me* anything? My mind went back to that first housegroup and my obsessionally incessant questioning about how God actually communicates with men and women. Here, if Simon had been a man with less virtue and more imagination, was an ideal opportunity to get a bit of his own back. *How* had I heard so clearly from God? What was I really talking about? Suddenly I wanted to say it was all a mistake and run home and hide (not for the first time) in the bottom of our big wardrobe, where darkness was more welcome and desirable than Narnia. It had all been in my mind – wishful thinking because I so wanted something to happen for Dip. It was just so much rubbish – all of it. God, the church, prayer, worship and all the rest of the clutter we'd invented or dragged together to make existence on this planet half bearable.

'What exactly would you see as being Elizabeth's role in this special communion service?'

Eileen's forehead was wrinkled with frowning concern. It should have made me feel worse, but as a matter of interest it didn't. Considering how lost and panic-stricken I had felt only a second ago, it seemed to make my mind very clear – oddly clear.

'Dip gave her aborted child a name,' I said calmly. 'She called him David. I think what we need to do is leave a gap somewhere in the service, just before we actually take communion perhaps, so that God can do anything he likes about Dip and David, and Dip can respond to it. We can't plan it any more than that. We'll just have to – to trust.'

Eileen pursed her lips judiciously.

'There are warnings in scripture,' she said slowly, with a side-ways look at Simon, 'about the dangers of dabbling in anything that might be said to smack of communication with the dead. I think we should be cautious. Perhaps the sensible way forward would be for some of us to gather around Elizabeth at the next meeting and simply pray that she will find peace of mind.'

'Perhaps the sensible way forward would be to take a risk,' offered my sweety-pie of a risk-detesting husband. 'If the Holy Spirit intends to do something that will help Dip, I'd rather find out what it was than rush around filling up all the gaps with stuff we vaguely hope is a good idea – don't you agree?'

'Katherine,' queried Eileen, 'may I ask exactly how the Lord spoke to you about these things?'

I sighed. I was going to have to go through this after all, just as I thought I'd managed to avoid it.

'All right, but first of all, please, please believe me when I say I'm not claiming that there's anything special about me at all. If I was God I'd choose someone much better and more sensible and consistent and non-judgmental than me if I was going to say something through them – I honestly would. And I'd be the first to say that I could be totally deluded. Of course I could.' I paused, then said, in the interests of truth, 'But I don't happen to think I am. And I will try to explain what happens. The only problem with trying to describe this sort of thing in words is that it's like – it's like trying to wrap a cat in sheets of tissue-paper. Cats keep changing shape because they're alive, and they strongly object to being wrapped in tissue-paper, and they do their very best to *avoid* being wrapped in tissue-paper. Do you know what I mean?'

Eileen stared uncomprehendingly at me. Oh, dear, not a lot of cat-wrapping in this one's background, I thought. Let's try another angle. I thought for a moment, then went on.

'Eileen, you know how, when you're a child, you don't just believe the things grown-ups tell you – you *know* them. They are *facts*. And they go on being facts even when you've grown up yourself and you find that they weren't really true.'

I noticed that, as well as still looking blank, Eileen had moved her hand slightly so that her fingertips were just touching the Bible on her lap. It was as if she was saying, 'Tell me which verse you base this on, so that I feel safe enough to travel with you, and then it won't matter if I don't understand what you're talking about.'

Burying my head in my hand, I searched for a way to clarify what I was saying.

'Look,' I said, surfacing, 'I'm sure you'll think what I just said sounds silly, and I don't blame you, so I'll give you an example of what I mean. In my head – in my more or less sensible grown-up head – I know perfectly well that it's possible to go and buy a new bicycle pump, right? It's simple. All I have to do is just go up to the bike shop and say what I want and they'll give it to me and I'll pay for it and that's that. I've got a brand new pump. Easy. But the child inside me, the child who grew up in a house where, for years and years, there was hardly enough money to buy food for everyone to live on, let alone any spare money, knows that actually it's not that simple. That child knows for a fact that bicycle pumps come approximately five thousand, nine hundred and fifty-seventh on the list of priorities that need to be bought with the money that is available, and that she's jolly well got to mend the old one, or find the coloured bendy bit that got lost in the garage, or borrow one from the boy next door, because you simply *do not buy new pumps, my girl*! Even now, if I had to go and buy a pump, something in me would say that it just doesn't make sense. Foolish? Course it is, but it's true.'

I had another thought, and rattled on.

'You just think, Eileen, what that could mean to someone who, let's say, was sexually abused when she was little. Uncle Bob next door used to tell her that the things he made her do were perfectly all right, and even if she felt a little uneasy about what was going on, she believed him because he was one of the big people who know things. Then, as she grows up, she begins to realize that what happened was a long way from being all right, and she has to look back at all those memories from years ago and see them for what they were. One great big problem for her, though, is that the little girl who believed what Uncle Bob told her still believes – she *knows* – that it was perfectly all right, and she has an awful long journey to make in her head and her feelings before those two true and opposite facts can come together and make sense. Are you with me?'

She was with me all right, but neither of us were quite in the place where I had thought we were. All my annoyance and impatience with Eileen had melted away to be replaced with a sort of shocked compassion as I read on that crumpled, thirteen-year-old face, like the headline on one of those old yellowed newspapers you find under the floorboards, the clear message that there had once been an Uncle Bob in her life, and that she had never told a living soul about it. If I hadn't already been sitting down I would have gone weak at the knees. What was going on? I hadn't come here for this. I hadn't even finished making my point yet. Mike and Simon appeared to be oblivious to what was happening.

'So, Eileen,' I continued, but with a sort of croaking gentleness that must have been utterly bewildering in contrast with the slightly combative tone I had just been using, 'when I was speaking to Dip on the phone, I was suddenly filled up with that same sort of childlike knowing, as though it had always been there, and the thing I knew was that we ought to – you know, have a communion service and help Dip to overcome the past. But, don't you think – '

I did the previously unthinkable. Moving across to Eileen's chair I sat on the arm so that I could take one of her hands in both of mine. I didn't know where I was going now, but as I'd chickened out and surrendered the navigation to someone else it didn't seem to matter too much.

'Eileen, don't you think it's marvellous that God might have a good plan for Dip, or anybody, for that matter, to sort out some of the bad things that have happened to us in our lives?'

Eileen nodded but said nothing. She knew and I knew that if she opened her mouth at this moment, more than a quarter of a century's worth of grief would demand expression, and it certainly couldn't be allowed to happen in front of two men. I looked at Mike, wide-eyed and with his jaw resting gently in his lap. We were pretty well practised in the giving and interpretation of looks. He came to with a start, picked his jaw up and addressed Simon.

'Err, Simon, I've got an idea that Kath and Eileen want to spend a little bit of time together, if that's all right. Perhaps we could just pop into the other room and, err, do some more talking about this communion – or something.'

Simon blinked and wondered, but they left, and for the next half hour I listened, and said very little. The things that sad little

Eileen managed to tell me during those thirty minutes do not need to be recorded here, but it is a matter of heavenly record that, between us, we got through enough tissue to wrap many, many cats.

2

Driving home afterwards, I told Mike a little about Eileen, including my own shame as I now faced the fact that I had determinedly kept her out of my life, other than for the unavoidable hour or two of contact on Thursday evenings. That would have to change. He nodded agreement and told me in return that, during the period of their joint banishment to the grease-free Davenport kitchen, Simon had been unexpectedly enthusiastic about the idea of the communion, which was to happen this coming Thursday, as we had hoped.

'When I say it was unexpected, Kath, I mean I thought he would be a lot more cautious than he was, and need to go and discuss it with the vicar or something before making a final decision, but he didn't. He just said he thought we should really go for it. He opened up quite a bit – saying how he's always longed to see God really healing hurt people, people whose hearts have been broken, people like Eileen – and Dip, of course. And how useless he's felt sometimes because people don't really move on much. He's a bit like me, old Simon, pretty well controlled most of the time. It was good to see a spot of passion in him.'

As we drove on without speaking for a minute or two, a steady rain was beginning to fall. I've always loved being the passenger in a car at night when the heavens are opening outside, feeling protected and cosy and sleepy while someone else takes responsibility.

'Mike,' I said drowsily.

'Yes, Kath?'

'Do you think our car is the only one in the world that does animal impressions?'

'I beg your pardon!'

'Well, for a start, there's the cats' paws.'

Flapping a lazy hand, I pointed out hundreds of little paw-marks on the windscreen made by heavy drops of rain flattened as we drove against the wind.

'Now close your eyes and tell me if the noise our worn out old wipers make on the glass isn't just like sea-lions at feeding time.'

'I think I'll pass on closing my eyes, if that's all right with you,' he said, 'otherwise we shall have the ultimate spiritual experience a bit before our time, but you're right. Perhaps we should get it a variety agent.'

'P'raps it'll do well on one of those talent shows like – *Cars in Their Eyes*.'

'Not if it tells jokes like that, it won't.'

'You know, you're a funny bloke, Mike.'

'Am I?'

'Yes, I mean, how can you go from sulking like you did yesterday, to being as grown-up and in-charge as you are at school and like you were tonight?'

'I suppose it's not that different from the sort of people who are – let's say – grumpy and awkward one minute, and loyal and loving the next, do you think?'

I pinched his arm.

'We're lucky to have each other, aren't we, Mike?'

'Well, *you* are – lucky to have me, that is. You really fell on your feet there, didn't you? Yes, we are, Kath, we're very lucky. We must try to remember that when our next argument starts.'

'Perhaps we'll never have another argument.'

'Perhaps pigs will fly.'

'For all you know there's an aircraft somewhere that does a very good pig impression, and – '

'Kathy.'

'Yes?'

'Why don't you just let yourself doze off – I'll wake you when we get home.'

I nestled even more closely into his shoulder.

'Mmmmallright …'

four

Tuesday

1

I woke on Tuesday remembering that I still hadn't done anything about Joscelyn. I felt really bad about the things I'd said to her on that stinky morning, and it was no use trying to tell myself there had been some lofty prophetic content in the words that I had snapped out. I did actually have a go at convincing myself that there might have been, but it was no good. In some theologically sound sense, I was on my own with this. My little tantrum had been born out of pure impatience and irritability, and I needed to do something about it before the housegroup got together on Thursday for Dip's special meeting.

People who are unfortunate enough to be constructed like me are very good at allowing this sort of thing to hang over every aspect of ordinary existence like the darkest of dark clouds. This has a ridiculously devastating effect on one's sense of perspective. Eternal night falls, like winter in the Arctic Circle. There are no scraps of enjoyable melancholy to be grabbed and indulged in, just sick despair arising from the dismal certainty that there is only one possible remedy, namely to actually do the thing that is causing the despair in the first place. And, of course, the longer you delay the dreadful deed, the more difficult it is to do.

In the end I decided to create an extra stepping-stone for myself by phoning Joscelyn to suggest we meet for coffee in town on Wednesday, but translating even that decision into action was another matter. I spent most of Monday morning after Felicity had gone to school dithering uselessly around the house, hungrily seeking any excuse to put off making the call. I was so afraid that John would answer it and tell me off for upsetting his wife, or that Joscelyn would pick up the phone and announce that she had cancelled all her meetings and magazine-writing commitments because her faith was in rags since hearing from me.

At midday, clean out of excuses, I made myself sit by the phone and pray a little prayer. God must have forgiven me for using him as another aid to procrastination, because immediately after finishing I picked up the phone and dialled Joscelyn's number. Drumming my fingertips nervously on the table beside me, I counted the ringing-tones, just as I had done when I called Dip on the Saturday, telling myself that, this time, I would be generous enough to let it ring ten times before giving up. The silence followed by a buzz followed by a click that you hear when an answering machine is turning itself on usually annoys me intensely – I *hate* speaking to answering machines, leaving a recorded message in response to a recorded message – but on this occasion I punched the air with my free hand like Mark does when his football team scores.

'This is the home of Joscelyn and John Wayne,' announced Joscelyn's resonantly confident, disembodied voice – recorded before Saturday, no doubt, I thought guiltily. 'We are not here to take your call at the moment, but we are very grateful to you for taking the trouble to ring us. Please leave a message and your name and number after the long tone, and we will look forward to speaking to you later. Thank you.'

After a series of short beeps the long tone invited me to say something. I stumbled into speech.

'Ah, err, Joscelyn – or John – this is Kathy Robinson here with a message for Joscelyn – I just wondered if we could possibly meet for coffee tomorrow, Joscelyn – Wednesday, I mean, at Wickham's in town around ten-thirty, just to – well, to talk.' Cowardice struck. 'Don't bother phoning back if you can make it. I'll just assume you'll be there. Bye.'

I put the phone down and wooshed with relief. At least I'd *done* something about it now, and nothing else need happen until tomorrow. My philosophy in these matters tends to be mad but effective. The world might end before tomorrow, I told myself, or I might develop a serious illness that will mean I can't be there on Wednesday and the Waynes will have to feel sorry for me, or perhaps John will be attacked and eaten by a lion on his way home from work this afternoon and Joscelyn will have to rearrange our date, or – well, anything might happen. I hummed with the relief of it all as I headed upstairs to make my bed. I was still humming as I answered the phone in the bedroom a couple of minutes later. Why did it never occur to me that it could be Joscelyn returning my call?

'Hello, could I speak to Kathy, please?'

'Joscelyn – '

'Kathy, I'm so sorry I didn't answer your call just now, but I was upstairs – if you know what I mean – and by the time I got down the thing had come on and you'd finished your message. I'm really glad you've called actually, because there is something I have been very much wanting to say to you.'

Joscelyn's voice wasn't at all subdued today. On the contrary, she sounded more confident and buoyant than ever. She certainly didn't give the impression of being cross or resentful. Perhaps she was going to make what they called an assertive response to my attack on her. Best for me to eat a good slice of humble pie before she said anything else, I decided.

'Well, I wanted to say something to you as well, Joscelyn, about the stuff I came out with on the phone on Saturday morning. I had just been through an awful night, but I know that's no excuse, and I really am most terribly – '

'But that's exactly what I wanted to talk to you about, Kathy!'

Oh dear.

'Well, I don't blame you, Joscelyn, I really don't. Please say whatever you want.'

I braced myself.

'Kathy, I want to thank you from the bottom of my heart.'

'To *thank me*?'

'Yes, to thank you for just being so obedient.'

'Being so – ?'

'Thank you, Kathy, for being obedient to God when he told you to say those things to me.'

'But it wasn't – '

'I have to confess that at first I did feel just a little bit upset, but then I realized that, through you, I had actually been given something very special indeed. You were right in what you said, Kathy, and I applaud your courage in being so honest. Apart from anything else, those words you spoke to me have been an enormous inspiration on the professional level. I'm just in the process of finishing a magazine article entitled "Sin and forgiveness – the simple heart of the gospel", and when I do my next After-dinner in a month or so, I shall be placing the story of that phone call of ours at an absolutely central point in my talk – assuming you have no objection of course, Kathy.'

'I don't – '

'I knew you wouldn't. I told John you wouldn't. Kathy, you do know what that phone call has done, don't you?'

Uh-oh! The last nail in the coffin of my lingering hope that God might really have spoken through me on that piscine morning was about to be driven in.

'What's that then, Joscelyn?' I asked resignedly.

'Well, I honestly do feel that through your words God has totally transformed me in the most *amazing* way ...'

2

Later that day, when Mike came home from school, I sat him down at the kitchen table, poured him a cup of tea and told him about my conversation with Joscelyn.

'The whole thing worries me a bit, Mike,' I said. 'I mean, you can bet your life that by the time that Saturday morning telephone conversation gets into one of Joscelyn's talks, it's not going to bear much resemblance to what was actually said. Just think how embarrassing it would be if I went along and crept in at the back one day and heard my side of the conversation coming out with its spiritual content cubed. I feel as if I'm just aiding and abetting her in being deluded and passing on her delusions to everybody else. That can't be right, can it, surely?'

Mike smiled and shook his head.

'I don't think you ought to worry yourself about it too much, Kath. I mean – nothing's really altered, has it? From what you say, Joscelyn feels that her life has been completely changed by the realization that her life has not, in fact, been completely changed on all those occasions when she thought it was completely changed, and that'll last for a while until the next thing comes along, and then her life will be – well, it'll be completely changed again. You've just been part of the pattern for a while, that's all. If it comes to that, I suppose we all behave in patterns, don't we? Joscelyn's is easier to identify than most, that's the only difference. From what I've seen, hardly anybody manages to break out of being what they are in any radical sort of way – always assuming that breaking out is a good idea in the first place. Maybe it isn't.'

I considered this for a moment, absent-mindedly holding my ginger biscuit in my tea for so long that the submerged section melted and disappeared into the depths of the cup.

'Damn! I mean blast! I mean blow!' I fished for bits of soggy biscuit with my spoon as I went on. 'Isn't that a bit of a depressing outlook for Christians, though, Mike? I thought we were supposed to believe that following Jesus changes us – renewing of the inner man, new creature in Christ, and all that stuff. What about all that?' Inspiration struck. 'Paul! What about Paul?'

'What about Paul?'

'Well, he was definitely changed, wasn't he? One minute he's single-mindedly hunting down Christians and killing them, the next minute there's a flash of light, he has his Damascus thing, and not only is he preaching Christ to the gentiles in most of the known world, but he's writing half the New Testament in his spare time without benefit of a word processor. If that isn't a change I'd like to know what is.'

Mike placidly stirred his second cup of tea and dunked a biscuit for precisely the correct length of time.

'Paul, eh? Now there, as it happens, you've chosen an excellent example of what I'm trying to say, and the clue to what I mean is in the way you described Paul before he was converted.'

'It is?'

'Well, what did you call him?'

'Paul?'

You have to stand up to these junior teachers with their infernal focused questioning, you know. Mike ploughed on patiently.

'How did you describe Paul before he was a Christian?'

'I dunno – can't remember. I said he was determined, didn't I?'

'No, what you actually said was that he was single-minded. You said that he single-mindedly hunted down Christians and murdered them, right?'

'Right ...'

'Right, well, now tell me how he set about preaching Christ to the gentiles and all the other things he did.'

I had a distinct feeling that if I played my cards right I was about to be awarded a gold star and a large red tick for good work in the classroom.

'He did it single-mindedly?'

'That's it – exactly! Good. Paul didn't stop being Paul. He just became the best possible version of himself that God was able to make him. King David's another good example – no holds barred, whether it was sin or obedience to God. He was extravagant in everything. Never stopped being the kind of person he was, but the things he applied it to were vastly different. I reckon that for most of us it's actually a sort of spiral thing, isn't it?'

'What's a sort of spiral thing?'

'Christian progress. We move round and round in circles, but, all things being equal, we're also moving upwards, perhaps without even realizing it – see what I mean?'

I nodded slowly.

'Or downwards, presumably.'

'Well, yes, some of us.'

'A bit like those swing-ball games where two of you hit a tennis-ball around on the end of a string trying to make it go up or down, and the winner's the one who gets to the top or the bottom first?'

'Err, yes, perhaps.'

'Right, so, as you are moving round your own idiosyncratic Mike Robinson-type circles – let's say, for instance, in our relationship – there should be lots of minor improvements and adjustments going on as you allow God to direct you upward into being the best possible *you* in relation to me?'

'Precisely! You've got it.'

'A positive accretion, as it were?'

He was really impressed with that. Another gold star, I thought, or possibly even a certificate of merit.

'Well, yes, Kathy, that's a very good way of putting it.'

So innocently, schoolmasterishly happy did Mike appear with the fact that the two of us were having what he fondly imagined to be an intelligent, grown-up discussion without arguing, that I almost let him off the next bit of the conversation – only almost, though.

'Well, can I put in a formal application for a special bit of accretion on the next go round, a few minor improvements and adjustments – only little ones?'

Mike looked as wary as he always did when I forced him to descend from the general to the particular.

'What sort of, err, special bit of accretion were you thinking of?'

'It's to do with all this business of us being a bit more – you, know – more romantic. I sometimes wish ...'

Mike was looking worried now. I deliberately waited for him to ask me what it was that I sometimes wished, but I could have waited until the millennium. He obviously wasn't going to.

'Come on, Mike, ask me what it is that I sometimes wish.'

'What do you sometimes wish, Kath?'

'Well, you know how you talk to Felicity – I've often wished that you could bring yourself to call me the same as you call her.'

Pause.

'You want me to call you Felicity?'

I suppose he felt he owed it to me after my deliberately dumb 'Paul' answer.

'Mike, I would be much obliged if you could see your way clear to removing that serious, puzzled look from your face immediately. That is one of the most blatant pieces of deliberate not-understanding that I've ever witnessed. Just explain to me why on earth I would find it more romantic to be called by my daughter's name.' I looked at my watch. 'You have two minutes, and your time starts – now!'

Mike smiled ruefully.

'I suppose you're talking about a general sort of – being affectionate, are you?' He thought for a moment. 'But you do know I love you, don't you?'

I shrugged.

'Well, yes, but you used to come out and say it quite a lot when we were younger. I have to prise it out of you these days like a midwife helping a ferret give birth to a giraffe.' Mike blenched at my simile, as I knew he would, but I ignored him. 'Nowadays, you voluntarily saying you love me is an event that comes up about as regularly as Oberammergau.' I sighed theatrically. 'Oh, well, I suppose once every ten years isn't that bad, really. A decade passes very quickly when you know you've got something to look forward to.'

'Oh, come on, Kath, it's not as bad as – '

'I've never really thought properly about this before, but ever since Felicity first came along you seem to have been able to talk to her in ways that you've never ever been able to use with anyone else – certainly not me – well, not since we were first courting, anyway.'

Frowning worriedly and blowing air out through puffed cheeks, Mike pushed his chair back a few inches and folded his arms. I couldn't help smiling for a moment at this little amalgam of blatantly symbolic behaviour. It reminded me (no doubt because of my reference to our courting days) of the time, not long after we had first met and fallen in love in beautiful Durham, when the mild-mannered, inwardly rather intense and self-conscious young man I had fallen for so heavily announced, as we walked back after Morning Prayer at St Nick's one Sunday, that he had been reading a most interesting book on the subject of body language. Extracting it eagerly from the bag in which he was wont also to transport his large, black, coffin-like Bible, he showed me the garishly jacketed volume.

Clearly aimed at the money-spending reading masses by an anthropologist of the popular school, this heavily illustrated tome set out to analyse normal human behaviour and to explain it in the context of survival, conflict strategy and tribal behaviour. Fundamentally, the writer confidently asserted, we humans were nothing more than animals walking on our hind legs, and just about all of our habitual behaviours could be understood and explained in those terms.

That Sunday, as we continued with the latest of our darling dawdles along by the river, Mike explained with enthusiasm that the bit of the book he had found really interesting was the section on attack and defence. According to the writer, when we performed simple actions like folding our arms or crossing our legs, we were actually expressing the fact that we felt threatened in some way. In effect, unconsciously, we were guarding our hearts and our genitals ('other vulnerable areas' was the term that I think Mike used for those unspeakable items at the time) against an aggressor. In the context of modern-day living, people who habitually tied their limbs in knots in this way whenever they were in the company of others were, broadly speaking, likely to be defensive types of men and women, unable or unwilling to be truly vulnerable or to let others in on their lives. Those who felt safe and secure in themselves, on the other hand, had no need to erect these barriers.

Thinking about it, Mike said, he had realized that he did indeed have a depressingly consistent tendency to fold his arms and cross his legs whenever he was in the company of people he didn't know very well. As a Christian, he went on to explain earnestly to me, he was seriously concerned about this. It might give non-Christians the idea that he was not open to their involvement in his life. As a human being he was worried that it might be making him look a nervous idiot. As a result of this two-fold concern he had already begun a campaign of monitoring his own limb-folding activities and counteracting the tendency as soon as it manifested itself.

I felt a rush of relief on hearing all this. At church that morning, and during the coffee time afterwards, I had observed Mike behaving in a seriously odd way, and I had been wondering how to approach the subject with him. Seated next to me during the service he had two or three times performed very strange physical manoeuvres, reminiscent of a mechanical toy rather than a human being. His arms would move into the normal folded position, for instance, then abruptly fly apart, as though a button had been pushed or an electrical contact made. His legs also appeared to have acquired a life of their own, folding and then explosively unfolding every now and then in a dervish-like little dance that bore no relation to what was happening in the upper part of his body.

Sharing a pew for an entire Anglican service with a human windmill who occasionally broke into what would nowadays be called a riverdance had been disconcerting enough, but afterwards, sitting and chatting over coffee with some of the other young people who went to the church, things were worse. It was difficult to decide whether Mike was exhausted, or whether he was revealing a streak of exhibitionism hitherto unsuspected by me or anyone else. Instead of adopting his more or less normal sitting posture, he slumped back in one of the plastic chairs, his arms dangling loosely over the sides, his knees pushed as far apart as the resistance of his trouser fabric would allow. This simian pose was punctuated at unnervingly irregular intervals by enfoldings and eruptions of upper and lower limbs as before, the whole phenomenon suggestive of an actor obsessionally rehearsing the portrayal of death-throes. In fact, of course, Mike was practising the appearance of vulnerability, and finding out just how difficult it really was to stop being yourself when no genuine change has taken place.

My smile turned into a laugh as I remembered the alarmed expression on my future husband's face when I gently informed him in the course of that walk that, far from projecting an image of relaxed vulnerability, his bizarre behaviour was likely to get him sectioned if it continued. He did stop after that, which was just as well, because I couldn't have married him if he hadn't.

'What are you laughing at?'

The arms were still folded.

'Oh, I'm sorry, Mike. I was just remembering when you had that dreadful book in Durham before we got married, remember? The one that made you think you'd put everyone off if you folded your arms or crossed your legs, and I had to tell you – '

'All right, all right!' Unfolding his arms in an impressively smooth and rational manner, Mike smiled sheepishly. 'Of course I remember the stupid book. I don't think I've ever felt such a twit in all my life.'

He pushed his chair up to the table again and we sat in silence for a while. I was remembering lots of other things to do with being in Durham. I'm sure he was as well.

'You call her "sweetheart" and "darling" and "love" and – and things like that.'

'Do I?'

'You know you do.'

Looking down into the remnants of his tea, Mike held the end of a teaspoon between the very tips of his finger and thumb, letting it make little dinging noises as it dangled against the inside of the china cup.

'I suppose,' he said slowly and thoughtfully, 'it's all about confidence. Having Felicity is the first time in my life that I've sort of been in charge of a relationship with a female right from the beginning. I know she's not far off swapping roles now that she's reached the ripe old age of ten, but I've been rather pleased – proud, in a funny sort of way – that I've been able to call her those things. It's nice.' He looked up. 'It doesn't matter, does it?'

'Good heavens, no, I didn't mean that. I love the relationship you have with her, I really do. It's just that ...'

'You wish I'd say the same things to you.'

'Mmm ... I feel silly now.'

'Well, I'll try. It might sound a bit forced at first – sweetheart.'

We both burst into laughter. It sounded ridiculous and unnatural, but I knew Mike. He wouldn't give up now that he'd said he was going to try. For a moment the thought of how the rest of the family were going to enjoy this for all the wrong reasons made me wish I'd never said anything. Still, perhaps it would become more natural with practice, and it was nice ...

'Come and sit here, Kath.'

Dropping his spoon into his cup and swinging his knees away from the table, Mike patted his lap invitingly. Gosh, I thought, there's nothing like memories of Durham for shifting the old passion up a gear. I thought about those days again as I cuddled up to him.

'We never did do it before we got married, did we, Mike?'

'Never did do what?'

I groaned.

He smiled and shook his head.

'Sorry – no, we didn't. We were very good, weren't we, Kath? Good Christian young people, that's what we were.'

'We wouldn't have been if I'd had my way, though, would we? I suppose I was potentially a bit of a trollop when it came to it, wasn't I? Do you remember after we got engaged, me going on and on about how we were going to get married anyway, so what difference would it make? And you used to say, all serious, that of course you wanted to do it, but the Bible made it quite clear that we should wait until we were married. Remember?'

'Of course I remember – I still think that.'

'You were so *stern* and responsible.'

'Hmm ...'

I tilted my head and looked up at the abashed expression on his face.

'What?'

'I was just thinking, Kath, that actually – what was it Oscar Wilde said?'

Our treasured large tomes of collected writings, essential to dedicated kitchen-dwellers, lived on a shelf high on the long side-wall opposite the fable. Raising an arm I waved it in the direction of the complete works of O. Wilde.

'All that.'

'No, I mean, what was it he said epigrammatically about people using what they ought to do or not do as an excuse for not doing or doing something that they actually don't want to do because they're too frightened?'

'I'm not sure, but something tells me he put it a little more concisely than that. You should have married the milkgirl.'

'I wouldn't have minded, she's rather pretty. He did put it better than that. Wait a minute – I've got it! I remember what it was. "Conscience is oft misnamed cowardice." '

' "Conscience is oft misnamed cowardice", eh?' I rolled the thought round my mind. 'I get it – so, what you're saying is that it wasn't so much the teaching of the Bible that was stopping you as cold feet, but you didn't want to admit that, so you got all high and mighty and moral? You were a fraud, Michael Robinson.'

'Well, I was a bit, I suppose. Nervous about being a lousy lover, and worried about doing something I thought was wrong. Ah, well, God does use whatever he can to sort things out, doesn't he? And it's not as if I didn't believe what I was saying. Anyway, whatever the reason, I'm glad now that we didn't sleep together before we got married, aren't you?'

I thought about this, and nodded slowly.

'Yes, I am – I wasn't at all then – but I am glad now.'

'What are you glad about, Mummy?'

So absorbed had we been in our conversation that neither of us had registered the sound of the front door opening and closing. As usual, Felicity slam-dunked the accoutrements of her school life on to one end of the kitchen table and collapsed into a chair as if she had just emerged from eight hours at the coalface instead of a forty-five-minute netball practice. She knitted her brows.

'Why are you sitting on Daddy's lap, Mummy, and what are you glad about?'

'I'm sitting on Daddy's lap because I *like* sitting on Daddy's lap, and I'm gla-a-ad about something else I was talking to Daddy about. Can I get you a drink, darling? Did you have a good day at school? Looking forward to your week off?'

Felicity knew she was being fobbed off, but, as an experienced ten-year-old, she also knew that allowing yourself to be fobbed off without making a fuss has solid commercial value in the parent/child market-place.

'Yes, I am. Can you make me a hot chocolate, and can I go and get the news things from upstairs that me and Jack were doing on Saturday that you never heard, an' read them to you?'

'What a good idea, darling – are you thinking of getting changed while you're up there?' enquired Mike pleasantly

Parents are delightfully naive sometimes. How could Mike, who deals with kids all day and every day, have so easily forgotten that commands phrased as questions are almost always wasted on intelligent children.

'No,' replied Felicity, precisely echoing her father's pleasant tones, 'I'm not. I'm thinking of doing it afterwards.'

A few minutes later, unchanged, and with her hot chocolate steaming in front of her, Felicity read with occasional stumbles from a sheet of Jack's computer paper.

'Right – here is the news. This week historians announced that the story of Goldilocks we usually hear is wrong. Recent research shows that in the real story, the porridge Goldilocks ate in the cottage belonged to her great-great-grandfather, her great-great-grandmother, her great-grandfather and her great-grandmother. So the story should actually have been called "Goldilocks and the Forebears".'

We tittered dutifully.

'Why is that funny?' asked Felicity, looking up.

'Well, it's – I'll explain later,' said Mike. 'Go on to the next bit.'

'Right, the next one is about a man who was killed in his

cottage in the country. Do you think that's good news or bad news?'

'It sounds like bad news,' suggested Mike warily.

'But he died with a huge beam on his face.'

'Oh, well, that's quite good news, isn't it?'

'No, it's not, because the huge beam was part of the cottage ceiling that fell on his head.'

Mike's protest, 'But that's just horrible!' was completely lost on our young newsreader, who had gone off into fits of laughter over the black humour of her second story. I waited for her to recover.

'Is that it, then, sweetheart? Any more ghastly tales for us?'

Felicity sipped her chocolate expertly without lifting it, waving her hand wildly as she did so to signal that we should stay put.

'No, the next one's about you and Mark, Mummy.'

'Oh dear.'

'At ten o'clock yesterday afternoon Mrs Kathy Robinson accompanied her son, Mark Robinson, to the local osteopath, where he was treated for a leg injury. Asked if she had been upset by the visit, Mrs Robinson replied, "No, on the contrary, it was nice to see him being manipulated for a change." I don't understand why that's funny either.'

We did.

Felicity continued.

'Police said today that most crime is committed by petty crooks, and they are just the small-fry. The real big bosses organize everything from inside prison, and they are the stir-fry. Jack's mad. None of these are funny. There's another one about motorways being boring, especially the M6 because it's a major turn-off, and there's one about a man who – '

'That's enough now. Drink your hot chocolate, darling, or it'll get cold.'

'All right.'

A slurp-filled pause. Peace. Mike and I exchanged smiles. Felicity looked up over the top of her mug.

'What were you glad about when I came in, Mummy . . . ?'

five

Wednesday

1

'Mike, can you write down for us to remember to get a red bulb?'

I have already mentioned the patterns that make up much of family life. I suppose Mike's good old rising spirals are part of that as well, but most of these domestic designs are things you only really recognize when you sit down and think hard about what's happening, or what's happened repeatedly in the past. There are certain such patterns, though, that you can get very worked up about before they even start to appear. More often than not, these are manifested in the form of arguments.

For example (Dip has described this in chilling detail elsewhere), there is the vast gulf that lies between my idea of the best way to pack suitcases for a long journey, and the method favoured by my dear husband. Briefly, mine is chaotic and occupies an evening, whereas Mike's, if anyone was ever plain foolish enough to let him put it into practice, is exceptionally well organized and would take just short of a year. Every time we go away for a family holiday we engage in precisely the same argument in almost exactly the same detail, and it is an argument that has already begun in our hearts, as it were, long before the subject is actually mentioned.

Tonight, I just knew that it was going to be about getting the house cleaned and ready for my party, and the irritation had already begun to seethe around in me as I made coffee in the kitchen to take through to the living-room for Mike and me.

Wednesday evening was our first real chance to plan the party. Jack and Mark had gone out to some pub quiz together, giving us the chance to chat peacefully (that was the theory, anyway) for a couple of hours. Felicity was in, but she had been allowed to choose and rent a video to watch upstairs with her friend, the infamous, high-pitched Caroline Burton, before going to bed. As far as Felicity was concerned, this had not worked out quite as smoothly as it might have done. Caroline's stated preference for films about 'fairies and imps and that' was starkly at variance with our dear daughter's ongoing and so far unsuccessful campaign to persuade us to let her watch a '15', but the one they eventually chose seemed a reasonable compromise, and all was quiet as I set a tray down on the coffee-table in front of Mike at about seven o'clock.

Mike and I think in such different ways. He had equipped himself with a neat little notebook and a new pencil from his special drawer in the bedroom, and would, I am quite sure, have produced a printed agenda if past experience had not taught him that she who constituted the committee was likely to immediately make it into a paper dart and send it on a long-haul flight. I knew that he would be sitting down with a head full of ideas and headings and calculations, whereas I had only two things in my head. One was that rising tide of impatience at the thought of our forthcoming, inevitable conflict over getting the house ready, and the other was a determination to make sure that, whatever else we might remember or forget, there must be at least one room in the house on the night of the party that would be lit by a red light-bulb. Hence my opening gambit.

It went down with more of a glug than the *Titanic*. If ever anything was calculated to drive Mike mad with exasperation, it was having random points made at times when a little clear thinking was called for. His sigh sounded as if it was scraping its way over heavy-duty sandpaper.

'Kathy, we'll come to the trivial details in a minute when we've looked at the broad spectrum of what's entailed. I'd really appreciate it if, just for a change, we could discipline ourselves into doing things in some sort of order.'

One of my long-term private ambitions is to creep up behind the broad spectrum of what is entailed, and strangle it.

'What you mean, of course,' I replied grimly, 'is that you'd appreciate it if *I* could discipline *my*self, because, as we all know, you are the most disciplined person on the face of the earth.'

This brief analysis was so palpably true that, although Mike went through all the headshaking, hand-waving, tongue-and-teeth-clicking activity that commonly precedes a denial, he was unable to actually produce any words to match his pantomime. Not that I allowed him much opportunity to do so if he *had* thought of anything to say.

'I consider myself to be adequately disciplined in the small but perfectly formed, non-trivial area of making sure that we have a red light-bulb in one of the rooms,' I continued coldly. 'I want us to start with that, and I refuse to talk about anything else until we've sorted that out, so there!'

I sat back on the sofa and folded my arms. Being made to feel small brings out the very worst in me, and has sometimes resulted in clashes of very heavy artillery between Mike and me.

I shall never forget, for instance, one notable occasion which was quite decidedly only funny in retrospect. We had been house-hunting for some weeks, and the whole tedious process was beginning to get both of us down. Apart from anything else, it had taken some time to learn the language of house-selling well enough to translate 'within easy reach of local transport systems' into 'next to the lorry depot behind the railway station', and 'enormous potential for development' into 'a collapsing wreck'. On this typically stressful day I became increasingly furious with Mike. In our interminable interviews with estate agents and the like, he had been tending to take over altogether, as though he was the adult and I was his little girl who was obliged to tag along with him, sitting quietly while the grown-ups attended to their important business. On the one occasion when I was graciously permitted to take a leading role, he had interrupted and qualified the things I said to such an extent that he might as well have done all the talking in the first place. By the time we reached the fourth or fifth of these glorified brick-merchants there was murder in my heart, and, knowing this, Mike must have decided that the time had come for me to be appeased in some way.

'Okay, Kathy,' he communicated in an oleaginous whisper, as we sat by one of the desks waiting for someone to get off the phone and be free to see us, 'this one's all yours. You're the boss this time, okay?'

If he hadn't expressed this invitation in such a condescending way, all might have been well. As it was, his words only served to anger me even further. By the time our professionally smiling, classically uniformed estate agent joined us at the desk, I was way past caring what happened. As far as I can recall, I said, in the most natural manner possible, something along the following lines.

'Good morning. This is my husband. He'll be interrupting and correcting me at regular intervals in the most infuriating manner possible. I shall seethe but say nothing in front of you, then get very cross with him afterwards. He'll begin by being upset, but end by losing his temper. I shall sulk and there'll be an uneasy tension between us for a few hours. Later, I shall be having trouble remembering quite why I was so hugely justified in being angry, but be sure that I was. By the end of the day practical requirements will have forced us back into talking normally to each other until the next time. How do you do?'

What the poor young man who had sat down in such an estate-agentish manner to interview us might have replied to this must for ever remain a mystery, because at this point Mike stood up and more or less dragged me out into the street. Later, in my mind's eye, I could still see that young man's face with its open mouth and staring eyes, as clearly as if I had taken a snapshot. Mike and I drove home in silence, and I very much fear that the sun went down on our wrath that night. I was quite ashamed afterwards, but, by George, it felt good at the time!

Now, I watched Mike rubbing his eyes heavily as he tried to work out how to deal with the 'Red Bulb' threat.

'All right,' he said at last, with a sort of weary annoyance, 'I will write down "red bulb", if that's what you really want, and then perhaps we can get on. It is your party we're talking about, you know.'

He wrote for a moment, then held the pad up high for me to look at.

'There, you see, I've written it in great big letters right in the very middle of the first page. Now we'll remember it, won't we? Is that sufficient, or did you want me to put my coat on and pop out to the all-night garage and get one before we go any further?'

Sarcasm may be the lowest form of wit, but it can also be the most annoying. And we hadn't even started about the house yet!

'No,' I replied glacially, 'that won't be necessary, thank you. I would hate to think that you were using up so much energy on something so trivial. You want to get on, so let's get on, shall we?'

Mike peered suspiciously at me for a moment, wondering whether he could possibly take my words at face value.

'Very well,' he said, 'well, let's begin with – '

'Mike, I do just want to sort one thing out straight away. We are intending to have the place cleaned and ready for when people actually arrive, aren't we?'

He very slowly closed the notebook and replaced it on the table without taking his eyes from my face.

'Cleaned and – of course we are. What on earth makes you think we wouldn't, Kathy?'

I gestured vaguely with both hands and shrugged.

'Oh, nothing really – just the trivial fact that on every other occasion when we've done anything like this, we've ended up still rushing madly around tidying up even as guests are coming through the door. Just once – just for *once* – couldn't we try to be ready and calm and cool and holding glasses of wine in our hands when the doorbell goes, instead of one of us being in the shower, and coming out on the landing dripping wet and scream-ing down the stairs that we haven't got a towel, and the other one creating deliberate and inexplicable mayhem in the kitchen just at the very moment when mayhem in the kitchen is the very last thing we need?'

Mike stared.

'Presumably you're talking about *me* creating mayhem in the kitchen, are you?'

'Well, it's unlikely to be me, isn't it? You must admit I am usefully superficial enough to appreciate the need to do a swift manicure on the house on these occasions, using any cheating shortcuts I can, for the very trivial reason that our visitors might prefer to walk straight into a pleasant environment.'

'Oh, I see, and what is it that I do?'

'What is it that you do? Well, let's see now.'

I settled back and prepared to indulge myself a little.

'For an occasion like this, Michael, your first move would probably be to climb up into the loft and give the purlins and the joists and the rafters a really good scrub, all ready for no-one at all to go up there during the party. Then you'd haul our bed right out and clean under that, just in case one of the guests decides he's unwilling to commit his nice clean coat to the top of a bed that might have a thin layer of dust underneath it. Oh, then there's the gutters and the drains! I forgot about the gutters and the drains. Of course, you'd have to clear all the gutters and make sure whatever goes into them can run away easily, so that if, in the course of the evening, someone from our party finds him or herself on the roof – as may well happen, let's face it – and urgently needs to deposit something or other into the gutter, they can do it without worrying.

'What next? Well, *up* with all the floor-coverings, wash the floorboards, hoover the underside of the carpets, and take the wallpaper off – very carefully, of course – so that you can wipe the walls before sticking it back up. And, of course, it goes without saying that, before doing any of these things, you would have popped up to work and completely tidied and polished your office, so that if the subject of school comes up at the party you'll be able to discuss it without suffering from the nagging feeling that you would be ashamed for whoever you were chatting with to see it if they were there instead of here. What else … ?'

'I have never been able to understand,' said Mike with

severe dignity, 'why you insist on regarding my preference for carrying work out carefully and in order as some kind of vice. Come on – you tell me. What exactly is wrong with doing things properly?'

'Doing things properly? Doing things *properly*? Is that what you call the way you behave? Mike, you make Hercule Poirot look like – like Sir Les Patterson. You're so maddeningly, infuriatingly, immovably *thorough* in all that you so perfectly do! You remind me of that man in the Ray Bradbury story – remember? Remember the man who'd burgled a house or something, and before leaving he decided to make sure he hadn't left any fingerprints? So he went round with a cloth wiping every surface that he might have been in contact with, but he got obsessional about it, and ended up polishing the underside of some fruit in a bowl that he hadn't even touched, and when the police came he was still in the house cleaning away like a loony, so he got caught. Remember?'

Mike nodded his head laboriously as though it had trebled in weight.

'Yes, I remember the story very well, and it has absolutely nothing to do with how I am. I just don't like being – '

'Cosmetic? Is that the word you're groping for?'

'You didn't give me any time to grope for – '

'If it is, you're absolutely right, because that's exactly what you don't like being. You don't like being cosmetic. You will not do a cosmetic job on anything, and you think it doesn't matter because you're going to know deep down that, even if you haven't got round to such petty trifles as the way things actually look, you've been *thorough*, so it doesn't matter what anyone else thinks. It's a matter of inner integrity. Am I right?'

'Forgive me, I'll make a special effort to be more shallow in future. Kathy, may I ask once again why you seem to be going out of your way to pick a fight when all we're doing is trying to organize *your* party – *sweetheart*?'

I clamped my lips shut and punched downward at the seat on either side of me with clenched fists. I wanted to find a way to tell myself that Mike was being unfair, but I knew he was right. I had deliberately picked the fight that I was sure we were going to end up having anyway. My eyes fell on Mike's closed notebook, never used before, with the words 'KATH'S PARTY' written neatly across the top of the cover, and his shiny new green pencil, both lying neatly on the table between us, and I remembered how much I loved him. I bit my lip. I've been biting my lip like that since I was two years old.

'Mike, I'd really like to start again and ...'

'Kath, I'm sorry I was sarcastic about ...'

I don't know if Mike's thought processes had been similar to mine, but they produced more or less the same result at exactly the same moment. We both laughed.

'You go ahead, Kath.'

'No, you say what you were going to say – I'm really sorry I got so het up. I don't know why I do it. I think it's just that I get all nervy waiting for us to lock horns, and I try to – sort of hurry it along, so we can get on with it and get it over with. Go on, you say what you were going to say.'

Mike leaned forward, opened his notebook, and tore off the first page, the one on which he had written 'LIGHT-BULB' in such risibly huge letters. On the next page he wrote it again, but in proper-sized letters, next to a neat number one in a circle.

'Right – item one in our discussion concerns the need for a red light-bulb to be purchased, said bulb to be employed throughout forthcoming party in the – hold on a minute, Kath, darling, just a small detail, where are we going to put this red bulb and what's it for?'

He called me darling!

'Oh, Mike, you can't have forgotten the red lights they always had at parties when we were in our teens. There was always at least one room where the lighting made everyone look as if they'd just done something they were really ashamed of – come to think of it, they probably had, when I think of some of the parties I went to. Anyway, that's all it was. I'd like there to be one room where I can get lost in David Bowie and dance badly with you in the middle of a crowd of people who all look red in the face. It's important to me.'

'Okay,' said Mike equably, 'it shall be done. Now you've got to tell me what you were going to say.'

'I was going to say that I wanted us to start again and see – just see – if we could talk about what I got all upset about without either of us getting as upset as we usually get. I think Oscar Wilde would have put that better as well, wouldn't he?'

'Look, you tell me calmly and clearly what it is that you want to change about the way I go about doing this party.'

'Clearly and calmly?'

'Yes, and I'll listen without interrupting.'

'Goodness! This is rather like one of those moments in *2001* when the stone pillar comes shooting up out of the ground, isn't it? I'm going to be clear and calm, and you're going to listen without interrupting. A new era has dawned.'

'A new day will have dawned if we don't get on with it, Kath. We've still got a number of important rows to get through tonight, and we've only had one so far. That was a joke, by the way.'

'Oh, good, I'm glad it was a joke, because just for one itsy-bitsy moment I did wonder if it might possibly have been a deliberately inflammatory comment, and that would have been a shame, wouldn't it, darling?'

'Absolutely not, dear sweet light of my life. Shall I open a bottle of wine?'

Armed with a glass each of the heavy, dark, blackcurranty wine that we both enjoyed so much, the evening seemed set to move into a different and more interesting gear altogether, but I was committed to my clear, calm, adult explanation.

'All it is, Mike,' I said, trying to express myself in a clear, calm, adult manner, but probably sounding more like a reception teacher addressing her new intake on their first day, 'is that sometimes, when we've done this sort of thing before, and you've been in charge of the food as usual, we seem to have ended up with you still doing things in the kitchen right up to the very last moment, because you've been so busy – and rightly so, of course,

I hasten to add – making sure that the house is nice and clean and tidy – darling.'

There was a pause while Mike checked that he wouldn't be interrupting.

'Right,' he said practically, 'if that's the problem, I think I can suggest an answer. I'll simply adjust my timetable so that I'm aiming to have everything finished an hour before the party starts. If we invite people to come at, say, seven-thirty, then I'll – we'll – make sure everything's completely done by half-past six. How would that be?'

I winked extravagantly, like a pirate, and said, 'That'll be just fine, cap'n, just fine!'

And who could tell? Perhaps it would.

Mike *so* loved being able to write down in his beautiful little book that the party was going to start at seven-thirty. You could see him thinking, 'Good, we've made a start at last.' This is a man, I thought, as I watched his tongue-between-the-teeth concentration, who must once have been a little boy who loved doing his homework and handing it in the next day.

After that we really got on with it, and the further down the bottle we went – I mean, of course, the more we went into responsibly considered issues – the more truly excited I began to feel about celebrating my advanced age. And I must say it was lovely sitting there with Mike, talking earnestly about what we were going to do and how we were going to do it – just being us, warm and together. No doubt the party itself would turn out to be wonderful, but I enjoyed that hour or two of planning as much as I was likely to ever enjoy anything.

You know, there are times when I really do fancy my husband.

Details? Well, the music pretty well decided itself. As well as all the prodigious best of David Bowie, we would have Elvis, the Beatles, the Stones, Bob Dylan, the Everly Brothers (no Cilia Black – surprise, surprise!) and any other obviously significant items of sixties musical culture that we could borrow or find in our own collection.

We decided to have lots and lots of food, which would be laid out on the table in our big kitchen, sufficient to avoid the normal phenomenon of latecomers picking dismally through left-over crumbs and crusts and bits of fatty ham. Folk were certain to bring lots of bottles of this and that, but we would get in a reasonable amount of wine and beer ourselves and put it somewhere at a good distance from the food, together with plenty of soft drinks for drivers, non-imbibers and weaker brothers and sisters.

'And,' proposed Mike, 'as well as all the people we've already asked, let's invite just about anybody else we can think of, apart from one or two of your killer relatives, otherwise we're sure to miss somebody important out and they'll hear about it afterwards and be upset.'

I agreed with him. Apart from anything else, that would ensure that the house was as packed with bodies as it needed to be to create a genuinely chaotic sixties atmosphere. At the same time, we could create extra space for people who didn't want to be crushed to death, by using the whole three storeys of the house – even Mark's room, I suggested, assuming that it could be fumigated and exorcized in the short time remaining to us.

I really was beginning to feel quite excited.

2

Later, after Caroline had gone home and Felicity was safely tucked up in bed, Mark and Jack rolled in, very slightly the worse for wear. Jack collapsed bonelessly on the other end of the settee while Mark parked himself on the floor in front of the television.

'Got it all sussed, Mumsy?'

Jack's voice was mellow and sleepy.

'Yes, we haven't done at all badly, have we, Mike? We were saying earlier that we'd quite like – Mark, don't turn the telly on, I want to ask you something.'

'It's *Frasier*. I'm leaving the sound down.'

'No you're not. You can't just walk in and change the whole atmosphere. You've had the sort of evening you wanted out there somewhere, but we're still having ours. Turn it right off, please.'

'How do you know I've had the sort of evening I wanted. I might have had a rotten time – you don't know. Why do you always think you know about me?'

Not for the first time, I reflected on the fact that I was rarely allowed any credit by Mark. Cash on the table seemed to be his unvarying terms as far as our relationship was concerned. Very good things that had happened in the same week, or the day before, or even on the same day, very seldom retained enough of their benign influence to temper his response to me on occasions like this. How could he *possibly* think that it was all right to be that rude and spoil the end of our evening?

'Please turn it off, Mark,' said Mike, his voice tinged with a combination of warmth and respect that I had never been able to manage in dealing with my middle child.

Sighing heavily, Mark leaned forward to turn off the television, then turned to face us, drawing his knees up under his chin and wrapping his arms around his legs.

'What? We came second, by the way.'

'Thank you. Congratulations. What was the prize?'

'Beer.'

'We just wanted to ask you if it would be all right for us to use your room for the party. We're going to have loads of people here, so we need all the space we can get. What do you think?'

'Course,' shrugged Mark, somewhat anticlimactically. 'No problem. Might have to give it a bit of a tidy.'

'A bit of a tidy!' Jack flung a lazy arm over the back of the sofa and guffawed spontaneously at this masterpiece of understatement. 'Tell you what,' he said, 'why not leave it as it is and make it into a party game where people have to guess whose room it is, like *Through the Keyhole* where the bloke with the funny voice goes round people's houses?'

He continued with a passable imitation of Lloyd Grossman's drawling tones.

'Who would live in a room like this? Let's take a look at the evidence – the stack of three-day-old unwashed dinner-plates with bits of bacon-rind stuck in congealed tomato sauce, the empty beer cans stacked in a pyramid on the windowsill, the ankle-deep layer of stale socks and underwear on the floor, the loose CDs that might have been used as Frisbees, the lights and television that are always left on when the owner's out in case someone happens to pop in, the half-drunk mugs of coffee covered in green mould, the bed that Big Daddy and Giant Haystacks have wrestled on for an hour. What kind of person *would* be prepared to live in a room like this? Party guests, it's over to you!'

'I might remind you, Jack,' commented Mike mildly, 'that there was a time just a few years ago when your room was more often than not a forest of empty milk bottles.'

'Anyway, my room's not all that bad,' grinned Mark, completely unabashed by his brother's comments. 'At least I'm better at cleaning my room than Jack is at impressions. Can my friends come to the party, Dad?'

'Ask your mother. It's her birthday party, not mine.'

'Can they, Mum? Pretend you're not cross with me.'

Two options remained. I could grab the nearest heavy object and batter him to death, or I could take the very unusual step of getting down on the floor to tickle him.

You should have heard him scream ...

six

Thursday

1

Shortly after eight o'clock on Thursday evening, I found myself saying a private prayer of gratitude for the way in which Simon Davenport had set up this difficult meeting with such sensitivity. From the offset he established an ideal atmosphere of hushed reverence and expectation very simply and effectively, by his manner as he welcomed people at the door and showed them through to the meeting. He had got the lighting in his living-room just right as well. Apart from a large candle burning in the middle of the coffee table, the only other light source was a small adjustable lamp, placed on a shelf at shoulder level behind Simon and Mike, so that they could see to lead and speak. I could feel the relief in Dip, sitting tensely beside me on the sofa, that whatever happened would happen in near-darkness.

Most of our Bible study group were there, thirteen people in all, including Joscelyn without John (guilty relief!), and Eileen, who was sitting on my other side. Eileen had rung me up on the Tuesday to ask if I thought her new wish to grapple with the past might also be mentioned during the communion service. After a brief and extremely childish wrestling match with God over the fact that it was supposed to be 'Dip's Meeting' – he won by two falls and a submission, by the way – I rang Simon to pass on Eileen's request, and he agreed immediately.

Fortunately, Simon had taken the time and trouble earlier

in the week to make sure that every member of the group knew, more or less, why we were having this special communion, so embarrassing explanations were unnecessary. After a brief welcome and introduction, the service began with quite a long period of silence, which Simon said should be used to reflect on the fact that Jesus was with us, as clear and in control as he had ever been when he walked the earth two thousand years ago, and that his promise of healing for the broken-hearted was one that would certainly be kept.

I'm not terribly good at silences. In the middle of this one I thought and felt so many things as I gazed, owl-eyed, at the very faintly flickering candle in the centre of our circle.

I began by thinking about the fact that, in my experience, lots of broken-hearted people *didn't* seem to be healed, and suddenly my faith plummeted. Then I thought about the small number of individuals I knew who actually had been given a new heart through their walk with Jesus, and I felt ashamed of my doubt. I moved on from there to feeling a shadow of worry as I once again faced the fact that I was the one who had originally suggested the idea of a communion service. Coincidentally, the candle flame did an extra little flicker at that very moment, and I had to stifle a giggle. It was as if the Holy Spirit had borrowed the candle for a second to say, 'Excuse me, *who* originally suggested it?' Finally, I thought about Jesus, my friend, and tears filled my eyes as I silently implored him to allow some lightening of the burdens carried by our mutual friends.

2

By the time Simon began the celebration itself, the air in the room really did seem alive with possibility, and as we moved nearer and nearer to the sharing of bread and wine, the words of the service, so familiar that at other times they had become mere patterns of sound to me, seemed to ring with fresh depth and meaning.

'Almighty God, to whom all hearts are open, all desires known, and from whom no secrets are hidden; cleanse the thoughts of our hearts by the inspiration of your Holy Spirit, that we may perfectly love you ...'

'We have sinned against you, and against our fellow men, in thought and word and deed, through negligence, through weakness, through our own deliberate fault. We are truly sorry ...'

'We believe in one God, the Father, the almighty, maker of heaven and earth, of all that is seen and unseen ...'

'Lord Jesus Christ, only son of the Father, Lord God, Lamb of God, you take away the sins of the world; have mercy on us ...'

After the Gloria, Mike took over.

'Right, I'd like to read you two quite short Bible extracts before I speak for a little while. The first is from one of my favourite chapters of the Old Testament – well, the whole Bible – Isaiah sixty-one.

' "The Spirit of the Sovereign Lord is on me, because the Lord has appointed me to preach good news to the poor. He has sent me to bind up the broken-hearted, to proclaim freedom for the captives, and release from darkness for the prisoners, to proclaim the year of the Lord's favour and the day of vengeance of our God, to comfort all who mourn, and provide for those who grieve in Zion – to bestow on them a crown of beauty instead of ashes, the oil of gladness instead of mourning, and a garment of praise instead of a spirit of despair. They will be called oaks of righteousness, a planting of the Lord for the display of his splendour." '

Pausing, he found another place in his Bible.

'And the second reading is one that quite a bit of the communion service comes from: Luke, chapter twenty-two, verses fourteen to twenty.

' "When the hour came, Jesus and his apostles reclined at the table. And he said to them, 'I have eagerly desired to eat this Passover with you before I suffer. For I tell you, I will not eat it again until it finds fulfilment in the kingdom of God.' After taking the cup, he gave thanks and said, 'Take this and divide it among you. For I tell you I will not drink again of the fruit of the vine until the kingdom of God comes.' And he took bread, gave thanks and broke it, and gave it to them, saying, 'This is my body given for you; do this in remembrance of me.' In the same way, after the supper he took the cup, saying, 'This cup is the new covenant in my blood, which is poured out for you.' " '

Mike closed his Bible and laid it down on the floor by his feet. For a few seconds he said nothing. Someone sitting on the opposite side shivered suddenly, but not with the cold. The whole room felt to me like a gently breathing, living thing, the light from the candle at its heart. When Mike did begin to speak, it was without notes.

'In a moment we shall be saying one of my favourite prayers, the one we call the Prayer of Humble Access. There are two prayers to choose from at that point in the service, and I think they're both beautiful. The slightly less well known of them begins with these words: "Most merciful Lord, your love compels us to come in ..."

'Communion means so much to me – to all of us – and it doesn't really matter whether it's held in a magnificent cathedral or in this very comfortable sitting-room. And it is a sacrament of cosmic extremes, isn't it? So rich and so poor, so vast and so small, so distant and so near, deeply rooted in the past and yet still flowering miraculously in the present, so ineffably mystical and so very ordinary, so sad and so full of joy.

'It struck me, as I was trying to think what I should say this evening, that these latter extremes of sadness and joy are very significant and necessary parts of the celebration that we are all about to be part of.

'What could possibly be sad about communion? Well, communion has always been sad for me because it makes me think of Jesus in the upper room, on the same dreadful night that he was betrayed, gazing yearningly round the table at the faces of his friends as they enjoyed a final meal together. I would imagine that parents suffering from terminal illness must feel that same rush of love and pain as they gaze into the faces of their small children, knowing with stomach-lurching certainty, not just that parting is inevitable, but that, in the midst of grieving, their little ones will struggle in vain to understand why the person they loved and needed so much can no longer be with them. I feel so sad for Jesus – for the man God became.

'Communion also makes me sad for the far less worthy but no less important reason that it demands, over and over again, my assent to the proposition that the whole of my world and my ways, negative and positive, must be left with Bible, hymn book and spectacles on my chair as I approach to receive the bread and wine – those wonderful, rich, earthy symbols of heavenly, unearned salvation. Yes, his love compels us to come in, but for some of us, there is a little death to die every single time we yield to that compulsion. Like Simon Peter centuries ago, we yet again instinctively move to draw the sword of our own will and attributes, only to feel the gentle but firmly restraining pressure of his hand upon our arm. At that same moment we hear his voice softly telling us that if we cannot come with hands that are as empty of virtues as they are of sins, we cannot come at all.

'The joys of communion? Well, they are certainly not the opposite side of the coin. They are the same side of the same coin, seen with exactly the same eyes, but cleared by the power of the Spirit, able to recognize the stamp of the King, and to perceive the truly inestimable value of what is being put into these empty hands of ours at this very special time. We stand, equals in spiritual poverty, before our heavenly Father, brothers and sisters united in a desire to meet the God of our salvation, ready to bow our heads humbly before him and to say, "Thank you – so much – that we do not have to trust in our own righteousness."

'Now, a little later we're going to offer each other the bread and wine, and we know that there are at least two people here who will find that quite – traumatic, because they are facing really big and difficult issues in their lives after years of trying to push them away and pretending they don't exist. Let me, as humbly as I can, say something very important to you.'

Mike dropped his eyes so that he did not seem to be addressing anyone in particular, and his voice became, if anything, even quieter, but the words remained crystal clear.

'All of us have to face up to and say sorry for the sins we commit in thought and word and deed, things we should have done, and things we shouldn't have done, just as the old Anglican prayer says. But listen – here is a promise for you. I promise you that God will never, never blame us for the things that are not our fault, and I think that, tonight, he would very much like to say exactly that. Dear Dip, dear Eileen, the things that happened to you all those years ago, the things that have caused you so much pain for such a long time – it's all right, they were not your fault ...'

On the sofa beside me, Eileen began to cry softly. On the other side Dip gripped my hand even more tightly, hardly seeming to breathe, let alone make a sound.

'As far as you are able,' continued Mike, 'when the bread and the wine comes to you, by an effort of the will put those terrible things down for just a moment, open your hearts and your hands, and receive the comfort and love of God in the body and blood of his Son. It has always been kept safely there for you anyway, earning interest, and whatever has happened in the past, whatever happens now, and regardless of what happens in the future, nothing in heaven or on earth can ever take it away from you. Do it in remembrance of him. Amen.'

Rightly or wrongly, I felt so proud of Mike.

After Simon had actually said the Prayer of Humble Access, he introduced Grumpy Norman's favourite part of the proceedings, the Sharing of the Peace, by saying the following words:

'Christ is our peace. He has reconciled us to God in one body by the cross. We meet in his name and share his peace. The peace of the Lord be always with you.'

'And also with you,' responded the rest of us.

'Let us offer one another a sign of peace.'

Sometimes, when God does something, it takes a moment to catch on, doesn't it? The fact is that, after Simon said that, *nobody moved*. Possibly it was just that no-one wanted to be first, but I don't think so. I believe that it was my cue, and because an imp of narrowness was muttering in my ear, I was a razor's width from missing it.

'Jesus is here now, Dip,' I said, my voice barely rising above a whisper, 'and David is with him, holding his hand. In some way that we can't understand he's done all his growing up and falling over and having his knees kissed better. He's what he would have been, and you can say whatever you need to say to him.'

Huge single tears reflected the candlelight as they rolled slowly down Dip's cheeks. When she licked her lips before speaking I could almost taste the salt.

'David – darling, I always loved you, you know – always. I have always. I've thought about you every single day. I so wish we could have been together. I'm so very sorry that – that it wasn't possible. Thank you, Jesus, for loving him and looking after him for me. Please help me to let this wound heal. I never want the scar to go, but I – I honestly don't think I can stand the pain any more.' She let her head drop on my shoulder like an exhausted child. 'Can't say any more ...'

I fear I must be very shallow. As poor little Eileen, her eyes bright with relieved happiness, ministered the symbols of the body and blood of Jesus to me a few minutes later, I was horrified to find myself wishing that I was receiving them from someone else, someone more substantial. As I sipped the wine, some words of Dip's echoed in my mind.

'You can't measure the value of the post by the quality of the postman.'

Sighing heavily, I told myself and God that I had a very long way to go, and as I turned to offer the wine to Dip, I saw the candle flame flicker once more, almost as though it was nodding in agreement.

seven

Friday

Early the next morning I confessed my awful thought about Eileen to Mike, and I was still ploughing my furrow as he opened the back door to leave for work.

'Christianity is so blinking difficult,' I complained. 'I mean, why can't there be really neat endings to things? How can it be possible that I listened to that excellent talk of yours, and said those things to Dip, and then had such a miserable, half-baked, uncharitable thought about Eileen? I don't like her any more than I did before, you know – just feel very sorry for her. And we both know it's only a matter of time before Mark and I start biting great lumps out of each other again, don't we? How can it make sense that – '

Mike placed his fingers against my lips.

'Kathy, darling,' – good – 'I do in fact know the answers to every single one of your questions, but I haven't time to give them to you now because if I don't go I shall get told off for being late.'

'Who by? You're the headmaster.'

'By God,' said Mike, with mock piety. 'Bye!'

Ten seconds later the front door bell rang. It was Mike.

'I've had an inspiration,' he said. 'I think I have the answer to your questions. It's unrepented sin in your life.'

'What!'

'Unrepented sin. She's at the end of the road and approaching fast. Bye!'

I thumbed my nose at Mike and his unsuccessful attempt at humour as he departed hurriedly, but he was right about this being as good a time as any to make my peace with the girl who delivered our milk.

I really couldn't blame her for being a little wary. When I opened the front door a few minutes later to find her bending over the crate on the step, she let a couple of empties clatter noisily back into their spaces and peered up the stairs with a rich mixture of apprehension and fascination. For all she knew, naked teenagers telling bad jokes were part of our daily routine.

'I'm glad I caught you,' I began, 'only – '

She straightened.

'There's no need to pay anything today, Mrs Robinson, nor tomorrow, because this week I'm having to treat Friday as though it was Tuesday, so that I can catch up on – '

'No, no,' I interrupted hastily, 'it wasn't about paying.'

'Oh,' she said, smiling brightly and twiddling a ringlet between finger and thumb. 'What was it, then?'

'Well, I just wanted to apologize for – for Mark appearing in that state last Saturday.'

She giggled.

'Well, I was a bit s'prised, but I've got two older brothers myself, and they're both mad.'

Passing over this doubtful reassurance, and rubbing my hands up and down my sides in embarrassment, I moved on.

'The other thing I wanted to say to you was that I, err, I'm really, really sorry I was so rude to you that morning. I'd had a bad beginning to the day, but that was no excuse for taking it out on you, so please forgive me.'

She looked at me with wide eyes.

'Honestly, there's nothing to forgive, Mrs Robinson. Honestly. You were just the same as you always are – honestly.'

'Oh. Oh, right.'

We parted with mutual expressions of goodwill, and a promise from her that she would come to my party the next day if she felt brave enough, but I couldn't help feeling that, from my point of view, the encounter had been less than satisfactory. In her eyes, I was a person with a mad son and a consistently irritable manner. Oh well, I reflected as I closed the door and returned to party preparations, God must have decided that all these loose ends were good for my soul.

'Never mind,' I said to the creator of the universe as I set off up the stairs, 'as long as you give me a nice birthday present tomorrow.'

It was a silly prayer, and I didn't really mean it, but I think he must have been listening ...

eight

Saturday

1

'The house looks wonderful, Dip. Tell you what – let's cancel this evening and just sit in the middle of it and enjoy the weird feeling of being more or less organized.'

Mike, Dip and I, with unexpectedly energetic assistance from Jack, had worked hard since early morning on Saturday, which was my birthday, and the day of my party. Three of us started at the top of the house and worked slowly downwards, while Mike shopped, prepared food and sorted out the kitchen. Mark, who wasn't working that day, gutted his own room to the point where it was merely a disgusting mess, and then agreed to contribute to the general effort by taking Felicity out for the day in order to shop, have lunch and go to the cinema, in that order. He had been allowed to perform this selfless act of service on the strict condition that he didn't abandon his little sister in the section of the cinema where something suitable for her was showing, while he trotted off happily to watch *Confessions of a Brain-Damaged Wombat*.

It was after five o'clock now. All was quiet, the house looked and felt abnormally clean (even a trifle museum-like), and I felt so tired that I couldn't begin to imagine summoning up the energy to greet and mix with all the people who would be arriving at my party to congratulate me on being fifty while secretly wondering why I looked seventy.

Leaving Jack to beat an honourable retreat to his room to listen to music, Dip and I had finally agreed to ditch our cleaning materials and flop like an old pair of rubber gloves in the kitchen. There was more than ample evidence that Mike had vastly exceeded his promise of the other evening, for not only was the kitchen perfectly clean and completely tidied, but, as far as we could tell, he had managed to prepare and arrange everything in the food line a good *two and a half hours* before the party was due to begin. I was very impressed. Our long kitchen table, lengthened by the addition of a smaller folding table borrowed from the hall, was groaning with heavily laden bowls, baskets and plates, all decently covered over with two large red tablecloths. The slightly unfortunate overall effect of this, enhanced by the positioning of three or four vertical half-baguettes at the 'foot' end, was that of two rather knobbly corpses laid out under a blanket on a mortuary slab.

'Where *is* Mike?' I wondered out loud. 'I haven't seen or heard him for half an hour or so. Did you see him when you came downstairs just now, Dip? Are you going to put the kettle on?'

'I think he went out to get some more drinks or something,' replied Dip vaguely. 'How about if you put the kettle on and I'll actually make it when it boils?'

'You really have got a bit of a blind spot when it comes to understanding what personal Christian service ought to mean, haven't you, Dip?'

'Absolutely right, Kathy,' she nodded sadly, settling back comfortably in her chair as I hauled myself to my feet. 'I am grossly deficient in that area, whereas you – well, awesome is not the word. The joy of caring for others lights you up like a beacon of hope to those of us who dwell miserably in the eternal darkness of greed and grasping selfishness. Could you get the biscuits out while you're up? Actually, I think Mike said something earlier about getting your present from him to give you at the party, so he might have gone to do that. I don't think he'd mind me telling you that.' She leaned forward. 'Has it struck you, by the way, that everyone who comes tonight is probably going to bring you a card and a present of some sort? We'll have to find a table or something to put them all on, won't we?'

'Oo, you make me feel quite greedy,' I said, shining like the beacon that I was as I put teabags into two mugs and added two sugars to mine. 'I've already had loads of presents from Mike and the kids this morning. Felicity made me a lovely card with fifty kisses all over it, and Jack and Mark got me perfume between them. As for *you* – wasting far too much money on that beautiful thirties lady I was foolish enough to covet out loud when we went to Brighton. I keep sneaking into the bedroom just to prove to myself it's there. And more tonight! I can't believe it. This is turning out to be like the sort of Christmas I used to fantasize about in my fat, avaricious little childhood soul – piles and heaps and mountains of presents, all for *me*. Now you mention it, I really hadn't thought about everyone bringing something. Gosh, how exciting! I'll share them with you, Dip.'

'I'm still enjoying the present I was given on Thursday,' smiled Dip. 'I don't need anything else at the moment.'

The kettle boiled. I filled the two mugs, added milk from the fridge, and took them back to the table. We looked at each other for a few moments without speaking. I badly wanted to know what kind of difference that communion had really made, but it was difficult to find words that didn't sound like a line from a bad soap.

'Dip, do you feel better about – about David?'

Dip gazed into nowhere for a second or two.

'I have been thinking about that,' she said softly, 'and I'll tell you what I was thinking. There are different kinds of pain, aren't there? There's the pain you get in your teeth, for instance. You know how I hate and loathe and detest going to the dentist, Kathy – '

'The one you've got now has been good, hasn't she?'

'Yes, I was just going to say – to be fair, the one I've got now never hurts me. But I just hate it. And whenever I do get toothache the physical pain seems to be doubled by that awful heart-sinking knowledge that there's only one way of dealing with it. So off I go every time full of misery and tension on the day of my appointment, and I have the injection and the filling, or even an extraction, and then I go home and wait for the anaesthetic to wear off. And sometimes – usually – the pain I get then is as bad or even worse than what I was feeling before. The huge difference, though, is that it's the pain of getting better – the pain of healing. The weight of worry and fear has gone, so, given a couple of tablets and a spot of distraction, I can handle it. I know it will fade in the end, you see.'

'And, it's like that with – ?'

'It's not as easy as that, Kathy. I mean, yes, I hope and pray and half think that it is like that with David. I'll be honest. Confronting the whole thing so totally – so specifically – on Thursday evening, well, it was like one great scream of pain without any anaesthetic, and the pain's still here inside me, the same as – well, probably worse than before, when I used all sorts of tricks to deal with it just to survive.' Her eyes misted over a little as she continued. 'But, Kathy, I'm beginning to think it might be different. This feels to me as if it could just be the pain of getting better, of healing. I do feel as if that awful weight has gone from round my neck – so, I'm going to believe it'll be all right. That's what I'm going to do.' She smiled. 'In the meantime, getting ready for your party is the equivalent to at least three paracetamol tablets, so I'm on track, thank God.'

Yes – thank you!

'I'm so pleased, Dip.'

'Err, I'm afraid I do have one little bone to pick with you, though,' said Dip very seriously. 'I wasn't going to mention it, but I'm afraid I really think I have to.'

My heart sank.

'What is it?'

'You've forgotten to get the biscuits out ...'

2

Being ready so early felt very peculiar indeed. By seven fifteen we were all at action stations, but with nothing left to do.

Mike had eventually returned from his undercover mission at about five thirty, clutching a mysterious-looking package and looking very pleased with himself. He was now sitting calmly in the kitchen listening to *The Carpenters' Greatest Hits* on our little portable stereo and contentedly jotting things in his little notepad.

Jack had retired to the sitting-room with the door closed (to block out *The Carpenters' Greatest Anagram*, as he insisted on calling it for some reason I hadn't worked out yet) doing some last minute sorting-out of a stack of CDs for use during the party.

Mark was upstairs, recovering from a 'well good' outing with his sister, and probably marvelling at the acres of space revealed by the army of giant earth-moving machines that Dip and I had driven through his room earlier in the day.

Felicity was curled up like a hamster, reading a new book in the window ledge on the stairs, every now and then pushing up on to her knees and peering out through the unfrosted pane at the top to see if her friends, Caroline and Jenny, had arrived for their 'friend's mum's party'.

As soon as Mike got back, Dip zoomed off home to make herself beautiful (out with the earth-moving equipment again, I suggested – how we laughed!) and that just left me – me, the reason for it all – roaming restlessly up and down my spotless hall, wondering why we had ever thought it a good idea for me to make myself this vulnerable. In my mind's eye I pictured the vast majority of our guests stepping out of the shower at this very moment, suddenly remembering that they'd forgotten to buy me a present and wondering if they would be able to find something in the garage shop down the road that didn't look as if it had been bought in the garage shop down the road. I could almost hear the conversations:

'How much do you think we ought to go to?'

'Well, it's a fiftieth, so we can't really get away with less than fifteen, can we?'

'Oh, do you reckon? I was thinking more like ten.'

'Let's say no more than twelve fifty, shall we?'

'Okay – bottle of something a bit posh, perhaps – in one of those fancy boxes. Can't go too far wrong with that, can we? Thank God for off-licences, eh?'

'Good idea. And they do cards up at the late shop. They're a bit crap, but at least we'll have got one. Don't forget to bring a pen in the car ...'

These unworthy imaginings, based entirely on my own experience, were abruptly interrupted by a ringing on the doorbell. Such a sudden loud noise shattered the unnatural calm that had fallen over our little world, and catapulted every member of the family into action. Mark came thundering down the stairs like a ton of coal, followed and clung to from behind, poultice-style, by Felicity, who must have got so absorbed in her book that she'd forgotten to check the street for a while, while Jack and Mike dead-heated at the end of the hall just as I was opening the front door to admit my first guest.

The fact that this very first guest turned out to be a strange-looking man in a dingy suit standing uneasily on the step holding a large bunch of carrots requires a little explaining.

Daniel Wigley, a member of our church who has been described elsewhere by Dip as 'one of those square-shaped, friendless men who need to shave twice a day but don't', was in his mid-fifties, and without question one of the oddest people we knew. He was one of those folk who fret so hard over how to do the right thing that they almost invariably worry themselves into doing something inappropriate. During his time in our church, Daniel had developed 'taking offence' to the point where it was a multifaceted art form, reaching its (for him) dangerous peak a few years ago, during a period when we were just beginning to get to know him a little better. Mike made one terrible mistake around this very time when he most untypically completely forgot that the whole family, together with Dip, had been invited as honoured and sole guests to Daniel's fiftieth birthday dinner, and we had flown off in blissful ignorance to America for a holiday, leaving Dip to pick up the pieces.

A providential coincidence had just about saved our bacon

when it came to the crunch, but ever since that fiasco Mike had worked really hard on his relationship with the other man, to the point where Daniel was now able to actually laugh – or make a strange rasping noise, at least – about his tendency to opt for being upset when people made him feel foolish or inadequate.

Mike had been really clever over one aspect of this. He pointed out to Daniel that when anyone used the phrase 'don't take offence' it sounded as if they were trying to talk someone out of stealing posts and barbed wire. Daniel found this sadly unfunny observation highly amusing, and it became much more than a joke between the two of them. Whenever Mike noticed Daniel starting to get upset about what he imagined someone had said or done to him, he would wink conspiratorially at him, and say, 'Oi, bring that barbed wire back!' It usually worked, probably because Daniel enjoyed the intimacy of sharing a secret – perhaps for the first time in his life.

This, then, was the person who confronted five pairs of Robinson eyes at exactly seven thirty on the evening of my party, and I suppose it was predictable that he should be the only guest who arrived dead on time. It occurred to me that he had probably been waiting outside, just round the corner, checking his watch to make sure that he didn't commit the awful social gaff of turning up thirty seconds early or fifteen seconds late.

My children have been capable of all sorts of appalling things within the bosom of the family, but there has never been any doubt about their compassion for outsiders who struggle painfully with the business of living. They knew about Daniel. That's why they didn't burst into laughter at the sight of the large and leafy bunch of carrots that he was clutching in his hand. The effort required for such control was, however, a fairly sizeable one. We all stared, and then frowned determinedly. A good two seconds must have elapsed before anyone said anything. Mike recovered first.

'Daniel! Welcome, my old mate! You're the very first to arrive. Come on in. Felicity, take Daniel's coat, darling, and put it in – '

'I *know*!' said Felicity, slightly irritably. She had volunteered herself and her two not-yet-arrived friends for the role of official coat depositors some time ago and didn't want telling. 'You don't have to say it, Daddy.'

As I closed the door and Felicity dashed off up the stairs with our visitor's coat, Daniel turned to me and spoke in his deep, fussy voice.

'A very happy birthday to you, Kathy. I was very unsure about what kind of present to bring you, but in the end I decided that on this very special birthday it would be right to give you something that has a great deal of meaning for me.'

Solemnly, he offered me the bunch of carrots. Solemnly, I took it. I was conscious of Jack and Mark hastily turning away at that moment. I wished I could join them.

'Why are carrots so important to you, Daniel?' asked Mike seriously.

'My father grew carrots on our allotment,' said Daniel. 'I helped.'

Poor, sad Daniel.

'Actually, Daniel,' I said, 'it's just occurred to me that a lot of people like to eat pieces of raw carrot at parties. I could slice them up and put them out with some dips. Thanks ever so much.'

He was radiant – in a low-wattage sort of way.

Beginnings of parties are so strange, aren't they? I know it is one of the most over-used clichés of all, but people do seem reluctant to come early and be the ones who get the thing stoked up for the ones who come late. After all our preparations and envisionings, the next half hour felt as though we must have made some terrible miscalculation. The only other guests to arrive during that period were Mark's tadpole friends, Jason and Richard, who were so excruciatingly embarrassed by being at *my* party instead of simply visiting their friend as usual that they could hardly breathe. They came and hung about dutifully in the kitchen for a while because I happened to be there slicing Daniel's carrots. Here, they became increasingly purple, and performed a terror-stricken little circular dance, battling continually to gain and regain the coveted status of being 'the one standing with his back to me'. My attempts to strike up conversation with these two resulted in abject failure, but I did try. A major problem was their voices, which seemed to be emerging from faulty tubes that had become much too small and flattened to allow the words to exit properly.

ME: How's the course going, Jason?

JASON: Glub ...

ME: I can't remember which subjects you're doing ...

JASON: Glubber 'n' glubglub ...

ME: Good, good, and how's your mum, Richard? I haven't seen her down at the Centre for a while.

RICHARD: Mnlub. Mnlubberly umbnlub ...

ME: Ah, right, yes, of course ...

Taking pity on them and myself after a couple of these unproductive exchanges, I suggested to Mark that, since nothing much was happening yet, he should take Jason and Richard and a can or two of beer up to his room. I couldn't help giggling to myself as I listened to them shuffling gratefully away along the hall and up the stairs. It was like magic. Two seconds after departing from my abominable presence, Jason and Richard started to turn into human beings again, and the language of earthlings could once more be heard on their lips.

By eight o'clock, with Daniel happily settled down beside Jack in the sitting-room, clicking his fingers with wild lack of rhythm to Bowie's singles collection and probably hoping against hope that no-one else would arrive to stretch his social skills, and Mark and his tadpoles villainously quaffing ale upstairs and wishing exactly the same thing, it really had begun to feel as if world history had probably finished and nothing else was ever going to happen. Even Dip hadn't arrived yet, and I had been expecting her for half an hour.

Just after eight, though, everything changed. They all came. We hardly had time to close the door between one arrival and the next. It was like the electricity coming back after a power cut, when you've forgotten that you left all your appliances switched on. They came thick and fast, did my guests, some thick, some fast, but all bearing gifts and cards and bottles and the odd very welcome dish of this or that to add to Mike's mortuary slab. Fortunately, Felicity's friends, Caroline and Jenny, were in the vanguard of this procession of visitors. I must say that the speed with which they breathlessly but instantly metamorphosed from party guests into cloakroom attendants was very impressive.

It was wonderful, but more than a little overwhelming and embarrassing to find myself so solidly at the centre of attention, kissed and congratulated and plied with presents by an endless succession of friends and relatives coming through the door. Jack took the brightly wrapped parcels and packages of fascinatingly varied sizes and shapes from me as they were presented, carting them through to the sitting-room and piling them, unopened, on a pair of card-tables that Dip had set up in a corner before she left. It seemed a very great privilege that all these kind people had, at the very least, scoured the aforementioned local garage shop or off-licence just to find something suitable to give me. (Much later, when I had time to open all my presents with Felicity's excited assistance, I was to repent of these uncharitable assumptions. It was clear that one or two people had been forced as a matter of urgency to make hurried visits to the off-licence, or to search through the strangely focused retail world of road atlases and household coal, but most of those gifts had a lot of love and thought behind them. It made me feel like crying.)

Included in that early spate of guests were Joscelyn and John Wayne. I had, of course, seen Joscelyn on Thursday at Dip's communion, but this was the first time I had seen John since that dreadful telephone conversation with his wife last Saturday. After Joscelyn had enfolded me in her arms and offered effusive greetings and congratulations, John gave me a neat hug, then drew his head back and looked me directly in the eyes for just a second or two, with a little smile playing around his lips and one eyebrow slightly raised. In that moment I understood that it was he who had done the hard work in transforming Joscelyn's perception of my plonking discouragement into a sense of God having radically changed her life yet again, and I blushed for shame. Oddly enough, at that moment it also struck me that there was something about small men that was by no means unattractive.

By eight thirty the house felt – no, the house really was – excitingly full of people, noise and music. After an early tendency on the part of our guests to create one congealed block of humanity in the hall and kitchen, we had finally managed to persuade people that it was all right to spread into most of the other rooms, including the dining-room, where item one on Mike's planning list, my beloved red bulb, cast a nostalgic glow over all those who entered, and over the table laden with bottles and glasses that had doubtless attracted many of them.

Some brave souls even investigated Mark's room on the top floor, where, according to reports, they were greeted with polite but subtly repelling cordiality if they were too old and hadn't got any beer, or wildly inclusive enthusiasm if they were young-ish and armed with cans. No doubt a little splinter party was well under way up there. Some mother's instinct told me that this extra celebration was not entirely unplanned, but I had already switched my attitude as firmly as possible to a 'not worrying about it' setting.

Popping my head into our room on the first floor at one point, I found a huge heap of coats laid out and arranged on the bed with great care by our industrious door-girls. These three, finding themselves largely redundant as cloakroom attendants after the first big rush, had exited the house through the sitting-room French windows, and, as far as I knew, were now working out dances on the patio. Glancing once more at the pile of coats before turning away to go back downstairs, I thought about what had happened to my friend all those years ago, and prayed fleetingly that this would be a good evening for her.

Good old Dip. She had given me good advice while we were cleaning up earlier – 'don't drink much at your own party' – and she was absolutely right. Mind you, I didn't really want to, anyway. It was intoxicating enough to move from room to room, savouring the fact that the most important people in my life were richly layered together in one place – well, very nearly all the most important people in my life. By nine o'clock I still hadn't seen any sign of Dip, though the place was so packed by now that it was difficult to know who was there and who wasn't. When I mentioned it to Mike he assured me he had seen and talked to her only a few minutes earlier, and anyway, he pointed out, her car was parked directly outside our house at that very moment. I checked, and he was right.

Once or twice, too, right in the middle of laughing and chatting with folk, I had felt a sudden stab of pain about my stupidity in refusing that once-only opportunity to cross the world and be with my brother and his family, but I did my best to push those thoughts away. This was not the night for stabs of pain. This was a night for celebration.

'Sitting-room, everybody! Felicity, can you go right up to the top of the house, please – yes, you *do* have to, the other two can help you – and tell everyone you meet and everyone you don't meet that they've got to come downstairs. Go on – off you go! Sitting-room, everybody! Time to embarrass Kathy!'

3

There really is no point at all in trying to resist junior headmasters, you know. They expect to be obeyed. The human pools and tributaries that were filling our house began to flow with sluggish obedience down towards the biggest landlocked sea, which was the sitting-room.

Jack steered me firmly in the same direction. On reaching our destination at last, he indicated a little space at the garden end of the room with a high stool in the middle of it, this being the spot where his father's master plan presumably demanded that I should park myself.

I did maintain a more or less appropriate smirk on my face as I sat like a lemon on my stool, watching everyone trying to squeeze into a space that was nowhere near large enough for comfort, but inwardly I was the teeniest bit miffed. It sounds ungrateful, but I had just begun to really enjoy the unstructured bustle and noise of my party. Especially, I had been feeling obscurely flattered by the sight of people engaged in conversation and laughing with each other in our house – in a situation that *we* had created. Perhaps it was a similar satisfaction to the one felt by those lucky people who write plays and create sets, then watch actors and actresses playing out their dreams like puppets. Probably it was much more childish than that.

'Right, squeeze in everybody,' shouted Mike over the hubbub, 'bring your glass with you or grab another one. Make sure there's something in it. Come on, push up at the front and push in at the back. We don't want anyone to end up gnashing their teeth in the hall.'

I don't know if Mike pictured everyone sitting in neat cross-legged rows with a grown-up on a chair at the end of each line. If so, he must have been sorely disappointed. Shrieks and squeals of hysterical laughter from those who enjoyed this kind of thing accompanied chaotic efforts by all those present to obey Mike's command, but in the end, by some sacrificial, floor-dwelling, lap-sitting, intertwining miracle of limb redistribution, the entire assembly was at last corked tightly into the room, and Mike held up a hand for hush.

'Right, I want to start,' he said, 'by thanking you all very much for your good wishes and your gifts, but thank you most of all for simply being here to help us celebrate Kathy's sixtieth birthday tonight.'

I swung my arm stiffly like one of those entry gates in the supermarket, hitting him jovially but quite firmly with the back of my fist. Much laughter.

'Sorry, Kath, I meant fiftieth, of course. Time passes so quickly when you're having fun – so I've been told.'

More laughter.

'I don't think we've ever had so many friends and family all together at exactly the same time. It really is so lovely to see you all in our home. So, let's start by giving each other a big round of applause for being here at all.'

As people clapped furiously, I scanned the sea of faces before me. The whole world seemed to be squashed into our sitting-room. Jack, Mark and Felicity were sitting on the floor, more or less at my feet. I could sense a very natural excitement in them, but there was an excitement within their excitement that rather puzzled me.

Carefully selected relatives beamed in my direction from various points in the room (they had been selected on the basis of beaming potential and discretion). Simon Davenport was there, as well as Eileen and the rest of our housegroup, together with other friends from the church. The girl who delivered the milk had plucked up her courage and come. There she was now by the door, looking very pretty out of uniform, and happy, if a little confused. Colleagues from Mike's school had come, and folk from the immediate neighbourhood, including the increasingly frail but unquenchably feisty Mrs Van Geeting from next door, a particular across-the-fence favourite with Dip and me. Even Mark's tadpoles were jammed into an impossibly small space in the angle of the wall behind the television in the far corner. Everyone was there, in fact, except – I swept the room with my eyes one more time to make sure – everyone except Dip. She was nowhere to be seen. My heart sank.

'Mike!' I hissed, as the applause began to subside. 'Dip's *not* here. She must have got cold feet. I think we should – '

'Dip's fine,' he interrupted in a whisper, laying a hand on my shoulder. 'Trust me!'

So, after looking into his eyes for a moment, and although it didn't make any sense, I trusted him.

'Okay!' Mike clapped his hands together and rubbed his palms expectantly. 'Our three children are here in front of us, and before I make my little speech they've all got something to say.' Pause. 'I'm very proud of my children – '

'Uh-oh!' I interrupted. 'Joke on the starboard bow – fire at will.'

Cheers from many and machine-gun noises from a few.

'No, no, I mean it. We're glad we had Jack, Mark and Felicity, despite friends advising us early in our marriage that we should avoid having children for the same reason that we shouldn't change our car from petrol to diesel. They told us that, compared with petrol, diesel was noisy, smelly, and lacked acceleration.'

Laughter, groans, the odd cry of 'Shame!' and a disapproving glare from Felicity, who had reached the age where jokes of that sort had to be about other people. Even a light-hearted suggestion that she might be noisy, smelly and slow didn't go down at all well. I directed a reassuring, he-was-only-joking smile at her, but she brightened up anyway at Mike's next words.

'I know that Felicity and Jack have something to do for you now, so I'll hand you over to them. Jack and Felicity!'

Amid tumultuous, floor-thumping applause, Jack and Felicity got to their feet and stood on either side of me facing the populace, each clutching a sheet of paper.

'Felicity and I would like to perform a sort of tribute to Mum,' announced Jack gravely, as soon as there was quiet.

I sensed everyone gearing up to being deeply moved, but none of them knew Jack as well as I did. I smiled inside and did my level best to look as sombre as my son.

'Yes,' said Felicity with equal gravity, 'we wrote down all the things about Mum that came into both our heads an' turned them into a poem. Well, Jack did most of the turning, but I helped.'

'A serious poem,' added Jack, 'about a person we deeply respect.'

Felicity nodded in earnest agreement, but her whole body was bobbing and quivering infinitesimally with the joy of the moment.

'We're going to read a verse alternatively,' she said.

'Alternately,' corrected Jack.

'Alternately – a verse each at a time.'

'That's right, with Flitty starting.'

The doggerel that my daughter and her oldest brother then proceeded to recite was so heavily punctuated and interrupted by laughter, cat-calls and applause that an accurate record of the event itself is virtually impossible. Here, however, is a bald transcription of the verses that they read:

Mummy lives in Daddy's house,
She gets all red and cross,
She watches Friends on telly,
And she really fancies Ross.

Mummy says, 'Be good at meals,'
And shouts when we don't do it,
She picked a bowl of leeks up once,
And jolly nearly threw it.

Mummy does aerobics,
With some younger, thinner mothers,
She wears long shirts and leggings,
And she hides behind the others.

Mummy told her best friend, Dip,
About her favourite dream,
She falls into a river,
And it's made of Bristol Cream.

Born with three-score years and ten,
Of fifty she's bereft,
Or, turned into a fraction,
She's got three-sevenths left.

Mummy was a writer once,
She even wrote a book,
But since the 'blasted kids' arrived,
She's forced to clean and cook.

For almost half her life on earth,
Our mum has loved us best.
Thank you, Mum, we promise,
We will love you for the rest.

There was no doubting the success of this item. Thunderous appreciation threatened to lift the roof off our faithful old centurion of a house, as Felicity, her face flushed with pleasure and pride, threw her arms around my neck, kissed me on the cheek, and wished me a happy birthday.

I had to check a tear at this point, not, as it happens, in response to the last verse of the poem (I knew all too well that my children loved me), but because of the reference to my writing. This reaction took me by surprise. It was not unlike another moment in the recent past when I had become aware that I was no longer mourning my mother's death with the same suffocating pungency of grief as in the early days after losing her. I had felt ashamed of overcoming the worst of my pain, as though I had let her down.

But this was about writing. I had once been a writer. Now I was fifty, and I was not a writer any more. Okay, I accepted it, but what was I? How do you find out what you are?

I hugged Felicity hard, wishing, as I buried my face in the warm material of her sweatshirt, that my mother could be here at my party, fiddling around endlessly in the kitchen, scolding me for getting het up, pointing out what was wrong with my life in private and defending me to the death in public. If she could have just – been here. All the old God stuff had jolly well better be right, I thought. I pulled myself together as Mike spoke again.

'Thank you very much, Jack and Felicity. Felicity will be – '

'Hey, hold on,' I broke in, 'surely I'm allowed to say just a word or two in my own defence, aren't I?'

'Mmm, I don't know – well, okay, I'll put it to the vote,' said Mike. 'All those in favour of Kathy being allowed to say a word or two in her own defence, please raise a hand.'

A veritable garden-centre of hands shot up.

'Thank you very much for your kind permission. First of all, I thought it was an excellent poem, and very well read – well done, Felicity and Jack. Having said that, I must insist on salvaging what remains of my good name and my reputation for sanity by pointing out that I most certainly do *not* fancy Ross. As Jack and Felicity know full well, I would regard going out with him as the rough equivalent of marrying my great-aunt. When the last trump sounds and all is revealed, the communion of saints on earth and in heaven will learn that his name was only put on the end of the last line because it rhymes with "cross", an adjective that I suppose might occasionally be applied to me ...'

341

Exaggerated gasps of incredulity from all the members of my immediate family, and from one or two others present as well.

'As for the bowl of leeks, I deeply resent the suggestion that I nearly threw it. I *did* throw it – well, I slid it as hard as I could and it would have fallen on the floor if Mike hadn't caught it at the other end . . .'

Riotous applause, received by Mike with a gracious bow, after which I continued.

'It was an extraordinarily satisfying thing to do, and I would thoroughly recommend it to all those whose children react to the sight of their mother's choicer dishes by sticking their fingers in their mouths and pretending to vomit. As for the rest of the poem, the aerobics, the – what was the other thing? – ah, yes, the sherry dream, only having three-sevenths of my life left, and calling this lot 'the blasted kids' on one or two occasions, I confess to them all, but I absolutely refuse to repent, as it's my birthday. Thank you.'

'As I was about to say before I was so predictably interrupted,' continued Mike as soon as calm returned once more, 'Felicity will be doing one other thing a little later on, but I know that Jack and Mark want to say a few words now.'

Jack, still standing beside me, cleared his throat.

'I don't want to say much, just that I love my mum and I hope she has a really good party, and a happy birthday and, most important of all, I hope God forgives her for lying about Ross. Happy birthday, Mumsy.'

The smile he gave me before sitting down was a much better speech. I shook my head in wonder. Imagine my first baby becoming a proper grown-up.

I felt quite worried for Mark as he dragged himself to his feet, his dark features unusually pink and nervous. Secretly I was amazed that he had decided to say anything at all in public. This was certainly not his sort of thing, and it can't have been made any easier by the fact that there was a complete absence of noise as he turned to face the room. It was as if all those people some-how sensed the fragility of his confidence, and were afraid that a slight sound might kill it altogether. When he did start to speak, it was quietly, and definitely in the manner of one who has abandoned his prepared speech.

'Mum an' I don't always get on.'

The silence, into which these seven words fell like sparrows' eggs onto a snowdrift, was made to seem even more profound by a very faint hiccup of ten-year-old satirical laughter from Felicity, who was sitting cross-legged on the floor next to me, staring at her ankles. At the back of the room the tadpoles were transfixed behind the telly, rigid with horror as they imagined themselves committing such an appalling act of self-exposure.

'We are sort of like each other really – well, in ways, you know …'

Mark turned towards me, a fierce frown on his face.

'But, it doesn't mean – I mean, just because we sometimes fall out doesn't mean that we don't – you know. I try an' she tries …'

Oh, Mark …

'Anyway – happy birthday, Mum.'

As Mark put his arms round me and kissed me awkwardly, I realized for the first time what people meant when they talked about 'filling up' with emotion. The cumulative effect of the last few days and the things that were happening this evening was pretty powerful. I wasn't keen to overflow in front of all my guests, but I wasn't sure how long I could hold out.

'Just a couple more things!' Mike raised his voice and flapped his arms to quell the explosion of approval that had greeted Mark's speech. 'Just two more things before we all go and have some food and get on with the party. First of all, I'd like you all to raise your glasses and drink a toast to Kathy. She and I don't always get on either …'

Comfortable laughter.

'But she's still my sweetheart and I really do love her very much. Kath, darling, I wish you the happiest birthday of your whole life. To Kathy!'

'To Kathy!' echoed the assembly, tilting their glasses with gusto, as assemblies do.

'*Just* one more thing.'

Goodness, what now?

Reaching over to one of the present tables, Mike picked up the mysteriously shaped package he had brought home just before the party began, and made a signal to Felicity, who immediately turned and produced her violin and bow from somewhere behind the place where she had been sitting.

'Stand up, sweetheart, that's it. Ready? Good! Now, everybody, the final thing I want to do is give Kathy her birthday present from me. And before I hand it over, Felicity's going to give her a very subtle little musical clue as to what it is. Listen carefully, Kath. Right, off you go, darling.'

If I live to be a hundred I shall never forget the strangeness of the next minute or so. It says something about my state of mind that, for twenty seconds at least, the name of the very familiar piece of music Felicity started to play escaped me completely. I found myself concentrating intently on my daughter's fingers as they danced on the neck of her instrument, dimly aware that this lilting tune had enormous significance if I could only clear my mind enough to recognize it. At the instant when it finally clicked that, of course, the tune was 'Waltzing Matilda', I felt a sudden rush of cold air from behind me and heard a gasp from one of my relatives at the back of the room. Turning, the only thing my eyes focused on at first was Dip standing by the open French windows, flushed and excited, with what appeared to be the keys of *our* car dangling from her fingers. I remember frowning in real bewilderment and actually trying to move towards her to ask what was going on, but making no progress at all because I was blocked by a tall stranger in an overcoat, who grabbed my shoulders and tilted my chin so that I was forced to look up into his face. I came near to fainting on the spot when I recognized the barely altered features of the older brother I had feared I would never see again this side of heaven. From somewhere beside me Mike said quietly, 'Happy birthday, darling,' and after that I couldn't stop the tears any more.

nine

Sunday

1

'Come on now, Kathy, be honest. Did you have any idea what was going to happen?'

'Mmm, well, I was a bit puzzled about how the children were. I don't know – they were just that bit more quiveringly excited than you might have expected, given what was going on. And then, when you didn't seem to be around after the party got under way, Dip, well, that was a mystery and a real worry. I suppose it occurred to me there must be *something* in the air, but I honestly and truthfully hadn't the remotest notion that Mike had sorted out the money for Pete to fly over on one of those standby efforts. And at such incredibly short notice, too! The lying rat told me we couldn't afford it any more and I believed him. Apart from anything else, if you remember, he arrived back a couple of hours before the party with what now turns out to be an awkwardly shaped old bit of wood nicely wrapped up in pretty paper, didn't he? All a cover for his nefarious plans. When he picked it up just before Felicity did her bit on the violin I really did think that was what he was about to present me with. Gosh, he was never that good a liar before, Dip, I'm going to have to watch him in future.' I clapped, a hand to my head. 'Hold on a minute, what am I saying? You're just as bad, aren't you, my so-called best friend? You've been keeping it under your hat all week.'

Dip tried to look contrite, but succeeded only in looking as smugly pleased with herself as she had done ever since yesterday evening, when she had been personally responsible to Mike for driving to the airport and back (in our car, so that Pete's luggage could be accommodated) to collect, entertain at her house until the right moment, and finally deliver the best birthday present I had ever been given.

It was Sunday afternoon. By mutual consent no-one had been to church that morning. Pete was upstairs (my brother Pete, upstairs in one of *our* rooms, in our house, at that very moment) sleeping the sandbagged sleep of the severely jetlagged, while Mike had driven the others up on to the hills with their kites on this crisp, breezy day, presumably feeling that an hour or two of intensive unravelling practice would do them good. Dip and I, pleasantly dozy as a result of not getting to bed until the early hours, were sprawled in the sitting-room, relishing the process of reviewing an event that had not only been hugely successful and enjoyable, but, just as importantly, was now safely in the past. Between us we had managed to clear away all unwanted traces of yesterday's celebrations, and now, for an hour or so anyway, there was nothing left to do but relax and natter. Dip leaned forward to take a birthday chocolate and pour a little more sherry into my glass.

'What was your favourite bit of the party?' she asked.

'Apart from your Cilia Black impression, do you mean?'

'I thought it was more like *This Is Your Life* myself. Apart from that, yes.'

I leaned back in my chair and considered for a moment, twirling my glass in my fingers like a posy of flowers as the memory returned.

'Oh, I think it was when I danced with Pete in the red bulb room. The surprise-surprise part was wonderful, of course it was, but it sort of took my breath away, and we were both in tears in any case. But then, when we did that little smooch later on in the dining-room – ' I sighed. 'Having Pete there and the whole atmosphere and everything, it seemed to bring so much of the past back with a – a warm whoosh! And I felt *really* happy, Dip. It's reassuring for someone like me to know that it's possible to feel as all right as that, even if it only lasts for a few minutes. Makes you look forward to heaven a bit more. What was your favourite bit?'

Dip turned her head to one side and thought.

'Sharing a secret. Being a small part of making it happen. Seeing your face when it did. Not ending up talking about cloud formations to Daniel for the *entire* evening in the angle of the kitchen doorway. Those were the highlights.'

'Actually, Dip, to be deadly serious for a moment, I think, if you're honest with yourself, the Lord has been telling you for a long time that you should marry Daniel. He's certainly been making it very clear to me.'

'Now, if you meant that,' said Dip sardonically, 'it would be a very good example of what one might call anti-evangelism. Fond as I am of Daniel, if I ever seriously thought the divine will was demanding that we spend the rest of our lives together, I would bend my knee to the nearest available idol and cancel my monthly standing order to the Church of England. Your brother, now – that's another matter. Shame he's married.'

'Mmm, that would've been neat, wouldn't it? Nice foursome we'd have made, eh? Hard luck. By the way, Pete says there's a chance he'll be coming back on business in a couple of years, and they might let him bring Dawn and the girls. Wouldn't that be great? I'd really love it. It's so wonderful to have just him for a little while, though.' I shook my head. 'I still can't get over Mike doing that. Amazing – simply amazing.'

'Those fears of yours about ruining everything when you met – all gone up in a puff of smoke, have they?'

I rolled my shoulders impatiently on the back of the sofa, clicking my tongue in annoyance at the memory of my own foolishness.

'Of course they bloomin' well have, Dip. I don't know how I could have been so stupid. I suppose it was just that it had been so long, and it meant so much to me. I lost confidence and got scared. No, the moment I recognized Pete all that rubbish just – did whatever you said.'

'Went up in smoke?'

'Mm, that's it.'

We sat happily without speaking for a little while. Glancing through the window beside me I saw that the sky had blackened angrily, threatening rain. The kite-flyers would be starting to make their way back by now. An old-fashioned Sunday tea would be nice if we ever managed to stand up again. Inside, the late afternoon gloom of the sitting-room was only faintly relieved by the last of our birch logs flaming and glowing in the grate. It felt to me like the kind of atmosphere in which great thoughts might possibly find expression.

'Bacon,' said Dip solemnly.

'I beg your pardon?'

'I used the word "anti-evangelism" just now. Well, I've just solved the whole problem of how to evangelize really effectively.'

'Using bacon?'

'Yes,' she continued dreamily. 'I don't see how you could go wrong. You set up a huge tent near the middle of the town one day, and when you're ready for the meeting to begin you start frying loads of bacon inside. Then, when the heavenly scent has drawn lots of people in, as it's bound to, you sit them down, preach at them for a while, and then tell them that anyone who makes a commitment can have some bacon, and anyone who doesn't can stay hungry and clear off. Can't fail, can it? I don't understand why no-one's tried it before.'

'No, God must be kicking himself for starting the whole movement off in a part of the world where that ploy was unlikely to work. Hmm, I wonder how people like Billy Graham would react to the news that they're potentially slightly less effective than a couple of rashers of unsmoked back?'

'Oh, well, we visionaries have to put up with a lot of misunderstanding and prejudice. We accept that. I gather the kids did really well just before I arrived last night, Kathy?'

'Dip, they were wonderful. I felt as if we were one of those real families you read about in American paperbacks. Mark was especially – oh, I don't know what he especially was, but I wished we could just hold on to that little bit of time and never have any more of our rotten battles. You will pray for Mark and me, won't you?'

She shook her head at my silliness.

'Don't worry. Praying for you and your kids has become almost as much of a habit as breathing, and I wasn't planning to give up either of those essential activities for the next few years.'

I looked at her speculatively.

'And *I* shall pray about what's going to happen for *you* during those next few years. Do you think it's possible that anything – different could be on the cards?'

'Different? What do you mean – different?'

'Oh, you know – different.'

'Well, it's possible,' said Dip, stroking her chin and looking straight at me, 'it is possible.'

2

Very late that evening, when everyone else had finally gone to bed, Mike and I sat on opposite sides of the round table by the big window at the back of the sitting-room and drank a glass of wine together. Quietly but clearly through our music system, Jacqueline du Pre and Edward Elgar yet again celebrated the rich autumnal mulch of beauty and sadness offered by a world in which life, however vibrant, is inescapably a prelude to physical decline and death. I found myself tingling with something that was greater than expectation, because my tingle was born in what was happening *now*. Such immaculately mellow times were rare enough in our hectic lives, but this seemed distinctively special to me, one of those mysterious, unplanned occasions, so artlessly shaped by circumstance, and so infused with significance that each one has almost the nature of a sacrament. As I sat and sipped my wine, I thought about all that I had and all those I loved, and from there I moved to thinking about all that the swiftly passing years might do to take those things and those people away from me, or to take me away from them. Suddenly, abruptly, typically, there was no mellowness and the moment had gone. I felt like a child lost in the dark, and I was filled with dread.

'Mike,' I said in a small voice, 'is it going to be all right?'

Mike transferred his gaze to me from the one or two stars visible in the night sky through the open curtains, and raised his eyebrows.

'Is what going to be all right?'

'Everything. Is everything going to be all right?'

'Ah, I see, everything – yes, I see what you mean. Sorry, I wasn't quite sure what you meant exactly.'

'Do you think it is?'

He paused before speaking again.

'Is it definitely my turn to be sure?'

We both laughed a little at that, and Mike topped up our glasses from the dark bottle that gleamed in the light from the lamp at the centre of the table. Then he reached across to the little bookcase beside the window and took down the Bible that I had put there for when visitors wanted to look something up and I wanted to look as if we always had one handy. After flicking through the pages for a second or two, he found what he wanted and began to read softly:

' "Then Jesus went with his disciples to a place called Gethsemane, and he said to them, 'Sit here while I go over there and pray.' He took Peter and the two sons of Zebedee along with him, and he began to be sorrowful and troubled. Then he said to them, 'My soul is overwhelmed with sorrow to the point of death. Stay here and keep watch with me.' Going a little farther, he fell with his face to the ground and prayed, 'Father, is everything going to be all right – ?' " '

Some sweet, sorrowful element of that deliberate misquote seemed to wrap around us like arms, as pain and joy struggled to their inevitable climax in Elgar's great hymn of triumph and despair. Joining hands across the table, we said a short prayer for Dip, for David, for Pete and Dawn and the girls, for the rest of our family, and for each other, and then we went to bed.

Silver Birches

A Novel

*Adrian Plass, Internationally
Bestselling Author*

When David Herrick receives an invitation to a reunion from a long-forgotten acquaintance, his first reaction is to refuse. He isn't feeling very sociable since his wife, Jessica, died six months ago.

But the invitation comes from Angela, one of his wife's oldest friends – and mysteriously, she has something for him from his beloved Jessica. Reluctant but curious, he visits Headly Manor.

When the friends gather, they no longer resemble the fresh-faced group of twenty years ago. One has been deserted by her husband, another has lost his faith, and another is filled with anger and bitterness. As they have less than forty-eight hours with each other, they decide to be vulnerable and bear their souls.

This poignant and moving story blends Adrian Plass's rich style of writing with his knack for addressing the deep issues we all face, such as faith, grief, love … and fear.

Available in stores and online!

Share Your Thoughts

With the Author: Your comments will be forwarded to
the author when you send them to *zauthor@zondervan.com*.

With Zondervan: Submit your review of this book
by writing to *zreview@zondervan.com*.

Free Online Resources at

www.zondervan.com

Zondervan AuthorTracker: Be notified whenever your favourite
authors publish new books, go on tour, or post an update
about what's happening in their lives at www.zondervan.com/
authortracker.

Daily Bible Verses and Devotions: Enrich your life with daily
Bible verses or devotions that help you start every morning
focused on God. Visit www.zondervan.com/newsletters.

Free Email Publications: Sign up for newsletters on Christian
living, academic resources, church ministry, fiction, children's
resources, and more. Visit www.zondervan.com/newsletters.

Zondervan Bible Search: Find and compare Bible passages in
a variety of translations at www.zondervanbiblesearch.com.

Other Benefits: Register yourself to receive online benefits
like coupons and special offers, or to participate in research.

ZONDERVAN.com/
AUTHORTRACKER
follow your favorite authors